Unseen Academicals

A Discworld® Novel

BOOKS BY TERRY PRATCHETT

The Discworld® series

Other books about Discworld

THE ART OF DISCWORLD
(with Paul Kidby)

THE WIT AND WISDOM OF DISCWORLD
(edited by Stephen Briggs)

THE FOLKLORE OF DISCWORLD
(with Jacqueline Simpson)

--- Discworld maps ---

THE STREETS OF ANKH-MORPORK
(with Stephen Briggs)

THE DISCWORLD MAPP
(with Stephen Briggs)

A TOURIST GUIDE TO LANCRE –
A DISCWORLD MAPP
(with Stephen Briggs, illustrated by Paul Kidby)

DEATH'S DOMAIN
(with Paul Kidby)

A complete list of other books based on the Discworld series – illustrated
screenplays, graphic novels, comics and plays, can be found on
www.terrypratchett.co.uk

--- Non-Discworld books ---

GOOD OMENS (with Neil Gaiman)

STRATA

THE DARK SIDE OF THE SUN

THE UNADULTERATED CAT (illustrated by Gray Jolliffe)

--- Non-Discworld novels for younger readers ---

THE CARPET PEOPLE

TRUCKERS

DIGGERS

WINGS

ONLY YOU CAN SAVE MANKIND*

JOHNNY AND THE DEAD

JOHNNY AND THE BOMB

NATION

*www.ifnotyouthenwho.com

UNSEEN
ACADEMICALS

Terry Pratchett

Doubleday

LONDON · TORONTO · SYDNEY · AUCKLAND · JOHANNESBURG

TRANSWORLD PUBLISHERS
61–63 Uxbridge Road, London W5 5SA
A Random House Group Company
www.rbooks.co.uk

First published in Great Britain
in 2009 by Doubleday
an imprint of Transworld Publishers

A CIP catalogue record for this book
is available from the British Library.

ISBN 9780385609340

Addresses for Random House Group Ltd companies outside the UK
can be found at: www.randomhouse.co.uk
The Random House Group Ltd Reg. No. 954009

The Random House Group Limited supports The Forest Stewardship
Council (FSC), the leading international forest-certification organization. All our
titles that are printed on Greenpeace-approved FSC-certified paper carry the FSC logo.
Our paper procurement policy can be found at
www.rbooks.co.uk/environment

Typeset in 11.5/15pt Minion by
Falcon Oast Graphic Art Ltd.
Printed and bound in Great Britain by
Clays Ltd, Bungay, Suffolk

2 4 6 8 10 9 7 5 3 1

Mixed Sources
Product group from well-managed
forests and other controlled sources
www.fsc.org Cert no. TT-COC-2139
© 1996 Forest Stewardship Council
FSC

This book is dedicated to Rob Wilkins, who typed most
of it and had the good sense to laugh occasionally.
And to Colin Smythe for his encouragement.

The chant of the goddess Pedestriana is a parody of the wonderful
poem 'Brahma' by Ralph Waldo Emerson, but of course you knew
that anyway.

Note from the Publisher

For extra information on the folklore background to *Unseen Academicals*, see *The Folklore of Discworld* (new Corgi paperback edition).

I T WAS MIDNIGHT in Ankh-Morpork's Royal Art Museum.*

It occurred to new employee Rudolph Scattering about once every minute that on the whole it might have been a good idea to tell the Curator about his nyctophobia, his fear of strange noises and, he now knew, his fear of absolutely every thing he could see (and, come to that, not see), hear, smell and feel crawling up his back during the endless hours on guard during the night. It was no use telling himself that everything in here was dead. That didn't help at all. It meant that he stood out.

And then he heard the sob. A scream might have been better. At least you are certain when you've heard a scream. A faint sob is something you have to wait to hear again, because you can't be sure.

* Technically, the city of Ankh-Morpork is a Tyranny, which is not always the same thing as a monarchy, and in fact even the post of Tyrant has been somewhat redefined by the incumbent, Lord Vetinari, as the only form of democracy that works. Everyone is entitled to vote, unless disqualified by reason of age or not being Lord Vetinari.
  And yet it does work. This has annoyed a number of people who feel, somehow, that it should not, and who want a monarch instead, thus replacing a man who has achieved his position by cunning, a deep understanding of the realities of the human psyche, breathtaking diplomacy, a certain prowess with the stiletto dagger, and, all agree, a mind like a finely balanced circular saw, with a man who has got there by being born.†
  However, the crown has hung on anyway, as crowns do – on the Post Office and the Royal Bank and the Mint and, not least, in the sprawling, brawling, squalling consciousness of the city itself. Lots of things live in that darkness. There are all kinds of darkness, and all kinds of things can be found in them, imprisoned, banished, lost or hidden. Sometimes they escape. Sometimes they simply fall out. Sometimes they just can't take it any more.

† A third proposition, that the city be governed by a choice of respectable members of the community who would promise not to give themselves airs or betray the public trust at every turn, was instantly the subject of music-hall jokes all over the city.

He raised his lantern in a shaking hand. There shouldn't be anyone in here. The place was securely locked; no one could get in. Or, now he came to think about it, out. He wished he *hadn't* thought about it.

He was in the basement, which was not among the most scary places on his round. It was mostly just old shelves and drawers, full of the things that were almost, but very definitely not entirely, thrown away. Museums don't like things to be thrown away, in case they turn out to be very important later on.

Another sob, and a sound like the scraping of . . . pottery?

A rat, then, somewhere on the rear shelves? Rats didn't sob, did they?

'Look, I don't want to have to come in there and get you!' said Scattering with heartfelt accuracy.

And the shelves exploded. It seemed to him to happen in slow motion, bits of pottery and statues spreading out as they drifted towards him. He went over backwards and the expanding cloud passing overhead crashed into the shelves on the other side of the room, which were demolished.

Scattering lay on the floor in the dark, unable to move, expecting at any moment to be torn apart by the phantoms bubbling up from his imagination . . .

The day staff found him there in the morning, deeply asleep and covered in dust. They listened to his garbled explanation, treated him kindly, and agreed that a different career might suit his temperament. They wondered for a while about what he had been up to, night watchmen being rather puzzling people at the best of times, but put it out of their heads . . . because of the find.

Mr Scattering then got a job in a pet shop in Pellicool Steps, but left after three days because the way the kittens stared at him gave him nightmares. The world can be very cruel to some people. But he never told anyone about the gloriously glittering lady holding a large ball over her head who smiled at him before she vanished. He did not want people to think he was strange.

*

But perhaps it is time to talk about beds.

Lectrology, the study of the bed and its associated surroundings, can be extremely useful and tell you a great deal about the owner, even if it's only that they are a very knowing and savvy installations artist.

The bed of Archchancellor Ridcully of Unseen University, for example, is at the very least a bed and a half, being an eight-poster. It encompasses a small library and a bar, and artfully includes a shut-away privy, of mahogany and brass throughout, to save those long cold nocturnal excursions with their concomitant risk of tripping over slippers, empty bottles, shoes and all the other barriers presented to a man in the dark who is praying that the next thing that stubs his toe will be porcelain, or at least easy to clean.

The bed of Trevor Likely is anywhere: a friend's floor, in the hayloft of any stable that has been left unlocked (which is usually a much more fragrant option), or in a room of an empty house (though there are precious few of those these days); or he sleeps at work (but he is always careful about that, because old man Smeems never seems to sleep *at all* and might catch him at any time). Trev can sleep anywhere, and does.

Glenda sleeps in an ancient iron bed,* whose springs and mattress have gently and kindly shaped themselves around her over the years, leaving a generous depression. The bottom of this catenary couch is held off the floor by a mulch of very cheap, yellowing romantic novels of the kind to which the word 'bodice' comes naturally. She would die if anyone found out, or possibly they will die if she finds out that they have found out. Usually there is, on the pillow, a very elderly teddy bear called Mr Wobble.

Traditionally, in the lexicon of pathos, such a bear should have only one eye, but as the result of a childhood error in Glenda's sewing, he has three, and is more enlightened than the average bear.

---

* That is to say Glenda officially sleeps in the old iron bedstead; in reality most of her sleeping is done in a huge and ancient armchair in the Night Kitchen, where she has very nearly mastered the art of doing without proper sleep altogether. So many crumbs, spoons, bits of pie dough, books and spilt drinks have gone down the sides of the cushions of that chair that it might well now harbour a small, thriving civilization.

Juliet Stollop's bed was marketed to her mother as fit for a princess, and is more or less like the Archchancellor's bed, although almost all less, since it consists of some gauze curtains surrounding a very narrow, very cheap bed. Her mother is now dead. This can be inferred from the fact that when the bed collapsed under the weight of a growing girl, someone raised it up on beer crates. A mother would have made sure that at least they were, like everything else in the room, painted pink with little crowns on.

Mr Nutt was seven years old before he found out that sleeping, for some people, involved a special piece of furniture.

Now it was two o'clock in the morning. A cloying silence reigned along the ancient corridors and cloisters of Unseen University. There was silence in the Library; there was silence in the halls. There was so much silence you could hear it. Everywhere it went, it stuffed the ears with invisible fluff.

Gloing!

The tiny sound flew past, a moment of liquid gold in the stygian silence.

Silence ruled again above stairs, until it was interrupted by the shuffling of the official thick-soled carpet slippers of Smeems, the Candle Knave, as he made his rounds throughout the long night from one candlestick to another, refilling them from his official basket. He was assisted tonight (although, to judge from his occasional grumbling, not assisted enough) by a dribbler.

He was called the Candle Knave because that was how the post had been described in the university records when it was created, almost two thousand years before. Keeping the candlesticks, sconces and, not least, the candelabra of the university filled was a never-ending job. It was, in fact, the most important job in the place, in the mind of the Candle Knave. Oh, Smeems would admit under pressure that there were men in pointy hats around, but they came and went and mostly just got in the way. Unseen University was not rich in windows, and without the Candle Knave it would be in darkness within a day. That the wizards would simply step outside and from the teeming crowds hire another man capable of climbing ladders with pockets full of candles had never featured in his thoughts. He was irreplaceable, just like every other Candle Knave before him.

And now, behind him, there was a clatter as the official folding stepladder unfolded.

He spun around. 'Hold the damn thing right!' he hissed.

'Sorry, master!' said his temporary apprentice, trying to control the sliding, finger-crushing monster that every stepladder becomes at the first opportunity, and often without any opportunity at all.

'And keep the noise down!' Smeems bellowed. 'Do you want to be a dribbler for the rest of your life?'

'Actually, I quite like being a dribbler, sir—'

'Ha! Want of ambition is the curse of the labouring class! Here, give me that thing!'

The Candle Knave snatched at the ladder just as his luckless assistant closed it.

'Sorry about that, sir . . .'

'There's always room for one more on the wick-dipping tank, you know,' said Smeems, blowing on his knuckles.

'Fair enough, sir.'

The Candle Knave stared at the grey, round, guileless face. There was an unshakeably amiable look about it that was very disconcerting, especially when you knew what it was you were looking at. And he knew what it was, oh yes, but not what it was called.

'What's your name again? I can't remember *everybody*'s name.'

'Nutt, Mister Smeems. With two t's.'

'Do you think the second one helps matters, Nutt?'

'Not really, sir.'

'Where is Trev? He should be on tonight.'

'Been very ill, sir. Asked me to do it.'

The Candle Knave grunted. 'You have to look smart to work above stairs, Nutts!'

'Nutt, sir. Sorry, sir. Was born not looking smart, sir.'

'Well, at least there's no one to see you now,' Smeems conceded. 'All right, follow me, and try to look less . . . well, just try not to look.'

'Yes, master, but I think—'

'You are not paid to think, young . . . man.'

'Will try not to do so, master.'

Two minutes later Smeems was standing in front of the Emperor, watched by a suitably amazed Nutt.

A mountain of silvery-grey tallow almost filled the isolated junction of stone corridors. The flame of this candle, which could just be made out to be a mega-candle aggregated from the stubs of many, many thousands of candles that had gone before, all dribbled and runnelled into one great whole, was a glow near the ceiling, too high to illuminate anything very much.

Smeems's chest swelled. He was in the presence of History.

'Behold, Nutts!'

'Yes, sir. Beholding, sir. It's Nutt, sir.'

'Two thousand years look down on us from the top of this candle, Nutts. Of course, they look further down on you than on me.'

'Absolutely, sir. Well done, sir.'

Smeems glared at the round, amiable face, and saw nothing there but a slicked-down keenness that was very nearly frightening.

He grunted, then unfolded his ladder without much more than a pinched thumb, and climbed it carefully until it would take him no further. From this base camp generations of Candle Knaves had carved and maintained steps up the hubward face of the giant.

'Feast your eyes on this, lad,' he called down, his ground-state bad temper somewhat moderated by this contact with greatness. 'One day you might be the . . . man to climb this hallowed tallow!'

For a moment, Nutt looked like someone trying hard to disguise the expression of a person who seriously hopes that his future holds more than a big candle. Nutt was young and as such did not have that reverence for age that is had by, mostly, the aged. But the cheerful not-quite-smile came back. It never went away for long.

'Yessir,' he said, on the basis that this generally worked.

Some people claimed that the Emperor had been lit on the very night that UU was founded, and had never gone out since. Certainly the Emperor was huge, and was what you got when, every night for maybe two thousand years, you lit a new fat candle from the guttering remains of the last one and pressed it firmly into the warm wax. There was no visible candlestick now, of course. That was somewhere in the vast accumulation of waxy dribbles on the next floor down.

Around a thousand years ago, the university had had a large hole made in the ceiling of the corridor below, and already the Emperor was seventeen feet high up here. There was thirty-eight feet in total of pure, natural, dribbled candle. It made Smeems proud. He was keeper of the candle that never went out. It was an example to everyone, a light that never failed, a flame in the dark, a beacon of tradition. And Unseen University took tradition very seriously, at least when it remembered to.

As now, in fact . . .

From somewhere in the distance came a sound like a large duck being trodden on, followed by a cry of 'Ho, the Megapode!' And then all hell eventuated.

A . . . creature plunged out of the gloom.

There is a phrase 'neither flesh nor fowl nor good red herring'. This thing was all of them, plus some other bits of beasts unknown to science or nightmare or even kebab. There was certainly some red, and a lot of flapping, and Nutt was sure he caught a glimpse of an enormous sandal, but there were the mad, rolling, bouncing eyes, the huge yellow and red beak and then the thing disappeared down another gloomy corridor, incessantly making that flat honking noise of the sort duck hunters make just before they are shot by other duck hunters.

'Aho! The Megapode!' It wasn't clear where the cry came from. It seemed to be coming from everywhere. 'There she bumps! Ho, the Megapode!'

The cry was taken up on every side, and from the dark shadows of every corridor, bar the one down which the beast had fled, galloped

15

curious shapes, which turned out to be, by the flickering light of the Emperor, the senior faculty of the university. Each wizard was being carried piggy-back by a stout bowler-hatted university porter, whom he was urging onward by means of a bottle of beer on a string held, as tradition demanded, ahead of the porter's grasp on a long stick.

The doleful quack rang out again, some distance away, and a wizard waved his staff in the air and yelled: 'Bird is Flown! Ho, the Megapode!'

The colliding wizardry, who'd already crushed Smeems's rickety ladder under the hobnailed boots of their steeds, set off at once, butting and barging for position.

For a little while 'Aho! The Megapode!' echoed in the distance. When he was certain they had gone, Nutt crept out from his refuge behind the Emperor, picked up what remained of the ladder, and looked around.

'Master?' he ventured.

There was a grunt from above. He looked up. 'Are you all right, master?'

'I have been better, Nutts. Can you see my feet?'

Nutt raised his lantern. 'Yes, master. I'm sorry to say the ladder is broken.'

'Well, do something about it. I'm having to concentrate on my hand-holds here.'

'I thought I wasn't paid to think, master.'

'Don't you try to be smart!'

'Can I try to be smart enough to get you down safely, master?'

No answer was the stern reply. Nutt sighed, and opened up the big canvas tool bag.

Smeems clung to the vertiginous candle as he heard, down below, mysterious scrapings and clinking noises. Then, with a silence and suddenness that made him gasp, a spiky shape rose up beside him, swaying slightly.

'I've screwed together three of the big snuffer poles, master,' said Nutt from below. 'And you'll see there's a chandelier hook stuck in the top, yes? And there's a rope. Can you see it? I think that if you can make a loop around the Emperor it won't slip much and you ought to be

16

able to let yourself down slowly. Oh, and there's a box of matches, too.'

'What for?' said Smeems, reaching out for the hook.

'Can't help noticing that the Emperor has gone out, sir,' said the voice from below, cheerfully.

'No it hasn't!'

'I think you'll find it has, sir, because I can't see the—'

'There is no room in this university's most important department for people with bad eyesight, Nutts!'

'I beg your pardon, master. I don't know what came over me. Suddenly I can see the flame!'

From above came the sound of a match being struck, and a circle of yellow light expanded on the ceiling as the candle that never went out was lit. Shortly afterwards Smeems very gingerly lowered himself to the floor.

'Well done, sir,' said Nutt.

The Candle Knave flicked a length of congealed candle dribble off his equally greasy shirt.

'Very well,' he said. 'But you'll have to come back in the morning to recover the—' But Nutt was already going up the rope like a spider. There was a clanging on the other side of the great candle as the lengths of snuffer pole were dropped, and then the boy abseiled back down to his master with the hook under his arm. And now he stood there all eagerness and scrubbed (if somewhat badly dressed) efficiency. There was something almost offensive about it. And the Candle Knave wasn't used to this. He felt obliged to take the lad down a peg, for his own good.

'All candles in this university must be lit by long taper from a candle that still burns, boy,' he said sternly. 'Where did you get those matches?'

'I wouldn't like to say, sir.'

'I dare say you wouldn't, indeed! Now tell me, boy!'

'I don't want to get anyone into trouble, master.'

'Your reluctance does you credit, but I insist,' said the Candle Knave.

'Er, they fell out of your jacket when you were climbing up, master.'

Off in the distance was one last cry: 'The Megapode is catched!' But around the Emperor silence listened with its mouth open.

'You are mistaken, Nutts,' said Smeems slowly. 'I think you will find that one of the gentlemen must have dropped them.'

'Ah, yes, that's certainly what must have happened, sir. I must learn not to jump to conclusions.'

Once again, the Candle Knave had that off-balance feeling. 'Well, then, we will say no more about it,' was all he managed.

'What was it that happened just then, sir?' said Nutt.

'Oh, that? That was all part of one of the gentlemen's magically essential magical activities, lad. It was vital to the proper running of the world, I'll be bound, oh yes. Could be they was setting the stars in their courses, even. It's one of them things we have to do, you know,' he added, carefully insinuating himself into the company of wizardry.

'Only it looked like a skinny man with a big wooden duck strapped to his head.'

'Ah, well, it may have looked like that, come to think of it, but that was because that's how it looks to people like us, what are not gifted with the ocular sight.'

'You mean it was some sort of metaphor?'

Smeems handled this quite well in the circumstances, which included being so deeply at sea with that sentence that barnacles would be attracted to his underwear. 'That's right,' he said. 'It could be a meta for something that didn't look so stupid.'

'Exactly, master.'

Smeems looked down at the boy. It's not his fault, he thought, he can't help what he is. An uncharacteristic moment of warmth overtook him.

'You're a bright lad,' he said. 'There's no reason why you shouldn't be head dribbler one day.'

'Thank you, sir,' said Nutt, 'but if you don't mind I was rather hoping for something a bit more in the fresh air, so to speak.'

'Ah,' said Smeems, 'that could be a bit . . . tricky, as you might say.'

'Yes, sir. I know.'

'It's just that there's a lot of— well, look, it's not me, it's . . . it's . . . well, you know. It's people. You know what people are like.'

'Yes. I know what people are like.'

Looks like a scarecrow, talks posh like one of the gentlemen, Smeems thought. Bright as a button, grubby as a turd. He felt moved to pat the little . . . fellow on his curiously spherical head, but desisted.

'Best if you stay down in the vats,' he said. 'It's nice and warm, you've got your own bedroll, and it's all snug and safe, eh?'

To his relief the boy was silent as they walked down the passages, but then Nutt said, in a thoughtful tone of voice, 'I was just wondering, sir . . . How often has the candle that never goes out . . . not gone out?'

Smeems bit back the stinging retort. For some reason he knew it could only build up trouble in the long run.

'The candle that never goes out has failed to go out three times since I've been Candle Knave, lad,' he said. 'It's a record!'

'An enviable achievement, sir.'

'Damn right! And that's even with all the strangeness there's been happening lately.'

'Really, sir?' said Nutt. 'Have stranger than usual things been happening?'

'Young . . . man, stranger than usual things happen all the time.'

'One of the scullery boys told me that all the toilets on the Tesseractical floor turned into sheep yesterday,' said Nutt. 'I should like to see that.'

'I shouldn't go further than the sculleries, if I was you,' said Smeems, quickly. 'And don't worry about what the gentlemen do. They are the finest minds in the world, let me tell you. If you was to ask 'em . . .' He paused, trying to think of something really difficult, like, 'What is 864 times 316 . . .?'

'273,024,' said Nutt, not quite under his breath.

'What?' said Smeems, derailed.

'Just thinking aloud, master,' said Nutt.

'Oh. Right. Er . . . Well that's it, see? They'd have an answer for you in a brace of shakes. Finest minds in the world,' said Smeems, who believed in truth via repetition. 'Finest minds. Engaged in the business of the universe. Finest minds!'

'Well, that was fun,' said Mustrum Ridcully, Archchancellor of the university, throwing himself into a huge armchair in the faculty's Uncommon Room with such force that it nearly threw him out again. 'We must do it again some time.'

'Yes, sir. We will. In one hundred years,' said the new Master of The Traditions smugly, turning over the pages in his huge book. He reached the crackling leaf headed Hunting the Megapode, wrote down the date and the amount of time it had taken to find the aforesaid Megapode, and signed his name with a flourish: Ponder Stibbons.

'What is a Megapode, anyway?' said the Chair of Indefinite Studies, helping himself to the port.

'A type of bird, I believe,' said the Archchancellor, waving a hand towards the drinks trolley. 'After me.'

'The original Megapode was found in the under-butler's pantry,' said the Master of The Traditions. 'It escaped in the middle of dinner and caused what my predecessor eleven hundred years ago called . . .' he referred to the book, ' "a veritable heyhoe-rumbelow as all the Fellows pursued it through the college buildings with much mirth and good spirits".'

'Why?' said the head of the Department of Post-Mortem Communications, deftly snatching the decanter full of good spirits as it went past.

'Oh, you can't have a Megapode running around loose, Doctor Hix,' said Ridcully. 'Anyone'll tell you that.'

'No, I meant why do we do it again every hundred years?' said the head of the Department of Post-Mortem Communications.*

The Senior Wrangler turned his face away and murmured, 'Oh, good gods . . .'

* Strictly speaking, Dr Hix, spelled with an X, was the son of Mr and Mrs Hicks, but a man who wears a black robe with nasty symbols on it and has a skull ring would be mad, or let us say even madder, to pass up the chance to have an X in his name.

'It's a tradition,' the Chair of Indefinite Studies explained, rolling a cigarette. 'We have to have traditions.'

'They're traditional,' said Ridcully. He beckoned to one of the servants. 'And I don't mind saying that this one has made me somewhat peckish. Can you fetch the cheeseboards one to five, please? And, um, some of that cold roast beef, some ham, a few biscuits and, of course, the pickle carts.' He looked up. 'Anyone want to add anything?'

'I could toy fitfully with a little fruit,' said the Professor of Recondite Phenomena. 'How about you, Librarian?'

'Ook,' growled the figure hogging the fire.

'Yes, of course,' said the Archchancellor. He waved a hand at the hovering waiter. 'The fruit trolley as well. See to it, please, Downbody. And . . . perhaps that new girl could bring it up? She ought to get used to the Uncommon Room.'

It was as if he had just spoken a magic spell. The room, its ceiling hazy with blue smoke, was suddenly awash with a sort of heavy, curiously preoccupied silence mostly due to dreamy speculation, but in a few rare cases owing to distant memory.

The new girl . . . At the mere thought, elderly hearts beat dangerously.

Very seldom did beauty intrude into the daily life of UU, which was as masculine as the smell of old socks and pipe smoke and, given the faculty's general laxness when it came to knocking out their pipes, the smell of smoking socks as well. Mrs Whitlow, the housekeeper, she of the clanking chatelaine and huge creaking corset that caused the Chair of Indefinite Studies to swoon when he heard it, generally took great care to select staff who, while being female, were not excessively so, and tended to be industrious, clean in their habits, rosy cheeked and, in short, the kind of ladies who are never too far from gingham and an apple pie. This suited the wizards, who liked to be not far away from an apple pie themselves, although they could take gingham or leave it alone.

Why, then, had the housekeeper employed Juliet? What could she have been thinking of? The girl had come into the place like a new world in a solar system, and the balance of the heavens was subtly wobbling. And, indeed, as she advanced, so was Juliet.

By custom and practice, wizards were celibate, in theory because women were distracting and bad for the magical organs, but after a week of Juliet's presence many of the faculty were subject to (mostly) unfamiliar longings and strange dreams, and were finding things rather hard, but you couldn't really put your finger on it: what she had went beyond beauty. It was a sort of distillation of beauty that travelled around with her, uncoiling itself into the surrounding ether. When she walked past, the wizards felt the urge to write poetry and buy flowers.

'You may be interested to know, gentlemen,' said the new Master of The Traditions, 'that tonight's was the longest chase ever recorded in the history of the tradition. I suggest we owe a vote of thanks to tonight's Megapode . . .'

He realized the statement had plummeted on to deaf ears. 'Er, gentlemen?' he said.

He looked up. The wizards were staring, in a soulful sort of way, at whatever was going on inside their heads.

'Gentlemen?' he said again, and this time there was a collective sigh as they woke up from their sudden attack of daydreaming.

'What say?' said the Archchancellor.

'I was just remarking that tonight's Megapode was undoubtedly the finest on record, Archchancellor. It was Rincewind. The official Megapode headdress suited him very well, all things considered. I think he's gone for a lie down.'

'What? Oh, that. Well, yes. Indeed. Well done, that man,' said Ridcully, and the wizards commenced that slow handclapping and table-thumping which is the mark of appreciation amongst men of a certain age, class and girth, accompanied by cries of 'Ver', ver' well done, that man!' and 'Jolly good!' But eyes stayed firmly fixed on the doorway, and ears strained for the rattle of the trolley, which would herald the arrival of the new girl and, of course, one hundred and seven types of cheese, and more than seventy different varieties of pickles, chutneys and other tracklements. The new girl might be the very paradigm of beauty, but UU was not the place for a man who could forget his cheeses.

Well, she was a distraction at least, Ponder thought as he snapped the book shut, and the university needed a few of them right now. It had been tricky since the Dean had left, very tricky indeed. Whoever heard of a man resigning from UU? It was something that simply did not happen! Sometimes people left in disgrace, in a box or, in a few cases, in bits, but there was no tradition of resigning at all. Tenure at Unseen University was for life, and often a long way beyond.

The office of Master of The Traditions had fallen inevitably on Ponder Stibbons, who tended to get all the jobs that required someone who thought that things should happen on time and that numbers should add up.

Regrettably, when he'd gone to check on things with the previous Master of The Traditions, who, everyone agreed, had not been seen around and about lately, he'd found that the man had been dead for two hundred years. This wasn't a wholly unusual circumstance. Ponder, after years at Unseen, still didn't know the full size of the faculty. How could you keep track of them in a place like this these days, where hundreds of studies all shared one window, but only on the outside, or rooms drifted away from their doorways during the night, travelled intangibly through the slumbering halls and ended up docking quite elsewhere?

A wizard could do what he liked in his own study, and in the old days that had largely meant smoking anything he fancied and farting hugely without apologizing. These days it meant building out into a congruent set of dimensions. Even the Archchancellor was doing it, which made it hard for Ponder to protest: he had half a mile of trout stream in his bathroom, and claimed that messin' about in his study was what kept a wizard out of mischief. And, as everyone knew, it did. It generally got him into trouble instead.

Ponder had let that go, because he now saw it as his mission in life to stoke the fires that kept Mustrum Ridcully bubbling and made the university a happy place. As a dog reflects the mood of its owner, so a university reflects its Archchancellor. All he could do now, as the university's sole self-confessed entirely sensible person, was to steer things as best he could, keep away from squalls involving the person previously known as the Dean, and find ways of keeping the Archchancellor too occupied to get under Ponder's feet.

Ponder was about to put the Book of Traditions away when the heavy pages flopped over.

'That's odd.'

'Oh, those old book bindings get very stiff,' said Ridcully. 'They have a life of their own, sometimes.'

'Has anyone heard of Professor H. F. Pullunder, or Doctor Erratamus?'

The faculty stopped watching the door and looked at one another.

'Ring a bell, anyone?' said Ridcully.

'Not a tinkle,' said the Lecturer in Recent Runes, cheerfully.

The Archchancellor turned to his left. 'What about you, Dean? You know all the old—'

Ponder groaned. The rest of the wizards shut their eyes and braced themselves. This might be bad.

Ridcully stared down at two empty chairs, with the imprint of a buttock in each one. One or two of the faculty pulled their hats down over their faces. It had been two weeks now, and it had not got any better.

He took a deep breath and roared: 'Traitor!' – which was a terrible thing to say to two dimples in leather.

The Chair of Indefinite Studies gave Ponder Stibbons a nudge, indicating that he was the chosen sacrifice for today, again.

Again.

'Just for a handful of silver he left us!' said Ridcully, to the universe in general.

Ponder cleared his throat. He'd really hoped the Megapode hunt would take the Archchancellor's mind off the subject, but Ridcully's mind kept on swinging back to the absent Dean the way a tongue plunges back to the site of a missing tooth.

'Er, in point of fact, I believe his remuneration is at least—' he began, but in Ridcully's current mood no answer would be the right one.

'Remuneration? Since when did a wizard work for wages? We are pure academics, Mister Stibbons! We do not care for mere money!'

Unfortunately, Ponder was a clear logical thinker who, in times of mental confusion, fell back on reason and honesty, which, when dealing with an angry Archchancellor, were, to use the proper academic term, unhelpful. And he neglected to think strategically, always a mistake when talking to fellow academics, and as a result made the mistake of employing, as at this point, common sense.

'That's because we never actually pay for anything very much,' he said, 'and if anyone needs any petty cash they just help themselves from the big jar—'

'We are part of the very fabric of the university, Mister Stibbons! We take only what we require! We do not seek wealth! And most certainly we do not accept a "post of vital importance which includes an attractive package of remuneration", whatever the hells that means, "and other benefits including a generous pension"! A pension, mark you! When ever has a wizard retired?'

'Well. Doctor Earwig—' Ponder began, unable to stop himself.

'He left to get married!' snapped Ridcully. 'That's not retirin', that's the same as dyin'.'

'What about Doctor Housemartin?' Ponder went on.

The Lecturer in Recent Runes kicked him on the ankle, but Ponder merely said, 'Ouch!' and continued. 'He left with a bad case of work-related frogs, sir!'

'If you can't stand the heat, get off the pot,' muttered Ridcully. Things were subsiding a bit now, and the pointy hats were tentatively raised. The Archchancellor's little moments only lasted a few minutes. This would have been more comforting were it not for the fact that at approximately five-minute intervals something suddenly reminded him of what he considered to be the Dean's totally treasonable activity, to wit, applying for and getting a job at another university via a common advertisement in a newspaper. That was not how a prince of magic behaved. He didn't sit in front of a panel of drapers, greengrocers and bootmakers (wonderful people though they may be, salt of the earth, no doubt, but even so . . .) to be judged and assessed like some champion terrier (had his teeth counted, no doubt!). He'd let down the entire brotherhood of wizardry, that's what he'd done—

There was a squeaking of wheels out in the corridor, and every wizard stiffened in anticipation. The door swung open and the first overloaded trolley was pushed in.

There was a series of sighs as every eye focused on the maid who was pushing it, and then some rather louder sighs when they realized that she was not, as it were, the intended.

She wasn't ugly. She might be called homely, perhaps, but it was quite a nice home, clean and decent and with roses round the door and a welcome on the mat and an apple pie in the oven. But the thoughts of the wizards were, astonishingly, not on food at this point, although some of them were still a bit hazy as to why not.

She was, in fact, quite a pleasant looking girl, even if her bosom had clearly been intended for a girl two feet taller; but she was not Her.*

The faculty was crestfallen, but it brightened up considerably as the caravan of trolleys wound its way into the room. There was nothing like a 3 a.m. snack to raise the spirits, everyone knew that.

Well, Ponder thought, at least we've got through the evening without anything breaking. Better than Tuesday, at least.

It is a well-known fact in any organization that, if you want a job done, you should give it to someone who is already very busy. It has been the cause of a number of homicides, and in one case the death of a senior director from having his head shut repeatedly in quite a small filing cabinet.

In UU, Ponder Stibbons was that busy man. He had come to enjoy it. For one thing, most of the jobs he was asked to do did not need doing, and most of the senior wizards did not care if they were not

---

* The Egregious Professor of Grammar and Usage would have corrected this to 'she was not she', which would have caused the Professor of Logic to spit out his drink.

26

done, provided they were not not done by themselves. Besides, Ponder was very good at thinking up efficient little systems to save time, and was, in particular, very proud of his system for writing the minutes of meetings, which he had devised with the help of Hex, the university's increasingly useful thinking engine. A detailed analysis of past minutes, coupled with Hex's enormous predictive abilities, meant that for a simple range of easily accessible givens, such as the agenda (which Ponder controlled in any case), the committee members, the time since breakfast, the time to dinner, and so on, in most cases the minutes could be written beforehand.

All in all, he considered that he was doing his bit in maintaining UU in its self-chosen course of amiable, dynamic stagnation. It was always a rewarding effort, knowing the alternative, to keep things that way.

But a page that turns itself was, to Ponder, an anomaly. Now, while the sound of the pre-breakfast supper grew around him, he smoothed out the page and read, carefully.

Glenda would have cheerfully broken a plate over Juliet's sweet, empty head when the girl finally turned up in the Night Kitchen. At least, she would cheerfully have thought about it, in quite a deliberate way, but there was no point in losing her temper, because its target was not really much good at noticing what other people were thinking. There wasn't a nasty bone in Juliet's body, it's just that she had a great deal of trouble homing in on the idea that someone was trying to be unpleasant to her.

So Glenda made do with 'Where have you been? I told Mrs Whitlow you'd gone home ill. Your dad'll be worried sick! And it looks bad to the other girls.'

Juliet slumped into a chair, with a movement so graceful that it seemed to sing.

'Went to the football, didn't I. You know, we were playing those buggers in Dimwell.'

'Until three in the morning?'

'That's the rules, innit? Play until full time, first dead man or first score.'

'Who won?'

'Dunno.'

'You don't know?'

'When we left it was being decided on head wounds. Anyway, I went with Rotten Johnny, didn't I.'

'I thought you'd broken up with him.'

'He bought me supper, didn't 'e.'

'You shouldn't have gone. That's not the sort of thing you should do.'

'Like you know?' said Juliet, who sometimes thought that questions were answers.

'Just do the washing-up, will you?' said Glenda. And I'll have to do it again after you, she thought, as her best friend drifted over to the line of big stone sinks. Juliet didn't exactly wash dishes, she gave them a light baptism. Wizards weren't the type of people who noticed yesterday's dried egg on the plate, but Mrs Whitlow could see it from two rooms away.

Glenda liked Juliet, she really did, although sometimes she wondered why. Of course, they'd grown up together, but it had always amazed her that Juliet, who was so beautiful that boys went nervous and occasionally fainted as she passed, could be so, well, dumb about everything. In fact it was Glenda who had grown up. She wasn't sure about Juliet; sometimes it seemed to Glenda that she had done the growing up for both of them.

'Look, you just have to scrub a bit, that's all,' she snapped after a few seconds of listless dipping, and took the brush out of Juliet's perfect hand, and then, as the grease was sent down the drain, she thought: I've done it again. Actually, I've done it again again. How many times is that? I even used to play with her dolls for her!

Plate after plate sparkled under Glenda's hands. Nothing cleans stubborn stains like suppressed anger.

Rotten Johnny, she thought. Ye gods, he smells of cat wee! He's the only boy stupid enough to think he's got a chance. Good grief, she's got a figure like that and all she ever dates are total knobheads! What would she do without me?

After this brief excitement, the Night Kitchen settled into its routine and those who had been referred to as 'the other girls' got on with their familiar tasks. It has to be said that girlhood for most of them had ended a long time previously, but they were good workers and Glenda was proud of them. Mrs Hedges ran the cheeseboards like a champion. Mildred and Rachel, known officially on the payroll as the vegetable women, were good and reliable, and indeed it was Mildred who had come up with the famous recipe for beetroot and cream cheese sandwiches.

Everybody knew their job. Everybody *did* their job. The Night Kitchen was reliable and Glenda liked reliable.

She had a home to go to and made sure she went to it at least once a day, but the Night Kitchen was where she lived. It was her fortress.

Ponder Stibbons stared at the page in front of him. His mind filled up with nasty questions, the biggest and nastiest of which was simply: Is there any way at all in which people can make out that this is my fault? No. Good!

'Er, there is one tradition here that regrettably we don't appear to have honoured for some considerable time, Archchancellor,' he said, managing to keep the concern out of his voice.

'Well, does that matter?' said Ridcully, stretching.

'It is traditional, Archchancellor,' said Ponder reproachfully. 'Although I might go so far as to say that not observing it has now, alas, become the tradition.'

'Well, that's fine, isn't it?' said Ridcully. 'If we can make a tradition of not observing another tradition, then that's doubly traditional, eh? What's the problem?'

'It's Archchancellor Preserved Bigger's Bequest,' said the Master of The Traditions. 'The university does very well out of the Bigger estates. They were a very rich family.'

'Hmm, yes. Name rings a faint bell. Decent of him. So?'

'Er, I would have been happier had my predecessor paid a little more attention to some of the traditions,' said Ponder, who believed in drip-feeding bad news.

'Well, he *was* dead.'

'Yes, of course. Perhaps, sir, we should, ahem, start a tradition of checking on the health of the Master of The Traditions?'

'Oh, he was quite healthy,' said the Archchancellor. 'Just dead. Quite healthy for a dead man.'

'He was a pile of dust, Archchancellor!'

'That's not the same as being ill, exactly,' said Ridcully, who believed in never giving in. 'Broadly speaking, it's stable.'

Ponder said, 'There is a condition attached to the bequest. It's in the small print, sir.'

'Oh, I never bother with small print, Stibbons!'

'I do, sir. It says: ". . . and thys shall follow as long as the University shall enter a team in the game of foot-the-ball or Poore Boys' Funne".'

'Porree boy's funny?' said the Chair of Indefinite Studies.

'That's ridiculous!' said Ridcully.

'Ridiculous or not, Archchancellor, that is the condition of the bequest.'

'But we stopped taking part in that years ago,' said Ridcully. 'Mobs in the streets, kicking and punching and yelling . . . and they were the players! Mark you, the spectators were nearly as bad! There were hundreds of men in a team! A game could go on for days! That's why it was stopped.'

'Actually, it has never been stopped as such, Archchancellor,' said the Senior Wrangler. '*We* stopped, yes, and so did the guilds. It was no longer a game for gentlemen.'

'Nevertheless,' said the Master of The Traditions, running a finger down the page, 'such are the terms. There are all sorts of other conditions. Oh, dear. Oh, calamity. Oh, surely not . . .'

His lips moved silently as he read on. The room craned as one neck.

'Well, out with it, man!' roared Ridcully.

'I think I'd like to check a few things,' said the Master of The

Traditions. 'I would not wish to worry you unduly.' He glanced down. 'Oh, hells' bells!'

'What are you talking about, man?'

'Well, it looks as though— No, it would be unfair to spoil your evening, Archchancellor,' Ponder protested. 'I must be reading this wrongly. He surely can't mean— Oh, good heavens . . .'

'In a nutshell, please, Stibbons,' growled Ridcully. 'I believe I am the Archchancellor of this university? I'm sure it says so on my door.'

'Of course, Archchancellor, but it would be quite wrong of me to—'

'I appreciate that you do not wish to spoil my evening, sir,' said Ridcully. 'But I would not hesitate to spoil your day tomorrow. With that in mind, what the hells are you talking about?'

'Er, it would appear, Archchancellor, that, er . . . When was the last game we took part in, do you know?'

'Anyone?' said Ridcully to the room in general. A mumbled discussion produced a consensus on the theme of 'Around twenty years, give or take.'

'Give or take what, exactly?' said Ponder, who hated this kind of thing.

'Oh, you know. Something of that order. In the general vicinity of, so to speak. Round about then. You know.'

'About?' said Ponder. 'Can we be more *precise*?'

'Why?'

'Because if the university hasn't played in the Poor Boys' Fun for a period of twenty years or more, the bequest reverts to any surviving relatives of Archchancellor Bigger.'

'But it's banned, man!' the Archchancellor insisted.

'Er, not as such. It's common knowledge that Lord Vetinari doesn't like it, but I understand that if the games are outside the city centre and confined to the back streets, the Watch turns a blind eye. Since I would imagine that the supporters and players easily outnumber the entire Watch payroll, I suppose it is better than having to turn a broken nose.'

'That's quite a neat turn of phrase there, Mister Stibbons,' said Ridcully. 'I'm quite surprised at you.'

'Thank you, Archchancellor,' said Ponder. He had in fact got it from a leader in the *Times*, which the wizards did not like much because it either did not print what they said or printed what they said with embarrassing accuracy.

Emboldened, he added, 'I should point out, though, that under UU law, Archchancellor, a ban doesn't matter. Wizards are not supposed to take notice of such a ban. We are not subject to mundane law.'

'Of course. But nevertheless it is generally convenient to *acknowledge* the civil power,' said Ridcully, speaking like a man choosing his words with such care that he was metaphorically taking some of them outside to look at them more closely in daylight.

The wizards nodded. What they had heard was: 'Vetinari may have his little foibles, but he's the sanest man we've had on the throne in centuries, he leaves us alone, and you never know what he's got up his sleeve.' You couldn't argue with that.

'All right, Stibbons, what do you suggest?' said Ridcully. 'These days you only ever tell me about a problem when you've thought up a solution. I respect this, although I find it a bit creepy. Got a way to wriggle us out of this, have you?'

'I suppose so, sir. I thought we might, well, put up a team. It doesn't say anything about winning, sir. We just have to play, that's all.'

It was always beautifully warm in the candle vats. Regrettably, it was also extremely humid and rather noisy in an erratic and unexpected way. This was because the giant pipes of Unseen University's central heating and hot water system passed overhead, slung from the ceiling on a series of metal straps with a greater or lesser coefficient of linear expansion. That was only the start, however. There were also the huge pipes for balancing the slood differential across the university, the pipe for the anthropic particle flux suppressor, which did not work properly these days, the pipes for the air circulation, which had not worked either since the donkey had been ill, and the very ancient tubes that were all that remained of the ill-fated attempt by a previous arch-chancellor to operate a university communication system by means of trained marmosets. At certain times of the day all this piping broke into a subterranean symphony of gurgles, twangs, upsetting organic trickling sounds and, occasionally, an inexplicable boinging noise that would reverberate through the cellar levels.

The general ad hoc nature of the system's construction was enhanced by the fact that, as an economy measure, the big iron hot water pipes were lagged with old clothing held on by string. Since some of these items had once been wizards' apparel, and however hard you scrubbed you could never get all of the spells out, there were sporadic showers of multicoloured sparks and the occasional ping-pong ball.

Despite everything, Nutt felt at home down among the vats. It was worrying; in the high country, people in the street had jeered at him that he'd been made in a vat. Although Brother Oats had told him that this was silly, the gently bubbling tallow called to him. He felt at peace here.

He ran the vats now. Smeems didn't know, because he hardly ever troubled to come down here. Trev knew, of course, but since Nutt doing his job for him meant that he could spend more time kicking a tin can around on some bit of wasteground he was happy. The opinion of the other dribblers and dippers didn't really count; if you worked in the vats it meant that, as far as the job market was concerned, you had been still accelerating when you'd hit the bottom of the barrel and had been drilled into the bedrock. It meant that you no longer had enough charisma to be a beggar. It meant that you were on the run from something, possibly the gods themselves, or the demons inside you. It meant that if you dared to look up you would see, high above you, the dregs of society. Best, then, to stay down here in the warm gloom, with enough to eat and no inconvenient encounters and, Nutt added in his head, no beatings.

No, the dippers were no problem. He did his best for them when he could. Life itself had beaten them so hard that they had no strength left to beat up anyone else. That was helpful. When people found out that you were a goblin, all you could expect was trouble.

He remembered what the people in the villages had shouted at him when he was small and the word would be followed by a stone.

Goblin. It was a word with an ox-train-load of baggage. It didn't matter what you said or did, or made, the train ran right over you. He'd shown them the things he'd built, and the stones had smashed them while the villagers screamed at him like hunting hawks and shouted more words.

That had stopped on the day Pastor Oats rode gently into town, if a bunch of hovels and one street of stamped mud could be called a town, and he had brought . . . forgiveness. But on that day, no one had wanted to be forgiven.

In the darkness, Concrete the troll, who was so gooned out on Slab, Slice, Sleek and Slump, and who would even snort iron filings if Nutt didn't stop him, whimpered on his mattress.

Nutt lit a fresh candle and wound up his home-made dribbling aid. It whirred away happily, and made the flame go horizontal. He paid attention to his work. A good dribbler never turned the candle when he dribbled; candles in the wild, as it were, almost never dripped in more than one direction, which was away from the draught. No wonder the wizards liked the ones he made; there was something disconcerting about a candle that appeared to have dribbled in every direction at once. It could put a man off his stroke.*

He worked fast, and was putting the nineteenth well-dribbled candle in the delivery basket when he heard the clank of a tin can being bowled along the stone floor of the passage.

---

* Employing professional dribblers might seem extravagant for a body like Unseen University. Nothing could be further from the truth. No traditional wizard worth his pointy hat could possibly work by the light of pure, smooth, dare one say virgin undribbled candles. It would just not look right. The ambience would be totally shattered. And when it did happen, the luckless wizard would mess about, as people do, with matchsticks and bent paperclips, to try to get nice little dribbles and channels of wax, as nature intended. However, this sort of thing never really works and invariably ends with wax all over the carpet and the wizard setting himself on fire. Candle dribbling, it has been decreed, is a job for a dribbler.

'Good morning, Mister Trev,' he said, without looking up. A moment later an empty tin can landed in front of him, on end, with no more ceremony than a jigsaw piece falling into place.

'How did you know it was me, Gobbo?'

'Your leitmotif, Mister Trev. And I'd prefer Nutt, thank you.'

'What's one o' them motifs?' said the voice behind him.

'It is a repeated theme or chord associated with a particular person or place, Mister Trev,' said Nutt, carefully placing two more warm candles in the basket. 'I was referring to your love of kicking a tin can about. You seem in good spirits, sir. How went the day?'

'You what?'

'Did Fortune favour Dimwell last night?'

'What are you on about?'

Nutt pulled back further. It could be dangerous not to fit in, not to be helpful, not to be careful. 'Did you *win*, sir?'

'Nah. Another no-score draw. Waste of time, really. But it was only a friendly. Nobody died.' Trev looked at the full baskets of realistically dribbled candles.

'That's a shitload you've done there, kid,' he said kindly.

Nutt hesitated again, and then said, very carefully, 'Despite the scatological reference, you approve of the large but unspecified number of candles that I have dribbled for you?'

'Blimey, what was that all about, Gobbo?'

Frantically, Nutt sought for an acceptable translation. 'I done okay?' he ventured.

Trev slapped him on the back. 'Yeah! Good job! Respect! But you gotta learn to speak more proper, you know. You wu'nt last five minutes down our way. You'd probably get a half-brick heaved at yer.'

'That has, I mean *'as* been known to . . . 'appen,' said Nutt, concentrating.

'I never seen why people make such a to-do,' said Trev generously. 'So there were all those big battles? So what? It was a long time ago and a long way away, right, an' it's not like the trolls and dwarfs weren't as bad as you lot, ain't I right? I mean, goblins? What was that all about? You

35

lot jus' cut throats and nicked stuff, right? That's practically civilized in some streets round here.'

Probably, Nutt thought. No one could have been neutral when the Dark War had engulfed Far Uberwald. Maybe there had been true evil there, but apparently the evil was, oddly enough, always on the other side. Perhaps it was contagious. Somehow, in all the confusing histories that had been sung or written, the goblins were down as nasty cowardly little bastards who collected their own earwax and were always on the other side. Alas, when the time came to write their story down, his people hadn't even had a pencil.

Smile at people. Like them. Be helpful. Accumulate worth. He liked Trev. He was good at liking people. When you clearly liked people, they were slightly more inclined to like you. Every little helped.

Trev, though, seemed genuinely unfussed about history, and had recognized that having someone in the vats who not only did not try to eat the tallow but also did most of his work for him and, at that, did it better than he could be bothered to do it himself, was an asset worth protecting. Besides, he was congenially lazy, except when it came to foot-the-ball, and bigotry took too much effort. Trev never made too much effort. Trev went through life on primrose paths.

'Master Smeems came looking for you,' said Nutt. 'I sorted it all out.'

'Ta,' said Trev, and that was that. No questions. He *liked* Trev.

But the boy was standing there, just staring at him, as if trying to work him out.

'Tell you what,' Trev said. 'Come on up to the Night Kitchen and we'll scrounge breakfast, okay?'

'Oh no, Mister Trev,' said Nutt, almost dropping a candle. 'I don't think, sorry, fink, I ought to.'

'Come on, who's going to know? And there's a fat girl up there who cooks great stuff. Best food you ever tasted.'

Nutt hesitated. **Always agree, always be helpful, always be becoming, never frighten anyone.**

'I fink I will come with you,' he said.

*

There's a lot to be said for scrubbing a frying pan until you can see your face in it, especially if you've been entertaining ideas of gently tapping someone on the head with it. Glenda was not in the mood for Trev when he came up the stone steps, kissed her on the back of the neck and said cheerfully, ''ullo, darlin', what's hot tonight?'

'Nothing for the likes of you, Trevor Likely,' she said, batting him away with the pan, 'and you can keep your hands to yourself, thank you!'

'Not bin keeping somethin' warm for your best man?'

Glenda sighed. 'There's bubble and squeak in the warming oven and don't say a word if anyone catches you,' she said.

'Just the job for a man who's bin workin' like a slave all night!' said Trev, patting her far too familiarly and heading for the ovens.

'You've been at the football!' snapped Glenda. 'You're always at the football! And what kind of working do you call that?'

The boy laughed, and she glared at his companion, who backed away quickly as though from armour-piercing eyes.

'And you boys ought to wash before you come up here,' she went on, glad of a target that didn't grin and blow kisses at her. 'This is a food-preparation area!'

Nutt swallowed. This was the longest conversation he'd ever had with a female apart from Ladyship and Miss Healstether and he hadn't even said anything.

'I assure you, I bath regularly,' he protested.

'But you're grey!'

'Well, some people are black and some people are white,' said Nutt, almost in tears. Oh, why had he, why had he left the vats? It was nice and uncomplicated down there, and quiet, too, when Concrete hadn't been on the ferrous oxide.

'It doesn't work like that. You're not a zombie, are you? I know they do their best, and none of us can help how we die, but I'm not having all that trouble again. Anyone might get their finger in the soup, but rolling around in the bottom of the bowl? That's not right.'

'I am alive, miss,' said Nutt helplessly.

'Yes, but a live what, that's what I'd like to know.'

'I'm a goblin, miss.' He hesitated as he said it. It sounded like a lie.

'I thought goblins had horns,' said Glenda.

'Only the grown-up ones, miss.' Well, that was true, for some goblins.

'You lot don't do anything nasty, do you?' said Glenda, glaring at Nutt.

But he recognized it as a kind of residual glare; she'd said her piece, and now it was just a bit of play-acting, to show she was the boss here. And bosses can afford to be generous, especially when you look a little fearful and suitably impressed. It worked.

Glenda said, 'Trev, fetch Mister . . . ?'

'Nutt,' said Nutt.

'Fetch Mister Nutt some bubble and squeak, will you? He looks half-starved.'

'I have a very fast metabolism,' said Nutt.

'I don't mind about that,' said Glenda, 'so long as you don't go showing it to people. I have enough—'

There was a crash from behind her.

Trev had dropped the tray of bubble and squeak. He was stock still, staring at Juliet, who was returning the stare with a look of deep disgust. Finally, she said, in a voice like pearls, ''ad your bleedin' eyeful? You got a nerve, largin' it in here wiv that rag round your neck! Everyone knows Dimwell are well pants. Beasly couldn't carry the ball in a sack.'

'Oh yeah right? Well, I hear that the Lobbins walked all over you last week. Lobbin Clout! Everyone knows they're a bunch o' grannies!'

'Oh yeah, that's all you know! Staple Upwright was let out of the Tanty the day before! See if you Dimmers like him stamping all over you!'

'Old Staple? Ha! He'll clog away, yeah, but he can't run above a canter! We'll run rings around—'

Glenda's frying pan clanged loudly on top of the iron range. 'Enough of that, the pair of you! I've got to clean up for the day, and I don't want football dirtying up my nice surfaces, you hear me? You wait here, my girl, and you, Trevor Likely, you get back to your cellar, and I shall want that dish cleaned and back here by tomorrow night or you can try begging your meals off some other girl, right? Take your little friend with you. Nice to meet you, Mister Nutt, but I wish I could find you in better company.'

She paused. Nutt looked so lost and bewildered. Gods help me, she thought, I'm turning into my mum again. 'No, wait.' She reached down, opened one of the warming ovens and came back again with another large dish. The scent of cooked apples filled the kitchen. 'This is for you, Mister Nutt, with my compliments. You need fattening up before you blow away. Don't bother to share it with this scallywag, 'cos he's a greedy beggar, ask anyone. Now, I've got to clean up, and if you boys don't want to help, get out of my kitchen! Oh, and I'll want that dish back as well!'

Trev grabbed Nutt's shoulder. 'Come on, you heard what she said.'

'Yes, and I don't mind helping—'

'Come on!'

'Thank you very much, miss,' Nutt managed, as he was dragged down the stairs.

Glenda folded her oven cloth neatly as she watched them go.

'Goblins,' she said thoughtfully. 'Have you ever seen a goblin before, Jools?'

'What?'

'Have you ever seen a goblin?'

'Dunno.'

'Do you think he's a goblin?'

'What?'

'Mr Nutt. Is he a goblin, do you think?' said Glenda, as patiently as possible.

'He's a posh one, then. I mean, he sounded like he reads books and stuff.'

This was a discrimination that was, in Glenda's view, at practically forensic standards of observation for Juliet. She turned around and found to her surprise that Juliet had gone back to reading something, or at least staring intently at the words. 'What have you got there?' she asked.

'It's called *Bu-bubble*. It's like, what important people are doing.'

Glenda looked over her friend's shoulder as she leafed through the pages. As far as she could tell all the important people shared one smile and were wearing unsuitable clothes for this time of year. 'So what is it that makes them important?' she asked. 'Just being in a magazine?'

'There's fashion tips too,' said Juliet defensively. 'Look, it says here chrome and copper micromail is the look for the season.'

'That's the page for dwarfs,' sighed Glenda. 'Come on, get your things and I'll take you home.'

Juliet was still reading as they waited for the horse bus. Such sudden devotion to a printed page worried Glenda. The last thing she wanted was to see her friend getting ideas in her head. There was such a lot of room in there for them to bounce around and do damage. Glenda herself was reading one of her cheap novels wrapped in a page of the *Times*. She read the way a cat eats: furtively, daring anyone to notice.

While the horses plodded up towards Dolly Sisters, she took her scarf out of her bag and absent-mindedly wrapped it around her wrist. Personally, she hated the violence of the football, but it was important to belong. Not belonging, especially after a big game, could be dangerous to your health. It was important to show the right colours on your home turf. It was important to fit in.

For some reason, that thought immediately turned her mind to Nutt. How strange he was. Kind of ugly, but very clean. He had stunk of soap and seemed so nervous. There was something about him . . .

The air in the Uncommon Room had gone as cold as meltwater.

'Are you telling us, Mister Stibbons, that we should be seen to enter a game for bullies, louts and roughs?' said the Chair of Indefinite Studies. 'That would be impossible!'

'Unlikely, yes. Impossible? No,' said Ponder wearily.

'Most certainly not possible!' said the Senior Wrangler, nodding at the Chair. 'We would be trading kicks with people from the gutters!'

'My grandfather scored two goals in a match against Dimwell,' said Ridcully, in a quiet, matter-of-fact voice. 'Most people never managed one in their lives, in those days. I think the most number of goals scored by one man in his whole life is four. That was Dave Likely, of course.'

There was a ripple of hurried rethinking and retrenchment.

'Ah, well, of course, those were different times,' said the Senior Wrangler, suddenly all syrup. 'I'm sure that even skilled workmen occasionally took part in a spirit of fun.'

'It wasn't much fun if they ran into Granddad,' said Ridcully, with a faint little grin. 'He was a prizefighter. He knocked people down for money and pubs sent for him if there was a really dangerous brawl. Of course, in a sense, this made it even more dangerous, but by then most of it was out in the street.'

'He threw people out of the buildings?'

'Oh yes. In fairness, it was usually from the ground floor and he always opened the window first. He was a very gentle man, I understand. Made musical boxes for a living, very delicate, won awards for them. Teetotal, you know, and quite religious as well. The punching was just a job of casual work. I know for a fact he never tore off anything that couldn't be stitched on again. A decent chap, by all accounts. Never met him, unfortunately. I've always wished I had something to remember the old boy by.'

As one wizard, the faculty looked down at Ridcully's huge hands. They were the size of frying pans. He cracked his knuckles. There was an echo.

'Mister Stibbons, all we need to do is engage another team and lose?' he said.

'That's right, Archchancellor,' said Ponder. 'You simply forfeit the game.'

'But losing means being seen not to win, am I right?'

'That would be so, yes.'

'Then I rather think we ought to win, don't you?'

'Really, Mustrum, this is going too far,' said the Senior Wrangler.

41

'Excuse me?' said Ridcully, raising his eyebrows. 'May I remind you that the Archchancellor of this university is, by college statute, the first among equals?'

'Of course.'

'Good. Well, I am he. The word *first* is, I think, germane here. I see you scribbling in your little notebook, Mister Stibbons?'

'Yes, Archchancellor. I'm looking to see if we could manage without the bequest.'

'Good man,' said the Senior Wrangler, glaring at Ridcully. 'I knew there was no reason to panic.'

'In fact I'm pleased to say that I think we could rub along quite well with only a minimal cut in expenditure,' Ponder went on.

'There,' said the Senior Wrangler, looking triumphantly at the first among equals, 'you see what happens if you don't simply panic.'

'Indeed,' said Ridcully calmly. With his gaze still fixed on the Senior Wrangler he added, 'Mister Stibbons, would you be so kind as to enlighten the rest of us: to what, in reality, does a "minimal cut in expenditure" equate?'

'The bequest is a trust,' said Ponder, still scribbling. 'We have the use of the significant income from the very wise investments of the Bigger trustees, but we cannot touch the capital. Nevertheless, the income is enough to cover – I'm sorry to be imprecise – about eighty-seven point four per cent of the university's food bill.'

He waited patiently until the uproar had died away. It was amazing, he thought, how people would argue against figures on no better basis than 'they must be wrong'.

'I'm sure the Bursar would not agree with those figures,' said the Senior Wrangler sourly.

'That is so,' said Ponder, 'but I'm afraid that is because he regards the decimal point as a nuisance.'

The faculty looked at one another.

'Then who is dealing with our financial affairs?' said Ridcully.

'Since last month? Me,' said Ponder, 'but I would be happy to hand the responsibility over to the first volunteer.'

This worked. Regrettably, it always did. 'In that case,' he said, in the sudden silence, 'I have worked out, with reference to calorific tables, a regime that will give every man here a nourishing three meals a day—'

The Senior Wrangler frowned. 'Three meals? *Three meals?* What kind of person has three meals a day?'

'Someone who can't afford nine,' said Ponder flatly. 'We could eke out the money if we concentrate on a healthy diet of grains and fresh vegetables. That would allow us to keep the cheeseboard with a choice of, say, three types of cheese.'

'Three cheeses isn't a choice, it's a penance!' said the Lecturer in Recent Runes.

'Or we could play a game of football, gentlemen,' said Ridcully, clapping his hands together cheerfully. 'One game. That's all. How hard would that be?'

'As hard as a face full of hobnails, perhaps?' said the Chair of Indefinite Studies. 'People get trodden into the cobbles!'

'If all else fails, we will find volunteers from the student body,' said Ridcully.

'Corpse might be a better word.'

The Archchancellor leaned back in his chair. 'What makes a wizard, gentlemen? A facility with magic? Yes, of course, but around this table we know this is not, for the right kind of mind, hard to obtain. It does not, as it were, happen like magic. Good heavens, witches manage it. But what makes a magic user is a certain cast of mind which looks a little deeper into the world and the way it works, the way its currents twist the fortunes of mankind, et cetera, et cetera. In short, they should be the kind of person who might calculate that a guaranteed double first is worth the occasional inconvenience of sliding down the street on their teeth.'

'Are you seriously suggesting that we give out degrees for mere physical prowess?' said the Chair of Indefinite Studies.

'No, of course not. I am seriously suggesting that we give out degrees for extreme physical prowess. May I remind you that I rowed for this university for five years and got a Brown?'

'And what good did that do, pray?'

'Well, it does say "Archchancellor" on my door. Do you remember why? The University Council at the time took the very decent view that it might be the moment for a leader who was not stupid, mad or dead. Admittedly, most of these are not exactly qualifications in the normal sense, but I like to think that the skill of leadership, tactics and creative cheating that I learned on the river also stood me in good stead. And thus for my sins, which I don't actually remember committing but must have been quite crimson, I was at the top of a shortlist of one. Was that a choice of three cheeses, Mister Stibbons?'

'Yes, Archchancellor.'

'I was just checking.' Ridcully leaned forward. 'Gentlemen, in the morning, correction, later this morning, I propose to tell Vetinari firmly that this university intends to once again play football. And the task falls to me because I am the first among equals. If any of you would like to try your luck in the Oblong Office, you have only to say.'

'He'll suspect something, you know,' said the Chair of Indefinite Studies.

'He suspects everything. That is why he is still Patrician.' Ridcully stood up. 'I declare this meet— this overly extended snack . . . over. Mister Stibbons, come with me!'

Ponder hurried after him, books clutched to his chest, happy for the excuse to get out of there before they turned on him. The bringer of bad news is never popular, especially when it's on an empty plate.

'Archchancellor, I—' he began, but Ridcully held his finger to his lips.

After a moment of cloying silence, there was a sudden festival of scuffling, as of men fighting in silence.

'Good for them,' Ridcully said, heading off down the corridor. 'I wondered how long it would take them to realize that they might be seeing the last overloaded snack trolley for some time. I'm almost tempted to wait and see them waddle out with their robes sagging.'

Ponder stared at him. 'Are you enjoying this, Archchancellor?'

'Good heavens no,' said Ridcully, his eyes sparkling. 'How could you suggest such a thing? Besides, in a few hours I have to tell Havelock

Vetinari that we are intending to become a personal affront. The unschooled mob hacking at one another's legs is one thing. I don't believe he will be happy with the prospect of our joining in.'

'Of course, sir. Er, there is a minor matter, sir, a small conundrum, if you will . . . Who is Nutt?'

There seemed to Ponder to be a rather longer pause than necessary before Ridcully said, 'Nutt would be . . .?'

'He works in the candle vats, sir.'

'How do you know that, Stibbons?'

'I do the wages, sir. The Candle Knave says Nutt just turned up one night with a chitty saying he was to be employed and paid minimal wage.'

'Well?'

'That's all I know, sir, and I only found that out because I asked Smeems. Smeems says he's a good lad but sort of odd.'

'Then he should fit right in, don't you think, Stibbons? In fact, we are *seeing* how he fits in.'

'Well yes, sir, no problem there, but he's a goblin, apparently, and generally, you know, it's a sort of odd tradition, but when the first people from other races first come to the city they start out in the Watch . . .'

Ridcully cleared his throat, loudly. 'The trouble with the Watch, Stibbons, is that they ask too many questions. We should not emulate them, I suggest.' He looked at Ponder and appeared to reach a decision. 'You know that you have a glowing future here at UU, Stibbons.'

'Yes, sir,' said Ponder gloomily.

'I would advise you, with this in mind, to forget all about Mister Nutt.'

'Excuse me, Archchancellor, but that simply will not do!'

Ridcully swayed backwards, like a man subjected to an attack by a hitherto comatose sheep.

Ponder plunged on, because when you have dived off a cliff your only hope is to press for the abolition of gravity.

'I have twelve jobs in this university,' he said. 'I do all the paperwork.

I do all the adding up. In fact, I do everything that requires even a modicum of effort and responsibility! And I go on doing it even though Brazeneck have offered me the post of Bursar! With a staff! I mean real people, not a stick with a knob on the end. Now . . . Will . . . You . . . Trust . . . Me? What is it about Nutt that is so important?'

'The bastard tried to lure you away?' said Ridcully. 'How sharper than a serpent's tooth it is to have a thankless Dean! Is there nothing he will not stoop to? How much did—'

'I didn't ask,' said Ponder quietly.

There was a moment of silence and then Ridcully patted him a couple of times on the shoulder.

'The problem with Mister Nutt is that people want to kill him.'

'What people?'

Ridcully stared into Ponder's eyes. His lips moved. He squinted up and down like a man engaged in complex calculation. He shrugged.

'Probably everybody,' he said.

'Please have some more of my wonderful apple pie,' said Nutt.

'But she gave it to you,' said Trev, grinning. 'I'd never 'ear the end of it if I ate your pie.'

'But you are my friend, Mister Trev,' said Nutt. 'And since it is my pie I can decide what to do with it.'

'Nah,' said Trev, waving it away. 'But there is a little errand you can do for me, me being a kind and understanding boss what lets you work all the hours you want.'

'Yes, Mister Trev?' said Nutt.

'Glenda will come in around midday. To be honest, she hardly ever leaves the place. I would like you to go and ask her the name of that girl who was up there tonight.'

'The one who shouted at you, Mister Trev?'

'The very same,' said Trev.

'Of course I will do that,' said Nutt. 'But why don't you ask Miss Glenda yourself? She knows you.'

Trev grinned again. 'Yes, she does and that's why I know she won't tell me. If I am any judge, and I'm pretty sound, she would like to know you better. I've never met a lady so good at feelin' sorry for people.'

'There's not much of me to know,' said Nutt.

Trev gave him a long, thoughtful glance. Nutt had not taken his eyes off his work. Trev had never seen anyone who could be so easily engrossed. Other people who ended up working in the vats were a bit weird, it was almost a requirement, but the little dark-grey fellow was somehow weird in the opposite direction. 'You know, you ought to get out more, Mister Nutts,' he said.

'Oh, I don't think I should like that at all,' said Nutt, 'and may I kindly remind you my name is not plural, thank you.'

''ave you ever seen a game of football?'

'No, Mister Trev.'

'Then I'll take you to the match tomorrow. I don't play, o'course, but I never miss a game if I can 'elp it,' said Trev. 'No edged weapons, prob'ly. The season starts soon, everyone's warming up.'

'Well, that is very kind of you, but I—'

'Tell you what, I'll pick you up down 'ere at one o'clock.'

'But people will look at me!' said Nutt. And in his head he could hear Ladyship's voice, calm and cool as ever: **Do not stand out. Be part of the crowd.**

'No, they won't. Trust me on that,' said Trev. 'I can sort that out. Enjoy your pie. I'm off.'

He pulled a tin can out of his coat pocket, dropped it on to his foot, flicked it into the air, toed it a few times so it spun and twinkled like some celestial object and then kicked it very hard so it sailed off down the huge gloomy room a few feet above the vats, rattling slightly. Against all probability it stopped in its flight a few feet from the far wall, spun for a moment and then started to come back with, it seemed to the amazed Nutt, a greater speed than before.

Trev caught it effortlessly and dropped it back into his pocket.

'How can you do that, Mister Trev?' said Nutt, astonished.

'Never thought about it,' said Trev. 'But I always wonder why everyone else can't. It's just about the spinning. It's not hard. See yer tomorrow, okay? And don't forget that name.'

The horse buses were not much faster than walking, but it wasn't *you* doing the walking, and there were seats and a roof and a guard with a battle-axe and all in all it was, in the damp grey hours before dawn, good value for tuppence. Glenda and Juliet sat side by side, rocking gently to the sway, lost in their thoughts. At least Glenda was; Juliet could get lost in half a thought, if that.

But Glenda had become an expert at knowing when Juliet was going to speak. It was rather like the sense a sailor has that the wind is going to change. There were little signs, as if a thought had to get the beautiful brain warmed up and spinning before anything could happen.

'Who was that boy what come up for his bubble and squeak?' she asked nonchalantly, or what she probably thought was nonchalantly, or again, what she might have thought was nonchalantly had she known that there was a word like nonchalantly.

'That's Trevor Likely,' said Glenda. 'And you don't want anything to do with him.'

'Why not?'

'He's a Dimmer! Fancies himself as a Face, too. And his dad was Big Dave Likely! Your dad would go mad if he heard you'd even talked to him.'

'He's got a lovely smile,' said Juliet, with a wistfulness that rang all kinds of alarms for Glenda.

'He's a scallywag,' she said firmly. 'He'll try on anything. Can't keep his hands to himself, too.'

'How come you knows that?' said Juliet.

That was another worrying thing about Juliet. Nothing much seemed to be going on between those perfect ears for hours on end and then a question like that would come spinning towards you with edges on it.

'You know, you should try to speak better,' Glenda said, to change the subject. 'With your looks you could snag a man who thinks about more than beer and footie. Just speak with a little more class, eh? You don't have to sound like—'

'My fare, lady?'

They looked up at the guard, who was holding his axe in a way that was very nearly not threatening. And when it came to looking up, this was not a long way. The axe's owner was very short.

Glenda gently pushed the weapon out of the way. 'Don't wave it about, Roger,' she sighed. 'It doesn't impress.'

'Oh, sorry, Miss Glenda,' said the dwarf, what was visible of his face behind the beard colouring with embarrassment. 'It's been a long shift. That will be fourpence, ladies. Sorry about the axe, but we've been getting people jumping off without paying.'

'He ought to be sent back to where he came from,' muttered Juliet, as the guard moved on along the bus. Glenda chose not to rise to this. As far as she had been able to tell, up until today, at least, her friend had no opinions of her own, and simply echoed anything other people said to her. But then she couldn't resist. 'That would be Treacle Mine Road, then. He was born in the city.'

'He's a Miners fan, then? I suppose it could be worse.'

'I don't think dwarfs bother much about football,' said Glenda.

'I don't fink you can be a real Morporkian an' not shout for your team,' was the next piece of worn-out folk wisdom from Juliet. Glenda let this one pass. Sometimes, arguing with her friend was like punching mist. Besides, the plodding horses were laboriously passing their street. They got off without missing a step.

The door to Juliet's house was covered in the ancient remnants of multiple layers of paint, or, rather, multiple layers of paint that had bubbled up into tiny little mountains over the years. It was always the cheapest paint possible. After all, you could afford to buy beer or you could afford to buy paint and you couldn't drink paint unless you were Mr Johnson at number fourteen, who apparently drank it all the time.

'Now, I won't tell your dad that you were late,' said Glenda, opening the door for her. 'But I want you in early tomorrow, all right?'

'Yes, Glenda,' said Juliet meekly.

'And no thinking about that Trevor Likely.'

'Yes, Glenda.' It was a meek reply, but Glenda recognized the sparkle. She'd seen it in the mirror once.

But now she cooked an early breakfast for widow Crowdy, who occupied the house on the other side and couldn't get about much these days, made her comfortable, did the chores in the rising light, and finally went to bed.

Her last thought as she plummeted into sleep was: Don't goblins steal chickens? Funny, he doesn't look the type . . .

At half past eight, a neighbour woke her up by throwing gravel at her window. He wanted her to come and look at his father, described as 'poorly', and the day began. She had never needed to buy an alarm clock.

Why did other people need so much sleep? It was a permanent puzzle for Nutt. It got boring by himself.

Back in the castle in Uberwald there had always been someone around to talk to. Ladyship liked the night-time and wouldn't go out in bright sunshine at all, so a lot of visitors came then. He had to stay out of sight, of course, but he knew all the passages in the walls and all the secret spy-holes. He saw the fine gentlemen, always in black, and the dwarfs with iron armour that gleamed like gold (later, down in his cellar that smelled of salt and thunderstorms, Igor showed him how it was made). There were trolls, too, looking a bit more polished than the ones he'd learned to run away from in the forests. He especially remembered the troll that shone like a jewel (Igor said his skin was made of living diamond). That alone would have been enough to glue him into Nutt's memory, but there had been that moment, one day when the diamond troll was seated at the big table with other trolls and dwarfs, when the diamond eyes had looked up and had seen Nutt, looking through a tiny, hidden spy-hole at the other end of the room. Nutt was convinced of it. He'd jerked away from the hole so quickly that he'd banged his head on the wall opposite.

He'd grown to know his way around all the cellars and workshops in Ladyship's castle. **Go anywhere you wish, talk to everyone. Ask any questions; you will be given answers. When you want to learn, you will be taught. Use the library. Open any book**.

Those had been good days. Everywhere he went, men stopped work to show him how to plane and carve and mould and fettle and smelt iron and make horseshoes – but not how to fit them, because any horse went mad when he entered the stables. One once kicked the boards out of the rear wall.

That particular afternoon he went up to the library, where Miss Healstether found him a book on scent. He read it so fast that his eyes should have left trails on the paper. He certainly left a trail in the library: the twenty-two volumes of Brakefast's *Compendium of Odours* were soon stacked on the long lectern, followed by Spout's *Trumpet of Equestrianism*, and then, via a detour through the history section, Nutt plunged into the folklore section, with Miss Healstether pedalling after him on the mobile library steps.

She watched him with a kind of gratified awe. He'd been barely able to read when he'd arrived, but the goblin boy had set out to improve his reading as a boxer trains for a fight. And he was fighting something, but she wasn't sure in her own mind what it was and, of course, Ladyship never explained. He would sit all night under the lamp, book of the moment in front of him, dictionary and thesaurus on either side, wringing the meaning out of every word, punching ceaselessly at his own ignorance.

When she came in the next morning there was a dictionary of Dwarfish and a copy of Postalume's *The Speech of Trolls* on the lectern too.

Surely it's not right to learn like this, she told herself. It can't be settling properly. You can't just fork it into your head. Learning has to be digested. You don't just have to know, you have to comprehend.

She mentioned this to Fassel, the smith, who said, 'Look, miss, he came up to me the other day and said he'd watched a smith before, and could he have a go? Well, you know her ladyship's orders, so I gave him a bit of bar stock and showed him the hammer and tongs and next minute he was going at it like – well, hammer and tongs! Turned out a nice little knife, very nice indeed. He thinks about things. You can see his ugly little mush working it all out. Have you ever met a goblin before?'

'Strange you should ask,' she told him. 'Our catalogue says we've got one of the very few copies of J. P. Bunderbell's *Five Hours and Sixteen Minutes Among the Goblins of Far Uberwald*, but I can't find it anywhere. It's priceless.'

'Five hours and sixteen minutes doesn't sound very long,' said the smith.

'You'd think so, wouldn't you? But according to a lecture Mr Blunderbell gave to the Ankh-Morpork Trespassers' Society,'* said Miss Healstether, 'it was about five hours too long. He said they ranged in size from unpleasantly large to disgustingly small, had about the same level of culture as yogurt and spent their time picking their own noses and missing. A complete waste of space, he said. It caused quite a stir. Anthropologists are not supposed to write that sort of thing.'

'And young Nutt is one of them?'

'Yes, that puzzled me, too. Did you see him yesterday? There's something about him that frightens horses, so he came to the library and found some old book about the Horseman's Word. They were a kind of secret society, which knew how to make special oils that would make horses obey them. Then he spent the afternoon down in Igor's crypt, brewing up gods know what, and this morning he was riding a horse around the yard! It wasn't happy, mind you, but he was winning.'

'I'm surprised his ugly little head doesn't explode,' said Fassel.

'Ha!' Miss Healstether sounded bitter. 'Stand by, then, because he's discovered the Bonk School.'

'What's that?'

'Not that, them. Philosophers. Well, I *say* philosophers, but, well . . .'

* Originally the Explorers' Society until Lord Vetinari forcibly insisted that most of the places 'discovered' by the society's members already had people living in them, who were already trying to sell snakes to the newcomers.

'Oh, the mucky ones,' said Fassel cheerfully.

'I wouldn't say mucky,' said Miss Healstether, and this was true. A ladylike librarian would not employ that word in the presence of a smith, especially one who was grinning. 'Let's say "indelicate", shall we?'

There is not a lot of call for delicacy on an anvil, so the smith continued unabashed: 'They are the ones who go on about what happens if ladies don't get enough mutton, and they say cigars are—'

'That is a fallacy!'

'That's right, that's what I read.' The smith was clearly enjoying this. 'And Ladyship lets him read this stuff?'

'Indeed, she very nearly insists. I can't imagine what she's thinking.' Or him, come to that, she thought to herself.

There was a limit to how many candles he should make, Trev had told Nutt. It looked bad if he made too many, Trev explained. The pointy hats might decide that they didn't need all the people. That made sense to Nutt. What would No Face and Concrete and Weepy Mukko do? They would have nowhere else to go. They had to live in a simple world; they too easily got knocked down by life in this one.

He'd tried wandering around the other cellars, but there was nothing much happening at night, and people gave him funny looks. Ladyship did not rule here. But wizards are a messy lot and nobody tidied up much and lived to tell the tale, so all sorts of old storerooms and junk-filled workshops became his for the use of. And there was so much for a lad with keen night vision to find. He had already seen some luminous spoon ants carrying a fork, and, to his surprise, the forgotten mazes were home to that very rare indoorovore, the Uncommon Sock Eater. There were some things living up in the pipes, too, which periodically murmured, 'Awk! Awk!' Who knew what strange monsters made their home here?

He cleaned the pie plates very carefully indeed. Glenda had been kind to him. He must show that he was kind, too. It was important to be kind. And he knew where to find some acid.

*

Lord Vetinari's personal secretary stepped into the Oblong Office with barely a disturbance in the air. His lordship glanced up. 'Ah, Drumknott. I think I shall have to write to the *Times* again. I am certain that one down, six across and nine down appeared in that same combination three months ago. On a Friday, I believe.' He dropped the crossword page on to the desk with a look of disdain. 'So much for a Free Press.'

'Well done, my lord. The Archchancellor has just entered the palace.'

Vetinari smiled. 'He must have looked at the calendar at last. Thank goodness they have Ponder Stibbons. Show him straight in after the customary wait.'

Five minutes later, Mustrum Ridcully was ushered in.

'Archchancellor! To what urgent matter do I owe this visit? Our usual meeting is not until the day after tomorrow, I believe.'

'Er, yes,' said Ridcully. As he sat down, a very large sherry was placed in front of him.* 'Well, Havelock, the fact of the matter is—'

'But it is in fact quite providential that you have arrived just now,' Vetinari went on, ignoring him, 'because a problem has arisen on which I would like your advice.'

'Oh? Really?'

'Yes, indeed. It concerns this wretched game called foot-the-ball . . .'

'It does?'

The glass, now in Ridcully's hand, trembled not a fraction. He'd held his job for a long time, right back to the days when a wizard who blinked died.

'One has to move with the times, of course,' said the Patrician, shaking his head.

'We tend not to, over the road,' said Ridcully. 'It only encourages them.'

'People do not understand the limits of tyranny,' said Vetinari, as if talking to himself. 'They think that because I can do what I like I can do what I like. A moment's thought reveals, of course, that this cannot be so.'

'Oh, it is the same with magic,' said the Archchancellor. 'If you flash

* There are those who say that sherry should not be drunk early in the morning. They are wrong.

spells around like there's no tomorrow, there's a good chance that there won't be.'

'In short,' Vetinari continued, still talking to the air, 'I am intending to give my blessing to the game of football, in the hope that its excesses can be more carefully controlled.'

'Well, it worked with the Thieves' Guild,' Ridcully observed, amazed at his own calmness. 'If there has to be crime, then it should be organized, I think that's what you said.'

'Exactly. I have to admit to the view that all exercise for any purpose other than bodily health, the defence of the realm and the proper action of the bowels is barbaric.'

'Really? What about agriculture?'

'Defence of the realm against starvation. But I see no point in people just . . . running about. Did you catch your Megapode, by the way?'

How the hells does he do it? Ridcully wondered. I mean, how? Aloud, he said, 'Indeed we did, but surely you are not suggesting that we were merely "running about"?'

'Of course not. All three exceptions apply. Tradition is at least as important as bowels, if not quite so useful. And, indeed, the Poor Boys' Fun has some remarkable traditions of its own, which some might find it worthwhile exploring. Let me be frank, Mustrum. I cannot enforce a mere personal dislike against public pressure. Well, I can, strictly speaking, but not without going to ridiculous and indeed tyrannical lengths. Over a game? I think not. So . . . as things stand, we find teams of burly men pushing and shoving and kicking and biting in the faint hope, it seems to me, of propelling some wretched object at some distant goal. I have no problem with them trying to kill one another, which has little in the way of a downside, but it has now become so popular once more that property is being damaged, and that cannot be tolerated. There have been comments in the *Times*. No, what the wise man cannot change he must channel.'

'And how do you intend to do that?'

'By giving the job to you. Unseen University has always had a fine sporting tradition.'

' "Had" is the right word,' sighed Ridcully. 'In my day we were all so . . . so relentlessly physical. But if I was to suggest so much as an egg and spoon race these days they'd use the spoon to eat the egg.'

'Alas, I did not know your day was over, Mustrum,' said Lord Vetinari, with a smile.

The room, never normally noisy, sank into deeper silence.

'Now look here—' Ridcully began.

'This afternoon I shall be speaking to the editor of the *Times*,' said Vetinari, gently surfing his voice over that of the wizard with all the skill of a born committee manipulator, 'who is, as we know, a very civic-minded person. I'm sure he will welcome the fact that I am asking the university to tame the demon foot-the-ball, and that you have, after careful thought, agreed to the task.'

I don't have to do this, Ridcully thought carefully. On the other hand, since it is what I want, and thereby don't have to ask for, this may be unwise. Damn! This is so like him!

'You would not object if we raise our own team?' he managed.

'Indeed, I positively demand that you do so. But no magic, Mustrum. I must make that clear. Magic is not sporting, unless you are playing against other wizards, of course.'

'Oh, I am a very sporting man, Havelock.'

'Capital! How is the Dean settling in at Brazeneck, by the way?'

If it had been anyone else asking, Ridcully thought, that would simply be a polite enquiry. But this is Vetinari, isn't it . . .

'I've been too busy to find out,' he said loftily, 'but I'm sure he will be fine when he finds his feet.' Or manages to see them without a mirror, he added to himself.

'I'm sure you must be pleased to see your old friend and colleague making his way in the world,' said Vetinari, innocently. 'And so is Pseudopolis itself, of course. I must say, I admire the sturdy burghers of that city for embarking on their noble experiment in this . . . this democracy,' he went on. 'It is always good to see it attempted again. And sometimes amusing, too.'

'There is something to be said for it, you know,' grunted Ridcully.

'Yes, I believe you practise it at the university,' said the Patrician, with a little smile. 'However, on the matter of football we are in accord. Capital. I will tell Mister de Worde what you are doing. I'm sure that the keen players of foot-the-ball will be interested, when someone explains the longer words to them. Well done. Do try the sherry. I am told it is highly palatable.'

Vetinari stood up, a signal that, in theory at least, the business of the meeting was concluded, and strolled over to a polished stone slab, set into a square wooden table. 'On a different note, Mustrum . . . How is your young visitor?'

'My visit— Oh, you mean the . . . uh . . .'

'That's right.' Vetinari smiled at the slab as if sharing a joke with it. 'The, as you put it, Uh.'

'I note the sarcasm. As a wizard, I must tell you that words have power.'

'As a politician, I must tell you I already know. How is he getting along? Concerned minds would like to know.'

Ridcully glanced at the little carved men on the playing slab as if they were listening to him. In a roundabout way, they probably were. Certainly it was well known now that the hands that guided half the pieces lived in a big castle in Uberwald, and were female and belonged to a lady who was mostly rumour.

'Smeems says he keeps himself to himself. He says he thinks the boy is cunning.'

'Oh, good,' said Vetinari, still seeming to find something totally engrossing in the layout of playing pieces.

'Good?'

'We need cunning people in Ankh-Morpork. We have a Street of Cunning Artificers, do we not?'

'Well, yes, but—'

'Ah, then it is *context* that has power,' said Vetinari, turning around with a look of unmasked delight. 'Did I say that I am a politician? Cunning: artful, sly, deceptive, shrewd, astute, cute, on the ball and, indeed, arch. A word for any praise and every prejudice. Cunning . . . is a cunning word.'

'You don't think that maybe this . . . experiment of yours might be a step too far?' said Ridcully.

'People said that about the vampires, did they not? It's alleged that they have no proper language, but I am told he speaks several languages fluently.'

'Smeems did say he talked la-di-da,' Ridcully admitted.

'Mustrum, compared with Natchbull Smeems, trolls speak la-di-da.'

'The . . . boy was brought up by a priest of some sort, I know that,' said Ridcully. 'But what will he become when he grows up?'

'By the sound of him, a professor of linguistics.'

'You know what I mean, Havelock.'

'Possibly, although I wonder if *you* do. But he is, I suggest, unlikely to become a ravening horde all by himself.'

Ridcully sighed. He glanced towards the game again, and Vetinari noticed.

'Look at them. Ranks, files,' he said, waving a hand over the little stone figures, 'locked in everlasting conflict at the whim of the player. They fight, they fall, and they cannot turn back because the whips drive them on, and all they know is whips, kill or be killed. Darkness in front of them, darkness behind them, darkness and whips in their heads. But what if you could take one out of this game, get him before the whips do, take him to a place without whips – what might he become? One creature. One singular being. Would you deny them that chance?'

'You had three men hanged last week,' said Ridcully, without quite understanding why.

'They had their chances. They used them to kill, and worse. All we get is a chance. We don't get a benison. *He* was chained to an anvil for seven years. He should get his chance, don't you think?'

Suddenly Vetinari was smiling again.

'Let us not get sombre, however. I look forward to your ushering in a new era of lively, healthy activity in the best sporting tradition.

Indeed, tradition will be your friend here, I am sure. Please don't let me trespass any further on your time.'

Ridcully drained the sherry. That at least was palatable.

It's a short walk from the palace to Unseen University; positions of power like to keep an eye on one another.

Ridcully walked back through the crowds, occasionally nodding at people he knew, which, in this part of the city, was practically everyone.

Trolls, he thought, we get along with trolls, now that they remember to look where they're putting their feet. Got 'em in the Watch and everything. Jolly decent types, bar a few bad apples, and gods know we have enough of those of our own. Dwarfs? Been here for ages. Can be a bit tricky, can be as tight as a duck's arse – here he paused to think and edited that thought to 'drive a hard bargain'. You always know where you are with them, anyway, and of course they are short, which is always a comfort provided you know what they are doing down there. Vampires? Well, the Uberwald League of Temperance seemed to be working. Word on the street – or in the vault or whatever – was that they policed their own. Any unreformed bloodsucker who tried to make a killing in the city would be hunted down by people who knew exactly how they thought and where they hung out.

Lady Margolotta was behind all that. She was the person who, by diplomacy, and probably more direct means, had got things moving again in Uberwald, and she had some sort of . . . relationship with Vetinari. Everyone knew it, and that was all everyone knew. A dot dot dot relationship. One of those. And nobody had been able to join up the dots.

She had been to the city on diplomatic visits, and not even the well-practised dowagers of Ankh-Morpork had been able to detect a whisper of anything other than a businesslike amiability and international cooperation between the two of them.

And he played endless and complex games with her, via the clacks system, and apart from that, that was, well, that . . . until now.

And she'd sent him this Nutt to keep safe. Who knew why, apart from them? Politics, probably.

Ridcully sighed. One of the monsters, all alone. It was hard to think of it. They came in thousands, like lice, killing everything and eating the dead, including theirs. The Evil Empire had bred them in huge cellars, grey demons without a hell.

The gods alone knew what had happened to them when the Empire collapsed. But there was convincing evidence now that some still lived up in the far hills. What might they do? And one, right now, was making candles in Ridcully's cellars. What might he become?

'A bloody nuisance?' said Ridcully aloud.

''ere, 'oo are you calling a nuisance, mister? It's my road, same as yours!'

The wizard looked down at a young man who appeared to have stolen his clothes only from the best washing lines, though the tattered black and red scarf around his neck was probably his own. There was an edginess to him, a continual shifting of weight, as though he might at any moment run off in a previously unguessable direction. And he was throwing a tin can up in the air and catching it again. For Ridcully it brought back memories so sharp that they stung, but he pulled himself together.

'I am Mustrum Ridcully, Archchancellor and Master of Unseen University, young man, and I see you are sporting colours. For some game? A game of football, I suggest?'

'As it happens, yes. So what?' said the urchin, then realized that his hand was empty when it should now, under normal gravitational rules, be full again. The tin had not fallen back from its last ascent, and was in fact turning gently twenty feet up in the air.

'Childish of me, I know,' said Ridcully, 'but I did want your full attention. I want to witness a game of football.'

'Witness? Look, I never saw nuffin'—'

Ridcully sighed. 'I mean I want to watch a game, okay? Today, if possible.'

'You? Are you sure? It's your funeral, mister. Got a shilling?'

There was a clink, high above.

'The tin will come back down with a sixpence in it. Time and place, please.'

''ow do I know I can trust you?' said the urchin.

'I don't know,' said Ridcully. 'The subtle workings of the brain are a mystery to me, too. But I'm glad that is your belief.'

'What?' With a shrug, the boy decided to gamble, what with having had no breakfast.

'Loop Alley off the Scours, 'arp arsed one, an' I've never seen you before in my life, got it?'

'That is quite probable,' said Ridcully, and snapped his fingers.

The tin dropped into the urchin's waiting hand. He shook out the silver coin and grinned. 'Best o' luck to you, guv.'

'Is there anything to eat at these affairs?' said Ridcully, for whom lunchtime was a sacrament.

'There's pies, guv, pease pudding, jellied eel pies, pie and mash, lobster . . . pies, but mostly they are just pies. Just pies, sir. Made of pie.'

'What kind?'

His informant looked shocked. 'They're pies, guv. You don't ask.'

Ridcully nodded. 'And as a final transaction, I'll pay you one penny for a kick of your can.'

'Tuppence,' said the boy promptly.

'You little scamp, we have a deal.'

Ridcully dropped the can on the toe of his boot, balanced it for a moment, then flicked it into the air and, as it came down, hit it with a roundhouse kick that sent it spinning over the crowd.

'Not bad, granddad,' said the kid, grinning. In the distance there was a yell and the sound of someone bent on retribution.

Ridcully plunged a hand into his pocket and looked down. 'Two dollars to start running, kid. You won't get a better deal today!' The boy laughed, grabbed the coins and ran. Ridcully walked on sedately, while the years fell back on him like snow.

He found Ponder Stibbons pinning up a notice on the board just outside the Great Hall. He did this quite a lot. Ridcully assumed it made him feel better in some way.

He slapped Ponder on the back, causing him to spill drawing pins all over the flagstones.

'It is a bulletin from the Ankh Committee on Safety, Archchancellor,' said Ponder, scrabbling for the spinning, wayward pins.

'This is a university of magic, Stibbons. We have no business with safety. Just being a wizard is unsafe, and so it should be.'

'Yes, Archchancellor.'

'But I should pick up all those pins if I were you, you can't be too careful. Tell me – didn't we use to have a sports master here?'

'Yes, sir. Evans the Striped. He vanished about forty years ago, I believe.'

'Killed? It was dead men's shoes in those days, you know.'

'I can't imagine who would want his job. Apparently he evaporated while doing press-ups in the Great Hall one day.'

'Evaporated? What kind of death is that for a wizard? Any wizard would die of shame if he just evaporated. We always leave *something* behind, even if it's only smoke. Oh, well. Cometh the hour, cometh the . . . whatever. General comethness, perhaps. What is that thinking engine of yours doing these days?'

Ponder brightened. 'As a matter of fact, Archchancellor, Hex has just discovered a new particle. It travels faster than light in two directions at once!'

'Can we make it do anything interesting?'

'Well yes! It totally explodes Spolwhittle's Trans-Congruency Theory!'

'Good,' said Ridcully cheerfully. 'Just so long as something explodes. Since it's finished exploding, set it to finding either Evans or a decent substitute. Sports masters are pretty elementary particles, it shouldn't be difficult. And call a meeting of the Council in ten minutes. We are going to play football!'

Truth is female, since truth is beauty rather than handsomeness; this, Ridcully reflected as the Council grumbled in, would certainly explain the saying that a lie could run around the world before Truth has got its, correction, *her* boots on, since she would have to choose which pair – the idea that any woman in a position to choose would have just one pair of boots being beyond rational belief. Indeed, as a goddess she would have lots of shoes, and thus many choices: comfy shoes for home truths, hobnail boots for unpleasant truths, simple clogs for universal truths and possibly some kind of slipper for self-evident truth. More important right now was what kind of truth he was going to have to impart to his colleagues, and he decided not on the whole truth, but instead on nothing but the truth, which dispensed with the need for honesty.

'Well, go on, then, what did he say?'

'He responded to reasoned argument.'

'He did? Where's the catch?'

'None. But he wants the rules to be more traditional.'

'Surely not! Gather they are practically prehistoric as it is!'

'And he wants the university to take the lead in all this, and quickly. Gentlemen, there is a game going to be played in about three hours' time. I suggest we observe it. And to this end, I will require you to wear . . . trousers.'

After a while Ridcully took out his watch, which was one of the old-fashioned imp-driven ones and was reliably inaccurate. He flipped up the gold lid and stared patiently as the little creature pedalled the hands around. When the expostulating had not stopped after a minute and a half, he snapped the lid shut. The click had an effect that no amount of extra shouting could have achieved.

'Gentlemen,' he said gravely. 'We must partake of the game of the people – from whom, I might add, we derive. Has any of us, in the last few decades, even seen the game being played? I thought not. We should get outside more. Now, I'm not asking you to do this for me, or even for the hundreds of people who work to provide us with a life in which discomfort so seldom rears its head. Yes, many other ugly heads have reared, it is true, but dinner has always beckoned. We are, fellow wizards, the city's last line of defence against all the horrors that can be thrown against it. However, none of them are as potentially dangerous as us. Yes, indeed. I don't know what might happen if wizards were really hungry. So do this, I implore you on this one occasion, for the sake of the cheeseboard.'

There had been some nobler calls to arms in history, Ridcully would be the first to admit, but this one was well tailored to its target audience. There was some grumbling, but that was the same as saying that the sky was blue.

'What about lunch?' said the Lecturer in Recent Runes suspiciously.

'We'll eat early,' said Ridcully, 'and I am told that the pies at the game are just – amazing.'

Truth, in front of her huge walk-in wardrobe, selected black leather boots with stiletto heels for such a barefaced truth.

Nutt was already waiting with a proud but worried look on his face when Glenda got in to the Night Kitchen. She didn't notice him at first, but she turned back from hanging her coat on its peg and there he was, holding a couple of dishes in front of him like shields.

She almost had to shade her eyes because they gleamed so brightly.

'I hope this is all right,' said Nutt nervously.

'What have you done?'

'I plated them with silver, miss.'

'How did you do that?'

'Oh, there's all kinds of old stuff in the cellars and, well, I know how to do things. It won't cause trouble for anyone, will it?' Nutt added, looking suddenly anxious.

Glenda wondered if it would. It shouldn't, but you could never be sure with Mrs Whitlow. Well, she could solve that problem by hiding them somewhere until they tarnished.

'It's kind of you to take the trouble. I generally have to chase people to get plates back. You are a real gentleman,' she said, and his face lit up like a sunrise.

'You are very kind,' he beamed, 'and a very handsome lady with your two enormous chests that indicate bountifulness and fecundity—'

The morning air froze in one enormous block. He could tell he'd said something wrong, but he had no idea what it was.

Glenda looked around to see if anyone had heard, but the huge gloomy room was otherwise empty. She was always the first one in and the last one out. Then she said, 'Stay right there. Don't you dare move an inch! Not an inch! And don't steal any chickens!' she commanded as an afterthought.

She should have trailed steam as she headed out of the room, her boots echoing on the flagstones. What a thing to come out with! Who did he think he was? Come to that, who did she think he was? And what did she think he was?

The cellars and undercrofts of the university were a small city in themselves, and bakers and butchers turned to look as she clattered past. She didn't dare stop now; it would be too embarrassing.

If you knew all the passages and stairs, and if they stayed still for five minutes, it was possible to get to just about anywhere in the university without going above ground. Probably none of the wizards knew the maze. Not many of them cared to know the dull details of domestic management. Hah, they thought the dinners turned up by magic!

A small set of stone steps led up to the little door. Hardly anyone used it these days. The other girls wouldn't go in there. But Glenda would. Even after the very first time that she had, in response to the bell, delivered the midnight banana, or rather had failed to deliver it on account of running away screaming, she knew she'd have to face it again. After all, we can't help how we're made, her mother had said, and nor can we help what a magical accident might turn us into through no fault of our own, as Mrs Whitlow had explained slightly more recently, when the screaming had stopped. And so Glenda had picked up the banana and had headed right back there.

Now, of course, she was surprised that anyone might find it odd that the custodian of all the knowledge that could be was a reddish brown and generally hung several feet above his desk, and she was pretty certain that she knew at least fourteen meanings of the word 'ook'.

As it was daytime, the huge building beyond the little door was bustling, insofar as the word can be applied to a library. She headed towards the nearest lesser librarian, who failed to look the other way in time, and demanded: 'I need to see a dictionary of embarrassing words beginning with F!'

His haughty glance softened somewhat when he realized she was a cook. Wizards always had a place in their hearts for cooks, because it was near their stomach.

'Ah, then I think Birdcatcher's *Discomforting Misusage* will be our friend here,' he said cheerfully, and led her to a lectern, where she spent several enlightening minutes before heading back the way she had come, a little wiser and a great deal more embarrassed.

Nutt was still standing where she'd told him to stand, and looked terrified.

'I'm sorry, I didn't know what you meant,' she said, and thought: abundant, productive and fruitful. Well, yes, I can see how he got there, worse luck, but that's not me, not really me. I think. I hope.

'Um, it was kind of you to say that about me,' she said, 'but you should have used more appropriate language.'

'Ah, yes, I'm so sorry,' said Nutt. 'Mister Trev told me about this. I should not talk posh. I should have said that you have enormous t—'

'Just stop there, will you? Trevor Likely is teaching *you* elocution?'

'Don't tell me, I know this one . . . You mean talkin' proper?' said Nutt. 'Yes, and he's promised to take me to the football,' he added proudly.

This led to some explanation, which only made Glenda gloomy. Trev was right, of course. People who didn't know long words tended to be edgy around people who did. That's why her male neighbours, like Mr Stollop and his mates, distrusted nearly everybody. Their wives, on the other hand, shared a much larger if somewhat specialized vocabulary owing to the cheap romantic novels that passed like contraband from scullery to washhouse, in every street. That's why Glenda knew 'elocution', 'torrid', 'boudoir' and 'reticule', although she wasn't too certain about 'reticule' and 'boudoir', and avoided using them, which in the general scheme of things was not hard. She was deeply suspicious about what a lady's boudoir might be, and certainly wasn't going to ask anybody, even in the Library, just in case they laughed.

'And he's going to take you to the football, is he? Mister Nutt, you will stand out like a diamond in a sweep's earhole!'

Do not stand out from the crowd. There were so many things to remember!

'He says he will look after me,' said Nutt, hanging his head. 'Er, I was wondering who that nice young lady was who was in here last night,' he added desperately, as transparent as air.

'He asked you to ask me, right?'

Lie. Stay safe. But Ladyship wasn't here! And the nice apple-pie lady was right here in front of him! It was too complicated!

'Yes,' he said meekly.

And Glenda surprised herself. 'Her name is Juliet, and she lives bang next door to me so he'd better not come round, okay? Juliet Stollop, see if he likes that.'

'You fear he will press his suit?'

'Her dad will press a lot more than that if he sees he's a Dimmer supporter!'

Nutt looked blank, so she went on: 'Don't you know anything? Dimwell Old Pals? The football team? The Dollies are Dolly Sisters Football Club. Dollies hate the Dimmers, the Dimmers hate the Dollies! It's always been like that!'

'What could have caused such a difference between them?'

'What? There is no difference between them, not when you've got past the colours! They're two teams, alike in villainy! Dolly Sisters wears white and black, Dimwell wears pink and green. It's all about football. Bloody, bloody, clogging, hacking, punching, gouging, silly football!' The bitterness in Glenda's voice would have soured cream.

'But you have a Dolly Sisters scarf!'

'When you live there, it's safer that way. Anyway, you have to support your own.'

'But is it not a game, like spillikins or halma or Thud?'

'No! It's more like war, but without the kindness and consideration!'

'Oh, dear. But war is not kind, is it?' said Nutt, bewilderment clouding his face.

'No!'

'Oh, I see. You were being ironic.'

She gave him a sideways look. 'I might have been,' she conceded. 'You are an odd one, Mister Nutt. Where are you from, really?'

The old panic contained again. **Be harmless. Be helpful. Make friends. Lie.** But how did you lie to friends?

'I must go,' he said, scurrying down the stone steps. 'Mister Trev will be waiting!'

Nice but odd, Glenda thought, watching him leap down the steps. Clever, too. To spot my scarf on a hook ten yards away.

The sound of a rattling tin can alerted Nutt to his boss's presence before he had even hurried through the old archway to the vats. The other habitués had paused in their work, which, frankly, given its usual snail-like progress, meant hardly any change at all, and were watching him listlessly. But they were watching, at least. Even Concrete looked vaguely alert, but Nutt saw a little dribble of brown in the corner of his mouth. Someone had been giving him iron filings again.

The can shot up as Trev caught it with his boot, flew over his head, and then came back obliquely, as if rolling down an invisible slope, and landed in his waiting hand. There was a murmur of appreciation from the watchers and Concrete banged his hand on the table, which generally meant approval.

'What kept you, Gobbo? Chatting up Glenda, were you? You've got no chance there, take it from me. Been there, tried that, oh yes. No chance, mate.' He threw a grubby bag towards Nutt. 'Get these on quick, else you'll stand out like a diamond in—'

'A sweep's earhole?' Nutt suggested.

'Yeah! You're gettin' it. Now don't hang about or we'll be late.'

Nutt looked doubtfully at a long, a very long scarf in pink and green and a large yellow woolly hat with a pink bobble on it.

'Pull it down hard so it covers your ears,' Trev commanded. 'Get a move on!'

'Er . . . pink?' said Nutt doubtfully, holding up the scarf.

'What about it?'

'Well, isn't football a rough man's game? Whereas pink, if you will excuse me, is rather a . . . female colour?'

Trev grinned. 'Yeah, that's right. Think about it. You are the clever one around here. And you can walk and think at the same time, I know that. Makes you stand out from the crowd in these parts.'

'Ah, I think I have it The pink proclaims an almost belligerent masculinity, saying as it does: I am so masculine I can afford to tempt you to question it, giving me the opportunity to proclaim it anew by doing violence to you in response. I don't know if you have ever read Ofleberger's *Die Wesentlichen Ungewissheiten Zugehörig der Offenkundigen Männlichkeit?*'

Trev grabbed his shoulder and spun him round. 'Wot do you fink, Gobbo?' he said, his red face a couple of inches from Nutt's. 'Wot is your problem? Wot are you all about? You come out with ten-dollar words an' you lay 'em down like a man doin' a jigsaw! So how come you're down in the vats, eh, workin' for someone like me? It don't make sense! Are you on the run from the Old Sam? No problem, there, unless you did up an old lady or somethin', but you got to tell me!'

Too dangerous, thought Nutt desperately. Change the subject! 'She's called Juliet!' he gasped. 'The girl you asked about! She lives next door to Glenda! Honestly!'

Trev looked suspicious. 'Glenda told you that?'

'Yes!'

'She was windin' you up. She knew you'd tell me.'

'I don't think she would lie to me, Mister Trev. She is my friend.'

'I kept thinkin' about her all last night,' said Trev.

'Well, she is a wonderful cook,' Nutt agreed.

'I meant Juliet!'

'Um, and Glenda said to tell you that Juliet's other name is Stollop,' said Nutt, hating to be the bearer of worse news.

'What? That girl is a Stollop?'

'Yes. Glenda said I was to see how you liked that, but I know the meaning of irony.'

'But it's like findin' a strawberry in a dogmeat stew, yeah? I mean, the Stollops are buggers, the lot of 'em, biters and cloggers to a man, the kind of bastards who'll kick your family jewels up into your throat.'

'But you don't play football, do you? You just watch.'

'Damn right! But I'm a Face, right? I'm known in all the boroughs. You can ask anyone. Everyone knows Trev Likely. I'm Dave Likely's lad. Every supporter in the city knows about him. Four goals! No one else scored that much in a lifetime! And gave as good as he got, did Dad. One game he picked up the Dolly bastard holding the ball and threw 'im over the line. He gave as good as 'e got, my dad, and then some.'

'So, he was a bugger and a clogger and a biter too, was he?'

'What? Are you pulling my tonker?'

'I would not wish to do so initially, Mister Trev,' said Nutt, so solemnly that Trev had to grin, 'but, you see, if he fought the opposing team with even more force than they used, does that not mean that he—'

'He was my dad,' said Trev. 'That means you don't try any fancy maths, okay?'

'Okay indeed. And you never wanted to follow in his footsteps?'

'What, and get brung home on a stretcher? I got my brains from my ol' mum, not from Dad. He was a good bloke and loved his football, but he wasn't flush with brains to start with an' on that day some of 'em were leakin' out of his ear. The Dollies got 'im in the melee and sorted 'im out good and proper. That's not for me, Gobbo. I'm smart.'

'Yes, Mister Trev, I can see that.'

'Get the gear on and let's go, okay? We don't want to miss anything.'

'Fing,' said Nutt automatically, as he started to wind the huge scarf around his neck.

'What?' said Trev, frowning.

'Wot?' said Nutt, his voice a little muffled. There was a lot of scarf. It was almost covering his mouth.

70

'Are you pulling my chuff, Gobbo?' said Trev, handing him an ancient sweater, faded and saggy with age.

'Please, Mister Trev, I don't know! There appears to be so much I might inadvertently pull!' He tugged on the big woolly hat with the pink pompom on it. 'They are so very pink, Mister Trev. We must be bursting with machismo!'

'I don't know what you person'ly are bursting with, Gobbo, but here's somethin' to learn. "Come on if you think you're hard enough." Now *you* say it.'

'Come on if you think you're hard enough,' said Nutt obediently.

'Well, okay,' said Trev, inspecting him. 'Just remember, if anyone starts pushing you around during the game, and givin' you grief, just you say that to 'em and they'll see you're wearing the Dimmer colours and they'll think twice. Got it?'

Nutt, somewhere in the space between the big bobbly hat and the boa constrictor of a scarf, nodded.

'Wow, there you are, Gobbo, a complete . . . fan. Your own mother wouldn't recognize you!'

There was a pause before a voice emerged from inside the mound of ancient woollens, which looked very much like a nursery layette made by a couple of giants who weren't sure what to expect.

'I believe you are accurate.'

'Yeah? Well, that's good, innit? Now let's go and meet the lads. Move fast, stay close.'

'Now remember, this is a pre-season friendly between the Angels and the Whoppers, right?' said Trev, as they stepped out into a fine rain which, because of Ankh-Morpork's standing cloud of pollution, was morphing gently into smog. 'They're both pretty crap, they'll never amount to anythin', but the Dimmers shout for the Angels, right?'

It took some explaining, but the core of it, as far as Nutt could understand it, was this: All football teams in the city were rated by Dimwell in proportion to their closeness, physical, psychological or general gut feeling, to the hated Dolly Sisters. It had just evolved that way. If you went to a match between two other teams, you automatically, according to some complex and ever-changing ready-reckoner of love and hate, cheered the team most nearly allied to your native turf or, more accurately, cobbles.

'Do you see what I mean?' Trev finished.

'I have committed what you said to memory, Mister Trev.'

'Oh Brutha, an' I'll bet you 'ave, at that. And it's just Trev when we're not at work, right? We shout together, right?' He punched Nutt play-fully on the arm.

'Why did you do that, Mister Trev?' said Nutt. His eyes, almost the only part of him visible, looked hurt. 'You struck me!'

'That wasn't me hitting you, Gobbo! That was just a friendly punch! Big difference! Don't you know that? It's a little tap on the arm, to show we're mates. Go on, do it to me. Go on.' Trev winked.

. . . You will be polite and, most of all, you will never raise your hand in anger to anyone . . .

But this wasn't like that, was it? Nutt asked himself. Trev was his friend. This was friendly. A friend thing. He punched the friendly arm.

'That was a punch?' said Trev. 'You call that a punch? A girl could punch better'n that! How come you're still alive with a weedy punch like that? Go on, try a proper punch!'

Nutt did.

Be one of the crowd? It went against everything a wizard stood for, and a wizard would not stand for anything if he could sit down for it, but even sitting down, you had to stand out. There were, of course, times when a robe got in the way, especially when a wizard was working in his forge, creating a magic metal or mobiloid glass or any of those other little exercises in practical magic where not setting fire to yourself is a happy bonus, so every wizard had some leather trousers and a stained, rotted-by-acid shirt. It was the shared dirty little secret, not very secret, but ingrained with deep-down dirt.

Ridcully sighed. His colleagues had aimed for the look of the common man, but had only a hazy grasp of what the common man looked like these days, and now they were sniggering and looking at one another and saying things like 'Cor blimey, don't you scrub down well, as it were, my ol' mate.' Beside them, and looking extremely embarrassed, were two of the university's bledlows, not knowing what to do with their feet and wishing that they were having a quiet smoke somewhere in the warm.

'Gentlemen,' Ridcully began, and then with a gleam in his eye added, 'or should I say, fellow workers by hand and brain, this afternoon we— Yes, Senior Wrangler?'

'Are we, in point of fact, workers? This is a university, after all,' said the Senior Wrangler.

'I agree with the Senior Wrangler,' said the Lecturer in Recent Runes. 'Under university statute we are specifically forbidden to engage, other than within college precincts, in any magic above level four, unless specifically asked to do so by the civil power or, under clause three, we really want to. We are acting as place holders, and as such, forbidden from working.'

'Would you accept "slackers by hand and brain"?' said Ridcully, always happy to see how far he could go.

'Slackers by hand and brain *by statute*,' said the Senior Wrangler primly.

Ridcully gave up. He could do this all day, but life couldn't be all fun.

'That being settled, then, I must tell you that I have asked the stalwart Mister Frankly Ottomy and Mister Alf Nobbs to join us in this little escapade. Mister Nobbs says that since we are not wearing football favours we should not attract unwanted attention.'

The wizards nodded nervously at the bledlows. They were, of course, merely employees of the university, while the wizards were, well, *were* the university, weren't they? After all, a university was not just about bricks and mortar, it was about people, specifically wizards. But to a man, the bledlows scared them.

They were all hefty men with a look of having been carved out of bacon. And they were all descendants of, and practically identical to, those men who had chased those wizards – younger and more limber, and it was amazing how fast you could run with a couple of bledlows behind you – through the foggy night-time streets. If caught, said bledlows, who took enormous pleasure in the prosecution of the university's private laws and idiosyncratic rules, would then drag you before the Archchancellor on a charge of Attempting to Become Rascally Drunk. That was preferable to fighting back, when the bledlows were widely believed to take the opportunity for a little class warfare. That was years ago, but even now the unexpected sight of a bledlow caused sullen, shameful terror to flow down the spines of men who had acquired more letters after their names than a game of Scrabble.

Mr Ottomy, recognizing this, leered and touched the brim of his uniform cap. 'Afternoon, gents,' he said. 'Don't you worry about a thing. Me and Alf here will see you right. We'd better get movin', though, they bully off in half an hour.'

The Senior Wrangler would not have been the Senior Wrangler if he did not hate the sound of silence. As they shuffled out of the back door, wincing at the unfamiliar chafing of trouser upon knee, he turned to Mr Nobbs and said, 'Nobbs . . . that's not a common name. Tell me, Alf, are you by any chance related to the famous Corporal Nobby Nobbs of the Watch?'

Mr Nobbs took it well, Ridcully thought, given the clumsy lack of protocol.

'Nosir!'

'Ah, a distant branch of the name, then . . .'

'Nosir! Different tree!'

In the greyness of her front room, Glenda looked at the suitcase, and despaired. She'd done her best with brown boot polish, week after week, but it had been bought from a shonky shop and the cardboard under the leather-ish exterior was beginning to show through. Her customers never seemed to notice, but she did, even when it was out of sight.

It was a secret part of a secret life that she lived for an hour or two on her half-day off once a week, and maybe a little longer if today's cold calls worked out.

She looked at her face in the mirror, and said in a voice that was full of jaunt: 'We all know the problem of underarm defoliation. It is so hard, isn't it, to keep the lichens healthy . . . But,' she flourished a green and blue container with a golden stopper, 'one spray with Verdant Spring will keep those crevices moist and forest fresh all day long . . .'

She faltered, because it really wasn't her. She couldn't do jaunty. The stuff was a dollar a bottle! Who could afford that? Well, a lot of troll ladies, that's who, but Mr Strongintherm said it was okay because they had the money, and anyway it did let the moss grow. She'd said all right, but a dollar for a fancy bottle of water with some plant food in it was a bit steep. And he'd said you are Selling the Dream.

And they bought it. That was the worrying part. They bought it and recommended it to their friends. The city had discovered the Heavy Dollar now. She'd read about it in the paper. There had always been trolls around, doing the heavy lifting and generally being there in the background if not being the actual background itself. But now they were raising families and running businesses, moving on and up and buying things, and that made them people at last. And so you got other people like Mr Strongintherm, a dwarf, selling beauty products to Miss and Mrs Troll, via ladies like Glenda, a human, because although dwarfs and trolls were officially great chums these days, because of something called the Koom Valley Accord, that sort of thing only meant much to the sort of people who signed treaties. Even the most well-intentioned dwarf would not walk down some of the roads along which Glenda, every week, dragged her nasty, semi-cardboard case, Selling the Dream. It got her out of the house and paid for the little treats. There was money to put away for a rainy day. Mr Strongintherm had the knack of coming up with new ideas, too. Who would have thought that lady trolls would go for fake-tan lotion? It sold. Everything sold. The Dream sold, and it was shallow and expensive and made her feel cheap. It—

Her ever-straining ears caught the sound of next door's front door opening very slowly. Ha! Juliet jumped as Glenda suddenly loomed beside her.

'Off somewhere?'

'Gonna watch the game, ain't I?'

Glenda glanced up the street. A figure was disappearing rapidly around the corner. She grinned a grim grin.

'Oh yes. Good idea. I wasn't doing anything. Just wait while I fetch my scarf, will you?' To herself she added, You just keep walking, Johnny!

With a thump that caused pigeons to explode away like a detonating daisy, the Librarian landed on his chosen rooftop.

He liked football. Something about the shouting and the fighting appealed to his ancestral memories. And this was fascinating, because, strictly speaking, his ancestors had been blamelessly engaged for centuries as upstanding corn and feed merchants and, moreover, were allergic to heights.

He sat down on the parapet with his feet over the edge, and his nostrils flared as he snuffed up the scents rising from below.

It is said that the onlooker sees most of the game. But the Librarian could smell as well, and the game, seen from outside, was humanity. Not a day went past without his thanking the magical accident that had moved him a few little genes away from it. Apes had it worked out. No ape would philosophize, 'The mountain is, and is not.' They would think, 'The banana is. I will eat the banana. There is no banana. I want another banana.'

He peeled one now, in a preoccupied way, while watching the evolving tableau below. Not only does said onlooker see most of the game, he might even see more than one game.

This street was indeed a crescent, which would probably have an effect on tactics if the players had any truck with such high-flown concepts.

People were pouring in from either end and also from a couple of alleyways. Mostly they were male – extremely so. The women fell into two categories: those who had been tugged there by the ties of blood or prospective matrimony (after which they could stop pretending that this bloody mess was in any way engrossing), and a number of elderly women of a 'sweet old lady' construction, who bawled indiscriminately, in a rising cloud of lavender and peppermint, screams of 'Get 'im dahn an' kick 'im inna nuts!' and similar exhortations.

And there was another smell now, one he'd learned to recognize but could not quite fathom. It was the smell of Nutt. Tangled with it were the smells of tallow, cheap soap and shonky-shop clothing that the ape part of him categorized as belonging to 'Tin Flinging Man'. He had been just another servant in the maze of the university, but now he was a friend of Nutt, and Nutt was important. He was also wrong. He had no place in the world, but he was in it, and the world was becoming aware of him soon enough.

The Librarian knew all about this sort of thing. There had been no space in the fabric of reality marked 'simian librarian' until he'd been dropped into one, and the ripples had made his life a very strange one.

Ah, another scent was riding the gentle updraught. It was easy: Screaming Banana Pie Woman. The Librarian liked her. Oh, she had screamed and run away the first time she'd seen him. They all did. But she had come back, and she'd smelled ashamed. She also respected the primacy of words, and, as a primate, so did he. And sometimes she baked him a banana pie, which was a kind act. The Librarian was not very familiar with love, which had always struck him as a bit ethereal and soppy, but kindness, on the other hand, was practical. You knew where you were with kindness, especially if you were holding a pie it had just given you. She was a friend of Nutt, too. Nutt made friends easily for someone who had come from nowhere. Interesting . . .

The Librarian, despite appearances, liked order. Books about cabbages went on the Brassica shelves, (blit) UUSSFY890-9046 (antiblit1.1), although obviously *Mr Cauliflower's Big Adventure* would be better placed in UUSS J3.2 (>blit) 9, while *The Tau of Cabbage* would certainly be a candidate for UUSS (blit+) 60-sp55-o9-hl (blit). To anyone familiar with a seven-dimensional library system in blit dimensional space it was as clear as daylight, if you remembered to keep your eye on the blit.

Ah, and here came his fellow wizards, walking awkwardly in the chafing trousers and trying so hard not to stand out in a crowd that they would have stood out even more if the rest of the crowd had been the least bit interested.

Nobody noticed. It was enthralling and exciting at the same time, Ridcully concluded. Normally the pointy hat, robe and staff cleared the way faster than a troll with an axe.

They were being pushed! And shoved! But it was not as unpleasant as the words suggested. There were moderate pressures on all sides as people poured in behind, as though the wizards were standing chest deep in the sea, and were swaying and shifting to the slow rhythm of the tide.

'My goodness,' said the Chair of Indefinite Studies. 'Is this football? It's a bit dull, isn't it?'

'Pies were mentioned,' said the Lecturer in Recent Runes, craning his neck.

'People are still coming in, guv,' said Ottomy.

'But however do we see things?'

'Depends on the Shove, guv. Usually people near the action shout out.'

'Ah, I see a pie seller,' said the Chair of Indefinite Studies. He took a couple of steps forward, there was a random shift and sway in the crowd, and he vanished.

'How is it now, Mister Trev?' said Nutt, as people surged around them.

'Hurts like buggery, excuse my Klatchian,' muttered Trev, clutching his injured arm to his coat. 'Are you sure you weren't holding a hammer?'

'No hammer, Mister Trev. I'm sorry, but you did ask me—'

'I know, I know. Where did you learn to punch like that?'

'Never learned, Mister Trev. I must never raise my hand to another person! But you went on so, and—'

'I mean, you're so skinny!'

'Long bones, Mister Trev, long muscles. I really am very sorry!'

'My fault, Gobbo, I didn't know your own strength—' Suddenly Trev shot forward, cannoning into Nutt.

'Where've you been, my man?' said the person who had just slapped him hard on the back. 'We said to meet at the eel-pie stall!'

Now the speaker looked at Nutt and his eyes narrowed. 'And who's this stranger who thinks he's one of us?'

He did not exactly glare at Nutt, but there was a definite sense of a weighing in the balance, and on unfriendly scales.

Trev brushed himself off, looking uncharacteristically embarrassed. 'Hi, Andy. Er, this is Nutt. He works for me.'

'What as? A bog brush?' said Andy. There was laughter from the group behind him. Andy always got a laugh. It was the first thing you noticed, after the glint in his eye.

'Andy's dad is captain of Dimwell, Gobbo.'

'Pleased to meet you, sir,' said Nutt, extending a hand.

'Ooo, pleased to meet you, sir,' Andy mimicked, and Trev grimaced as a calloused hand the size of a plate grasped Nutt's cheese-straw fingers.

'He's got hands like a girl,' Andy observed, taking a grip.

'Mister Trev has been telling me wonderful things about the Dimmers, sir,' said Nutt. Andy grunted. Trev saw his knuckles whiten with effort while Nutt chattered. 'The camaraderie of the sport must be a wonderful thing.'

'Yeah, right,' Andy grunted, finally managing to pull his hand away, his face full of angry puzzlement.

'And this is my mate, Maxie,' said Trev quickly, 'and this is Carter the Farter—'

'It's Fartmeister now,' said Carter.

'Yeah, right. And this is Jumbo. You want to watch out for him. He's a thief. Jumbo can pick a lock faster than you can pick your nose.'

The said Jumbo held up a small bronze badge. 'Guild, of course,' he said. 'They nail your ears to the door else.'

'You mean you break the law for a living?' said Nutt, horrified.

'Ain't you ever heard of the Thieves' Guild?' said Andy.

'Gobbo's new,' said Trev protectively. 'Hasn't got out much. He's a goblin, from the high country.'

'Coming down here, taking our jobs, yeah?' said Carter.

'Like, how often do you do a hand's turn?' said Trev.

'Well, I might want to one day.'

'Milking the cows when they come home?' said Andy. This got another laugh, on cue. And that was the introductions sorted out, to Nutt's surprise. He'd been expecting chicken theft to be mentioned. Instead, Carter pulled a couple of tin cans out of a pocket and tossed them to Nutt and Trev.

'Did a few hours' unloading down the docks, didn't I?' he said defensively, as though a bit of casual labour was some kind of offence. 'This come off a boat from Fourecks.'

Jumbo fished in his pocket again and pulled out someone else's watch.

'Game on in five minutes,' he declared. 'Let's shove . . . er, if that's all right with you, Andy?'

Andy nodded. Jumbo looked relieved. It was always important that things were all right with Andy. And Andy was still watching Nutt as a cat watches an unexpectedly cheeky mouse, while massaging his hand.

Mr Ottomy cleared his throat, causing his red Adam's apple to bob up and down like an indecisive sunset. Shouting in public, yes, he liked that, he was good at that. Speaking in public, now, that was a different kettle of humiliation.

'Well, er, gents, what we will have here is your actual football, what is basically about the Shove, which is what you gentlemen will be doing soon—'

'I thought we watched two groups of players vie with one another to get the ball in the opponents' goal?'

'Could be, sir, could very much be,' the bledlow conceded, 'but in the streets, see, your actual supporters on both sides try and endeavour to shorten the length of the field, as it were, depending on the flow of play, so to speak.'

'Like living walls, d'y'mean?' said Ridcully.

'That style of thing, sir, yes, sir,' said Ottomy loyally.

'What about the goals?'

'Oh, they're allowed to move the goals, too.'

'Sorry?' said Ponder. 'The spectators can move the goals?'

'You have put your finger firmly on it, sir.'

'But that's sheer anarchy! It's a mess!'

'Some of the old boys do say the game has gone downhill, sir, that is true.'

'Downhill, into and out through the bottom of the world, I'd say.'

'Good one to play with magic, though,' said Dr Hix. 'Well worth a try.'

'A word to the wise, sir,' said Ottomy with unwitting accuracy, 'but you'd be wearing your guts for garters if you tried it with some of the types who play these days. They take it seriously.'

'Mister Ottomy, I'm sure none of my blokes wear garters—' Ridcully stopped and listened to Ponder Stibbons's whispered interjection and continued, 'well, possibly one, two at most, and it would be a very dull world if we were all the same, that's what I say.' He looked around and shrugged. 'So, this is football, is it? Rather a wizened shell of a game, yes? I, for one, don't want to stand around all day in the rain while other people have all the fun. Let's go and find the ball, gentlemen. We are wizards. That must count for something.'

'I thought we were blokes now,' said the Lecturer in Recent Runes.

'Same thing,' said Ridcully, straining to see over the heads of the crowd.

'Surely not!'

'Well,' said Ridcully, 'isn't a bloke someone who likes drinking with his mates and without the company of women? Anyway, I'm fed up with this. Form up behind me, nevertheless. We're going to see some football.'

The progress of the wizards astonished Ottomy and Nobbs, who had hitherto seen them as fluffy plump creatures quite divorced from real life. But to get to be a senior wizard and stay there called for deep reserves of determination, viciousness and the sugared arrogance that is the mark of every true gentleman, as in 'Oh, was that your foot? I'm so *terribly* sorry.'

And, of course, there was Dr Hix, a good man to have in a tight spot because he was (by college statute) an officially bad person, in accordance with UU's happy grasp of the inevitable.*

A less mature organization than UU might have taken the view that the way forward would be to hunt such renegades down, at great risk and expense. UU, on the other hand, had given Hix and his team a department and a budget and a career structure, and also the chance to go out into dark caves occasionally and throw fireballs at unofficial evil wizards; it all worked rather well so long as nobody pointed out that the Department of Post-Mortem Communications was really, when you got right down to it, just a politer form of n*e*c*r*o*m*a*n*c*y, wasn't it?

And so Dr Hix was now tolerated as a useful, if slightly irritating member of the Council largely because he was allowed (by statute) to say some of the naughty things that the other wizards would really have liked to say themselves. Someone with a widow's peak, a skull ring, a sinister staff and a black robe was expected to spread a little evil around the place, although university statute had redefined acceptable evil in this case as being inconveniences on a par with shoelaces tied together or a brief attack of groinal itch. It wasn't the most satisfactory of arrangements, but it was in the best UU tradition: Hix occupied, amiably, a niche that might otherwise be occupied by someone who really got off on the whole mouldering corpses and peeled skulls thing. Admittedly, he was always giving fellow wizards free tickets to the various amateur dramatic productions he was obsessively involved with,

* In short, every wizard knew that, whatever you did, you'd get some wizards creeping off to do weird and messy magic in some cave somewhere.

but, on balance, they agreed, taking one thing with another, this was still better than peeled skulls.

For Hix, a crowd like this was too good to waste. Not only was there a plethora of bootlaces to be expertly tied together, but there were an awful lot of pockets as well. He always had some flyers for the next production in his robe,* and it wasn't the same as picking pockets. Quite the reverse. He stuffed them into any he could find.

The day was all a mystery to Nutt, and it stayed a mystery, becoming a little more mysterious with every passing minute. In the distance a whistle was blown and somewhere in this moving, jostling, crushing and in most cases drinking mob of people there was a game going on, apparently. He had to take Trev's word for it. There were *Oos* and *Aahs* in the distance and the crowd ebbed and flowed in response. Trev and his chums, who called themselves, as far as Nutt could make out over the din, the Dimwell Massive Pussy, took advantage of every temporary space to move nearer and nearer to the mysterious game, holding their ground when the press went against them and pushing hard when an eddy went their way. Push, sway, shove . . . and something in this spoke to Nutt. It came up through the soles of his feet and the palms of his hands, and slid into his brain with a beguiling subtlety, warming him, stripping him away from himself and leaving him no more than a beating part of the living, moving thing around him.

A chant came past. It had started somewhere at the other end of the game and, whatever it had been once, it was now just four syllables of roar, from hundreds of people and many gallons of beer. As it faded, it took the warm, belonging feeling away with it, leaving a hole.

Nutt looked into the eyes of Trev.

'Happened to you, did it?' Trev said. 'That was quick.'

'It was—' Nutt began.

'I know. We don't talk about it,' said Trev flatly.

---

* Hix had flatly refused to wear trousers. No self-disrespecting dark wizard would dream of wearing such common garb as a trouser, he declared. It totally spoiled the effect.

'But it spoke to me without—'

'We don't talk about it, okay? Not that sort of thing. Look! They're being pushed back. It's opening up! Let's shove!'

And Nutt was good at shoving . . . very good. Under his inexorable pressure people slid or gently spun out of the way, their hobnailed boots scraping on the stones as, short of an alternative, the owners were rolled and squeezed alongside Nutt and Trev and deposited behind them, somewhat dizzy, bewildered and angry.

Now, though, there was a frantic tugging at Nutt's belt.

'Stop pushing!' Trev shouted. 'We've left the others behind!'

'In fact my progress is now hindered by a pease pudding and chowder stand. I have been doing my best, Mister Trev, but it has really been slowing me down,' said Nutt over his shoulder, 'and also Miss Glenda. Hello, Miss Glenda.'

Trev glanced behind him. There was a fight going on back there, and he could hear Andy's battle cry. There was generally a fight going on around Andy, and if there wasn't, he started one. But you had to like Andy, because . . . well, you just had to. He— Glenda was up ahead? Surely that meant that *she* would be there too?'

There was a commotion further on and a vaguely oblong thing, wrapped now in tatters of cloth, rose up in the air and fell back, to cheers and catcalls from the crowd. Trev had been right up to the game face many times before. It was no big deal. He'd seen the ball dozens of times.

But how long had Nutt been pushing a pudding stall in front of him like a snowplough? Oh my, Trev thought, I've found a player! How can 'e do it? He looks half-starved all the time!

In the absence of any way round in the press of people, Trev scrambled between Nutt's legs, and for a moment looked down an avenue of coat hems, boots and, right in front of him, a pair of legs that were considerably more attractive than those of Nutt. He surfaced a few inches away from the milky-blue eyes of Juliet. She did not look surprised; surprise is an instant thing, and by the time Juliet could register surprise, she generally wasn't. Glenda, on the other hand, was the kind of person who instantly whacks surprise on the meat slab of indignation and hammers it into fury, and as their gazes locked and metaphorical bluebirds cleared their throats for the big number, she appeared between them and demanded: 'What the hells were you doing down there, Trevor Likely?'

The bluebirds evaporated.

'What are *you* doin' up front here?' said Trev. It wasn't repartee, but it was the best he could do now, with his heart pounding.

'We got shoved,' growled Glenda. 'You lot were shoving us!'

'Me? I never did!' said Trev indignantly. 'It was—' He hesitated. Nutt? Look at him standing there all nervous and skinny, like he's never had a good meal in his life. *I* wouldn't believe me, and I *am* me. 'It was them behind,' he said lamely.

'Trolls with big boots on, were they?' said Glenda, her voice all vinegar. 'We'd be in the game if it wasn't for Mister Nutt here, holding you all back!'

The unfairness of this took Trev aback, but he decided to stay there rather than argue with Glenda. Nutt could do no wrong in her eyes, and Trev could do no right, which he couldn't contest, but rather felt should be amended to 'never did any serious wrong'.

But there was Juliet, smiling at him. When Glenda looked away to talk to Nutt she slipped something into his hand and then turned her back on him as if nothing had happened.

Trev opened his hand, heart pounding, and there was a little enamel badge in black and white, the colours of the hated enemy. It was still warm from Her hand.

He closed his hand quickly and looked around to see if anyone had spotted this betrayal of all that was good and true, i.e. the good name of Dimwell. Supposing he got knocked down by a troll and one of the lads found it on him! Supposing Andy found it on him!

But it was a gift from Her! He put it into his pocket and rammed it down to the bottom. This was going to be really difficult, and Trev was not a man who liked problems in his life.

The owner of the pudding stand, having enterprisingly sold a number of portions to passing trade during its journey, strolled up to Trev and offered him a bag of hot pease.

'Tough mate you got there,' he said. 'Some kind of troll, is he?'

'Not troll. Goblin,' said Trev, as the sounds of the strife drew nearer.

'I thought they were little buggers—?'

'This one isn't,' said Trev, wishing the man would go away.

There was a sudden, localized silence. The kind of noise made by people who are holding their breath. He looked up and saw the ball, for the second time in the game.

There was a core of ash wood in there somewhere, then a leather skin and finally dozens of layers of cloth for grip, and it was dropping with pinpoint inevitability towards the beautiful, dreamy head of Juliet. Trev dived at her without a moment's thought, dragging her under the cart as the ball thumped on to the cobbles where She had been gracing the world with Her presence.

Many things went through Trev's mind as the ball hit the ground. She was in his arms, even if She was complaining about getting mud on her coat. He had probably saved Her life, which from a romantic point of view was money in the bank, and— oh, yes. Dimmer or Dolly, if one of the hardcore posses found out about this the next thing to go through his head would be a boot.

She giggled.

'Shush!' he managed. 'Not a good idea if you'd rather not know how you would look with that beautiful hair shaved off!'

Trev peeped out from under the stall, and attracted no attention at all.

This is because Nutt had picked up the ball and was turning it over and over in his hands with a frown on what was visible of, if you were kind, his face.

'Is this all it is?' he said to a bewildered Glenda. 'A most inappropriate ending to a pleasant social gathering with interesting canapés! Where is this wretched thing supposed to be, then?'

Glenda, hypnotized by the sight, pointed a wavering finger in the general direction of down the street.

'There's a big pole? Painted white . . . well, spattered with red at the bottom . . .'

'Oh yes, I see it. Well, in that case, I'll— Look, will you men please stop pushing?' Nutt added to the crowd, who were craning to see.

'But there's no way you'll ever get it there!' Glenda yelled. 'Just put it down and come away!'

Trev heard a grunt from Nutt and absolute silence from the rest of the world. Oh, no, he thought. Really no. It must be more than, what, a hundred and fifty yards to that goal, and those things fly like a bucket. There is no way that he could—

A distant *pock* broke the breathless silence, which healed itself instantly.

Trev peered over a shoulder as the sixty-foot goal post gave up its battle with termites, rot, weather, gravity and Nutt, and fell into its own base in a cloud of dust. He was so astonished that he hardly noticed Juliet standing up next to him.*

'Is that a kind of, like, sign?' said Juliet, who believed in such things.

At that moment, Trev believed in pointing a finger towards the other side of the street and shouting, 'He went that way!' and then hauling Juliet upright and butting Nutt in the stomach. 'Let's go!' he added. He couldn't do anything about Glenda, but that would not matter; while he held Juliet's hand Glenda would follow him like a homing vulture. People were trying to run towards the hidden goal; others were making for the apparent location of the long-distance scorer. Trev pointed in a random direction and yelled, 'He went down there! Big man with a black hat!' Confusion always helped, when it wasn't yours; when it was time for a hue and cry, make sure who was hue.

They halted a few alleys away. There was still a commotion far off, but a city crowd is easier to get lost in than a forest.

---

* In fact, Juliet's rising from beneath the cart passed relatively unnoticed by all except an art student who was almost blinded by the light at the spectacle, and many years later painted the picture known as *Beauty Arising from the Pease Pudding Cart Attended by Cherubs Carrying Hot Dogs and Pies*. It was widely regarded as a masterpiece, although no one could ever work out exactly what the hell it was all about. But it was beautiful and so it was true.

'Look, perhaps I should go back and apologize,' Nutt began. 'I could make a new pole quite easily.'

'I hate to tell you this, Gobbo, but I think you might have upset the kind of people who don't listen to apologies,' said Trev. 'Keep moving, everyone.'

'Why might they be upset?'

'Well, Mister Nutt, first, you are not supposed to score a goal when it is not your game, and anyway you are a watcher, not a player,' said Glenda. 'And second, a shot like that gets right up people's noses. You could have killed someone!'

'No, Miss Glenda, I assure you I could not. I deliberately aimed at the pole.'

'So? That doesn't mean you were sure to hit it!'

'Er, I have to say it does, Miss Glenda,' he mumbled.

'How did you do it? You took the pole to bits! They don't grow on trees! You'll get us all into trouble!'

'Why can't he be a player?' said Juliet, staring at her reflection in a window.

'What?' said Glenda.

'Bloody hell,' said Trev. 'With him on the team you wouldn't need a team!'

'That'd save a lot of trouble, then,' said Juliet.

'So you say,' said Glenda, 'and where would be the fun in that? That wouldn't be football any more—'

'We are being watched,' said Nutt. 'I am sorry to interrupt you.'

Trev glanced around. The street was busy, but mostly with its own affairs. 'There's no one interested, Gobbo. We're well away.'

'I can feel it on my skin,' Nutt insisted.

'What, through all that wool?' said Glenda.

He turned round, soulful eyes on her. 'Yes,' he said, and remembered Ladyship testing him on that. It had seemed like a game at the time.

He glanced up and a large head drew back quickly from a parapet. There was a very faint smell of bananas. Ah, that one. He was nice. Nutt saw him sometimes, going hand over hand along the pipes.

'You ought to get 'er home,' said Trev to Glenda.

Glenda shuddered. 'Not a good idea. Old Stollop'll ask her what she saw at the game.'

'Well?'

'She'll tell him. And who she saw—'

'Can't she lie?'

'Not in the way you can, Trev. She's just no good at making stuff up. Look, let's get back to the university. We all work there, and I often go in to catch up. We'll go directly now and you two go back the long way. We never saw one another, right? And for heavens' sake don't let him do anything silly!'

'Excuse me, Miss Glenda,' said Nutt meekly.

'Yes, what?'

'Which of us were you addressing?'

'I have let you down,' said Nutt, as they strolled through the post-match crowds. At least, Trev ambled; Nutt moved with a strange gait that suggested there was something wrong with his pelvis.

'Nah, it's fixable,' said Trev. 'Everything is fixable. I'm a fixer, me. What did anybody really see? Just a bloke in Dimmer kit. There's thousands of us. Don't worry. Er, how come you're so tough, Gobbo? You spent your life lifting weights, or what?'

'You are correct in your surmise, Mister Trev. Before I was born I did indeed use to lift weights. I was only a child then, of course.'

They strolled on and after a while Trev said, 'Could you say that again? It's got stuck in my head. Actually, I think part of it's stickin' out of my ear.'

'Ah, yes. Perhaps I have confused you. There was a time when my mind was full of darkness. Then Brother Oats helped me to the light, and I was born.'

'Oh, religion stuff.'

'But here I am. You asked why I am strong? When I lived in the dark of the forge, I used to lift weights. The tongs at first, and then the little hammer and then the biggest hammer, and then one

89

day I could lift the anvil. That was a good day. It was a little freedom.'

'Why was it so important to lift the anvil?'

'I was chained to the anvil.'

They walked on in silence again until Trev, picking each word with care, said, 'I guess things must be sort of tough in the high country?'

'It is not so bad now, I think.'

'Makes you count your blessin's, that sort of thing.'

'The presence of a certain lady, Mister Trev?'

'Yes, since you ask. I think about 'er all the time! I really like 'er! But she's a Dolly!' A small group of supporters turned to glance at them, and he lowered his voice to a hiss. 'She's got brothers with fists the size of a bull's arse!'

'I have read, Mister Trev, that love laughs at locksmiths.'

'Really? And what does it do when it's been smacked in the face by a bull's arse?'

'The poets are not forthcoming in that respect, Mister Trev.'

'Besides,' said Trev, 'locksmiths tend to be quiet blokes, you know? Careful and patient and that. Like you. I reckon you could get away with a bit of a joke. You must 'ave met girls. I mean, you're no oil painting, that's a fact, but they like a posh voice. I bet you 'ad them eatin' out of your 'and . . . well, after you'd washed it, obviously.'

Nutt hesitated. There had been Ladyship, of course, and Miss Healstether, neither of whom fitted easily into the category of 'girl'. Of course, there were the Little Sisters, who were certainly young and apparently female but it had to be said looked rather like intelligent chickens, and certainly weren't seen at their best when you watched them feeding – but once again, 'girls' did not seem the right word.

'I have not met many girls,' he volunteered.

'There's Glenda. She's taken a real shine to you. Watch out, though, she'll run your life for you if you let her. It's what she does. She does it to everyone.'

'You two have a history, I think,' said Nutt.

'You are a sharp one, aren't you? Quiet and sharp. Like a knife. Yeah,

I suppose it was a history. I wanted it to be more of a geography, but she kept slappin' my hand.' Trev paused to search for any flicker in Nutt's face. 'That was a joke,' he added, without much hope.

'Thank you for telling me, Mister Trev. I will decipher it later.'

Trev sighed. 'But I ain't like that any more, and Juliet . . . well, I'd crawl a mile over broken glass just to hold 'er 'and, no funny business.'

'Writing a poem is often the way to the intended's heart,' said Nutt.

Trev brightened. 'Ah, I'm good with words. If I wrote 'er a letter, you could give it to 'er, right? If I write it on posh paper, something like, let's see . . . "I think you are really fit. How about a date? No hanky panky, promise. Luv, Trev." How does that sound?'

'The soul of it is pure and noble, Mister Trev. But, ah, if I could assist in some way . . .?'

'It needs longer words, right? And more sort of curly language?' said Trev.

But Nutt was not paying attention.

'Sounds lovely to me,' said a voice above Trev's head. 'Who do you know what can read, smart boy?'

There was this to be said about the Stollop brothers: they weren't Andy. It was, in the great scheme of things, not a huge difference when you couldn't see for blood but, in short, Stollops knew that force had always worked, and so had never bothered to try anything else, whereas Andy was a stone-cold psychopath who had a following only because it was safer than being in front of him. He could be quite charming when the frantically oscillating mood swing took him; that was the best time to run. As for the Stollops, it would not take long for a researcher to realize that Juliet was the brains of the family outfit. One advantage from Trev's viewpoint was that they thought they were clever, because no one had ever told them otherwise.

'Ha, Mister so-called Trev,' said Billy Stollop, prodding Trev with a finger like a hippopotamus sausage. 'You full o' smarts, you tell us who broke the goal, right?'

'I was in the Shove, Billy. Didn't see a thing.'

'He gonna play for the Dimmers?' Billy persisted.

'Billy, not even your dad at his best could throw the ball half as far as everyone is saying. You know it, right? You couldn't do it. I'm hearing that the Angels' post just fell apart and someone made up a story. Would I lie to you, Billy?' Trev could make up lies that were very nearly truths.

'Yeah, 'cos you're a Dimmer.'

'All right, you got me, I'll come clean,' said Trev, holding out his hands. 'Respect and all that, Billy . . . It was Nutt here that threw that ball. That's my last offer.'

'I ought to smack your 'ead off for that,' said Billy, sneering at Nutt. 'That kid don't look like he could even lift the ball.'

And then a voice behind Trev said, 'Why, Billy, have they let you out without your collar on?'

Nutt heard Trev mutter, 'Oh gods, and I was doing so well,' under his breath, and then his friend turned and said, 'It's a free street, Andy. No 'arm in passin' the time, eh?'

'The Dollies killed your ol' man, Trev. Ain't you got no shame?'

The rest of the Massive Posse was standing behind Andy, their expressions a mix of defiance and the realization that, once again, they were going to be dragged into something. They were out in the main streets now. The Watch was not inclined to get involved in alley scuffles, but out in the open they had to do something in case the tax-payers complained, and since tired coppers didn't like having to do something, they did it good and hard, so with any luck they wouldn't have to do it again any time soon.

'What do you know about all this they're saying about a Dimmer man and a Dolly tart holding hands in the Shove?' Andy demanded. He put a heavy hand on Trev's shoulder. 'Come on, you're smart, you always know everything before anyone else.'

'Tart?' That was Billy; it was a long way from his ears to his brain. 'There's not a girl in Dolly Sisters who'd look at you poxy lot!'

'Ah, so that's where we got it from!' said Carter the Farter. This struck Nutt as inflammatory in the circumstances. Perhaps, he thought, the ritual is that childish insults shall be exchanged until both sides feel fully justified in attacking, just as Dr Vonmausberger noted in *Ritual Aggression in Pubescent Rats.*

But Andy had fished his short cutlass out of his shirt. It was a nasty little weapon, alien to the true spirit of foot-the-ball, which generally smiled indulgently on things that bruised, scared, fractured and, okay, worst case, heat of the moment and so on, blinded.* But then came Andy, who had issues. And once you had someone like Andy around you, you got other Andys around too, and every kid who might otherwise have gone to a match with a pair of brass knuckles for bravado noticeably clanked when he walked, and needed to be helped up if he fell over.

Now, weapons were being loosened here, too.

'Careful now, everyone,' Trev cautioned, stepping back and waving his empty hands in a conciliatory way. 'This is a busy street, okay? If the Old Sam catch you fightin', they'll be down on you with big, big truncheons and they'll beat you until you 'onk your breakfast, 'cos for why? 'cos they hate you, 'cos you're making paperwork for 'em and keepin' 'em out of the doughnut shop.'

He stepped back a little further. 'And then on account of you damagin' their weapons with your 'eads they'll run you down to the Tanty for a nice night in the Tank. Been there? Was it so much fun you want to go back again?'

He noted with satisfaction the looks of dismayed recollection on the faces of all except Nutt, who couldn't have any idea, and Andy, who was brother to the Tank. But even Andy was not inclined to go up against the Sam. Kill just one of them, and Vetinari would give you one chance to see if you could stand on air.

They relaxed a little, but not too much. All it took in these sphincter-taut circumstances was one idiot . . .

As it happened, one very clever person was able to do the job, when Nutt turned to Algernon, the youngest Stollop, and said cheerfully,

---

* But you'd got another eye, right? And now you had solid proof that you were a hard man, especially if you got one of those scars that run across the eye and down the cheek. Get a black eye-patch, and you would never have to wait to be served at a bar ever again.

'Do you know, sir, that your situation here is very similar to that described by Vonmausberger in his treatise on his experiment with rats?'

At this point, Algernon, after one second of what passed for Algernon as thought, whacked him hard with his club. Algernon was a big boy.

Trev managed to grab his friend before he hit the cobbles. The club had hit Nutt square in the chest and torn the ancient sweater open. Blood was soaking through the stitches.

'What did you 'ave to go and 'it him for, you bloody fool?' Trev said to Algernon, agreed even by his brothers to be as thick as elephant soup. 'He wasn't doin' a thing. What was that all about, eh?' He sprang to his feet and before Algernon could move Trev had ripped his own shirt off and was ministering to Nutt, trying to staunch the wound. He came back up again after half a minute and flung the sodden shirt at Algernon. 'There's no heartbeat, you moron! What did he ever do to you?'

Even Andy was frozen. No one had ever seen Trev like it, not old Trev. Even the Dollies knew Trev was smart. Trev was slick. Trev wasn't the sort to commit suicide by yelling at a bunch of men who were already tensed for a fight.

The luckless Algernon, with Trev's rage baking his face, managed, 'But, like . . . he's a Dimmer . . .'

'Who are yer? You're a bloody fool, that's what you are!' screamed Trev.

He rounded on the others, finger shaking. 'Who are yer? Who are yer? Nuffin! You're rubbish! You're all shite!'

He jabbed the finger at Nutt. 'And him? He made stuff. He knew things. And he'd never seen a game before today! He was only wearing the strip to fit in!'

'Don't you worry, Trev, mate,' Andy hissed and raised his cutlass menacingly. 'There's going to be a bloody war about this!' But Trev was suddenly in his face like a wasp.

'You what? You are mental! You just don't get it, do you?'

'I can see helmets, Andy,' said Jumbo urgently.

'Me? What did I do?'

'As much as the stupid Stollops. Dimmers and Dollies? I hope the gods shit thin shit on both of you!'

'They're getting really close, Andy.'

The Stollop boys, who were not altogether dumb, were already leaving. People in football strip were criss-crossing the city. The Watch couldn't chase everyone. But, well, belting some bloke who then bled a lot and stopped breathing, well, that was tantamount to murder, and the Old Sam could develop quite a turn of speed in those circumstances.

Andy shook a furious finger at Trev. 'It's a hard life in the Shove when you're a dumb chuff with no mates.'

'This ain't the Shove!'

'Better wake up, kid. It's all Shove.'

The Posse left at speed, although Jumbo turned for a moment to mouth 'sorry'. They weren't the only ones hurrying off. The street people were all for a free cabaret, but this one might have associated difficulties: for example the asking of dangerous metaphysical questions such as 'Did you see anything?' and similar. It was all very well for the Watch to say 'the innocent have nothing to fear', but what was that all about? Who cared about the innocent and their problems when the Watch were on their way?

Trev knelt by the cooling body of the late Nutt.

And now for the first time in a minute, it seemed to Trev, he started to breathe again. He had stopped when he had raged at Andy 'cos if you talked like that to Andy you were dead anyway, so why waste your breath?

There were things you had to do, weren't there? Weren't you supposed to keep banging on the chest to, like, show the broken heart how to beat again? But he didn't know how, and you didn't need much smarts to know that it was not a good idea to try to learn with the Watch on the way. It would not give a good first impression.

That was why, when two watchmen turned up at speed, Trev was walking unsteadily towards them with Nutt in his arms. He was relieved to see that in charge was Constable Haddock: at least he was one of the ones who asked questions first. Behind him, and eclipsing most of the scenery, was Troll officer Bluejohn, who could clear a whole street just by walking down the centre of it.

'Can you help me get him to the Lady Sybil, Mister Haddock? He's very heavy,' said Trev.

Constable Haddock pulled the sodden shirt aside, and made a sad little clicking sound. With experience comes familiarity.

'Morgue's closer, lad.'

'No!'

Haddock nodded. 'You're Dave Likely's son, aren't you?'

'I don't have to tell you!'

'No, 'cos I'm right,' said Constable Haddock evenly. 'Okay, Trev. Bluejohn here will take this man, who I expect you have never seen before in your life, and we'll both run to keep up. There was a decent thunderstorm the night before last. He might be lucky. And so might you.'

'I never did it!'

''course not. And now . . . let's see who's fastest at running, shall we? The hospital first.'

'I want to stay with him,' said Trev, as Bluejohn's huge hand gently cradled Nutt.

'No, lad,' said Haddock. 'You stay with me.'

It didn't stop with Constable Haddock. It never did. Everyone called him Kipper, and his calm unspoken message that since we're all in this together, why make it hard for one another often worked, but sooner or later you'd be handed over to a senior copper who manufactured hard, in a little room with another copper at the door. And this one had been working double shifts, by the look of her.

'I'm Sergeant Angua, sir, and I hope you are not in trouble.' She opened a notebook and smoothed down the page.

'Shall we go through the motions? You told Constable Haddock that you saw a fight going on and when you got there all the big boys had run away and, amazingly, you found your workmate, Mister Nutts, bleeding to death. Well, I bet I can name all the big boys, every last one of them. I wonder why can't you? And what, Trevor Likely, is *this* about?' She flicked a black-and-white enamel token across the table, and by luck or judgement its pin stuck in the wood a few inches from Trev's hand.

The unofficial motto of the Lady Sybil Free Hospital was 'Not everybody dies'. It was true that, subsequent to the founding of the Lady Sybil, the chances of death from at least some causes in the city were quite amazingly reduced. Its surgeons were even known to wash their hands *before* operating as well as after. But moving through its white corridors now was a figure who knew, from personal experience, that the unofficial motto was, in reality, entirely mistaken.

Death stood by the well-scrubbed slab and looked down. MISTER NUTT? WELL, THIS IS A SURPRISE, said Death, reaching into his robe. LET ME SEE WHAT I HAVE HERE.

YOU KNOW, he said, I USED TO WONDER WHY PEOPLE SCRABBLED SO. AFTER ALL, COMPARED WITH THE LENGTH OF INFINITY, PEOPLE DO NOT LIVE ANY TIME AT ALL. EVEN YOU, MISTER NUTT. ALTHOUGH I CAN SEE THAT SCRABBLING WOULD WORK A LITTLE MAGIC IN YOUR CASE.

'I can't see you,' said Nutt.

JUST AS WELL, said Death. YOU WILL NOT REMEMBER ME, IN ANY CASE, LATER ON.

'I'm dying, then,' said Nutt.

'YES. DYING AND THEN AGAIN LIVING. He fished out a life-timer from his robe and watched as the sand fell upwards. SEE YOU *LATER*, MISTER NUTT. I FEAR THAT YOU WILL HAVE AN INTERESTING LIFE.

'A Dolly favour on a good Dimmer boy? Gods bless my soul, I say, what can this be about? And you know what? I will find out. It's all a matter of shoving.'

Trev said nothing. He was out of options. Besides, he had seen the sergeant before, and she always seemed to be looking at his throat.

'Constable Haddock tells me the Igor's on duty down at the Lady Sybil. I hope he's got a heart in his vats that'll fit your friend, I really do,' she said. 'But it'll still be a murder case, even if he comes walking in here tomorrow. Lord Vetinari's rules: if it takes an Igor to bring you back, you were dead. Briefly dead, it's true, which is why the murderer will be briefly hanged. A quarter of a second usually does it.'

'I didn't touch 'im!'

'I know. But you have to keep solid with your mates, right? Jumbo and, of course, Carter, and, oh yes, Andy Shank, your mates, who aren't here. Look, you are not under arrest – yet – you are helping the Watch with their inquiries. That means you can use the privy, if you're feeling brave. If you're feeling suicidal, use the canteen. But if you try to run off I will hunt you down.' She sniffed and added, 'Like a dog. Understand?'

'Can't I go and see how Nutt is gettin' on?'

'No. Kipper's still down there now. That's Constable Haddock to you.'

'Everyone calls him Kipper.'

'Maybe, but not when it's you talking to me.' The sergeant twirled the favour around on the table in an absent-minded way. 'Has Mister Nutt got any next of kin? That means relatives.'

'I know what it means. He talks about people in Uberwald. That's all I know,' Trev lied instinctively. Saying that someone had spent his youth chained to an anvil was not going to help here. 'He gets on all right with the other guys in the vats.'

'How come he's in there?'

'We never ask. There's usually some bad story.'

'Anyone ever ask *you*?'

He stared at her. That was coppers for you. They came over all friendly, and just when you dropped your guard they stuck a pickaxe in your brain.

'Was that an official copper question, or were you just bein' nosy?'

'Coppers are never nosy, Mister Likely. However, sometimes we ask tangential questions.'

'So it wasn't official?'

'Not really . . .'

'Then shove it where the sun does not shine.'

Sergant Angua smiled a copper's smile. 'You've got no card in your hand that you dare play, and you come out with something like that. From Andy, yes, I'd expect it, but Kipper says you're smart. How smart does someone have to be to be as stupid as you?'

There was a tentative knock at the door and then a watchman put his head around it. Someone was shouting in the background in a large, authoritative voice. '—I mean, you deal with this sort of thing all the time, don't you? For heavens' sake, it's not that hard—'

'Yes, Nobby?'

'We've got a bit of a situation, sarge. That stiff that went to the Lady Sibyl? Doctor Lawn's here and he says the man's got up and gone home!'

'Did they get an Igor to look at him?'

'Yes. Sort of . . . er . . .'

The watchman was elbowed out of the way by an expansive man in a long green rubber robe who was clearly trying to balance angry and friendly at the same time. He was tailed by Constable Haddock, who was clearly trying to mollify him, and definitely failing.

'Look, we try to help, all right?' said Doctor Lawn. 'You people say you've got a murder case and I'll pull old Igor off his slab and hang the overtime. But you tell Sam Vimes from me that I'd like him to send his boys down when they're not busy for a bit of first-aid tuition, to wit, the difference between dead and sleeping. It's a fine line sometimes, but it's generally possible to spot the clues. The profession has always tended to consider walking about to be among the more reliable, although in this city we've learned to look on that as just a very good start. But when we pulled back the sheet he sat up and asked Igor if he had a sandwich, which is generally conclusive. Apart from a fever, he was fine. Strong heartbeat, which suggests he's got one. Not a scratch on him, but he could certainly do with a good dinner. He must have been hungry because he ate the sandwich Igor made for him. On the subject of dinners, frankly I could do with mine!'

'You let him go?' said Sergeant Angua, horrified.

'Of course! I can't keep a man in hospital for being inconveniently alive!'

She turned to Constable Haddock. 'And you let him go, Kipper?'

'It looked like a case of doctor's orders, sarge,' said Haddock, giving Trev a wretched look.

'He was covered in blood! He was really messed up!' Trev exploded.

'A prank, then?' Angua tried.

'I'd have sworn there wasn't a heartbeat, Sergeant,' Haddock volunteered. 'Maybe he's one of those monks from the Hub that do the hocus-pocus stuff.'

'Then someone has been wasting Watch time,' said Angua, glaring at Trev.

He spotted that one for the desperate throw it was. 'What would be in it for me?' he said. 'Do you think I want to be here?'

Constable Haddock cleared his throat. 'It's match night, sarge. The desk is heaving and there are supporters roaming around all over the place and someone's been feeding them a lot of rumours. We're stretched, that's all I'm saying. We've had a couple of big shouts already. And he did walk away, after all.'

'Not a problem for me,' said the doctor. 'Came in horizontal, went out upright. It's the preferred way. And I've got to get back, sergeant. We're going to have a busy night, too.'

The sergeant looked for someone to shout at, and there was Trev.

'You! Trev Likely. This one's down to you! Go and find your chum. And if there's any more trouble, there'll be . . . trouble. Is that clear?'

'Twice, sarge.' He couldn't resist it, he just couldn't, not even with the cold sweat rolling down his spine. But he felt light . . . uplifted . . . released. But some people just can't respect an epiphany when you're having one. It's not a cop skill.

'It's sergeant to you, Likely! Here!'

Trev managed to catch the favour as it was skimmed across the room.

'Thanks, sarge!'

'Get out!'

He got out, and was half expecting the shadowy shape that stepped up to him when he was clear of the building. There was a faint odour in the grey air. Well, at least it wasn't Andy. He could do without Andy right now.

'Yes, Carter?' he said to the fog.

'How did you know it was me?'

Trev sighed. 'I guessed.' He started to walk fast.

'Andy'll want to know what you said.'

'Don't worry, it's sorted.'

'Sorted! How?' Carter, always a bit overweight, had to scurry to keep up.

'Not going to tell you.' Oh, the joy of the moment.

'But can I tell him we're in the clear?'

'It's all sorted! Done and dusted! I blew it out. It's fixed. All gone away. It never happened.'

'Are you sure?' said Carter. 'He was pretty busted up.'

'Hey, what can I tell you?' Trev flung out his arms and twirled a pirouette. 'I'm Trev Likely!'

'Well, that's firm, then. Hey, I bet Andy'll let you back in the Posse now. That would be great, eh?'

'Do you know what Nutt thought the Posse was called, Carter?'

'No. What?'

Trev told him.

'Well, that's—' Carter began, but Trev interrupted.

'It's funny, Carter. It's funny, and sort of sad and hopeless. It really is.' Trev stopped walking so abruptly that Carter collided with him. 'And here's a tip: Carter the Farter isn't gonna take you anywhere. And that goes for the Fartmeister, too. Trust me.'

'But everybody calls me Carter the Farter,' the Fartmeister wailed.

'Punch the next one who does. See a doctor. Cut down on carbo-hydrates. Keep out of confined spaces. Use aftershave,' said Trev, speeding up again.

'Where are you going, Trev?'

'I'm gettin' out of the Shove!' Trev called over his shoulder.

Carter looked around desperately. 'What Shove?'

'Haven't you heard? It's all Shove!'

Trev wondered if he glowed as he trotted through the fog. Things were going to be different. As soon as Smeems got in, he'd go and see him about a better job or something . . .

A figure appeared out of the mist ahead of him. This was something of an achievement since the figure was a head shorter than him.

'Mithter Likely?' it said.

'Who's askin'?' said Trev and added, 'What's askin'?'

The figure sighed. 'I underthtand that you are a friend of the gentleman rethently admitted to the hothpital,' it said.

'What's that to you?'

'Quite a lot,' said the figure. 'May I athk if you know very much about the gentleman?'

'I don't have to talk to you,' said Trev. 'Everything's been fixed, okay?'

'Would that thith wath the cathe,' said the figure. 'I have to talk to you. My name ith Igor.'

'You know, I had a feelin' about that. Are you the one who made the sandwich for Nutt?' asked Trev.

'Yeth. Tuna, thpaghetti and jam, with thprinkleth. My thignature dith. Do you know anything about hith background?'

'Not a thing, mister.'

'Really?'

'Look. In the vats you stir up tallow, not the past, okay? You just don't, right? I know he's had some bad times, an' that's all I'm telling you.'

'I thought tho,' said Igor. 'I believe he cometh from Uberwald. Thome thtrange and dangerouth thingth come from Uberwald.'

'This might sound a stupid question, but do you come from Uberwald, by any chance?' said Trev.

'Thinth you athk, yeth,' said Igor.

Trev hesitated. You saw Igors around occasionally. The only thing most people knew was that they could stitch you up even better than the Watch and did strange things in cellars and only tended to come out much when there were thunderstorms.

'I think your friend may be very dangerouth,' said Igor.

Trev tried to picture Nutt as dangerous. It was quite hard until you remembered a throw that knocked down a whole goal post half a street away. He wished he didn't.

'Why should I listen to you? How do I know *you* are not dangerous?' he said.

'Oh, I am,' said Igor, 'believe me. And Uberwald containth thingth that I would not want to meet.'

'I am not gonna listen to you,' said Trev. 'And you are pretty hard to understand in any case.'

'Ith he thubject to thtrange moodth?' Igor ploughed on. 'Doth he get into a rage? Do you know anything about hith eating habitth?'

'Yes, he likes apple pies,' said Trev. 'What're you on about?'

'I can thee you are great friendth,' said Igor. 'I am thorry that I have trethpathed on your time.' 'Trethpathed' hanging in the air considerably added to the water drops hanging in the fog. 'I will give you thome advith. When you need me, jutht thcream. I regret that you will find it very eathy to thcream.' The figure turned and instantly vanished into the mist.

And Igors moved about oddly, Trev remembered. And you never saw one at a football game . . .

He noticed that last thought go past. What had he tried to tell himself? That someone who did not watch football was not a real person? He couldn't think of a proper answer. He was amazed that he had even asked the question. Things were changing.

Glenda arrived in the Night Kitchen with Juliet sworn to silence, and beneficently gave Mildred and Mrs Hedges the rest of the night off. That suited them both very well, as it always does, and a little favour had been done there that she could call upon when necessary.

She took her coat off and rolled up her sleeves. She felt at home in the Night Kitchen, in charge, in control. Behind black iron ranges she could defy the world.

'All right,' she said to the subdued Juliet. 'We weren't there today. Today did not happen. You were here helping me clean the ovens. I'll see you get some overtime so your dad won't suspect. Okay? Have you got that?'

'Yes, Glenda.'

'And while we're here we'll make a start on the pies for tomorrow night. It'll be nice to get ahead of ourselves, right?'

Juliet said nothing.

'Say "Yes, Glenda",' Glenda prompted.

'Yes, Glenda.'

'Go and chop some pork, then. Being busy takes your mind off things, that's what I always say.'

'Yes, Glenda, that's what you always say,' said Juliet.

An inflection caught Glenda's ear, and worried her a little. 'Do I always say that? When?'

'Every day when you come in and put your apron on, Glenda.'

'Mother used to say that,' said Glenda, and tried to shake the thought out of her head. 'And she was right, of course! Hard work never hurt anybody!' And she tried to unthink the treacherous thought: *except her.* Pies, she thought. You can rely on pies. Pies don't give you grief.

'I fink that Trev likes me,' Juliet muttered. 'He don't give me funny looks like the other boys. He looks like a little puppy.'

'You want to watch out for that look, my girl.'

'I fink I luvim, Glendy.'

Wild boar, thought Glenda, and apricots. There's some left in the cool room. And we've got mutton pies with a choice of tracklements . . . always popular. So . . . pork pies, I think, and there's some decent oysters in the pump room, so they'll do for the wet pie. I'll do Sea Pie and the anchovies look good, so there's always room for a Stargazey or two, even though I feel sorry for the little fishes, but right now I'll bake some blind pastries so that— 'What did you say?'

'I luvim.'

'You can't!'

'He saved my life!'

'That's no basis for a relationship! A polite thank you would have sufficed!'

'I've got a feelin' about him!'

'That's just silly!'

'Well? Silly's not bad, is it?'

'Now you listen to me, young— Oh, hello, Mister Ottomy.'

It is in the way of the Ottomies all around the worlds to look as if they have been built out of the worst parts of two men and to be annoyingly hushen-footed on thick red rubber soles, all the better to peep and pry. And they always assume that a free cup of tea is theirs by right.

'What a day, miss, what a day! Were you at the match?' he enquired, glancing from Glenda to Juliet.

'Been cleaning the ovens,' said Glenda briskly.

'Yes, today didn't happen,' Juliet added, and giggled. Glenda hated giggling.

Ottomy looked around slowly and without embarrassment, noting the absence of dirt, discarded gloves, cloths—

'And we've only just finished getting everything all neat and tidy,' Glenda snarled. 'Would you like a cup of tea, Mister Ottomy? And then you can tell us all about the game.'

It has been said that crowds are stupid, but mostly they are simply confused, since as an eyewitness the average person is as reliable as a meringue lifejacket. It became obvious, as Ottomy went on, that nobody had any clear idea about anything other than that some bloke threw a goal from halfway down the street, and even then only maybe.

'But, funny thing,' Ottomy went on, as Glenda metaphorically let out a breath, 'while we was in the Shove, I could've sworn I saw your lovely assistant here chatting to a lad in the Dimmer strip . . .'

'No law against that!' Glenda said. 'Anyway, she was here, cleaning the ovens.' It was clumsy, but she hated people like him, who lived for the exercise of third-hand authority and loved every little bit of power they could grab. He'd seen more than he'd told her, that was certain, and wanted her to wriggle. And out of the corner of her mind, she could feel him looking at their coats. Their wet coats.

'I thought you didn't go to the football, Mister Ottomy?'

'Ah, well, there you have it. The pointies wanted to go and watch a game, and me and Mister Nobbs had to go with them in case they got breathed on by ordinary people. Blimey, you wouldn't believe it! Tutting and complaining and taking notes, like they owned the street. They're up to something, you mark my words.'

Glenda didn't like the word 'pointies', although it was a good description. Coming from Ottomy, though, it was an invitation to greasy conspiracy. But however you baked it, wizards were nobs, people who mattered, the movers and the shakers: and when people like that got interested in the doings of people who by definition did not matter, little people were about to be shaken, and shook.

'Vetinari doesn't like football,' she said.

'Well, o'course, they're all in it together,' said Ottomy, tapping his nose. This caused a small lump of dried matter to shoot from his other nostril into his tea. Glenda had a brief struggle with her conscience over whether to point this out, but won.

'I thought you should know this, on account of how people up in the Sisters look up to you,' said Ottomy. 'I remember your mum. She was a saint, that woman. Always had a helping hand for everyone.' Yes, and didn't they grab, said Glenda to herself. She was lucky to die with all her fingers.

Ottomy drained his mug and plonked it on the table with a sigh. 'Can't stand around here all day, eh?'

'Yes, I'm sure you've got lots of other places to stand.'

Ottomy paused at the entrance arch, and turned to grin at Juliet.

'A girl the spit and image of you, I'd swear it. With a Dimmer boy. Amazing. You must have one of those double gangers. Well, it'll have to remain a mystery, as the man said when he found something that would have to remain a mystery. Toodle-oo—'

He stopped dead rather than walk into the silvery knife that Glenda was holding in a not totally threatening way quite close to his throat.

106

She had the satisfaction of seeing his Adam's apple pop back up and down again like a sick yoyo.

'Sorry about that,' she said, lowering it. 'I've always got a knife in my hand these days. We've been doing the pork. Very much like human flesh, pork, or so they say.' She put her spare hand across his shoulders and said, 'Probably not a good idea, spreading silly rumours, Mister Ottomy. You know how people can be so funny about that sort of thing. Nice of you to drop by and if you happen to be going past tomorrow I'll see that you get a pie. Do excuse us. I have a lot of chopping up to do.'

He left at speed. Glenda, her heart pounding, looked at Juliet; her mouth made a perfect O.

'What? What?'

'I fort you was goin' to stab 'im!'

'I just happened to be holding a knife. You are holding a knife. We hold knives. This is a kitchen.'

'D'you fink he's goin' to tell?'

'He doesn't really know anything.' Eight inches, she thought. That's as big as you can make a pie without a dish. How many pies could I make out of a weasel like Ottomy? The big mincer would make it easy. Ribcages and skulls must be a problem, though. Probably better, on the whole, to stick to pork.

But the thought blazed away at the back of her mind, never to become action but unfamiliar, exciting and oddly liberating.

What were the wizards doing at the game? Making notes about what? A puzzle to think about.

In the meantime, they were in a world of pies. Juliet could work quite well at repetitive jobs when she put her mind to it, and she had a meticulousness often found in people who were not very clever. Occasionally she sniffed, not a good thing when you are making pie filling. She was probably thinking about Trev, and pasting him, in her beautiful and not very overcrowded head, into one of those glittery dreams sold by *Bu-bubble* and other junk, where all you had to do to be famous was just 'be yourself'. Ha! While Glenda had always known what she wanted. She worked long, poorly paid hours to get it, and here it was: her own kitchen, and power, more or less . . . over pies! *A moment ago you were daydreaming of turning a man into pies!*

Why are you so angry all the time? What went wrong? I'll tell you what went wrong! When you got there, there was no there there. You wanted to see Quirm from an open carriage while a nice young man drank champagne out of your slipper, but you never did, because they were a funny lot in Quirm, and you couldn't trust the water, and how did that champagne thing work, anyway? Didn't it drip out? What would happen if your toe trouble played up again . . . ? So you never did. Never will.

'I never said Trev's a bad lad,' she said aloud. 'Not a gentleman, needs a slap to teach him manners and he takes life a good deal too easily, but he could make something of himself if he had reason to put his mind to it.'

Juliet did not seem to be listening, but you never could tell.

'It's just the football. You're on different sides. It won't work,' Glenda finished.

'S'posing I went and supported the Dimmers?'

A day ago that would have sounded like some kind of sacrilege; now it just presented a huge problem.

'For a start, your dad wouldn't speak to you ever again. Or your brothers.'

'They don't now, much, anyway, except to ask when their grub is goin' to be ready. D'you know, today was the first time I ever saw the ball up close? And you know what? It weren't worth it. Hey, and they're goin' to have a fashion show on at Shatta tomorrow. Why don't we go?'

'Never heard of it,' Glenda snorted.

'It's a dwarf store.'

'That sounds right. I can't imagine humans naming anything like that. You'd be hostage to the first misprint.'

'We could go. Might be fun.' Juliet waved a tattered copy of *Bu-bubble*. 'And the new micromails are going to be really good and soft, and don't chafe, it says here, plus, horned helmets are making a

108

return after too long in obs . . . curi . . . tea. Where's that? And there's this mat . . . in . . . a tomorrow.'

'Yes, but we're not the kind of women who go to fashion shows, Jules.'

'You're not. Why am I not?'

'Well, because . . . Well, I wouldn't know what to wear.' Glenda was getting desperate now.

'That's why you should go to fashion shows,' said Juliet smugly.

Glenda opened her mouth to snap a reply, and thought: it's not about boys and it's not about football. It's safe.

'All right. I suppose it might be fun. Look, we've done a woman's job this evening. I'll take you home now and do my chores and come back. Your dad might be worrying.'

'He'll be in the pub,' said Juliet accurately.

'Well, he would be worrying if he wasn't,' said Glenda.

She wanted some time to herself with her feet up. It hadn't just been a long day, it had been a long and deep one as well. She needed some time for things to settle.

'And we'll take a chair, how about that?'

'They're very expensive!'

'Well, you're only young once, that's what I say.'

'I never heard you say that before.'

Several troll chairs were waiting outside the university. They were expensive at fivepence for the ride, but the seats in panniers round the carrier's neck were much more comfy than the slats on the buses. Of course, it was posh, and curtains twitched and lips pursed. That was the strange thing about the street: if you were born there, people didn't like it if you started not to fit in. Granny had called it 'getting ideas above your station'. It was letting the side up.

She opened Juliet's door for her because the girl always fumbled with the lock, and watched it shut.

Only then did she open her own front door, which was as patched and peeling as the other one. She'd hardly taken her coat off when there was a hammering on the weatherbeaten woodwork. She flung it open to find Mr Stollop, Juliet's father, one fist still raised and a little cloud of powdered paint flecks settling around him.

'Heard you come in, Glendy,' he said. 'What's this all about?'

His other huge hand rose, holding a crisp off-white envelope. You didn't see many of these in Dolly Sisters.

'It's called a letter,' said Glenda.

The man held it out imploringly and now she noticed the large letter V on the dreaded government stamp, guaranteed to spread fear and despondency among those with taxes yet to pay.

'It's his lordship writing to me!' said Mr Stollop in distress. 'Why'd he want to go and write to me? I haven't done nothing!'

'Have you thought about opening it?' said Glenda. 'That's generally how we find out what's in letters.'

There was another of those imploring looks. In Dolly Sisters reading and writing was soft indoor work that was best left to the women. Real work required broad backs, strong arms and calloused hands. Mr Stollop absolutely fitted the bill. He was captain of the Dollies and in one match had bitten an ear off three men. She sighed and took the letter from a hand which she noticed was slightly trembling and slit it open with her thumbnail.

'It says here, Mister Stollop,' she said, and the man winced. 'Yes. That would be you,' Glenda added.

'Is there anything about taxes or anything?' he said.

'Not that I can see. He writes that "I would greatly appreciate your company at a dinner I am proposing to hold at Unseen University at eight o'clock Wednesday evening to discuss the future of the famous game foot-the-ball. I will be pleased to welcome you as the captain of the Dolly Sisters team."'

'Why has he picked on me?' Stollop demanded.

'He says,' said Glenda, 'because you're the captain.'

'Yes, but why me?'

'Maybe he's invited all the team captains,' Glenda volunteered. 'You could send a lad round with a white scarf and check, couldn't you?'

'Yeah, but supposing it's just me,' said Stollop again, determined to plumb the horror to its depths.

Glenda had a bright idea. 'Well then, Mister Stollop, it would look like the captain of the Dolly Sisters is the only one important enough to discuss the future of football with the ruler himself.'

Stollop didn't square his shoulders because he wore them permanently squared, but with a muscular nudge he managed to achieve the effect of cubed. 'Hah, he's got that one right!' he roared.

Glenda sighed inwardly. The man was strong, but his muscles were melting into fat. She knew his knees hurt. She knew he got out of breath rather quickly these days and in the presence of something he couldn't bully, punch or kick, Mr Stollop was entirely at a loss. Down by his sides his hands flexed and unflexed themselves as they tried to do his thinking for him.

'What's this all about?'

'I don't know, Mister Stollop.'

He shifted his weight. 'Er, would it be about that Dimmer boy that got himself hurt today, d'you think?'

Could be anyone, thought Glenda as cold dread blossomed. It's not as though it doesn't happen every week. It doesn't have to be either of them. It will be, of course, I know it, but I don't know it, can't possibly know it, and if I repeat that long enough it might all never have happened.

Got himself hurt, thought Glenda in the roar of panic. That quite likely means he happened to be standing in the wrong place in the wrong strip, which is tantamount to a self-inflicted wound. He got himself killed.

'My lads came in and said it was out in the street. That's what they just heard. He got killed, that's what they heard.'

'They didn't see anything?'

'That's right, they didn't see a thing.'

'But they were doing a lot of listening?'

That one went over Stollop's head without even bothering to climb.

'And it was a Dimmer boy?'

111

'Yes,' he said. 'They heard he died, but you know how those Dimwell buggers lie.'

'Where are your boys now?'

For a moment the old man's eyes blazed. 'They're stoppin' indoors or I'll thrash 'em. You get some nasty gangs out when something like that's been happening.'

'One less now, then,' said Glenda.

Stollop's face was painted in pigments of misery and dread. 'They're not bad boys, you know. Not at heart. People pick on them.'

Yes, down at the Watch House, she said to herself, where people say, 'That's them! The big ones! I'd know them anywhere!'

She left him shaking his head and ran down the road. The troll would never expect to get a fare up here and there was no sense in hanging around and getting covered in paint. She might just about be able to catch up with it on its way down town. After a minute or two she realized that someone was following her. *Chasing* her in the gloom. If only she'd remembered to bring the knife. She stepped into a patch of deeper shadow and, as the knife-wielding maniac drew level, stepped out and shouted, 'Stop following me!'

Juliet gave a little scream. 'They've got Trev,' she sobbed, as Glenda held her. 'I know they have!'

'Don't be silly,' said Glenda. 'There's fighting all the time after a big match. No sense in getting too worried.'

'So why were you running?' said Juliet sharply. And there was no answer to that.

The bledlow nodded him through the staff door with a grunt and he headed straight away for the vats. A couple of the lads were dribbling in their meticulous and very slow way, but there was no sign of Nutt until Trev risked his sanity and nasal passages by checking the communal sleeping area, where he found Nutt sleeping on his bedroll, clutching his stomach. It was an extremely large stomach. Given the usual neat shape of Nutt, it made him look a little like a snake that had swallowed an extremely large goat. The curious face of the Igor and his worried voice came back to him. He looked down beside the bedroll and saw a small piece of piecrust and some crumbs. It smelled like a very good pie. In fact, he could think of only one person who could ever make a pie quite so beguiling. Whatever it was that had been filling Trev, the invisible illumination that had made him almost dance here from the Watch House, drained out through his feet.

He headed through the stone corridors to the Night Kitchen. Any optimism he might have retained was dashed one hope at a time by the trail of pie crumbs, but the illumination rose again as he saw Juliet and, oh yes, Glenda, standing in what was left of the Night Kitchen, which was a mess of torn-open cupboards and pieces of piecrust.

'Oh, Mister Trevor Likely,' said Glenda, folding her arms. 'Just one question: who ate all the pies?'

The illumination swelled until it filled Trev with a kind of silvery light. It had been three nights since he had slept in an actual bed and it had not been your normal sort of day. He smiled broadly at nothing at all and was caught by Juliet as he hit the ground.

Trev woke up half an hour later, when Glenda brought him a cup of tea. 'I thought we'd better let you sleep,' she said. 'Juliet said you looked awful, so obviously she's coming to her senses.'

'He was dead,' said Trev. 'Dead as a doorknob, and then he wasn't. What's that all about?' He levered himself up and realized that he had been put to bed on one of the grubby bedrolls in the vats. Nutt was lying on the roll next to him.

'All right,' said Glenda. 'If you can do it without lying, tell me.' She sat down and watched the sleeping Nutt for a while as Trev tried to make sense of the previous evening. 'What was in the sandwich again? The one the Igor gave him?'

'Tuna, spaghetti and jam. With sprinkles,' said Trev, yawning.

'Are you sure?'

'It's not the kinda thing you forget.'

'What kind of jam?' Glenda insisted.

'Why ask?'

'I'm thinking it might work with quince. Or chilli. Can't see any place for sprinkles, though. They don't make any sense.'

'What? He's an Igor. It doesn't have to make sense!'

'But he warned you about Nutt?'

'Yes, but I don't think he meant "lock up your pies", do you? Are you gonna get into trouble about the pies?'

'No. I've got plenty more maturing in the cool room. They're at their best when matured. You have to keep ahead of yourself, with pies.'

She looked down at Nutt and went on, 'Are you really telling me he got all smashed up by the Stollop boys and then walked out of the Lady Sibyl?'

'He was as dead as a doorknob. Even old 'addock could spot that.'

This time they both stared at Nutt.

'He's alive now,' said Glenda, as if it was an accusation.

'Look,' said Trev, 'all I know about people who come from Uberwald is that some of them are vampires and some are werewolves. Well, I don't think vampires are much interested in pies. And it was a full moon last week and he didn't act odd; well, odder than normal.'

Glenda lowered her voice. 'Maybe he's a zombie— No, they don't eat pies either.' She continued to stare at Nutt, but another part of her said, 'There's going to be a banquet on Wednesday night. Lord Vetinari's up to something with the wizards. It's about the football, I'm sure of it.'

'Well?'

'For some plan, I expect. Something nasty. The wizards were at the game today taking notes! Don't tell me that's healthy. They want to shut down football, that's what it is!'

'Good!'

'Trevor Likely, how can you say that! Your dad—'

'Died because he was dumb,' said Trev. 'And don't tell me it was the way he would have wanted to go. No one would want to go like that.'

'But he loved his football!'

'So? What does that mean? The Stollop boys love their football. Andy Shank loves 'is football! And what does it mean? Not countin' today, how often have you seen the ball in play? Hardly ever, I bet.'

114

'Well, yes, but it's not about the football.'

'You're saying that football is not about football?'

Glenda wished she'd had a proper education, or, failing that, any real education at all. But she was not going to back off now. 'It's the sharing,' she said. 'It's being part of the crowd. It's chanting together. It's all of it. The whole thing.'

'I believe, Miss Glenda,' said Nutt from his mattress, 'that the work you are looking for is Trousenblert's *Der Selbst uberschritten durch das Ganze.*'

They looked down at Nutt again, mouths open. He had opened his eyes and appeared to be staring at the ceiling. 'It is the lonely soul trying to reach out to the shared soul of all humanity, and possibly much further. W. E. G. Goodnight's translation of *In Search of The Whole* is marred, while quite understandable, by the mistranslation of *bewußtseinsschwelle* as "haircut" throughout.'

Trev and Glenda looked at one another. Trev shrugged. Where could they start?

Glenda coughed. 'Mister Nutt, are you alive or dead or what?'

'Alive, thank you very much for asking.'

'I saw you killed!' Trev shouted. 'We ran all the way to the Lady Sybil!'

'Oh,' said Nutt. 'I am sorry, I do not recall. It would seem that diagnosis was in error. Am I right?'

They exchanged glances. Trev got the worst of it. When Glenda was angry, her glance might just possibly etch glass. But Nutt had a point. It was hard to argue with a man who insisted that he was not dead.

'Um, and then you came back here and ate nine pies,' said Glenda.

'Looks like they did you good,' said Trev, with brittle cheerfulness.

'But I can't see where they've gone,' Glenda finished. 'Belly-busters, every one of them.'

'You will be angry with me.' Nutt looked frightened.

'Let's all calm down, shall we?' said Trev. 'Look, I was pretty worried, my oath, yes. Not angry, okay? We're your friends.'

'I must be becoming. I must be helpful!' This came from Nutt's lips like a mantra.

Glenda took his hands. 'Look, I'm not bothered about the pies, really I'm not. I like to see a man with a good appetite. But you must tell us what's wrong. Have you done something you shouldn't?'

'I should be making myself worthy,' Nutt said, pulling away gently and not meeting her eyes. 'I must be becoming. I must not lie. I must gain worth. Thank you for your kindness.'

He got up, walked down the length of the vats, picked up a basket of candles, came back, wound up his dribbling machine and began to work, oblivious of their presence.

'Do you know what goes on in his head?' Glenda whispered.

'When he was young, he was chained to an anvil for seven years,' said Trev.

'What? That's terrible! Someone must have been very cruel to do something like that!'

'Or desperate to make sure he didn't get free.'

'Things are never all they seem, Mister Trev,' said Nutt, without looking up from his feverish activity, 'and the acoustics in these cellars are very good. Your father loved you, did he not?'

'Wot?' Trev's face reddened.

'He loved you, took you to the football, shared a pie with you, taught you to cheer for the Dimmers? Did he hold you on his shoulders so that you could see more of the game?'

'Stop talkin' about my dad like that!'

Glenda took Trev's arm. 'It's okay, Trev, it's all right, it's not a nasty question, really it isn't!'

'But you hate him, because he became a mortal man, dying on the cobbles,' said Nutt, picking up another undribbled candle.

'*That* is nasty,' said Glenda. Nutt ignored her.

'He let you down, Mister Trev. He wasn't the small boy's god. It turned out that he was only a man. But he was not only a man. Everyone who has ever watched a game in this city has heard of Dave Likely. If he was a fool, then any man who has ever climbed a mountain or swum a torrent is a fool. If he was a fool then so was the man who first tried to tame fire. If he was a fool then so was the man who tried

116

the first oyster, he was a fool, too – although I'm bound to remark that, given the division of labour in early hunter-gatherer cultures, he was probably a woman as well. Perhaps only a fool gets out of bed. But, after death, some fools shine like stars, and your father is such a one. After death, people forget the foolishness, but they do remember the shine. You could not have done anything. You could not have stopped him. If you could have stopped him he would not have been Dave Likely, a name that means football to thousands of people.' Nutt very carefully put down a beautifully dribbled candle and continued. 'Think about this, Mister Trev. Don't be smart. Smart is only a polished version of dumb. Try intelligence. It will surely see you through.'

'That's just a load of words!' said Trev hotly, but Glenda saw the glistening lines down his cheeks.

'Please think about them, Mister Trev,' said Nutt and added, 'There, I have done a complete basket. That is worth.'

It was the calmness. Nutt had been spinning, almost sick with anxiety. He'd been repeating himself, as if he'd had to learn things for a teacher. And then he was otherwise – totally reserved and collected.

Glenda looked from Trev to Nutt and back again. Trev's mouth hung open. She didn't blame it. What Nutt had said with quiet matter of factness had sounded like not an opinion but the truth, winched out of some deep well.

Then Trev broke the silence, speaking as if hypnotized, his voice hoarse.

'He gave me his old jersey when I was five. It was like a tent. I mean, it was so greasy I never got wet—' He stopped.

After a moment Glenda pushed at his elbow. 'He's gone all stiff,' she said, 'as stiff as a piece of wood.'

'Ah, catatonic,' said Nutt. 'He is overwhelmed by his feelings. We should lay him down.'

'These old mattresses they sleep on in here are rubbish!' said Glenda, looking around for a better alternative to cold flagstones.

'I know the very thing!' said Nutt, suddenly all action and plunging off down the passage. This left Glenda still holding a rigid Trev when

Juliet appeared from the direction of the kitchens. She stopped instantly when she saw them, and burst into tears.

'He's dead, isn't he?'

'Er, no—' Glenda began.

'I talked to some of the bakery lads coming in to work and they're telling me there's been fights all over the city and someone got himself murdered!'

'Trev's just had a bit of a shock, that's all. Mister Nutt's gone to find something for him to lie down on.'

'Oh.' Juliet sounded a little disappointed, presumably because 'a bit of a shock' was not sufficiently dramatic, but she rallied just as a loud, rough and uniquely wooden noise from the other direction heralded Nutt pushing a large couch, which shuddered to a halt in front of them.

'There's a big room piled up with old furniture up the hall,' he said, patting the faded velvet. 'It's a bit musty, but I think all the mice have fallen out on the way here. Quite a find actually. I believe it is a chaise longue from the workshop of the famous Gurning Upspire. I think I can probably restore it later. Let him down gently.'

'What happened to him?' said Juliet.

'Oh, the truth can be a little bit upsetting,' said Nutt. 'But he will get over it and feel better.'

'I would very much like to know the truth myself, Mister Nutt, thank you very much,' said Glenda, folding her arms and trying to look stern while all the time a voice in her head was whispering *Chaise longue! Chaise longue! When no one else is here you can have a go at languishing!*

'It's a kind of medicine with words,' said Nutt, carefully. 'Sometimes people fool themselves into believing things that aren't true. Sometimes that can be quite dangerous for the person. They see the world in a wrong way. They won't let themselves see that what they believe is wrong. But often there is a part of the mind that does know, and the right words can let it out.' He gave them a worried look.

'Well, that's nice,' said Juliet.

'It sounds like hocus pocus to me,' said Glenda. 'Folk know their own minds!' She folded her arms again, and saw Nutt glance at them.

'Well?' she demanded. 'Haven't you ever seen elbows before?'

'Never such pretty dimpled ones, Miss Glenda, on such tightly folded arms.'

Up until that point Glenda had never realized that Juliet had such a dirty laugh, to which, Glenda fervently hoped, she was not entitled.

'Glenda's got a bee-oh! Glenda's got a bee-ooh!'

'It's "beau", actually,' Glenda said, swiping to the back of her mind the recollection that it had taken her years to find that out herself. 'And I was just helping. We're helping him, aren't we, Mister Nutt?'

'Doesn't he look sweet lying there?' said Juliet. 'All pink.' She stroked Trev's greasy hair inexpertly. 'Just like a little boy!'

'Yes, he's always been good at that,' said Glenda. 'Why don't you go and get the little boy a cup of tea? And a biscuit. Not one of the chocolate ones. That'll take some time,' she said as the girl shimmied away. 'She tends to get distracted. Her mind wanders and amuses itself elsewhere.'

'Trev tells me that despite your more mature appearance you are the same age as her,' said Nutt.

'You really don't talk to many ladies, do you, Mister Nutt?'

'Oh dear, have I made another faux pas?' said Nutt, suddenly all nerves again, to such an extent that she took pity on him.

'Would this be "faux pas" that looks as if it should be said like "forks pass"?'

'Er, yes.'

Glenda nodded, satisfied, another literary puzzle solved. 'Better not use the word "mature" unless you are talking about cheese or wine. Not good to use it for ladies.'

She stared at him, wondering how to pose the next question. She opted for directness; she wasn't very good at anything else.

'Trev is sure you sort of died and came alive again.'

'So I understand.'

'Not many people do that.'

'The vast majority do not, I believe.'

'How did you do it?'

'I don't know.'

'This is rather late in the day, I must admit, but you don't feel any hunger for blood or brains, do you?'

'Not at all. Just pies. I like pies. I am very ashamed about the pies. It will not happen again, Miss Glenda. I fear my body was acting on its own. It needed instant nourishment.'

'Trev says you used to be chained to an anvil?'

'Yes. That was because I was worthless. Then I was taken to see Ladyship and she told me: You are worthless but, I think, not unworthy, and I will give you worth.'

'But you must have had parents!'

'I do not know. There are many things I don't know. There is a door.'

'What?'

'A door in my head. Some things are behind the door and I don't know them. But that is all right, Ladyship says.'

Glenda felt like giving up. Nutt answered questions, yes, but really all you ended up with was more questions. But she persevered. It was like stabbing away at a tin can, hoping to find a way in. 'Ladyship is a real lady, is she? Castles and servants and whatnot?'

'Oh, yes. Even a whatnot. She is my friend. And she is mature like cheese and wine, because she has lived for a long time and is not old.'

'But she sent you here, yes? Did she teach you . . . whatever it was you used on Trev?'

Beside Glenda, Trev stirred.

'No,' said Nutt. 'I read the works of the masters in the library all by myself. But she did tell me that people, too, were a kind of living book, and I would have to learn to read them.'

'Well, you read Trev well enough. Be told, though: don't try that stuff on me or you'll never see another pie!'

'Yes, Miss Glenda. Sorry, Miss Glenda.'

She sighed. What is it about me? The moment they look downcast I feel sorry for them! She looked up. He was watching her.

'Stop that!'

'Sorry, Miss Glenda.'

'But you got to see the football, at least. Did you enjoy it?'

Nutt's face lit up. 'Yes. It was wonderful. The noise, the crowds, the chanting, oh the chanting! It becomes a second blood! The unison! To not be alone! To be not just one but one and all, of one mind and purpose! . . . excuse me.' He had seen her face.

'So you quite liked it, then,' said Glenda. The intensity of Nutt's outburst had been like opening an oven door. It was a mercy her hair hadn't frizzled.

'Oh yes! The ambience was wonderful!'

'I didn't try those,' Glenda hazarded, 'but the pease pudding is usually good.'

The scrape of crockery and the tinkling of a teaspoon heralded the arrival of Juliet, or rather of the cup of tea that she was holding in front of her as if it were a grail, so that she drifted along behind it like a comet's tail. Glenda was impressed. The tea was in the cup instead of in the saucer and it was the acceptable brown colour that is usually characteristic of tea and was usually the only tea-like characteristic of tea made by Juliet.

Trev sat up, and Glenda wondered how long he might have been paying attention. All right, he might be good in an emergency, and at least he washed sometimes and owned a toothbrush, but Juliet was special, wasn't she? All she needed was a prince. Technically that meant Lord Vetinari, but he was far too old. Besides, no one was sure which side of the bed he got out of, or even if he went to bed at all. But one day a prince would come, even if Glenda had to drag him on a chain.

She turned her head. Nutt was watching her intently again. Well, her book was locked down tightly. No one was going to riffle through her pages. And tomorrow she would find out what the wizards were up to. That was easy. She'd be invisible.

In the stillness of the night, Nutt sat in his special place, which was yet another room, very close to the vats. Candles burned as he sat at a rescued table, staring at a piece of paper and absent-mindedly cleaning out his ear with the point of his pencil.

Nutt was technically an expert on love poetry throughout the ages and had discussed it at length with Miss Healstether, the castle librarian. He had also tried to discuss it with Ladyship, but she had laughed and said it was frivolity, although quite helpful as a tutorial on the use of vocabulary, scansion, rhythm and affect as a means to an end, to wit getting a young lady to take all her clothes off. At that particular point, Nutt had not really understood what she meant. It sounded like some sort of conjuring trick.

He tapped the pencil on the page. The castle library had been full of poetry and he'd read it avidly as he read all books, not knowing why it had been written or what exactly it was supposed to achieve. But generally poems written by men to women followed a very similar format. Now, with a world's worth of the finest poetry to choose from, he was lost for words.

Then he nodded to himself. Ah, yes, Robert Scandal's famous poem, 'Oi! To his Deaf Mistress'. It surely had the right shape and tempo. Of course, there had to be a muse. Oh, yes, all poetry needed a muse. That might present a difficulty. Juliet, while quite attractive, was also, in his mind, a kind of amiable ghost. Hmm. Ah, of course . . .

Nutt pulled the pencil out of his ear, hesitated and wrote:

> I sing, but not of love, for love is blind,
> but celebrate instead the muse of kindness . . .

The fires in the vats cooled, but Nutt's brain was suddenly ablaze.

Round about midnight, Glenda decided it was safe enough to leave the boys alone to get up to whatever it was boys got up to when women weren't around to look after them, and made sure that she and Juliet were on the late cross-town bus. That meant she actually got to sleep in her own bed.

She looked around the tiny bedroom by candlelight and met the gaze, which was quite difficult, of Mr Wobble, the three-eyed transcendental teddy bear. It would have been nice to have a bit of cosmic explanation at this point, but the universe never gave you explanations, it just gave you more questions.

She reached down surreptitiously, even though there was only a three-eyed teddy bear watching her, and picked up the latest Iradne Comb-Buttworthy from the cache unsuccessfully hidden below. After ten minutes of reading, which took her some way into the book (Ms Comb-Buttworthy producing volumes that were even slimmer than her heroines), she experienced déjà vu. Moreover, the déjà vu was squared, because she had the feeling of having had the déjà vu before.

'They're really all the same, aren't they?' she said to the three-eyed teddy bear. 'You know it's going to be Mary the Maid, or someone like her, and there's got to be two men and she will end up with the nice one, and there has to be misunderstandings, and they never do anything more than kiss and it's absolutely guaranteed that, for example, an exciting civil war or an invasion by trolls or even a scene with any cooking in it is not going to happen. The best you can expect is a thunderstorm.' It really had nothing to do with real life at all, which, although short on civil wars and invasions by trolls, at least had the decency to have lots of cooking.

The book dropped out of her fingers and thirty seconds later she was sound asleep.

Surprisingly, no neighbour needed her in the night so she got up, dressed and breakfasted in what was an almost unfamiliar world. She opened her door to take breakfast to widow Crowdy and found Juliet on the doorstep.

The girl took a step back. 'Are you goin' out, Glendy? It's early!'

'Well, you're up,' said Glenda. 'And with a newspaper, I'm pleased to see.'

'Isn't it exciting?' said Juliet, and thrust the paper at her.

Glenda took one look at the picture on the front page, took a second, closer look, and then grabbed Juliet and pulled her inside.

'You can see their tonkers,' Juliet observed, in a voice that was much too matter-of-fact for Glenda's liking.

'You shouldn't know what they look like!' she said, smacking the paper down on her kitchen table.

'What? I've got three brothers, ain't I? Everyone bathes in a tub in front of the fire, don't they? It's not like they're anything special. Anyway, it's culture, all right? Remember when you took me to that place full of people in the nuddy. You stayed in there hours.'

'It was the Royal Art Museum,' said Glenda, thanking her stars that they were indoors. 'That's different!'

She tried to read the story, but it was very difficult with that amazing picture beside it, just where an eye might stray again and again.

Glenda enjoyed her job. She didn't have a career; they were for people who could not hold down jobs. She was very good at what she did, so she did it all the time, without paying much attention to the world. But now her eyes were opened. In fact, it was time to blink.

Under the headline 'New Light on Ancient Game' was a picture of a vase or, rather more grandly, an urn, in orange and black. It showed some very tall and skinny men – their masculinity was beyond doubt, but possibly beyond belief. They were apparently struggling for possession of a ball; one of them was lying on the ground, and looked as if he was in some pain. The translation of the name of the urn was, said the caption, THE TACKLE.

According to the accompanying story, someone at the Royal Art Museum had found the urn in an old storeroom, and it contained scrolls which, it said here, had the original rules of foot-the-ball laid down in the early years of the century of the Summer Weevil, a thousand years ago, when the game was played in honour of the goddess Pedestriana . . .

Glenda skimmed through the rest of it, because there was a lot of rest to skim. An artist's impression of the aforesaid goddess adorned page three. She was, of course, beautiful. You seldom saw a goddess portrayed as ugly. This probably had something to do with their ability to strike people down instantly. In Pedestriana's case, she would probably have gone for the feet.

Glenda put the paper down, seething with anger, and as a cook she knew how to seethe. This wasn't football – except that the Guild of Historians said that it was, and could prove it not only with old parchments but also with an urn, and she could see that you were on the wrong end of an argument if you were up against an urn.

But it was too neat, wasn't it? Except . . . why? His lordship didn't like football, but here was an article saying that this game was very old and had its own goddess, and if there were two things this city liked, it was tradition and goddesses, especially if the goddesses were a bit short on the chiffon above the waist. Did his lordship let them put *anything* in the paper? What was going on? 'I've got business to attend to,' she said sternly. 'It's good that you bought a decent paper, but you don't want to read this kind of stuff.'

'I didn't. Who's interested in that? I got it for the advert. Look.'

Glenda had never bothered much about the adverts in the paper, because they were put there by people who were after your money. But there it was, right there. Madame Sharn of Bonk gives you . . . micromail.

'You said we could go,' said Juliet pointedly.

'Yes, well, that was before—'

'You said we could go.'

'Yes. But, well, has anyone from the Sisters ever gone to a fashion show? It's not our kind of thing, is it?'

'Doesn't say that in the paper. Says admission free. You said we could go!'

Two o'clock, thought Glenda. Suppose I could manage it . . . 'All right, meet at work at half past one, do you hear? Not a minute later! I've got things to do.'

The University Council meets every day at half past eleven, she thought to herself. Oh, to be a fly on that wall. She grinned . . .

Trev was sitting in the battered old chair that served as his office in the vats. Work was proceeding at its usual reliable snail's pace.

'Ah, I see you are in early, Mister Trev,' said Nutt. 'I am sorry not to have been here. I had to go and deal with an emergency candelabra upset.' He leaned closer. 'I have done what you asked, Mister Trev.'

Trev snapped out of his daydream of Juliet and said, 'Huh?'

'You asked me to write . . . to improve your poem for Miss Juliet.'

'You've done it?'

'Perhaps you would like to have a look, Mister Trev?' He handed the paper to Trev and stood nervously by the chair as a pupil stands by the teacher.

After a very short while Trev's forehead wrinkled. 'What's ee-er?'

'That's "e'er", sir, as in "where e'er she walks".'

'You mean, like, she walks on air?' said Trev.

'No, Mister Trev. I should just put it down to poetry if I were you.'

Trev struggled on. He had never had much to do with poetry, except the sort that started 'There was a young lady of Quirm', but this looked like the real stuff. The page seemed to be crowded and yet full of space as well. Also, the writing was extremely curly and that was a sure sign, wasn't it? You didn't get that sort of thing from the lady of Quirm. 'This is great stuff, Mister Nutt. This is really great stuff. This is poetry, but what really is it sayin'?'

Nutt cleared his throat. 'Well, sir, the essence of poetry of this nature is to create a mood that will make the recipient, that is to say, sir, the young lady who you are going to send it to, feel very kindly disposed to the author of the poem, which would be you, sir, in this case. According to Ladyship, everything else is just showing off. I have brought you a pen and an envelope; if you would kindly sign the poem I will ensure that it gets to Miss Juliet.'

'I bet no one's ever written her a poem before,' said Trev, skating quickly over the truth that he hadn't either. 'I'd love to be there when she reads it.'

'That would not be advised,' said Nutt quickly. 'The general consensus is that the lady concerned reads it in the absence of the hopeful swain, that is you, sir, and forms a beneficent mental picture of him. Your actual presence might actually get in the way, especially since I see you haven't changed your shirt again today. Besides, I am informed that there is a possibility that all her clothes will fall off.'

Trev, who had been struggling with the concept of 'swain', fast-forwarded to this information at speed. 'Er, say that again?'

'All her clothes might fall off. I am sorry about this, but it appears to be a by-product of the whole business of poetry. But broadly speaking, sir, it carries the message you have asked for, which is to say "I think you're really fit. I really fancy you. Can we have a date? No hanky panky, I promise." However, sir, since it is a love poem, I have taken the liberty of altering it slightly to carry the suggestion that if hanky or panky should appear to be welcomed by the young lady she will not find you wanting in either department.'

Archchancellor Ridcully rubbed his hands together. 'Well, gentlemen, I hope we have all seen the papers this morning, or glanced at them at any rate?'

'I thought that the front page was not the place,' said the Lecturer in Recent Runes. 'It quite put me off my breakfast. Metaphorically speaking, of course.'

'Apparently, the urn has been in the museum's cellars for at least three hundred years, but for some reason it makes its presence felt now,' said Ridcully. 'Of course, they have tons of stuff in there that's never really been looked at properly and the city was going through a prudish period then and didn't care to know about that sort of thing.'

'What, that men have tonkers?' said Dr Hix. 'That sort of news gets out sooner or later.'

He looked around at the disapproving faces and added, 'Skull ring, remember? Under college statute the head of the Department of Post-Mortem Communications is entitled, nay, required to make tasteless, divisive and moderately evil remarks. I'm sorry, but these are *your* rules.'

'Thank you, Doctor Hix. Your uncalled-for remarks are duly noted and appreciated.'

'You know, it seems very suspicious to me that this wretched urn has turned up at just this time,' observed the Senior Wrangler, 'and I hope I am not alone in this?'

'I know what you mean,' said Hix. 'If I didn't know that the Archchancellor had his work cut out to persuade Vetinari to let us play, I would think that this was some sort of plan.'

'Ye-ess,' said Ridcully thoughtfully.

'The old rules look a lot more interesting, sir,' said Ponder.

'Ye-ess.'

'Did you read the bit that said players were not allowed to use their hands, sir? And the high priest takes to the field of play to ensure that the rules are honoured?'

'I can't see that catching on these days,' said the Lecturer in Recent Runes.

'He's armed with a poisoned dagger, sir,' said Ponder.

'Ah? Well, that should make for a more interesting game, at least, eh, Mustrum? . . . Mustrum?'

'What? Oh, yes. Yes. Something to think about, indeed. Yes, indeed. One man, in charge . . . The onlooker who sees most of the game . . . the gamer, in fact . . . So what move have I missed?'

'Sorry, Archchancellor?'

Ridcully blinked at Ponder Stibbons. 'What? Oh, just composing my thoughts, as one does.' He sat up straight. 'In any case the rules don't concern us at this point. We have to play this game in any eventuality and so we will abide by them in the best traditions of sportsmanship until we have worked out where they may be most usefully broken to our advantage. Mister Stibbons, you are collating our studies of the game. The floor is yours.'

'Thank you, Archchancellor.' Ponder cleared his throat. 'Gentlemen, the game of football is clearly about more than the rules and the nature of the play. In any case, these are pure mechanical considerations; the chanting and, of course, the food are of more concern to us, I feel. They seem to be an integral part of the game. Regrettably, so do the supporters' clubs.'

'What is the nature of this problem?' Ridcully enquired.

'They hit one another over the head with them. It would be true to say that brawling and mindless violence, such as occurred yesterday afternoon, is one of the cornerstones of the sport.'

'A far cry from its ancient beginnings, then,' said the Chair of Indefinite Studies, shaking his head.

'Well, yes. I understand that in those days the losing team was throttled. However, I suppose this would be called mindful violence that took place with the enthusiastic consent of the entire community, or at least that part of it that was still capable of breath. Fortunately, we do not yet have supporters, so that this is not at present *our* problem, and I propose we go directly to the pies.'

There was a chorus of general agreement from the wizards. Food was their cup of tea, and if possible slice of cake too. Some of them were already watching the door in anticipation of the tea trolley. It seemed like an age since nine.

'Central to the game is the pie,' Ponder went on, 'which is generally of shortcrust pastry containing appropriate pie-like substances. I collected half a dozen and tested them on the usual subjects.'

'The students?' said Ridcully.

'Yes. They said they were pretty awful. Not a patch on the pies here, they said. They finished them off, however. Examination of the ingredients suggests that they consisted of gravy, fat and salt, and insofar as it was possible to tell, none of the students appears to have died . . .'

'So we are ahead on pies, then,' said Ridcully cheerfully.

'I suppose so, Archchancellor, although I do not believe that the pie quality plays any role—' He stopped, because the door had swung open to allow the ingress of a reinforced, heavy-duty tea trolley. Since it was not being propelled by Her, the wizards paid no further attention and settled down to the passing of cups, the handing round of the sugar bowl, the inspection of the quality of the chocolate biscuits with a view to taking more than one's entitlement and all the other little diversions without which a committee would be a clever device for making worth-while decisions quickly.

When the rattling had ceased, and the last biscuit had been fought for, Ridcully tinkled his teaspoon on the rim of his cup for silence, although since he was Ridcully this only added the crash of broken

129

crockery to the hubbub. Once the girl in charge of the trolley had sponged everybody down, he continued: 'The chanting, gentlemen, appears to be another inconsequentiality at first sight, but I have reason to believe that it has a certain power, and we will ignore it at our peril. I see the museum's translators say the modern chants were originally hymns to the goddess calling on her to grant her favours to the team of choice, while naiads danced on the edges of the field of play, the better to encourage the players to greater feats of prowess.'

'Naiads?' said the Chair of Indefinite Studies. 'They're water nymphs, aren't they? Young women with very thin damp clothing? Why would anyone want them around? Besides, didn't they drown sailors by singing to them?'

Ridcully let the thoughtful pause hang in the air for a while before volunteering: 'Fortunately, I don't think anyone these days would expect that we play football underwater.'

'The pies would float,' said the Chair of Indefinite Studies.

'Not necessarily,' said Ponder.

'What about clothing, Mister Stibbons? I assume there will be some?'

'Temperatures were somewhat warmer in olden days. I can assure you that no one will insist on nudity.'

Ponder might have noticed the rattle as the girl with the tea trolley almost dropped a cup, but was gracious enough not to notice that he had noticed. He went on. 'Currently the teams wear old shirts and short trousers.'

'How short?' said the Chair of Indefinite Studies, urgency in his voice.

'About mid-knee, I believe,' said Ponder. 'Is this likely to be a problem?'

'Yes, it is. The knees should be covered. It is a well-known fact that a glimpse of the male knee can drive women into a frenzy of libidinousness.' There was another rattle from the tea trolley, but Ponder ignored it because his own head had rattled a bit, too.

'Are you sure about that, sir?'

'It is established fact, young Stibbons.'

Ponder had found a grey hair on his comb that morning and was not in the mood to take this standing up.

'And precisely in what books does—' he began, but Ridcully interrupted with unusual diplomacy. Generally he liked little tiffs among the faculty.

'A few more inches to prevent mobbing by the ladies should present us with no problems, surely, Mister Stibbons? Oops . . .'

This last was to Glenda, who had dropped two spoons on the carpet. She gave him a cursory curtsy.

'Er, yes . . . and we should sport the university colours,' he went on, with a hint of nervousness. Ridcully prided himself on treating the staff well, and indeed did so whenever he remembered them, but the expression of intelligent amusement on the face of the dumpy girl had unnerved him; it was as if a chicken had winked.

'Um, yes, yes indeed,' he said. 'The good old red jersey we used to wear in my rowing days, with the big U's on the front, bold as brass . . .'

He glanced at the maid, who was frowning. But he was Archchancellor, wasn't he? It said so on his door, didn't it?

'That's what we'll do,' he declared. 'We'll look into pies, although I've seen a few pies that don't bear looking into, haha, and we'll adapt the good old red sweater. What's next, Mister Stibbons?'

'With regard to the chanting, sir. I've asked the Master of the Music to work on some options,' said Ponder smoothly. 'We need to select a team as soon as possible.'

'I don't see what the rush is,' said the Chair of Indefinite Studies, who had almost nodded off in the arms of a chocolate biscuit surfeit.

'The bequest, remember?' said the head of the Department of Post-Mortem Communications. 'We—'

'Pas devant la domestique!' snapped the Lecturer in Recent Runes.

Automatically, Ridcully turned again to look at Glenda, and got a distinct feeling that here was a woman about to learn a foreign language in a hurry. It was an odd but slightly exciting idea. Until this moment, he had never thought of the maids in the singular. They were all . . . servants. He was polite to them, and smiled when appropriate.

He assumed they sometimes did other things than fetch and carry, and sometimes went off to get married and sometimes just . . . went off. Up until now, though, he'd never really thought that they might think, let alone what they thought about, and least of all what they thought about the wizards. He turned back to the table.

'Who will be doing the chanting, Mister Stibbons?'

'The aforesaid supporters, fans, sir. It's short for fanatics.'

'And ours will be . . . who?'

'Well, we are the largest employer in the city, sir.'

'As a matter of fact I think Vetinari is, and I wish to all hells I knew exactly who he is employing,' said Ridcully.

'I'm sure our loyal staff will support us,' said the Lecturer in Recent Runes. He turned to Glenda, and to Ridcully's dismay said, glutinously, 'I'm sure you would be a fan, would you not, my child?'

The Archchancellor sat back. He had a definite feeling that this was going to be fun. Well, she hadn't blushed and she hadn't yelled. In fact, she had not done anything, apart from carefully pick up the china.

'I support Dolly Sisters, sir. Always have done.'

'And are they any good?'

'Having a poor patch at the moment, sir.'

'Ah, then I expect you will want to support our team, which will be very good indeed!'

'Can't do that, sir. You've got to support your team, sir.'

'But you just said they weren't doing well.'

'That's *when* you support your team, sir. Otherwise you're a numper.'

'A numper being . . . ?' said Ridcully.

'He's someone who's all cheering when things are going well, and then runs off to another team when there's a losing streak. They always shouts the loudest.'

'So you support the same team all your life?'

'Well, if you move away it's okay to change. No one will mind much unless you go to a real enemy.' She looked at their puzzled expressions, sighed and went on: 'Like Naphill United and the Whoppers, or Dolly

Sisters and Dimwell Old Pals, or the Pigsty Hill Pork Packers and the Cockbill Boars. You know?'

When they clearly didn't, she continued: 'They hate each other. Always have done, always will. They are the bad matches. The shutters go up for those. I don't know what my neighbours would say if they saw me cheering a Dimmer.'

'But that's dreadful!' said the Chair of Indefinite Studies.

'Excuse me, miss,' said Ponder, 'but most of those pairs are quite close to one another, so why do they hate one another so much?'

'That at least is easy,' said Dr Hix. 'It's hard to hate people who are a long way away. You forget how dreadful they are. But you see a neighbour's warts every day.'

'That's just the sort of cynical comment I'd expect from a post-mortem communicator,' grumbled the Chair of Indefinite Studies.

'Or a realist,' said Ridcully, smiling. 'But Dolly Sisters and Dimwell are quite far apart, miss.'

Glenda shrugged. 'I know, but it's always been like that. That's how it is. That's all I know.'

'Well, thank you . . . ?' There was no mistaking the hanging question.

'Glenda,' she said.

'I see there are a great many things we don't yet understand.'

'Yes, sir. Everything.' She hadn't meant to say that aloud. It just escaped of its own accord.

There was a stirring among the wizards, who were nonplussed because what had happened could not really have happened. The tea trolley might as well have neighed.

Ridcully banged his hand on the table before the others could summon up words.

'Well said, miss,' he chuckled, as Glenda waited for the floor to open and swallow her. 'And I'm sure that remark came from the heart, because I suspect it could not have come from the head.'

'Sorry, sir, but the gentleman did ask for my opinion.'

'Now, that one was from the head. Well done,' said Ridcully. 'So do, therefore, give us the benefit of your thinking, Miss Glenda.'

Still in a kind of shock, Glenda looked into the Archchancellor's eyes and saw that it was no time to be less than bold, but that was unnerving too.

'Well, what's this all about, sir? If you want to play, just go and do it, yes? Why change things?'

'The game of foot-the-ball is very behind the times, Miss Glenda.'

'Well, so are you— Sorry, sorry, but, well. You know. Wizards are always wizards. Not a lot changes in here, does it? And then you talk about some Master of the Music to make a new chant, and that's not how it goes. The Shove makes up the chants. They just happen. They just, like, come out of the air. And the pies are pretty awful, that's true, but when you're in the Shove, and it's mucky weather, and the water's coming through your coat, and your shoes are leaking, and then you bite into your pie, and you know that everyone else is biting into their pie, and the grease slides down your sleeve, well, sir, I don't have the words for it, sir, I really don't, sir. There's a feeling I can't describe, but it's a bit like being a kid at Hogswatch, and you can't just buy it, sir, you can't write it down or organize it or make it shiny or make it tame. Sorry to speak out of turn, sirs, but that's the long and the short of it. You must have known it, sir. Didn't your father ever take you to a game?'

Ridcully looked down the table at the Council and noted a certain moistness of eye. Wizards were, largely, of that generation from which grandfathers are carved. They were also, largely, large, and awash with cynical crabbiness and the barnacles of the years, but . . . the smell of cheap overcoats in the rain, which always had a tint and taste of soot in it, and your father, or maybe your grandfather, lifting you on to his shoulders, and there you were, above all those cheap hats and scarves, and you could feel the warmth of the Shove, watch its tides, feel its heartbeat, and then, certainly, a pie would be handed up, or maybe half a pie if times were hard, and if they were really bad it might be a handful of fat greasy pease which were to be eaten one at a time to make them last longer . . . or when times were flush there might be a real treat, like a hot dog you didn't have to share, or a plate of scouse, with yellow fat beading on the top and lumps of gristle you could chew at on the way home, meat which now you would not give to a dog but which was sacred lotus eaten with the gods, in the rain, in the cheering, in the bosom of the Shove . . .

The Archchancellor blinked. No time seemed to have passed, unless you count seventy years which had gone past like that. 'Er, very graphically argued,' he said, and pulled himself together. 'Interesting points well made. But, you see, we have a responsibility here. After all, this city was just a handful of villages before my university was built. We are concerned about the fighting in the streets yesterday. We heard a rumour that someone was killed because he supported the wrong team. We can't stand by and let this sort of thing happen.'

'So you'll be shutting down the Assassins' Guild, will you, sir?'

There was a gasp from every mouth, including her own. The only rational thought that didn't flee from her mind was: *I wonder if that job is still going in the Fools' Guild? The pay wasn't much, but they do know how to appreciate a pie.*

When she dared look, the Archchancellor was staring at the ceiling, while his fingers drummed on the table. *I should have been more careful*, Glenda whined in her own ear. *Don't get chatty with nobs. You forget what you are, but they don't.*

The drumming stopped. 'Good point, well put,' said Ridcully, 'and I shall marshal my responses thusly.' He flicked a finger and, with a smell of gooseberries and a *pop*, a small red globe appeared in the air over the table.

'One: the Assassins, while deadly, are not random, and indeed are mostly a danger to one another. Assassination is only to be feared, generally speaking, by those powerful enough to have a stab, as it were, at defending themselves.'

Another little globe appeared.

'Two: it is an article of faith with them that property is undamaged. They are invariably courteous and considerate and notoriously silent, and would never dream of inhuming their target in a public street.'

A third globe appeared.

'Three: they are organized and therefore amenable to civic influence. Lord Vetinari is very keen on that sort of thing.'

And another globe popped into life.

'And four: Lord Vetinari is himself a trained Assassin, majoring in stealth and poisons. I am not sure he would share your opinion. And he is a Tyrant even if he has developed tyranny to such a point of metaphysical perfection that it is a dream rather than a force. He does not have to listen to you, you see. He doesn't even have to listen to me. He listens to the city. I don't know how he does, but he does. And he plays it like a violin' – Ridcully paused, then went on – 'or like the most complicated game you can imagine. The city works, not perfectly, but better than it has ever done. I think it's time for football to change too.' He smiled at her expression. 'What is your job, young lady? Because you are wasted in it.'

It was probably meant as a compliment, but Glenda, her head so bewilderingly full of the Archchancellor's words that they were trickling out of her ears, heard herself say, 'I'm certainly not wasted, sir! You've never eaten better pies than mine! I run the Night Kitchen!'

The metaphysics of real politics were not a subject of interest to most of those present, but they knew where they were with pies. She was the centre of attention already, but now it blazed with interest.

'You do?' said the Chair of Indefinite Studies. 'We thought it was the pretty girl.'

'Really?' said Glenda brightly. 'Well, I run it.'

'So who does that wonderful pie you send up here sometimes, with the cheese pastry and the hot pickle layer?'

'The Ploughman's Pie? Me, sir. My own recipe.'

'Really? How do you manage to get the pickled onions to stay so hard and crispy in the baking? It's just amazing!'

'My own recipe, sir,' said Glenda firmly. 'It wouldn't be mine if I told anyone else.'

'Well said,' said Ridcully gleefully. 'You can't go around asking craftsmen the secrets of their trade, old chap. It's a thing you just don't do. Now, I am concluding this meeting, although what it has in fact concluded I shall decide later.' He turned back to Glenda. 'Thank you for coming here today, Miss Glenda, and I shall not enquire why a young lady who works in the Night Kitchen is pouring tea up here at nearly noon. Do you have any further advice for us?'

'Well,' said Glenda, 'since you ask . . . No, I really shouldn't say . . .'

'This is hardly the moment for bashfulness, do you think?'

'Well, it's about your strip, sir. That means your team colours. Nothing wrong with red and yellow, no one else uses those two, but, well, you want two big U's on the front, right? Like UU?' She waved her hands in the air.

'Yes, that is exactly right. After all, it's what we are.' Ridcully nodded.

'Are you sure? I mean, I know you gentlemen are bachelors and all, but . . . well, you'll look like you've got bosoms. Honestly.'

'Oh gods, sir, she's right,' said Ponder. 'It will make a rather unfortunate shape . . .'

'What kind of mind would see something like that in a pair of innocent letters?' the Lecturer in Recent Runes demanded angrily.

'I don't know, sir,' said Glenda, 'but every man watching the football has got one. And they would make up nicknames. They love doing that.'

'I suspect you may be right,' said Ridcully, 'but we never had any trouble when I was rowing in the old days.'

'Football followers are rather more robust in their language, sir,' said Ponder.

'Yes, and in those days we were pretty careless when it came to throwing fireballs, as I recall,' Ridcully mused. 'Oh dear, what a shame. I was looking forward to giving the old rag a bit of an airing again. Still, I'm sure we can change the design a little to save embarrassment all round. Thank you once again, Miss Glenda. Bosoms, eh? Narrow escape there, all round. Good day to you.' He shut the door after the trolley, which Glenda was pushing as if in a race . . .

Molly, the head maid in the Day Kitchen, was fretting at the end of the corridor beyond. She sagged with relief when Glenda came round the corner, teacups rattling.

'Was it all right? Did anything go wrong? I'll get into so

much trouble if anything went wrong. Tell me nothing went wrong!'

'It was all fine,' said Glenda. That got her a suspicious look.

'Are you sure? You owe me for this!'

The laws of favours are amongst the most fundamental in the multiverse. The first law is: nobody asks for just one favour; the second request (after the granting of the first favour), prefaced by 'and can I be really cheeky . . .?' is the asking of the second favour. If the aforesaid second request is not granted, the second law ensures that the need for any gratitude for the first favour is nullified, and in accordance with the third law the favour giver has not done any favours at all, and the favour field collapses.

But Glenda reckoned she'd won a lot of favours over the years, and was owed a few herself. Besides, she had reason to believe that Molly had been spending the welcome break in dalliance with her boyfriend, who worked in the bakery.

'Can you get me in to the banquet on Wednesday night?'

'Sorry, the butler chooses who gets those jobs,' said Molly.

Ah yes, the tall, thin girls, Glenda thought.

'Why in the world would you want to get in, anyway?' Molly said. 'It's a lot of running around and not much pay, when all's said and done. I mean, we get some decent leftovers after a big affair, but what's that to you? Everyone knows that you're the leftover queen!' She paused, too awkwardly. 'I mean, we all know you're really good at making wonderful food with always a little something left over,' she gabbled. 'That's all I meant!'

'I didn't think you meant anything else,' said Glenda, keeping her voice level. But she raised it again to add, as Molly scurried off: 'I can pay back the favour right now! You've got two floury handprints on your arse!'

The glare that came back was a small victory, but you have to take what you can get.

Still, that strange interlude, which she was sure she would regret, had taken up a lot of time. She had to get the Night Kitchen organized.

*

When the door had closed behind the rather forthright maid, Ridcully nodded meaningfully at Ponder. 'All right, Mister Stibbons. You were glancing at your thaumometer the whole time I was talking to her. Out with it.'

'Some kind of entanglement,' said Ponder.

'And there was me thinking that Vetinari was behind the business with the urn,' said Ridcully gloomily. 'I should have realized he's never that unsubtle.'

'Oh, I assumed it was going to be something like that right at the start,' said the Lecturer in Recent Runes.

'Indeed,' said the Chair of Indefinite Studies. 'It crossed my mind as soon as I saw it in the paper.'

'Gentlemen,' said Ridcully. 'I am humbled that as soon as I have an idea about what something is, it turns out that you all knew what it was. I am amazed.'

'Excuse me,' said Dr Hix, 'but I don't have a clue what you're talking about.'

'You are out of touch! You've been spending too long underground, sir!' said the Lecturer in Recent Runes sternly.

'You don't often let me out, that's why! And can I remind you that I have to maintain a vital line of cosmic defence in this establishment here with a staff of exactly one? And he's dead!'

'You mean Charlie? I remember old Charlie, keen worker nevertheless,' said Ridcully.

'Yes, but I have to keep rewiring him all the time,' sighed Hix. 'I do try to keep you abreast of things in my monthly reports. I hope you read them . . . ?'

'Tell me, Doctor Hix,' said Ponder, 'did you experience anything unusual when that young lady was speaking so eloquently?'

'Well, yes, I had a pleasant moment of happy recollection about my father.'

'So did we all, I am sure,' said Ponder. There was sombre nodding around the table. 'I never knew my father. I was brought up by my aunts. I had déjà vu *without the original vu.*'

'And it wasn't magic?' suggested the Lecturer in Recent Runes.

'No. Religion, I suspect,' said Ridcully. 'A god invoked, that sort of thing.'

'Not invoked, Mustrum,' said Dr Hix. 'Summoned by bloodshed!'

'Oh, I hope not,' said Ridcully, getting to his feet. 'I would like to try a little experiment this afternoon, gentlemen. We will not talk about football, we will not speculate about football, we will not worry about football—'

'You are going to make us play it, aren't you?' said the Lecturer in Recent Runes glumly.

'Yes,' said Ridcully, more than somewhat miffed at the spoiling of a perfectly good peroration. 'Just a little kick-about to help us get some hands-on experience of the game as it is played.'

'Er. Strictly, under the new rules, by which I mean the ancient rules we are taking as our model, hands-on experience means no hands,' said Ponder.

'Well pointed out, that man. Put the word out, will you? Football practice on the lawn after lunch!'

One thing you had to remember when dealing with dwarfs was that while they shared the same world as you did, metaphorically they thought about it as if it were upside down. Only the richest and most influential of dwarfs lived in the deepest caverns. For a dwarf, a penthouse in the centre of the city would be some kind of slum. Dwarfs liked it dark and cool.

It didn't stop there. A dwarf on the up and up was really on his uppers, and upper-class dwarfs were lower class. A dwarf who was rich, healthy and had respect and his own rat farm justifiably felt at rock bottom and was held in low esteem. When you talked to dwarfs, you turned your mind upside down. The city, too. Of course, when you dug down in Ankh-Morpork you just found more Ankh-Morpork. Thousands of years of it, ready to be dug out and shored up and walled in with the shiny dwarf brick.

It was Lord Vetinari's 'Grand Undertaking'. The city's walls corseted it like a fetishist's happiest dream. Gravity offered only a limited supply of up, but the deep loam of the plain had a limitless supply of down.

Glenda was surprised, therefore, to find Shatta right at the surface in the Maul, alongside the really posh dress shops that were for human ladies. That made sense, however; if you were going to make a scandalous profit selling clothes, it made sense to camouflage yourself amongst other shops doing the same thing. She wasn't sure about the name, but apparently *shatta* meant 'a wonderful surprise' in Dwarfish, and if you started to laugh about that sort of thing then you would never have time to pause for breath.

She approached the door with the apprehension of one who is certain that the moment she sets foot inside she will be charged five dollars a minute for breathing and then be held upside down and have all her wealth removed with a hook.

And it was, indeed, classy. But it was dwarf classy. That meant an awful lot of chain mail, and enough weaponry to take over a city – but if you paid attention, you realized it was female chain mail and weaponry. That was how things were happening, apparently. Dwarf women had got fed up with looking like dwarf men all the time and were metaphorically melting down their breastplates in order to make something a little lighter and with adjustable straps.

Juliet had explained this on the way down, although, of course, Juliet did not use the word 'metaphorically', it being several syllables beyond her range. There were battle-axes and war hammers, but all with that certain feminine touch: one war axe, apparently capable of cleaving a backbone lengthwise, was beautifully engraved with flowers. It was another world, and as she stood just inside the doorway looking around, Glenda felt relieved that there were other humans in the place. In fact, there were quite a few, and that was surprising. One of them, a young human woman with steel boots six inches high, gravitated towards them as if drawn by a magnet – and given the amount of ferrous metal on her body, a magnet was something she would never pass in a hurry. She was holding a tray of drinks.

'There's black mead, red mead and white mead,' she said, and then lowered her voice by a few decibels and three social classes. 'Actually, the red mead is really sherry and all the dwarf ladies are drinking it. They like not having to quaff.'

'Do we have to pay for this?' said Glenda nervously.

'It's free,' said the girl. She indicated a bowl of small black things on the tray, each one pierced with a cocktail stick, and said slightly hopelessly, 'And do try the rat fruit.'

Before Glenda could stop her, Juliet had taken one and was chewing enthusiastically.

'What part of a rat is its fruit?' asked Glenda. The girl with the tray did not look directly at her.

'Well, you know shepherd's pie?' she said.

'I know twelve different recipes,' said Glenda in a moment of rare smugness. This was actually a lie. She probably knew about four recipes because there was only so much you could do with meat and potatoes, but the glittering metallic grandeur of the place was getting on her nerves and she felt the need to stick up for herself. And then realization dawned. 'Oh, you mean like traditional shepherd's pie,' she said, 'made with the—'

'I'm afraid so,' said the girl, 'but they're very popular with the ladies.'

'Don't have any more, Jools,' said Glenda quickly.

'It's quite nice,' said Juliet. 'Can't I have one more?'

'Just one, then,' said Glenda. 'That should even up the rat.' She helped herself to a sherry and the girl, balancing carefully as she managed three different things with two different hands, handed her a glossy brochure.

Glenda glanced through it and knew her original impression had been right. This place was so expensive they didn't tell you the price of anything. You could always be sure things were going to be expensive when they didn't tell you the price. No point in looking through it, it'd suck your wages out through your eyeballs. Free drinks? Oh, yes.

With nothing else to do, she scanned the rest of the crowd. Everyone, except the growing and, in fact, quite large number of humans, had a beard. All dwarfs had beards. It was part of being a dwarf. Here, though, the beards were a little finer than you usually saw around the city and there had been some experimentation with perms and ponytails. There were mining pickaxes on view, it was true, but carried in expensively tooled bags as if the owner might spot a likely-looking coal seam on the way to the shops and wouldn't be able to help herself.

She shared this thought with Juliet, who pointed down at the feet of another well-heeled customer and said, 'Wot? And spoil those gorgeous boots? They're Snaky Cleavehelms, they are! Four hundred dollars a pop, an' you've to wait for six months!'

Glenda couldn't see the face of the boots' owner, but she did see the change in her body language. The hint of preening, even from the rear. Well, she thought, I suppose if you're going to spend all of a working family's yearly income on a pair of boots it's nice that someone notices.

When you watch people, you forget that people are watching you. Glenda was not very tall, which meant that from her point of view dwarfs were not very short. And she realized that they were being approached in a determined kind of way by two dwarfs, one of whom was extremely expansive around the waist and wearing a breastplate so beautifully hammered and ornamented that taking it into battle would be an act of artistic vandalism. He – and you had to remember that all dwarfs were he unless they asserted otherwise – had, when he spoke, a voice that sounded like the darkest and most expensive type of dark chocolate, possibly smoked. And the hand he offered had so many rings on each finger that you had to look with care to realize that he was not wearing a gauntlet. And she was a she, Glenda was sure of it: the chocolate was just too rich and fruity.

'So glad you could come, my dears,' she said, and the chocolate swirled. 'I am Madame Sharn. I wondered if you could be of assistance to me? I really would not dream of asking, but I am, as you would put it, between a rock and a hard one.'

All this was, to Glenda's annoyance, addressed to Juliet, who was eating rat fruit as if there was no tomorrow, which presumably there had not been for the rat. She giggled.

'She's with me,' said Glenda, and, without meaning to, added, 'Madame?'

Madame waved another hand and more rings glistened. 'This salon is technically a mine and that means that under dwarf law I am the king of the mine and in my mine my rules go. And since I am King, I declare that I am Queen,' she said. 'Dwarf law bends and creaks but is not broken.'

'Well,' Glenda began, 'we— Hey!'

This was to Madame's smaller companion, who was actually holding a tape measure up against Juliet. 'That is Pepe,' said Madame.

'Well, if he's going to take liberties like that I hope he's a woman,' said Glenda.

'Pepe is . . . Pepe,' said Madame calmly. 'And there is no changing him, as it were, or her. Labels are such unhelpful things, I feel.'

'Especially yours, 'cos you don't put the prices on them,' said Glenda, out of sheer nervousness.

'Ah yes, you notice these things,' said Madame, with a wink that disarmed to the point of melting.

Pepe looked up excitedly at Madame, who went on, 'I wonder if you, if she . . . if you *both* would mind joining me backstage? The matter is a little delicate.'

'Ooh, yes,' said Juliet immediately.

Out of nowhere, other human girls materialized among the crowd and carefully opened a path towards the back of the enormous room along which Madame progressed as though propelled by invisible forces.

Glenda felt that the situation had suddenly got away from her, but it had been a good measure of sherry and it whispered to her, 'Why not let a situation get away from you every once in a while? Or even just once.' She had no idea what she was expecting behind the gilded door at the far end, but she had not expected smoke and flames and shouting and someone screaming in a corner. The place looked like a foundry on the day they let the clowns in.

'Come on through. Don't let this disturb you,' said Madame. 'It's always like this at show time. Nerves, you know. Of course, everyone in this business is lowly strung and there is always this problem to begin with with the micromail. It's new, you see. According to dwarf law it must be hallmarked on every link and that would not only be sacrilege, but also bloody difficult to do.' Behind the scenes, it appeared that Madame became a little less chocolatey and a little more earthy.

'Micromail!' said Juliet, as if she had been shown the gateway to riches.

'You know what it is?' said Madame.

'She talks about nothing else,' said Glenda. 'Talks and talks.'

'Well, of course, it's wonderful stuff,' said Madame. 'Almost as soft as cloth, certainly better than leather—'

'—and it doesn't chafe,' said Juliet.

'Which is always a consideration for the more traditional dwarf who will not wear cloth,' said Madame. 'Old tribal customs, how they hold us back, always pull us back. We haul ourselves out of the mine, but somehow we always drag a bit of the mine with us. If I had my way, silk would be reclassified as a metal. What is your name, young lady?'

'Juliet,' said Glenda automatically, and then blushed. That was mumming, pure and simple. It was almost as bad as getting someone to spit on their handkerchief and wiping their face for them. The young lady with the drinks had followed them in and chose this moment to take Glenda's sherry glass and replace it with a full one.

'Would you mind just walking up and down a moment, Juliet?' said Madame.

Glenda wanted to ask why, but since her mouth was full of sherry as an anti-embarrassment remedy, she let that one pass.

Madame watched Juliet critically, one hand cupping the elbow of the other arm.

'Yes, yes. But I mean slowly, as if you were not in a hurry to get there and didn't care,' said Madame. 'Imagine you're a bird in the air, a fish in the sea. Wear the world.'

'Oh, right,' said Juliet and started again.

By the time Juliet was halfway across the floor for the second time,

Pepe had burst into tears. 'Where has she been? Where was she trained?' he, or conceivably she, squeaked while clapping his or her cheeks with both hands. 'You must hire her at once!'

'She's already got a good steady job at the university,' Glenda said. But the sherry said, 'Once in a while isn't over yet. Don't spoil it!'*

Madame, who clearly had an instinct for this kind of thing, put an arm around her shoulders. 'The problem with dwarf ladies, you see, is that a lot of us are a little shy about being the centre of attention. I also have to bear in mind that dwarf clothing is proving quite interesting to young humans of a certain turn of mind. Your daughter is human—' Madame turned briefly to Juliet. 'You are human, aren't you, dear? I find it pays to check.'

Juliet, apparently staring rapturously into a private world, nodded enthusiastically.

'Oh good,' said Madame. 'And while she is exquisitely well built and moves like a dream, she is not too much taller than the average dwarf and frankly, my dear, some of the ladies would aspire to being a little taller than they are. This may be letting the side up, but that walk, my word. Dwarfs have hips, of course, but they seldom know what to do with them . . . I'm sorry, have I said something wrong?'

The half-pint of sherry so recently consumed by Glenda finally gave way under the pressure of her rage. 'I am *not* her mother. She is my friend.'

Madame shot her another of those looks that gave her the feeling that her brain was being taken out and examined minutely. 'Then would you mind if I paid your friend' – there was a pause – 'five dollars to model for me this afternoon?'

'All right,' said the sherry to Glenda. 'You wondered where I was going to take you and here you are. Can you see the view? What are you going to do now?'

'Twenty-five dollars,' said Glenda.

* Dwarfs have a straightforward approach to alcoholic drink: beer, mead, wine, sherry – one large size fits all.

146

Pepe clapped her, or possibly his, cheeks again and screamed, 'Yes! Yes!'

'And a shop discount,' said Glenda.

Madame gave her a long-drawn-out stare. 'Excuse me one moment,' said the dwarf.

She walked over and took Pepe's arm, walking him at some speed to the corner. Glenda could not hear what was said over some nearby riveting and someone having hysterics. Madame came back smirking artificially, Pepe trailing her. 'I have a show starting in ten minutes and my best model has dropped her pickaxe on her foot. We shall negotiate any future engagements. And will you please stop that jumping up and down, Pepe?'

Glenda blinked. *I cannot believe I just did that*, she thought. *Twenty-five dollars for putting some clothes on! That's more than I earn in a month! That's just not right.* And the sherry said, 'What exactly is wrong here? Would you dress up in chain mail and parade in front of a lot of strangers for twenty-five dollars?'

Glenda shuddered. *Certainly not*, she thought.

'Well, there you are then,' said the sherry.

But it will all end in tears, thought Glenda.

'No, you're just saying that because part of you thinks it should,' said the sherry. 'You know there are far worse things that a girl could do for twenty-five dollars than put some clothes on. Take them off, for a start.'

But what will the neighbours say? was the last despairing argument from Glenda.

'They can stick it up their jumper,' said the sherry. 'Anyway, they won't know, will they? Dolly Sisters doesn't shop in the Maul, it's far too grand. Look, we're looking at twenty-five dollars. Twenty-five dollars to do what you couldn't stop her doing now with a length of lead pipe. Just look at her face! She looks as if someone has lit a lamp inside.'

It was true.

Oh, all right then, thought Glenda.

'Good,' said the sherry. 'And incidentally, I'm feeling lonely.'

And as the tray was at Glenda's elbow again, she reached out automatically.

Juliet was now surrounded by dwarfs and, by the sound of it, she was having a lightning education in how to wear clothing. But it wouldn't matter, would it? The truth of the matter was that Juliet would look good in a sack. Somehow, everything she wore fitted perfectly. Glenda, on the other hand, never found anything good in her size and indeed seldom found anything in her size. In theory, something should fit, but all she ever found was facts, which are so unbecoming.

'Well, we have a nice day for it,' said the Archchancellor.

'Looks like rain,' said the Lecturer in Recent Runes hopefully.

'I suggest two teams of five on a side,' said Ridcully. 'Only a friendly game, of course, just to get the hang of it.'

Ponder Stibbons made no comment. Wizards were competitive. It was a part of wizardry. Wizards have no more idea of a friendly game than cats have of a friendly mouse. The college lawns stretched out in front of them. 'Of course, next time we'll have proper jerseys,' said Ridcully. 'Mrs Whitlow already has her girls working on that. Mister Stibbons!'

'Yes, Archchancellor?'

'You shall be the keeper of the rules and adjudicate fairly. I will, of course, be captain of one of the teams and you, Runes, will captain the other. As Archchancellor, I suggest that I pick my team first and then you will be at liberty to choose yours.'

'It isn't actually supposed to work like that, Archchancellor,' said Ponder. 'You pick a team member and then he picks a team member until you have enough team members or have run out of team members who aren't grossly fat or trembling with nerves. At least that's how I remember it.' Ponder, in his youth, had spent far too long standing next to the fat kid.

'Oh well, if that's how it's done, then I suppose we shall have to do it that way,' said the Archchancellor with bad grace. 'Stibbons, it will be your task to penalize the opposing side for any infringements they make.'

'Don't you mean that I should penalize either side for any

infringements they make, Archchancellor?' he said. 'It has to be fair.'

Ridcully looked at him with his mouth open as if Ponder had mentioned a concept that was totally alien. 'Oh yes, I suppose it has to be like that.'

A variety of wizards had turned out this afternoon from curiosity, a suspicion that being there might turn out to be a good career move, and the prospect of maybe seeing some colleagues travelling across the lawn on their noses.

Oh dear, thought Ponder as the choosing began. It was just like school again, but at school nobody wanted the fat boy. Here, of course, it had to be a case of nobody wanted the fattest boy, which, since the departure of the Dean, was a matter of fine judgement.

Ponder reached into his robes and pulled out a whistle or, perhaps, the grandfather of all whistles, eight inches long and as thick as a generous pork sausage.

'Where did that come from, Mister Stibbons?' said Ridcully.

'As a matter of fact, Archchancellor, I found it in the study of the late Evans the Striped.'

'It's a fine whistle,' said Ridcully.

It was an innocent sentence that managed to hint quite silently that such a fine whistle should not be in the hands of Ponder Stibbons when it could be in the ownership of, for example, the Archchancellor of a university. Ponder spotted this because he had been expecting it. 'I shall need this to alert and control the behaviour of both teams,' he said haughtily. 'You made me the referee, Archchancellor, and I'm afraid that for the duration of the game I am, as it were,' he hesitated, 'in charge.'

'This university is a hierarchy, you understand, Stibbons?'

'Yes, sir, and this is a game of football. I believe that the procedure is to put the football down and when the whistle is blown each side will attempt to hit the goal of the opposing side with the ball while trying to prevent the ball hitting their own goal. Have we all understood that?'

'It seems pretty clear to me,' said the Chair of Indefinite Studies. There was a murmur of agreement.

'Nevertheless, before the game I demand a blow on the whistle.'

'Of course, Archchancellor, but then you must give it me back. I am the custodian of the game.' He handed over the whistle.

On Ridcully's first attempt at blowing he dislodged a spider that had been living a blameless yet frugal life for the last twenty years and deposited him in the beard of the Professor of Natural Studies, who was just passing.

The second blow shook free the fossilized pea inside and filled the air with echoes of liquid brass. And then . . .

Ridcully froze. His face flushed from the neck upwards at speed. The sound of his next drawn breath was like the vengeance of the gods. His stomach expanded, his eyes became pinpoints, thunder rolled overhead and he roared, 'WHY HAVEN'T YOU BOYS BROUGHT YOUR KIT?!'

St Elmo's fire roared along the length of the whistle. The sky darkened and fear gripped every watching soul as time reversed and there stood the giant, maniacally screaming Evans the Striped. The instigator of badly forged notes from your mother, the enthusiast for long runs in the sleet, the promoter of communal showers as a cure for adolescent shyness and the one who, if you didn't bring your proper gear, would make you PLAY IN YOUR PANTS. Venerable wizards who had faced down the most cunning of monsters through the decades trembled in damp adolescent fear as the scream went on and on, to be halted as sharply as it started.

Ridcully fell forward on to the turf.

'I do apologize for that,' said Dr Hix, lowering his staff. 'A slightly evil deed, of course, but I'm sure you'll agree that it was necessary in the circumstances. The skull ring, remember? University statute? And that was a clear case of possession by artefact if ever I saw one.'

The collected wizards, the cold sweat beginning to evaporate, nodded sagely. Oh, yes. It was regrettably necessary, they agreed. For his own good, they agreed. Had to be done, they agreed. And this verdict was echoed by Ridcully himself when he opened his eyes and said, 'What the hell was that?'

'Er, the soul of Evans the Striped, I think, Archchancellor,' said Ponder.

'In the whistle, was it?' Ridcully rubbed his head.

'Yes, I think so,' said Ponder.

'And who hit me?'

A general shuffling and murmuring indicated that by democratic agreement this was a question that could best be answered by Dr Hix.

'It was acceptable treachery under college statute, sir. Wouldn't mind the whistle for the Dark Museum, if nobody objects.'

'Quite so, quite so,' said Ridcully. 'Saw the problem, sorted it out. Well done that man.'

'Do you think I could be allowed an evil chuckle, sir?'

Ridcully brushed himself down. 'No. We shall forgo the whistle, Mister Stibbons. And now, gentlemen, let the game commence.'

And thus, after a certain amount of bickering, Unseen University's first football match in decades began. Instantly, from Ponder Stibbons's point of view, various problems arose. The most pressing one was that all the wizards were dressed as wizards, which was to say alike. Ponder ordered the teams to play hats on and hats off, which caused another row. And that particular problem was exacerbated further because there were so many collisions that even the officially hatted kept losing theirs. And then the game was paused because it was declared that the statue commemorating Archchancellor Scrubbs's discovery of blit was in fact three inches narrower than the venerable statue of Archchancellor Flanker discovering the Third Breakfast, thus giving an unfair advantage to the hatless squad.

But all these problems, foreseeable and inescapable, paled into insignificance compared with the problem of the ball. It was an official ball – Ponder had made certain of that. But pointy shoes, even if they have a very long point, cannot absorb the impact of the human foot kicking what is, when all is said and screamed, a piece of wood with a thin cloth and leather wrapping. Eventually, as another wizard was helped away with a sprained ankle, even Ridcully was moved to say, 'This is damn nonsense, Stibbons! There has got to be something better than this.'

'Bigger boots?' suggested the Lecturer in Recent Runes.

'The kind of boots you need for kicking this would slow you right down,' said Ponder.

'Besides, the men on the urn had nothing at all on their feet. I suggest we consider this research. What do we need, Stibbons?'

'A better ball, sir. And some attempt at running about. And a general consensus that it is not a good idea to stop to re-light your pipe in the middle of play. A more sensible type of goal, because running into a stone statue is painful. Some grasp, however small, of the notion of teamwork in a gaming situation. A resolution not to run away if a member of the opposing team is rushing towards you. An understanding of the fact that you do not handle the ball in *any* circumstances; may I remind you that I gave up stopping play because of this since you gentlemen, when you were excited, persisted in picking it up and, in one case, hiding it behind your back, and standing on it. I would like to point out at this juncture that a sense of direction is worth cultivating vis-à-vis the goal that is yours and the goal that is theirs; inviting as it may be, there is no point in kicking the ball into your own goal, and nor should you congratulate and pat on the back anyone who achieves this feat. Out of the three goals scored in our match, the number scored by players into their own goal was' – he paused and looked down at his clipboard – 'three. This is a commendably high level of scoring, compared with football as currently played, though once again I must stress that issues of direction and goal ownership are of pivotal importance. A tactic, which I admit looked promising, was for the players to cluster thickly around their own goal so there was no possibility of anything getting past them. I regret, however, that if both teams do this you do not have a game so much as a tableau. A more promising tactic, which seemed to be adopted by one or two of you, was to lurk near the opponents' goal so that if the ball came in your direction you would be ideally placed to get it past the custodian of the goal. The fact that in some cases you and the opposing custodian leaned companionably against the goal, sharing a cigarette and watching the play up-field, showed a decent spirit and may possibly be a good starting point for some more advanced tactics, but I do not think this should be encouraged. On this general topic, I have to assume that retiring from the field of play for the call of nature or a breather is acceptable, but doing so for a snack is not. My feeling, Archchancellor, is that our colleagues' general desire to be never more than twenty minutes from some savouries may be satisfactorily catered for by a pause in the middle of the game. Happily, if they changed ends at that point, that would satisfy the complaints about one goal being larger than the other. Yes?' This was to the Chair of Indefinite Studies.

'If we change ends,' said the Chair, who had put his hand up, 'will that then mean that the goals that were scored into our own goal will now become goals scored against the opposing team since that goal is now physically theirs?'

Ponder considered the metaphysics of answering this one and settled for, 'No, of course not. I have a whole list of other notes, Archchancellor, and regrettably they add up to us not being very good at football.'

The wizards fell silent. 'Let's start with the ball,' said Ridcully. 'I've got an idea about the ball.'

'Yes, sir. I thought you would.'

'Then come and see me after dinner.'

Juliet had been sucked into the manic circus that was the backstage area of Shatta, and no one was paying Glenda any attention whatsoever. Just for now, she was a hindrance, surplus, no use to anyone, an obstruction to be worked around, an onlooker in the game. A little way away, a handsome young dwarf with a double ponytail beard was waiting patiently while a temporary rivet was put into what looked like a silver cuirass. She was surrounded by workers in much the same way as a knight is when his vassals must dress him for combat. Standing a little apart from them were two taller dwarfs, whose weaponry looked slightly more functional than beautiful. They were male. Glenda knew this simply because any female of any sapient species knows the look of a man who has nothing very much to do in an environment that, for this time, is clearly occupied by and totally under the control of females. It looked as though they were on guard.

Propelled by the sherry, she wandered over. 'That must cost a lot of money,' she said to the nearest guard. He looked slightly embarrassed by the approach.

'You're telling me. Moonsilver, they call it. We're even having to walk down the catwalk with her. They say it's the coming thing, but I dunno. It won't take an edge and it wouldn't stop a decent blade. You need Igors to help you smelt it, too. They say it's worth even more than platinum. Looks good, though, and they say you hardly know you're wearing it. It's not what my granddad would have called a metal, but they say that we have to move with the times. Personally, I wouldn't even hang it on the wall, but there you go.'

'Girl's armour,' said the other guard.

'What about this micromail stuff?' said Glenda.

'Ah, different pocketful of rats entirely, miss,' said the first guard. 'I hear they set up and forge it right here in the city, 'cos the best crafts-men are here. Just the job, eh? Chain mail as fine as cloth and strong as steel! It'll get cheaper, too, they say, and most of all it doesn't—'

'Wotcher, Glendy, guess who?'

Someone tapped Glenda on the shoulder. She turned round and saw a vision of heavily but tastefully armoured beauty. It was Juliet, but Glenda only knew this because of the milky-blue eyes. Juliet was wear-ing a beard.

'Madame says I'd better wear this,' she said. 'It's not dwarf if it don't include a beard. What d'you think?'

This time the sherry got in first.

'It's actually rather attractive,' said Glenda, still in mild shock. 'It's very – silvery.'

It was a female beard, she could tell. It looked styled and stylish and didn't have bits of rat in it.

'Madame says there's a place saved for you in the front row,' said Juliet.

'Oh, I couldn't sit in the front row—' Glenda began, on automatic, but the sherry cut in with, 'Shut up, stop thinking like your mother, will you, and go and sit down in the damn front row.'

One of the ever-present young ladies chose this exact moment to take Glenda by the hand and lead her slightly unsteady feet through the settling chaos, out through the door and back into fairyland. There was indeed a seat waiting for her.

Fortunately, although in the front row it was off to one side. She would have died of shame had it been right in the middle. She clutched her handbag in both hands and risked a look along the row. It was packed. It wasn't exclusively dwarf, either; there were a number of human ladies, smartly dressed, a little on the skinny side (in her opinion), almost offensively at ease and all talking.

Another sherry mystically appeared in her hand and, as the noise stopped with rat-trap sharpness, Madame Sharn came out through the curtain and began to address the crowded hall. Glenda thought, I wish I'd worn a better coat . . . At which point the sherry tucked her up and put her to bed.

Glenda only started to think properly again some time later, when she was hit on the head by a bunch of flowers. They struck her just over the ear and as expensive petals rained around her she looked up at the beaming, radiant face of Juliet, at the very edge of the catwalk, halfway through the motions of shouting 'Duck!'

. . . And there were more flowers flying and people standing and cheering, and music, and in general the feeling of being under a waterfall with no water but inexhaustible torrents of sound and light.

Out of it all Juliet exploded, throwing herself at Glenda and flinging her arms around her neck.

'She wants me to do it again!' she panted. 'She says I could go to Quirm and Genua, even! She says she'll pay me more if I don't work for no one else and the world is an oyster. I never knew that.'

'But you've already got a steady job in the kitchen . . .' said Glenda, only three-quarters of her way into consciousness. Later, more often than she liked, she remembered saying those words while the applause thundered all around them.

There was a gentle pressure on her shoulder, and here was one of the interchangeable young women with a tray. 'Madame sends her compliments, miss, and would like to invite you and Miss Juliet to join her in her private boudoir.'

'That's nice of her, but I think we should be getting— A boudoir, you say?'

'Oh yes. And would you like another drink? It's a celebration, after all.'

Glenda looked around at the chattering, laughing and, above all, drinking crowd. The place felt like an oven.

'All right, but not that sherry, thank you all the same. Have you got something very cold and fizzy?'

'Why, yes, miss. Lots.' The girl produced a large bottle and expertly filled a tall fluted glass with, apparently, bubbles. When Glenda drank it, the bubbles filled her, too.

'Mm, quite nice,' she ventured. 'A bit like lemonade grown up.'

'That's how Madame drinks it, certainly.'

'Er, this boudoir,' Glenda tried, following the girl rather unsteadily. 'How big is it?'

'Oh, pretty large, I think. There must be about forty people in there already.'

'Really? That's a big boudoir.' Well, thank goodness, Glenda thought. That at least is sorted out. They really ought to put proper explanations in these novels.

She had never been sure, given that she had no idea what sort of thing a boudoir was, what sort of thing you would find in it when you did. She found that it contained people, heat and flowers – not flowers in bunches, but in pillars and towering stacks, filling most of the air with clouds of sticky perfume while the people below filled the rest of it with words, tightly packed. No one could possibly hear what they were saying, Glenda told herself, but perhaps that wasn't important. Perhaps what was important was being there to be seen to say it.

The crowd parted, and she saw Juliet, still in the glittering outfit, still in the beard ... being there. Salamanders were flashing on and off,

156

which meant people with iconographs, didn't it? The trashy papers were full of people glittering for the picture. She had no time for them. What made it worse was that her disapproval mattered not a fig to anyone. The people glittered anyway. And here was Juliet, glittering most of all.

'I think I could do with a little fresh air,' she mumbled.

Her guide led her gently to an unobtrusive doorway. 'Restrooms through here, ma'am.' And they were – except that the long, carefully lit room was like some kind of fairy tale, all velvet and drapes. Fifteen surprised visions of Glenda stared at her from as many mirrors. It was overpowering enough to make her sit down in a very expensive bendy-legged chair that turned out to be very restful, too . . .

When she jerked awake, she staggered out, got lost in a dark world of smelly passages choked with packing cases and finally blundered into a very large room indeed. It was more like a cavern; at the far end were a pair of double doors, probably ashamed to let in a grey light which did not so much illuminate as accuse. Another chaos of empty clothes racks and packing cases was scattered around the floor. In one place, water had dripped from the roof, and a puddle had formed on the stone, soaking some cardboard.

'There they are, in there with their glitter and their finery, and it's all muck and rubbish round the back, right, dear?' said a voice in the dark. 'You look like a lady who can spot a metaphor when she stares it in the face.'

'Something like that,' muttered Glenda. 'Who's doing the asking?'

An orange light glowed and faded in the gloom. Someone was smoking a cigarette in the shadows.

'It's the same all over, love. If there was an award for the arse end of things, there'd be a real bloody squabble for first place. I've seen a few palaces in my time and they're all the same: turrets and banners in the front, maids' bedrooms and water pipes round the back. Fancy a top-up? Can't be walking around here with an empty glass, you'll stand out.'

The cooler air was making her feel better. She still had a glass in her hand. 'What is this stuff?'

'Well, if this was any other party it'd probably be the cheapest fizzing wine you could strain through a sock, but Madame won't stint. It's the real stuff. Champagne.'

'What? I thought only nobby people drank that!'

'No, just people with money, love. Sometimes it's the same thing.'

She looked closer, and gasped. 'What? Are you Pepe?'

'That's me, love.'

'But you're not all . . . all . . .' She waved her hands frantically.

'Off duty, love. Don't have to worry about . . .' He waved his hands equally frantically. 'I've got a bottle here of our very own. Care to join me?'

'Well, I ought to be getting back in there—'

'Why? To fuss around her like an old hen? Leave her be, love. She's a duck who's just found water.'

Pepe looked taller in this gloom. Maybe it was the language and the lack of flapping. And, of course, anyone next to Madame Sharn would look small. He was willowy, though, like someone made of sinews.

'But anything could happen to her!'

Pepe's grin gleamed. 'Yes! But probably won't. My word, she sold micromail for us, and no mistake. Told Madame I had a good feeling. She's got a great career in front of her.'

'No, she's got a good, steady job in the Night Kitchen, with me,' said Glenda. 'It might not be big money, but it'll turn up every week. On the nail, and she won't lose it if someone prettier comes along.'

'Dolly Sisters, right? Sounds like the Botney Street area,' said Pepe. 'I'm sure of it. Not too bad, as I recall. I didn't get beaten up much down there, but at the end of the day they're all crab buckets.'

Glenda was taken aback. She'd expected anger or condescension, not this sharp little grin.

'You know a lot about our city for a dwarf from Uberwald, I must say.'

'No, love, I know a lot about Uberwald for a boy from Lobbin Clout,' said Pepe smoothly. 'Old Cheese Alley, to be precise. Local lad, me. Wasn't always a dwarf, you know. I just joined.'

'What? Can you do that?'

'Well, it's not like they advertised. But yeah, if you know the right people. And Madame knew the right people, ha, knew quite a lot about the right people. It wasn't hard. I've got to believe in a few things, there's a few observances, and of course I have to keep off the old booze—' He smiled as her glance pinned the glass in his hand, and went on: 'Too quick, love, I was going to add "when I'm working", and good job too. It doesn't matter if you are shoring up the mine roof or riveting a bodice, being a piss artist is bloody stupid. And the moral of all this is, you have to grab life or drop back into the crab bucket.'

'Oh yes, that's all very well to say,' Glenda snapped, wondering what crabs had got to do with anything. 'But in real life people have responsibilities. We don't have shiny jobs with lots of money, but they are real jobs doing things that people need! I'd be ashamed of myself, selling boots at four hundred dollars a go, which only rich people can afford. What's the point of that?'

'Well, you must admit that it makes rich people less rich,' said the chocolate voice of Madame behind her. Like many large people, she could move as quietly as the balloon she resembled. 'That's a good start, isn't it? And it goes to wages for the miners and the smiths. It all goes around, they tell me.'

She sat down heavily on a packing case, glass in hand. 'Well, we've got most of them out now,' she said, fumbling in her capacious breast-plate with her spare hand and pulling out a thick wad of paper.

'The big names want to be in on this and everyone wants it exclusively and we're going to need another forge. Tomorrow I'll go and see the bank.' She paused to dip into her metal bodice again. 'As a dwarf I was raised in the faith that gold is the one true currency,' she said, counting out some crisp notes, 'but I have to admit this stuff is a lot warmer. That's fifty dollars for Juliet, twenty-five from me and twenty-five from the champagne, which is feeling happy. Juliet said to give it to you to look after.'

'Miss Glenda thinks that we'll lead her treasure into a lifetime of worthless sin and depravity,' said Pepe.

'Well, that's a thought,' said Madame, 'but I can't remember when I last had some depravity.'

'Tuesday,' said Pepe.

'A whole box of chocolates is not depraved. Besides, you slid out the card between the layers, which confused me. I did not intend to eat the bottom layer. I did not want the bottom layer. It was practically assault.'

Pepe coughed. 'We're scaring the normal lady, love.'

Madame smiled. 'Glenda, I know what you're thinking. You're thinking we're a couple of louche evil clowns who booze away in a world of smoke and mirrors. Well, that's fairly accurate right now, but today was the end of a year's hard work, you see.'

And you bicker like an old married couple, Glenda thought. Her head was aching. She'd tried a rat fruit, that was the trouble, she was sure of it.

'In the morning I'm going to show these orders to the manager of the Royal Bank and ask him for a lot of money. If he trusts us, can you? We *need* Juliet. She just . . . sparkles.'

And you two are holding hands. Tightly. Something soft snapped inside Glenda.

'All right, look,' she said. 'It's like this. Jools is going to come back home with me tonight, to get her head straight. Tomorrow . . . well, we'll see.'

'We can't ask for more than that. Can we?' said Madame, patting Glenda on the knee. 'You know, Juliet thinks the world of you. She said she'd need you to say yes. She was telling all the society ladies about your pies.'

'She's been talking to society ladies?' said Glenda in astonishment laced with trepidation and tinted with wonder.

'Certainly. They all wanted a close look at the micromail, and she just chatted away, cheery as you like. I don't think anyone ever said "Wotcher!" to them in their lives before.'

'Oh no! I'm sorry!'

'Why be? They were rather taken by it. And apparently you can bake pickled onions into a pie so that they stay crunchy?'

'She told them that?'

'Oh, yes. I gather that they all intend to get their cooks to try it out.'

'Hah. They'll never find the way!' said Glenda with satisfaction.

'So Jools says.'

'We . . . generally call her Juliet,' said Glenda.

'She told us to call her Jools,' said Madame. 'Is there a problem?'

'Well, er, not really a problem,' Glenda began wretchedly.

'That's good, then,' said Madame, who clearly knew when not to notice subtleties. 'Now let's prise her away from her new friends, and you can see to it that she gets a good night's sleep.'

There was laughter, and the girls helping with the show streamed out into the clammy place that was the midwife to beauty. Juliet was among them, and with the loudest laugh. She broke away when she saw Glenda and gave her another hug. 'Oh, Glendy, isn't this great? It's like a fairy story!'

'Yes, well, it might be,' said Glenda, 'but they don't all have happy endings. Just you remember you have a good job now, with prospects and regular leftovers to take home. That's not to be lightly thrown away.'

'No, it should be hurled with great force,' said Pepe. 'I mean, what is this? Emberella? The wand has been waved, the court is cheering, a score of handsome princes are waiting to sign up for just a sniff of her slipper, and you want her to go back to work making pumpkins?'

He looked at their blank faces. 'All right, perhaps that came out a little confused, but surely you can follow the seam? This is a *big* chance! As big as it gets. A way out of the bucket!'

'I think we'll go home now,' said Glenda primly. 'Come along, Jools.'

'See,' said Pepe, when they had gone, 'it's a crab bucket.'

Madame peered into a bottle to see if, against all probability, one glassful yet remained. 'Did you know she more or less raised the kid? Jools will do what she says.'

'What a waste,' said Pepe. 'Don't take the world by storm, stay here and make pies? You think that's a life?'

'Someone has to make pies,' Madame said, with an infuriating calm reasonableness.

'Oh, pur-lease! Not her. Let it not be her. And for leftovers? Oh no!'

Madame picked up another empty bottle. She knew it was empty because it was in the vicinity of Pepe at the end of a long day, but she examined it anyway because thirst springs eternal.

'Hmm. It might not come to that,' she said. 'I have a feeling that Miss Glenda is just about to start thinking. There's a powerful mind behind that rather sad cloak and those awful shoes. Today might be its lucky day.'

Ridcully strode through the corridors of Unseen University with his robes flapping confidently behind him. He had a big stride and Ponder had to run in a semi-crabwise fashion to keep up with him, his clipboard clutched protectively to his chest. 'You know we did agree that it wasn't to be used for purposes other than pure research, Archchancellor. You actually signed the edict.'

'Did I? I don't remember that, Stibbons.'

'I remember it most distinctly, sir. It was just after the case of Mister Floribunda.'

'Which one was he?' said Ridcully, still striding purposefully ahead.

'He was the one who felt a little peckish and asked the Cabinet for a bacon sandwich to see what would happen.'

'I thought that anything taken out of the Cabinet had to be returned in 14.14 hours recurring?'

'Yes, sir. That is the case, but the Cabinet appears to have strange rules that we do not fully understand. In any case, Mister Floribunda's defence was that he thought the fourteen-hour rule didn't apply to bacon sandwiches. Nor did he tell anybody and so the students on his floor were only alerted when they heard the screams some fourteen hours later.'

'Correct me if I'm wrong,' said Ridcully, still covering the flagstones at an impressive rate, 'but would it not have been digested by that point?'

'Yes, sir. But it still went back to the Cabinet, of its own accord, you might say. That was quite an interesting discovery. We did not know that could happen.'

Ridcully stopped and Ponder bumped into him. 'What exactly did happen to him?'

'You wouldn't want me to draw a picture, sir. However, the good news is that he will soon be out of the wheelchair. In fact, I gather he's already walking quite well with a stick. How we discipline him is, of course, up to you, sir. The file is on your desk, as are, indeed, a considerable number of other documents.'

Ridcully strode off again. 'He did it to see what would happen, did he?' he said cheerfully.

'So he said, sir,' said Ponder.

'And this was against my express orders, was it?'

'Yes, absolutely definitely, sir,' said Ponder, who knew his Archchancellor and already had an inkling of how this one was going to end. 'And so therefore, sir, I must insist that he—' He walked into Ridcully again because the man had stopped outside a large door on which was a bright red notice saying, 'No Item To Be Removed From This Room Without The Express Permission Of The Archchancellor. Signed Ponder Stibbons pp Mustrum Ridcully.'

'You signed this one for me?' Ridcully said.

'Yes, sir. You were busy at the time and we had agreed on this one.'

'Yes, of course, but I don't think that you should pp just like that. Remember what that young lady said about the UU.'

Ponder produced a large key and opened the door. 'May I also remind you, Archchancellor, that we agreed a moratorium on the use of the Cabinet of Curiosity until we had cleaned up some of the residual magic in the building. We still don't seem to have got rid of the squid.'

'Did we agree, Mister Stibbons,' said Ridcully, turning around sharply, 'or did you agree with yourself pp me, as it were?'

'Well, er, I think I understood the spirit of your thinking, sir.'

'Well, this is the spirit of pure research,' said Ridcully. 'It's research into how we can hope to save our cheeseboard. Many would say there could be no greater goal. As for young Floribunda . . .'

'Yes, sir?' said Ponder wearily.

'Promote him. Whatever level he is, move him up one.'

'I think that'll send the wrong kind of signal,' Ponder tried.

'On the contrary, Mister Stibbons. It will send exactly the right message to the student body.'

'But he disobeyed an express order, may I point out?'

'That's right. He showed independent thinking and a certain amount of pluck, and in the course of so doing added valuable data to our understanding of the Cabinet.'

'But he might have destroyed the whole university, sir.'

'Right, in which case he would have been vigorously disciplined, if we'd been able to find anything left of him. But he didn't and he was lucky and we need lucky wizards. Promote him, on the direct order of me, not pp'd at all. Incidentally, how loud were his screams?'

'As a matter of fact, Archchancellor, the first one was so heartfelt that it kept going long after he'd run out of breath and apparently adopted an independent existence. Residual magic again. We've had to lock it in one of the cellars.'

'Did he actually say what the bacon sandwich was like?'

'Coming or leaving, sir?' said Ponder.

'Only coming, I think,' said Ridcully. 'I do have a vivid imagination after all.'

'He said it was the most delightful bacon sandwich he'd ever eaten. It was the bacon sandwich that you dream of when you hear the words bacon sandwich and never, ever quite get.'

'With brown sauce?' said Ridcully.

'Of course. Apparently, it was the bacon sandwich to end all bacon sandwiches.'

'It nearly did, for him, but isn't that what you already know about the Cabinet? That it always delivers a perfect specimen?'

'Actually, we know very little for certain,' said Ponder. 'What we do know is that it will hold nothing too large to fit inside a cube measuring 14.14 inches recurring on a side, that it will cease working if, we now know, a non-organic object is not replaced in it in 14.14 hours recurring, and that none of its contents are pink, although we do not know why this should be.'

'But bacon is definitely organic, Mister Stibbons,' said Ridcully.

Ponder sighed. 'Yes, sir, we don't know why that is either.'

The Archchancellor took pity on him. 'Perhaps it was one of those very crispy ones,' he suggested kindly. 'The kind that you can break between your fingers. I like that in a bacon sandwich.'

The door swung open and there it was. Small, in the centre of a *very* large room . . .

The Cabinet of Curiosity.

'Do you think this is wise?' said Ponder.

'Of course not,' said Ridcully. 'Now find me a football.'

On one wall was a white mask, such as one might wear to a carnival. Ponder turned towards it. 'Hex. Please find me a ball suitable for the game of football.'

'That mask is new?' said Ridcully. 'I thought Hex's voice travelled in blit space?'

'Yes, sir. It just comes out of the air, sir. But somehow, well, it feels better to have something to talk to.'

'What shape football do you require?' said Hex, his voice as smooth as clarified butter. 'Oval or spherical?'

'Spherical,' said Ponder.

Instantly the Cabinet shook.

The thing had always worried Ridcully. It looked too smug, for a start. It seemed to be saying: You don't know what you are doing. You use me as a kind of lucky dip and I bet you have never thought of how many dangerous things can fit into a fourteen-inch cube. In fact, Ridcully had thought about that, often at three in the morning, and never went into the room without a couple of sub-critical spells in his pocket just in case. And then there was Nutt . . . Well, hope for the best and prepare for the worst, that was the UU way.

A drawer slid out and went on sliding until it reached the wall and presumably continued to slide into some other hospitable set of dimensions, because it never turned up outside the room, no matter how often you looked.

'Very smooth today,' he observed, as another drawer rose up from under the floor and sprouted a further drawer exactly the same size as itself which began to move purposefully towards the far wall.

'Yes. The lads at Brazeneck have come up with a new algorithm for handling wave spaces in higher-level blit. It speeds up something like the Cabinet by getting on for 2,000 Drinkies.'

Ridcully frowned. 'Did you just make that up?'

'No, sir. Charlie Drinkie came up with it at Brazeneck. It's a shorter way of saying 15,000 iterations to the first negative blit. And it's a lot easier to remember.'

'So people you know at Brazeneck send you stuff?' said Ridcully.

'Oh, yes,' said Ponder.

'For free?'

'Of course, sir,' said Ponder, looking surprised. 'The free sharing of information is central to the pursuit of natural philosophy.'

'And so you tell them things, do you?'

Ponder sighed. 'Yes, of course.'

'I don't think I approve of that,' said Ridcully. 'I'm all for the free sharing of information, provided it's them sharing their information with us.'

'Yes, sir, but I think we're rather hampered by the meaning of the word "sharing".'

'Nevertheless,' Ridcully began and stopped. A sound so quiet that they had barely noticed it had stopped. The Cabinet of Curiosity had folded itself up and was once again just a piece of wooden furniture in the centre of the room, but as they looked at it its two front doors opened and a brown ball dropped on to the floor and bounced with a sound like *gloing!* Ridcully marched over and picked it up, turning it in his hands.

'Interesting,' he said, slamming it towards the floor. It bounced up past his head, but he was quick enough to catch it on the way down. 'Remarkable,' he said. 'What do you think of this, Stibbons?' He flicked the ball into the air and kicked it hard across the room. It came back towards Ponder, who, to his own amazement, caught it.

'Seems to have a life of its own.' Ponder dropped it on to the floor and tried a kick.

It flew.

Ponder Stibbons was the quintessential, all-time holder of the one-hundred-metre note from his auntie, which also asked for him to be excused all sporting activities on account of his athlete's ear, erratic stigmatism, a grumbling nose and a revolving spleen. By his own admission, he would rather run ten miles, leap a five-bar gate and climb a big hill than engage in any athletic activity.

The ball sang to him. It sang *gloing!*

A few minutes later, he and Ridcully walked back to the Great Hall, occasionally bouncing the ball on the flagstones. There was something about the sound of *gloing!* that made you want to hear it again.

'You know, Ponder, I think you've been doing it all wrong. There are more things in Heaven and Disc than are dreamed of in our philosophies.'

'I expect so, sir. I don't have many things in my philosophies.'

'It's all about the ball,' said Ridcully, slamming it down hard on the flagstones again and catching it. 'Tomorrow, we'll bring it here and see what happens. You gave the ball a mighty kick, Mister Stibbons, and yet you are, by your own admission, a wet and a weed.'

'Yes, sir, and a wuss, and I am proud of the appellation. I'd better remind you, Archchancellor, that the thing mustn't spend too long outside the Cabinet.'

Gloing!

'But we could make a copy, couldn't we?' said Ridcully. 'It's only leather stitched together, probably protecting a bladder of some sort. I bet any decent craftsman could make another one for us.'

'What, *now*?'

'The lights never go off on the Street of Cunning Artificers.'

By now, they were back in the Great Hall and Ridcully looked around until his gaze lighted on two figures pushing a trolley laden with candles. 'You lads, to me!' he shouted. They stopped pushing the trolley and walked over to him. 'Mister Stibbons here would like you to run an errand for him. It's of considerable importance. Who are you?'

'Trevor Likely, guv.'

'Nutt, Archchancellor.'

Ridcully's eyes narrowed. 'Yes . . . Nutt,' he said, and thought about the spells in his pocket. 'The candle dribbler, yes? Well, you can make yourselves useful. Over to you, Mister Stibbons.'

Ponder Stibbons held out the ball. 'Have you any idea what this is?'

Nutt took it out of his hands and bounced it on the tiles a couple of times.

Gloing! Gloing!

'Yes. It appears to be a simple sphere, although technically I believe it to be, in actual fact, a truncated icosahedron, made by stitching together a number of pentagons and hexagons of tough leather, and stitching means holes and holes let the air leak . . . Ah, there is lacing just here, you see? There must be some internal bladder – animal, probably. A balloon, as it were, for lightness and elasticity, encapsulated by leather, simple and elegant.' He handed the ball back to Ponder, who was open-mouthed.

'Do you know everything, Mister Nutt?' he said with the sarcasm of a born pedagogue.

Nutt's reply was concentrated and there was a lengthy pause before he said, 'I'm not sure about a lot of the detail, sir.'

Ponder heard a snigger behind him and felt himself redden. He'd been cheeked, by a dribbler, even if Nutt was the most incontinently erudite one he'd ever encountered.

'Do you know where a copy of this may be made?' said Ridcully loudly.

'I expect so,' said Nutt. 'I believe dwarf rubber will be our friend here.'

'There's plenty of dwarfs up at Old Cobblers who could knock one up, guv,' said Trev. 'They're good at this sort of thing, but they'd want paying, they always want paying. Nuffin's on credit when you're dealing with a dwarf.'

'Give these young gentlemen twenty-five dollars, Mister Stibbons, will you?'

'That's a lot of money, Archchancellor.'

'Yes, well, dwarfs, while the salt of the earth, don't have much of a grasp of small numbers and I want this in a hurry. I'm sure I can trust Mister Likely and Mister Nutt with the money, can't I?' He said it jovially, but there was an edge to his voice. Trev, at least, got the message very quickly; a wizard could trust you because of the hellish future he could unleash on you if his trust was betrayed.

'You can certainly trust us, guv.'

'Yes, I thought I could,' said Ridcully.

When they had gone, Ponder Stibbons said, 'You're entrusting them with twenty-five dollars?'

'Yes, indeed,' said Ridcully cheerfully. 'It will be interesting to see the outcome.'

'Nevertheless, sir, I have to say that it was an unwise move.'

'Thank you for your input, Mister Stibbons, but may I gently remind you who is the guv around here?'

Glenda and Juliet took a trolley bus home, another huge extravagance but, of course, Glenda was carrying more money than she had ever seen at one go. She had stuffed the notes into her bodice, à la Madame, and it seemed to generate a heat of its own. You were safe on a troll. Anyone wanting to mug a troll would have to use a building on a stick.

Juliet was quiet. This puzzled Glenda; she had expected her to bubble like a fountain full of soap flakes. The silence was unnerving.

'Look. I know it was a lot of fun,' Glenda said, 'but showing off clothes isn't like a real job, is it?' No. Real jobs pay a lot less, she thought.

Where had that come from? Jools hadn't opened her mouth and the troll was still covered in mountain lichen and had a single-syllable vocabulary. It came from me, she thought. This is about dreams, isn't it? She is a dream. I dare say the micromail is good stuff, but she made it sparkle. And what can I say? You help in the kitchen. You are useful and helpful, at least when you're not daydreaming, but you don't know how to keep accounts or plan a weekly menu. What would you do without me? How would you get on away from here, in foreign parts where folks are so odd?

'I'll have to open a bank account for you,' she said aloud. 'It'll be our little secret, all right? It'll be a nice little nest egg for you.'

'And if Dad don't know I've got the money he won't get it off me and piss it against the wall,' said Juliet, glancing up at the solemn, impassive face of the troll. If Glenda had known how to say '*Pas devant le troll*' she would have done so. But it was true: Mr Stollop commanded that all family earnings were pooled, with him holding the pool, which was then pooled with his friends in the bar of the Turkey & Vegetables, and ultimately pooled again in the reeking alley behind it.

She settled for: 'I wouldn't put it quite like that.'

Gloing! Gloing!

The new ball was magic, that's what it was. It bounced back to Trev's waiting hand as if by its own free will. For two pins he'd risk kicking it, but he and Nutt and the ball were already picking up a trail of curious street urchins such that he would be guaranteed never to see it again.

'Are you really sure you know 'ow it works?' he said to Nutt.

'Oh, yes, Mister Trev. It's a lot simpler than it looks, although the polyhedrons will need some work, but overall—'

A hand landed on Trev's shoulder. 'Well, now. Trev Likely,' said Andy. 'And his little pet, harder to kill than a cockroach, by all accounts. Something's going on, ain't it, Trev? And you're going to tell me what it is. Here, what's that you're holding?'

'Not today, Andy,' said Trev, backing away. 'You're lucky you didn't end up in the Tanty with Mister One Drop measurin' you up for a hemp collar.'

'Me?' said Andy innocently. 'I didn't do a thing! Can't blame me for what a thicko Stollop does, but something is going on with the football, ain't it? Vetinari wants to muck it about.'

'Just leave it alone, will you?' said Trev.

There was more than the usual gang behind Andy. The Stollop

brothers had sensibly spared the streets their presence lately, but people like Andy could always find followers. Like they said, it was better to be beside Andy than in front of him. And with Andy you never knew just when he was—

The cutlass was out in one movement. That was Andy. Whatever it was inside that held back the primeval rage could flick off just like that. And here came the blade with Trev's future written on it in very short words. And it stopped in mid air and Nutt's voice said, 'I believe I could squeeze with enough pressure, Andy, to make your bones grind and flow. There are twenty-seven bones in the human hand. I truly believe that I could make every one of them useless with the slightest extra pressure. However, I would like to give you a chance to revise your current intentions.'

Andy's face was a mix of colours: a white that was almost blue and a rage that was almost crimson. He was trying to pull away and Nutt stood calmly and was completely immoveable. 'Get 'im!' Andy hissed at the world in general.

'Could I regretfully remind you gentlemen that I have another hand?' said Nutt.

He must have squeezed because Andy yelped as his hand ground against the weapon's handle.

Trev knew all too well that Andy did not have friends, he had followers. They were looking at their stricken leader and they were looking at Nutt, and they could see very clearly not only that Nutt had a spare hand, but what he was capable of doing with it. They did not move.

'Very well,' said Nutt. 'Perhaps this has been nothing more than an unfortunate misunderstanding. I am about to release my grip just enough for you to drop the cutlass, Mister Andy, please.'

There was another intake of breath from Andy as the cutlass landed on the stones.

'Now, if you would excuse us, Mister Trev and I are going to walk away.'

'Take the bloody cutlass! Don't leave the cutlass on the ground,' said Trev.

'I am sure Mister Andy would not come after us,' said Nutt.

'Are you bloody mad?' said Trev. He reached down, snatched up the cutlass and said, 'Let 'im go and let's get a move on.'

'Very well,' said Nutt. He must have squeezed a little harder because now Andy slumped to his knees.

Trev pulled Nutt away and towed him through the permanent city crowd. 'That's Andy!' he said, hurrying them along. 'You don't expect logic with Andy. You don't expect him to "learn the error of his ways". Don't look for any sense when Andy's after you. Got that? Don't try talkin' to 'im as if 'e's a human being. Now, keep up with me.'

Dwarf shops were doing well these days, largely because they understood the first rule of merchandising, which is this: I have got goods for sale and the customer has got money. I should have the money and, regrettably, that involves the customer having my goods. To this end, therefore, I will not say 'The one in the window is the last one we have, and we can't sell it to you, because if we did no one would know we have them for sale', or 'We'll probably have some more on Wednesday', or 'We just can't keep them on the shelves', or 'I'm fed up with telling people there's no demand for them'; I will make a sale by any means short of physical violence, because without one I am a waste of space.

Glang Snorrisson lived by this rule, but he didn't like people much, an affliction that affects many who have to deal with the general public over a long period, and the two people on the other side of his counter were making him edgy. One was small and looked harmless, but something so deep down in Glang's psyche that it was probably stuffed in his genes was making him nervous. The other intru— customer was not much more than a boy and therefore likely to commit a crime any moment.

Glang dealt with the situation by not understanding anything they said and uttering silly insults in his native tongue. There was hardly a risk. Only the Watch learned Dwarfish, and it came as a surprise when the worryingly harmless one said, in better Llamedos Dwarfish than Glang himself spoke these days: 'Such incivility to the amiable stranger

172

shames your beard and erases the writings of Tak, ancient merchant.'

'What did you say to him?' Trev asked, as Glang spluttered out apologies.

'Oh, just a traditional greeting,' said Nutt. 'Could you pass me the ball, please?' He took the football and bounced it on the floor.

Gloing!

'I suspect you might know the trick of making brimstoned rubber?'

'That was my . . . my grandfather's name,' Glang stuttered.

'Ah, a good omen,' said Trev quickly. He caught the ball and batted it down again.

Gloing!

'I can cut out and stitch the outer cover if you will work on the bladder,' said Nutt, 'and we will pay you fifteen dollars and allow you a licence to make as many more as you wish.'

'You'll make a fortune,' said Trev encouragingly.

Gloing! Gloing! went the ball, and Trev added, 'That'd be a university licence, too. No one would dare mess with it.'

'How come you know about brimstoned rubber?' said Glang. He had the look about him of someone who knows that he is outnumbered but will go down fighting.

'Because King Rhys of the dwarfs presented a dress of brimstoned rubber and leather to Lady Margolotta six months ago, and I'm pretty sure I understand the principle.'

'Her? The Dark Lady? She can kill people with a thought!'

'She is my friend,' said Nutt calmly, 'and I will help you.'

Glenda wasn't quite sure why she tipped the troll tuppence. He was elderly and slow, but his upholstery was well kept and he had twin umbrellas and it was no fun for trolls to come this far, because the kid gangs would have graffitied them to the waist by the time they got out of there.

She felt hidden eyes on her as she walked up to her door, and it didn't matter.

'All right,' she said to Juliet. 'Have a night off, okay?'

'I'll go back to work with you,' said Juliet, to her surprise. 'We need the money and I can't tell Dad about the fifty dollars, can I?'

There was a small collision of expectations in Glenda's head as Juliet went on: 'You're right, it's a steady job and I want to keep it an' I'm so fick I'd prob'ly muck up the other one. I mean, it was fun and all that, but then, I thought, well, you always gave me good advice, an' I remembered that time you kicked Greasy Damien in the goolies so hard when he was messin' me around, he walked bent double for a week. Besides, if I go away with them it means leaving the street, and Dad and the lads. That's really scary. An' you said be careful about fairy stories, and you're right, half the time it's goblins. An' I don't know how I'd get on without you puttin' me right. You are solid, you are. I can't remember you not bein' around, and when one of the girls sniggered about your old coat I told her you work very hard.'

Glenda thought, I used to be able to read you like a book – one with big colourful pages and not many words. And now I can't. What's happening? You're agreeing with me and I ought to feel smug about it, but I don't. I feel bad about it, and I don't know why, and that hurts.

'Maybe you ought to sleep on it,' she suggested.

'No, I'd mess it up, I know I would.'

'Do you feel all right?' Something inside Glenda was shouting at her.

'I'm okay,' said Juliet. 'Oh, it was fun and that, but it's for nobby girls, not me. It's all glitter, nuffin' you can hold. But a pie's a pie, right? Solid! Besides, who'd look after Dad and the lads?'

No, no, no, screamed Glenda's voice in her own head, *not that! I didn't want that.* Oh, didn't I? Then what did I think I was doing, passing on all that old toot? She looks to me, and I've gone and given her a good example! Why? Because I wanted to protect her. She's so . . . vulnerable. Oh dear, I've taught her to be me, and I've even made a bad mess of that chore!

'All right, then, you can head back with me.'

'Will we see the banquet? Our dad has been fretting about the banquet. He reckons Lord Vetinari is going to have everyone murdered.'

'Does he do that a lot?'

174

'Yes, but it gets hushed up, our dad says.'

'There's going to be hundreds of people there. That would need a lot of hush.' And if I don't like what I hear, there won't be enough hush in all the world, she thought.

Trev mooched aimlessly around the shop while Nutt and the dwarf put their heads together over the ball. For some reason there was a faint scrabbling on the roof. It sounded like claws. Just a bird, he told himself. Even Andy wouldn't come in through the roof. There was another pressing matter. This place would have a privy, wouldn't it? There was at least a back door and that would inevitably lead to a back alley and, well, what is a back alley for except for sleeping tramps and the call of nature? Possibly in the same place if you were feeling cruel.

Trev unbuckled his belt, faced a noisome wall and stared upwards nonchalantly, as a man does in these circumstances. However, most men don't look up into the astonished faces of two birdlike women who were standing, no, *perching* on the roof. They screeched *Awk! Awk!* and flew up into the darkness.

Trev scuttled quickly and damply back into the shop. This city got bloody stranger every day.

After that, time flew past for Trev, and every second stank of sulphur. He'd seen Nutt dribbling candles, but that was at snail's pace compared with the speed at which the leather was cut for the ball. But that wasn't creepy, that was just Nutt. What was creepy was that he didn't measure anything. Eventually, Trev couldn't stand it any more, and stopped leaning against the wall, pointed to one of the multi-sided little leather strips and said, 'How long is that?'

'One and fifteen sixteenths of an inch.'

'How can you tell without measuring?'

'I do measure, with my eyes. It is a skill. It can be learned.'

'An' that makes you worthy?'

'Yes.'

'An' who judges?'

'I do.'

'Here we are, Mister Nutt, still warm,' said Glang, arriving from the back of the shop holding something that looked like something taken from an animal that was now, you hoped for its own sake, dead.

'Of course, I could do a lot better with more time,' he continued, 'but if you blow down this little tube . . .'

Trev watched in wonder, and it occurred to him that in all his life he'd made a few candles and a lot of mess. How much was he worth?

Gloing! Gloing!

Two balls in harmony, thought Trev, but clapped as Nutt and Glang shook hands, then, while they were still admiring their handiwork, he reached behind him and slipped a dagger off the bench and into his pocket.

He wasn't a thief. Oh, fruit off stalls, but everyone knew that didn't count, and picking a toff's pocket was just a case of social redistribution, everyone knew that, too, and maybe you found something that looked lost, well, someone would pick it up, so why not you?

Weapons got you killed, often because you were holding one. But things were going too far. He had heard Andy's bones creak and Nutt had brought the man to his knees without sweating. And there were two reasons for taking precautions right there. One was that if you put Andy down you'd better put him out, right out, because he would come back, blood around the corner of his mouth. And two, the worst, was that right now Nutt was more worrying than Andy. At least he knew what Andy was . . .

Carrying a ball each, they hurried back to the university, with Trev keeping a watchful eye on high buildings. 'It's amazin' what's turnin' up in this city,' he said. 'There were a couple of vampire types back there, did you know?'

'Oh, those? They work for Ladyship. They are there for protection.'

'Whose?' said Trev.

'Do not worry about them.'

'Hah! And do you know something even stranger has happened this evening?' said Trev, as the university hove into sight. 'You offered that dwarf fifteen dollars and he didn't even haggle. Like, that's unheard of. Must be the power of *gloing!*

'Yes, but I actually gave him twenty dollars,' said Nutt.

'Why? He didn't ask for anythin' more.'

'No, but he did work very hard and the extra five dollars will more than repay him for the dagger you stole while our backs were turned.'

'I never did!' said Trev hotly.

'Your automatic, unthinking and spring-loaded reply is noted, Mister Trev. As was the sight of the dagger on the bench, shortly followed by the sight of the empty space where the dagger had been. I am not angry, because I saw you most sensibly toss Mister Shank's wretched cutlass over a wall and I understand your nervousness, but nevertheless I must point out that this is stealing. And so I ask you, as my friend, to take the dagger back in the morning.'

'But that will leave 'im up by five dollars *and* his dagger back.' Trev sighed. 'But at least we've got a few dollars each,' he said, as they entered the back door of the university.

'Yes, and then again no, Mister Trev. You will take the remaining five dollars and this rather grubby although genuine receipt for twenty dollars to Mister Stibbons, who thinks you are no good, thus making him doubt his original assumption that you are a thief and a scallywag and assisting your progress in this university.'

'I'm not a—' Trev began and stopped, honest enough to acknowledge the knife in his coat. 'Honestly, Nutt, you're one of a kind, you are.'

'Yes,' said Nutt. 'I am coming to that conclusion.'

WOTCHER!

The word, in huge type, shouted out from the front page of the *Times*, next to a big picture of Juliet glittering in micromail and smiling right at the reader. Glenda, frozen for the last fifteen seconds in the act of raising a piece of toast to her mouth, finally bit.

Now she blinked and dropped the toast to read:

Mystery model 'Jewels' was the toast of an astounding fashion show at Shatta yesterday when she was the very incarnation of micromail, the remarkable metal 'cloth' about which there has been so much speculation in recent months and which, she confirms, Does Not Chafe. She chatted happily and with fetching straightforward earthiness to dignitaries to whom, this writer is certain, no one has ever said 'Wotcher' before. They appeared to find the experience refreshing and entirely without chafe . . .

Glenda stopped reading at this point because the question 'How much trouble are we going to get into about this?' was attempting to fill her whole head. And there was no trouble, was there? And there would not be. There couldn't be. First, who would think that the beauty in the silver beard, like some goddess of the forge, was a cook's assistant? And, second, there was no trouble to be had, unless someone tried to make it, in which case they would have to go through Glenda and Glenda would go through *them*, in very short order. Because Jools was wonderful. She had to admit it. The girl brought radiant sunshine to the page, and suddenly it was plain: it would be a crime to hide all that grace and beauty in a cellar. So what if she had a vocabulary of fewer than seven hundred words? There were more than enough people who were stuffed tight as an egg with words, and who would want to see any of *them* on the front page?

Anyway, she thought, as she pulled her coat on, it would be a nine-minute wonder in any case and besides, she added to herself, it wasn't as if anyone would spot it was Juliet. After all, she was wearing a beard and that was amazing, because there was no way that a woman in a beard should look attractive, but it worked. Imagine that catching on! You'd have to spend twice as long at the hairdresser's. Someone's going to think about that, she thought.

There was no sound from the Stollops' house. She wasn't surprised. Juliet did not have much grasp of the idea of punctuality. Glenda popped next door to see how the widow Crowdy was and then headed, in the drizzling rain, back to her safe haven of the Night Kitchen. Halfway there an all but forgotten pressure in her bodice reminded her of her duty and she dared go into the Royal Bank of Ankh-Morpork.

Trembling with fear and defiance, she walked up to a clerk at his desk, slapped fifty warm dollars in front of him and said, 'I want to start a bank account, all right?' She left five minutes later with a shiny account book and the delightful recollection that a posh-looking man at a posh-looking desk in a posh-looking building had called her madam, and enjoyed the sensation until it ran into the reality that madam had better roll up her sleeves and get to work.

There was a lot to do. She made pies at least a day ahead so that they could mature, and Mister Nutt's appetite last night had put quite a large dent in her pantry. But at least there wouldn't be much demand for pies tomorrow night. Even the wizards didn't call for a pie after a banquet.

Ah, yes, the banquet, she thought, as the rain started to soak into her coat. The banquet. She would have to see about the banquet. Sometimes if you wanted to go to the ball you had to be your own fairy godmother.

There were several obstacles requiring the touch of a magic wand: Mrs Whitlow did indeed operate a certain kind of apartheid between the Night and Day Kitchens, as if one flight of stairs actually changed who you were. The next difficulty was that Glenda did not have, according to the traditions of the university, the right kind of figure to serve at table, at least when there were visitors, and, lastly, Glenda did not have the temperament for serving at table. It wasn't that she didn't know how to smile; she was quite capable of smiling, if you gave her enough warning, but she positively hated having to smile at people who actually merited, instead, a flick around the earhole with a napkin. She hated taking away plates of unfinished food. She always had to suppress a tendency to say things like 'Why did you put it on your plate if you didn't intend to finish it?' and 'Look, you've left more than half of it and it cost a dollar a pound,' and 'Of course it's cold, but that's because you've been playing footsie with the young lady opposite and haven't been concentrating on your dinner,' and when all else failed

'There's little children in Klatch you know . . .' – it was a phrase of her mother's, but she'd obviously missed some significant part of it.

She hated waste, she thought to herself as she walked along the stone corridor towards the Night Kitchen. There never needed to be any if you knew your way around a kitchen and if your diners had the decency to take your food seriously. She was rambling to herself. She knew that. Occasionally she would pull the front page of the *Times* out of her bag and take a look at it again. It had all really happened and there was the proof. But, it was a funny thing: *every* day something happened that was important enough to be on the front page of the newspaper. She'd never bought it and seen a little sign that said 'Not much happened yesterday, sorry about that'. And tomorrow, wonderful though that picture was, it would be wrapping up fish and chips and everyone would have forgotten about it. That would be a load off her mind.

There was a polite cough. She recognized it as belonging to Nutt, who had the politest cough there could possibly be. 'Yes, Mister Nutt?'

'Mister Trev has sent me with this letter for Miss Juliet, Miss Glenda,' said Nutt, who had apparently been waiting by the steps. He held it out as if it were some double-edged sword.

'She's not come in yet, I'm afraid,' said Glenda as Nutt followed her up the steps, 'but I'll put it on the shelf over here where she'll be bound to see it.' She looked at Nutt and saw his eyes firmly fixed on the pie racks. 'Oh, and I do seem to have made one apple pie more than called for. I wonder if you could assist me by removing it from the premises?'

He gave her a grateful smile, took the pie and hurried away.

Alone again, Glenda looked at the envelope. It was the cheapest sort, the kind that looked as if it had been made from recycled lavatory paper. And somehow, it seemed to have got a bit bigger.

Inexplicably, she found herself recalling that the gum on those envelopes was so bad that when it came to sealing them it was probably better to just have a very bad cold. Anyone could simply open it up, see what it said, dig out a bit of earwax and no one would be any the wiser.

But that would have been a very bad thing to do.

Glenda thought that same thought fifteen times before Juliet walked

180

into the Night Kitchen, hung up her coat on the hook and put on her apron. 'There was a man on the bus readin' the paper and it had a picture of me on the front,' she said excitedly.

Glenda nodded and handed over her own paper.

'Well, I suppose it's me,' said Juliet, with her head on one side. 'What shall we do now?'

'Open the damn letter!' shouted Glenda.

'What?' said Juliet.

'Er, oh, Trev sent you a letter,' said Glenda. She snatched it from the shelf and held it out. 'Why don't you read it right *now*?'

'He's probably just mucking about.'

'No! Why don't you just read it right *now*? I haven't tried to open it!'

Juliet took the envelope. It opened more or less to a touch. Glenda's evil side thought, hardly any gum at all! I could have just flicked it open!

'I can't read with you standin' so close,' said Juliet. After some time moving her lips she went on, 'I don't get it. It's all kinda long words. Lovely curly writing, though. There's a bit here saying that I look like a summer's day. What's that all about, then?' She pressed it into Glenda's hand. 'Can you read it for me, Glendy? You know I'm not good at complicated words.'

'Well, I'm a bit busy,' said Glenda, 'but since you ask.'

'First time I've ever had a letter that's not all in capitals,' said Juliet.

Glenda sat down and started to read. A lifetime of what even she would call bad romantic novels suddenly bore fruit. It read as though someone had turned on the poetry tap and then absent-mindedly gone on holiday. But they were wonderful words, nevertheless. There was the word swain, for example, which was a definite marker, and quite a lot about flowers and quite a lot of what looked like pleading, wrapped up in fancy letters, and after a while she took out her handkerchief and fanned the air around her face.

'So, what's it all about?' said Juliet.

Glenda sighed. How to begin? How did you talk to Juliet about similes and metaphors and poetic licence all wrapped up in wonderful curly writing?

She did her best. 'Weeell, basically he's saying that he really fancies you, thinks you're really fit, how about a date, no hanky panky, he promises. And there's three little x's underneath.'

Juliet started to cry. 'That's loverlee. Fancy 'im sitting down and writing all those words just for me. Real poetry just for me. I'm gonna sleep with it under my pillow.'

'Yes, I suspect that he had something like that in mind,' said Glenda and thought, Trev Likely a poet? Not likely at all.

There was a dreadful load on Pepe's bladder, and he was stuck between a rock and a hard place, if that wasn't too offensive a description of lying between Madame and a wall. She was still asleep. She snored magnificently, using the traditional multi-part snore, known to those who are fortunate enough to have to listen to it every night as the 'errgh, errgh, errghh, blorrrt!' symphony. And she was lying on his leg. And the room was pitch dark. He managed to retrieve his leg, half of which had gone to sleep, and set out on the well-known search for porcelain, which began by him putting his foot down on an empty champagne bottle, which skittered away and left him flat on his back. In the gloom he groped for it, found it, tested it for true emptiness, because you never knew your luck, and, as it were, filled it again, putting it down on what was probably a table, but in his mind and the darkness could just as well have been an armadillo.

There was another sound syncopating with Madame's virtuoso performance. It must have been that which woke him. By groping, he located his shorts and after only three tries managed to get them the right way up and the right way round. They were a little chilly. That was the problem with micromail; it was, after all, metal. On the other hand, it did not chafe and you never had to wash it. Five minutes on the fire and it was as hygienic as anything. Besides, Pepe's version of the shorts held a surprise all of their own.

Thus feeling that he could face the world, or at least the part of it that would need to see only the top of him, he shuffled and stubbed his way to the shop's door, checking every bottle along the way for evidence of liquid content. Remarkably, a bottle of port had survived with fifty per cent remaining capacity. Any port in a storm, he thought, and drank his breakfast.

The shop's door was rattling. It had a small sliding aperture by which the staff could determine whether they wanted to let a prospective customer in, because when you are a posh shop like Shatta, you don't sell things to just anyone. Pairs of eyeballs zigzagged back and forth across his vision as people clustered on the other side of the door and fought for attention. Somebody said, 'We're here to see Jewels.'

'She's resting,' said Pepe. That was always a good line and could mean anything.

'Have you seen the picture in the *Times*?' said a voice. Then, 'Look,' as a vision of Juliet was held up in front of the door.

Blimey, he said to himself. 'She had a very tiring day,' he said.

'The public wants to know all about her,' said a sterner voice.

And a rather less aggressive female voice said, 'She seems to be rather amazing.'

'She is. She is,' said Pepe, inventing desperately, 'but a *very* private person and a bit artistic too, if you know what I mean.'

'Well, I've got a big order to place,' said yet another voice as the owner managed to shuffle for slot space.

'Oh, well, we don't have to wake her up for that. Just give me a moment and I'll be right with you.' He took another swig of the port. When he turned around, Madame, in a nightshirt that could have accommodated a platoon, at least if they were very friendly, was bearing down on him with a glass in one hand and the champagne bottle in the other.

'This stuff's gone horribly flat,' she said.

'I'll go and find some fresh,' he replied, snatching it from her quickly. 'We've got newspaper people and customers out there and they all want Jools. Can you remember where she lives?'

'I'm sure she told me,' said Madame, 'but it all seems a long time ago. That other one, Glenda I think, works at some big place in the city, as a cook. Anyway, why do they want to see her?'

183

'There's a wonderful picture in the *Times*,' said Pepe. 'You know when you said you thought we'd get rich? Well, it looks like you weren't thinking big enough.'

'What do you suggest, dear?'

'Me?' said Pepe. 'Take the order, because that's good business, and tell the others that Jools will see them later.'

'Do you think they'll go for that?'

'They'll have to, because we don't know where the hell she is. There's a million dollars walking around this city on legs.'

Rhys, Low King of the Dwarfs, paid particular attention to the picture of the wonderful girl. The definition wasn't too bad at all. The technique of translating the clacks semaphore signal into a black-and-white picture was quite well advanced these days. Even so, his people in Ankh-Morpork must have thought this particularly interesting to merit the expense of the bandwidth required. Certainly, it was exercising a lot of other dwarfs, but in the Low King's experience, it was possible to find someone, somewhere, who objected to anything. He looked at the grags in front of him. So simple for people like Vetinari, he thought. He just has religions to deal with. We don't have religions. Being a dwarf is a religion in itself, and no two priests ever agree, and sometimes it seems that every other dwarf is a priest. 'I see nothing here to disturb me,' he said.

'We believe the beard to be a false one,' said one of the grags.

'That is perfectly acceptable,' said the King. 'There is absolutely nothing in any precedent that bans false beards. They are a great salvation to those who find beards hard to grow.'

'But she looks, well, alluring,' said one of the other grags. They were indistinguishable under their tall, pointed leather cowls.

'Attractive, certainly,' said the King. 'Gentlemen, is this going to take long?'

'It must be stopped. It's not dwarfish.'

'Oh, but it manifestly is, is it not?' said the King. 'Micromail is one hundred per cent mail and you don't get any more dwarfish than that.

She is smiling and while I would agree that dwarfs do not appear to smile very much, certainly not when they come to see me, I think we could profit from her example.'

'It's positively an offence against morality.'

'How? Where? Only in your heads, I feel.'

The tallest grag said, 'So you intend to do nothing?'

The King paused for a moment, staring at the ceiling. 'No, I intend to do something,' he said. 'First of all, I shall see to it that my staff find out just how many orders there have been for micromail originating from here in Bonk today. I'm sure Shatta would not object to them seeing their records, especially since I intend to tell Madame Sharn that she can come back and establish her premises here.'

'You would do that?' said a grag.

'Yes, of course. We have nearly concluded the Koom Valley Accord, a peace with the trolls that no one ever thought they would see. And I am fed up, gentlemen, with your whining, moaning and endless, endless attempts to re-fight battles that you have already lost. As far as I am concerned, this young lady is showing us a better future and now, if you are not out of my office in ten seconds, I will charge you rent.'

'There will be trouble over this.'

'Gentlemen, there is always trouble! But this time I will be making it for you.'

As the door slammed shut behind them, the King sat back in his chair.

'Well done, sir,' said his secretary.

'They'll keep on. I can't imagine what being a dwarf would be like if we didn't argue all the time.' He squirmed a little in his chair. 'You know, they're right when they say it doesn't chafe and it's not as cold as you would imagine. Do ask our agent to express my thanks to Madame Sharn for her generous gift, will you?'

Even this early in the day, the Great Hall of the University was a general thoroughfare. Most of the tables were pushed back against the walls or, if someone felt like showing off, levitated to the ceiling, and the huge

185

black-and-white slabs of the floor, worn smooth by the footfalls of millennia, were polished still further as today's faculty and students took a short cut to various concerns, destinations and, very occasionally, when no viable excuse presented itself, to lectures.

The Great Chandelier had been swung down and off to one side for its daily replenishing of candles, but there was, fortunately for Mustrum Ridcully's purposes, a large expanse of clear floor.

He saw the figure he was waiting for hurrying towards him. 'How did it go, Mister Stibbons?'

'Extremely well, I have to say, sir,' said Ponder. He opened the sack he was carrying. 'One of these is our original ball and one of them is the ball that Nutt and Trevor Likely had made last night.'

'Ah, spot the ball,' said Ridcully. He picked them both up in his enormous hands and dropped them on the flagstones.

Gloing! Gloing!

'Perfectly identical,' he said.

'Trevor Likely said they had it made by a dwarf for twenty dollars,' said Ponder.

'Did he really?'

'Yes, sir, and he gave me the change and the receipt.'

'You seem puzzled, Mister Stibbons?'

'Well, yes, sir. I feel I have been rather misjudging him.'

'Possibly even small leopards can change their shorts,' said Ridcully, slamming him on the back convivially. 'Call it score one for human nature. Now, which of these balls is the one that's going back to the Cabinet?'

'Amazingly, sir, they did think to mark the new ball and there's a tiny little dot of white paint on this one here . . . I mean this one here . . . I think it was here . . . Ah! Here it is. It's ours. I'll send one of the students to put the other one back shortly. We still have an hour and a half.'

'No, I'd rather you did it yourself, Mister Stibbons, I'm sure it would only take a few minutes. Do hurry back, I'd like to try a little experiment.'

When Ponder returned, he found Ridcully loitering unobtrusively by one of the big doors. 'You have your notebook ready, Mister Stibbons?' he said quietly.

'And a fresh pencil, Archchancellor.'

'Very well, then. The experiment begins.'

Ridcully gently rolled the new football out on to the floor, straightened up and glanced at his stopwatch.

'Ah, the ball has been kicked aside by the Professor of Illiberal Studies, quite possibly by accident . . . Now one of the bledlows, Mister Hipney I think his name is, has kicked it somewhat uncertainly. One of the students, Pondlife, I believe, has prodded it back . . . We have momentum, Mister Stibbons. Undirected, it is true, but promising. Ah, but we can't have this . . .

'No touching the ball with your hands, gentlemen!' shouted the Archchancellor, deftly trapping the travelling ball with his boot. 'That's a rule! We really could do with that whistle, Stibbons.'

He bounced the ball on the stone floor.

Gloing!

'Don't just mess about like kids kicking a tin! Play football! I am the Archchancellor of this university, by Io, and I will rusticate, or otherwise expel, any man who skives off without a note from his mother, hah!'

Gloing!

'You will arrange yourself into two teams, set up goals and strive to win! No man will leave the field of play unless injured! The hands are not to be used, is that clear? Any questions?' A hand went up. Ridcully sought the attached face.

'Ah, Rincewind,' he said, and, because he was not a determinedly unpleasant man, amended this to, 'Professor Rincewind, of course.'

'I would like permission to fetch a note from my mother, sir.'

Ridcully sighed. 'Rincewind, you once informed me, to my everlasting puzzlement, that you never knew your mother because she ran away before you were born. Distinctly remember writing it down in my diary. Would you like another try?'

'Permission to go and find my mother?'

Ridcully hesitated. The Professor of Cruel and Unusual Geography had no students and no real duties other than to stay out of trouble. Although Ridcully would never admit it, it was against all reason an emeritus position. Rincewind was a coward and an unwitting clown, but he had several times saved the world in slightly puzzling circumstances. He was a luck sink, the Archchancellor had decided, doomed to being a lightning rod for the fates so that everyone else didn't have to. Such a person was worth all his meals and laundry (including an above-average level of soiled pants) and a bucket of coal every day even if he was, in Ridcully's opinion, a bit of a whiner. However, he was fast, and therefore useful.

'Look,' said Rincewind, 'a mysterious urn turns up and suddenly it's all about football. That bodes. It means something bad is going to happen.'

'Come now, it could be something wonderful,' Ridcully protested.

Rincewind appeared to give this due consideration. 'Could be wonderful, will be dreadful. Sorry, that's how it goes.'

'This is Unseen University, Rincewind. What is there to fear?' Ridcully said. 'Apart from me, of course. Good heavens, this is a sport.' He raised his voice. 'Arrange yourselves into two teams and play football!'

He stepped back and joined Ponder. The dragooned footballers, having been given clear instructions in a loud voice, went into a huddle to find out by hubbub what they should actually do instead.

'I can't believe this,' said Ridcully. 'Every boy knows what to do when they've found something to kick, don't they?' He cupped his hands. 'Come on, two captains step up. I don't care who it is.' This took rather more time than might have been expected since those who had not surreptitiously left the Hall could see that the post of football captain was one that offered a wonderful chance for being the target of the Archchancellor's mercurial wrath. Eventually two sacrifices were pushed forward and found it too difficult to push their way back into the ranks again.

'Now, I say again, pick the teams alternately.' He took off his hat and flung it to the ground. 'Now we all understand this! It's a boy thing! It's like little girls and the colour pink! You know how to do this! Pick the teams alternately so one of you ends up with the weird kid and the other with the fat kid. Some of the fastest mathematics of all time has been achieved by team captains trying not to end up with the weird kid— Stay where you are, Rincewind!'

Ponder gave an involuntary shudder as his schooldays came running back, jeering at him. The fat kid in his class had been the unfortunately named 'Piggy' Love, whose father owned a sweet shop, which gave the son some weight in the community, not to mention clout. That had left only the weird kid as the natural target for the other boys, which meant a chronic hell for Ponder until that wonderful day when sparks came out of Ponder's fingers and Martin Sogger's pants caught fire. He could smell them now. Best days of your life be buggered; the Archchancellor could be a bit crass and difficult at times, but at least he wasn't allowed to give you a wedgie—

'Are you listening to me, Stibbons?'

Ponder blinked. 'Er, sorry, sir, I was . . . calculating.'

'I said, who's the tall feller with the tan and the dinky beard?'

'Oh, that's Professor Bengo Macarona, Archchancellor. From Genua, remember? He's swapped with Professor Maidenhair for a year.'

'Oh, right. Poor old Maidenhair. Perhaps he won't get laughed at so much in a foreign language. And Mister Macarona's here to better himself, yes? Put a bit of polish on his career, no doubt.'

'Hardly, sir. He's got doctorates from Unki, QIS and Chubb, thirteen in all, and a visiting professorship at Bugarup, and he has been cited in two hundred and thirty-six papers and, er, one divorce petition.'

'What?'

'The rule about celibacy isn't taken seriously over there, sir. Very hot-blooded people, I understand, of course. His family owns a huge ranch and the biggest coffee plantation outside Klatch, and I think his grandmother owns the Macarona Shipping Company.'

'So why the hell did he come here?'

'He wants to work with the best, sir,' said Ponder. 'I think he's serious.'

'Really? Oh, well, he seems like a sensible chap, then. Er, the divorce thing?'

'Don't know much, sir, it got hushed up, I believe.'

'Angry husband?'

'Angry wife, as I heard it,' said Ponder.

'Oh, he was married, was he?'

'Not to my knowledge, Archchancellor.'

'I don't think I quite understand,' said Ridcully.

Ponder, who was not at all at home in this area, said very slowly, 'She was the wife of another man . . . I, er, believe, sir.'

'But I—'

To Ponder's relief, light dawned on Ridcully's huge face. 'Oh, you mean he was like Professor Hayden. We used to have a name for him . . .'

Ponder braced himself.

'Snakes. Very keen on them, you know. Could talk for hours about snakes with a side order of lizards. Very keen.'

'I'm glad you feel like that, Archchancellor, because I know that a number of the students—'

'And then there was old Postule, who was in the rowing team. Coxed us through two wonderful years.' Ponder's expression did not change, but for a few moments his face went pink and shiny. 'A lot of that sort of thing about, apparently,' said Ridcully. 'People make such a fuss. Anyway, in my opinion there's not enough love in the world. Besides, if you didn't like the company of men you wouldn't come here in the first place. I say! Well done, that man!' This was because, in the absence of Ridcully's attention, the footballers had at last started their own kick-about and some quite fancy footwork was emerging. 'Yes, what?'

A bledlow had appeared alongside Ridcully.

'Gentleman to see the Archchancellor, sir. He's a wizard, sir. The, er, the Dean, as was, only he says he's an Archchancellor too.'

Ridcully hesitated, but you'd have had to be an experienced Ridcully watcher, like Ponder, to notice the moment. When the Archchancellor spoke, it was calmly and carefully, every word hammered on the anvil of self-control.

'What a pleasant surprise, Mister Nobbs. Do show the Dean in. Oh, and please do not glance at Mister Stibbons for confirmation, thank you. I am still the Archchancellor in these parts. The only one, in fact. Is there a problem, Mister Stibbons?'

'Well, sir, it is a bit public in here—' Ponder stopped, because suddenly he had nobody's attention. He hadn't seen the ball bounce towards Bledlow Nobbs (no relation). Nor the vicious kick the latter gave it, just as he would an impertinent intrusion by a street urchin's tin can. Ponder did see the ball curving majestically through the air, heading for the other end of the Hall where, behind the organ, rose the stained-glass window dedicated to Archchancellor Abasti, which on a daily basis showed one of several thousand scenes of a mystical or spiritual nature. The intuition with which Ponder had successfully calculated the distance and trajectory of the ball told him that the current glowing picture of 'Bishop Horn realizing that the alligator quiche was an unwise choice' had appeared just in time to be extremely unlucky.

And then, like some new planet swimming into the ken of a watcher of the skies, as they are prone to do, a rusty red shape arose, unfolding as it came, snatched the ball out of the air and landed on the organ keyboard to the sound of *gloing!* in B flat.

'Well done, that ape!' the Archchancellor boomed. 'A beautiful save, but, regrettably, against the rules!'

To Ponder's surprise there was a murmur of dissent from all the players. 'I believe that decision may benefit from some consideration,' said a small voice behind them.

'Who said that?' said Ridcully, spinning round and looking into the suddenly terrified little eyes of Nutt.

'Nutt, sir. The candle dribbler. We met yesterday. I helped you with the ball . . . ?'

'And you are telling me I'm wrong. Are you?'

'I would rather you thought of me as suggesting a way in which you could be even more right.'

Ridcully opened his mouth and then shut it again. I know what he is, he thought. Does he? Or did they spare him that?

'Very well, Mister Nutt. Is there a point you wish to make?'

'Yes, sir. What is the purpose of this game?'

'To win, of course!'

'Indeed. Regrettably, it is not being played that way.'

'It isn't?'

'No, sir. The players all want to kick the ball.'

'And so they should, surely?' said Ridcully.

'Only if you believe the purpose of the game is healthy exercise, sir. Do you play chess?'

'Well, I have done.'

'And would you have thought it proper for all the pawns to swarm up the board in the hope of checkmating the king?'

For a moment, Ridcully had a mental vision of Lord Vetinari holding aloft a solitary pawn and saying what it might become . . .

'Oh, come now, that is quite different!' he burst out.

'Yes, but the skill lies in marshalling resources in the right way.'

Ridcully saw a face appear behind Nutt, like a rising moon of wrath.

'You don't talk to the gentlemen, Nutt, it is not your place to take up their time with your chatter—'

Ridcully writhed in sympathy with Nutt, all the more so because Smeems, as is the habit of such people, kept looking at the Archchancellor as if seeking and, worse, expecting approval of this petty tyranny.

But authority must back up authority, in public at least, otherwise there is no authority, and therefore the senior authority is forced to back up the junior authority, even if he, the senior authority, believes that the junior authority is a tiresome little tit.

'Thank you for your concern, Mister Smeems,' he said, 'but in fact I asked Mister Nutt his opinion of our little kick-about, since it is the game of the people and he is rather more people than I am. I will not keep him long from his duties, Mister Smeems, nor you from yours, which I know are both vital and pressing.'

Small, insecure authority can spot, if it is sensible, when a larger authority is giving it a chance to save face.

'Right you are, sir!' said Smeems after only a second's hesitation, and he scurried off to safety. The thing called Nutt appeared to be trembling.

He thinks he's done something wrong, Ridcully thought, and I shouldn't think of him as a thing. Some wizard's sense made him look round into the face of – what was the lad's name? – Trevor Likely.

'Do you have anything else to add, Mister Likely? Only I'm a bit busy at the moment.'

'I gave Mister Stibbons the change and the receipt,' said Trevor.

'What is it you do around here, young man?'

'I run the candle vats, guv.'

'Oh, do you? We're getting some very good dribbling from you fellows these days.'

Trev appeared to let this pass. 'Mister Nutt is not in any trouble, is he, guv?'

'Not to my knowledge.'

But what do I know? Ridcully asked himself. Mr Nutt, by definition, is trouble. But the Librarian says he potters about repairing things and is generally an amiable milksop, and he talks as though he's giving a lecture.* This little man, who actually, when you look at him, is not as little as he appears because he weighs himself down with humility . . . this little man was born with a name so fearsome some peasants chained him to an anvil because they were too scared to kill him. Perhaps Vetinari and his friends are right in their smug way and a leopard can change his shorts. I hope so, because if they aren't, a leopard will be a picnic. And any minute now, the Dean is coming, damn his treacherous hide.

'Only he's my friend, guv.'

'Well, that's good. Everyone should have a friend.'

'I'm not gonna let anyone touch 'im, guv.'

'A brave ambition, young man, if I may say so. Nevertheless, Mister

---

* You didn't get anywhere at Unseen University without being able to understand the vast number of meanings that can be carried by the word *ook*.

Nutt, why did you object when I pointed out that the Librarian, wonderful though his rising save was, was in infringement of the rules?'

Nutt didn't look up, but in a small voice said, 'It was elegant. It was beautiful. The game should be beautiful, like a well-executed war.'

'Oh, I don't think many people would say that war is very jolly,' said Ridcully.

'Beauty can be considered to be neutral, sir. It is not the same as nice or good.'

'I thought it was the same as truth, though,' said Ponder, trying to keep up.

'Which is often horrible, sir, but Mister Librarian's leap was both beautiful, sir, and good, sir, and therefore must be true and therefore the rule which should prevent him from doing it again would be proved to be neither beautiful nor true and would, indeed, be a false law.'

'That's right, guv,' said Trev. 'People will shout for that stuff.'

'Do you mean that they'd cheer for a goal not achieved?' said Ponder.

'Of course they will! And groan! It's something happening,' Ridcully snorted. 'You saw the game the other day! If you were lucky, you got a glimpse of a lot of large, grubby men fighting over a ball like a lump of wood. People want to see goals scored!'

'And saved, remember!' Trev pointed out.

'Exactly, young man,' agreed Ridcully. 'It must be a game of speed. This is the year of the Pensive Hare, after all. People get bored so easily. No wonder there are fights. We need, do we not, to make a sport that is more exciting than beating other people over the head with big weapons.'

'That one's always been very popular,' said Ponder doubtfully.

'Well, we are wizards, after all. And now I must go and greet the bloody, the so-called Archchancellor of Brazeneck so-called College in the correct damn spirit of fraternal goodwill!'

'So called,' murmured Ponder, not quite softly enough.

'What say?' the Archchancellor bellowed.

'Just wondering what you want me to do, Archchancellor?'

'Do? Keep 'em playing! See who's good at it! Work out what the most beautiful rules are,' Ridcully called out, heading out of the Hall at speed.

'By myself?' said Ponder, horrified. 'I've got a huge workload!'

'Delegate!'

'You know I'm hopeless at delegating, sir!'

'Then delegate the job of delegating to someone who isn't! Now, I must be off before he steals the silverware!'

It was very rare for Glenda to take time off. Being the head of the Night Kitchen was a mental state, not a physical one. The only meal she ever ate at home was breakfast, and that was always in a hurry. But now she'd stolen some time to sell the dream. May Hedges was looking after the kitchen and she was reliable and got on with everyone and so there were no worries there.

The sun had come out and now she knocked on the rear door of Mr Stronginthearm's workshop. The dwarf opened the door with rouge all over his fingers. 'Oh, hello, Glenda. How's it going?'

She thumped a wad of orders on the table proudly and opened the suitcase. It was empty. 'And I need a lot more samples,' she said.

'Oh, that's wonderful,' said the dwarf. 'When did you get these?'

'This morning.'

It had been *easy*. Door after door seemed to have opened for her and every time a little voice in her head said, 'Are you doing the right thing?' a slightly deeper voice, which sounded remarkably like Madame Sharn, said, 'He wants to make it. You want to sell it. They want to buy it. The dream goes round and round and so does the money.'

'The lipstick went down very well,' she said. 'Those troll girls put it on with a trowel and I'm not kidding. So what you ought to do, sir, is sell a trowel. A pretty one, in a nice box with sprinkles on it.'

He gave her an admiring look. 'This isn't like you, Glenda.'

'Not sure about that,' said Glenda, as more samples were dropped into the battered case. 'Have you thought about getting into shoes?'

'Do you think it would be worth a try? They don't normally wear shoes.'

'They didn't wear lipstick until they moved here,' said Glenda. 'It could be the coming thing.'

'But they've got feet like granite. They don't *need* shoes.'

'But they'll *want* them,' said Glenda. 'You could be in on the ground floor, as it were.'

Stronginthearm looked puzzled and Glenda remembered that even city dwarfs were used to the topsy-turvy language of home. 'Oh, sorry, I meant to say the top floor.'

'And then there's dresses,' said Glenda. 'I've been looking around and no one makes proper dresses for trolls. They're just outsized human dresses. And they're cut to make the troll look smaller, but they'd be better if they were cut to make them look bigger. More like a troll and less like a fat human. You know, you want the clothing to shout, "I'm a great big troll lady and proud of it".'

'Have you been hit on the head with something?' said Stronginthearm. 'Because, if so, I'd like it to drop on me.'

'Well, it's spreading the dream, isn't it?' said Glenda, carefully arranging the samples in her suitcase. 'It's a bit more important than I thought.'

She made fourteen more successful calls before calling it a day, posted the orders through Stronginthearm's letterbox and, with a light case and uncharacteristically light heart, went back to work.

Ridcully turned the corner and there, right in front of him, was . . . His mind spun as it sought for the correct mode of address: 'Archchancellor' was out of the question, 'Dean' too obvious an insult, 'Two Chairs' ditto with knobs on, and 'ungrateful, backstabbing, slimy bastard' took too long to say. What the hell was the bastard's name? Great heavens, they'd been friends since their first day at UU . . . 'Henry!' he exploded. 'What a pleasant surprise. What brings you here to our miserable and sadly out-of-date little university?'

'Oh, come now, Mustrum. When I left, the lads were pushing back the boundaries of knowledge. It's been a bit quiet since, I gather. By the way, this is Professor Turnipseed.'

There appeared from behind the self-styled Archchancellor of Brazeneck, like a moonlet moving out of the shadow of a gas giant, a sheepish young man who instantly reminded Ridcully of Ponder Stibbons, although for the life of him he couldn't make out why. Perhaps it was the look of someone permanently doing sums in his head, and not just proper sums either, but the sneaky sort with letters in them.

'Oh, well, you know how it is with boundaries,' Ridcully mumbled. 'You look at what's on the other side and you realize why there was a boundary in the first place. Good afternoon, Turnipseed. Your face is familiar.'

'I used to work here, sir,' said Turnipseed sheepishly.

'Oh yes, I recall. In the High Energy Magic Department, yes?'

'A coming man, our Adrian,' said the former Dean, proprietorially. 'We have our own High Energy Magic Building now, you know. We call it the Higher Energy Magic Building, but I stress that this is only to avoid confusion. No slight on good old UU is intended. Adopt, adapt, improve, that's my motto.'

Well, if you adapted it then it's now grab, copy and look innocent, Ridcully thought, but carefully. Senior wizards never rowed in public. The damage was apt to be appalling. No, politeness ruled, but with sharpened edges.

'I doubt there will be any confusion, Henry. We are the senior college, after all. And of course I am the *only* Archchancellor in these parts.'

'By custom and practice, Mustrum, and times are changing.'

'Or being changed, at least. But I wear the Archchancellor's Hat, Henry, as worn by my predecessors down the centuries. The Hat, Henry, of supreme authority in the affairs of the Wise, the Cunning and the Crafty. The hat, in fact, on my head.'

'It isn't, you know,' said Henry cheerfully. 'You are wearing the everyday hat that you made yourself.'

'*It would be on my head if I wanted it to be!*'

Henry's smile was glassy. 'Of course, Mustrum, but the authority of the Hat has often been challenged.'

'Almost correct, old chap. In fact, it is the ownership of the Hat that has, in the past, been disputed, but the Hat itself, never. Now, I note that you yourself are wearing a particularly spiffy hat of a magnificence that goes beyond the sublime, but it is just a hat, old boy, just a hat. No offence meant, of course, and I am sure that in another millennium it will have become weighted with dignity and wisdom. I can see that you have left plenty of room.'

Turnipseed decided to make a run for the lavatories right now, and with a muted apology pushed past Ridcully and sped away.

Oddly enough, the sudden lack of an audience lowered the tension rather than increased it.

Henry pulled a slim packet out of his pocket. 'Cigarette? I know that you roll your own, but Verdant and Scour make these specially for me and they are rather fine.'

Ridcully took one, because a wizard, however haughty, who would not accept a free smoke or a drink would be in his coffin, but he took care not to notice the words 'Archchancellor's Choice' in garish type on the packet.

As he handed the packet back, something small and colourful dropped out on to the floor. Henry, with an agility unexpected in a wizard so far up the main sequence as described in the well-known Owlspring/Tips Diagram,* reached down quickly and snatched it up, muttering something about 'not letting it get dirty'.

'You could eat your dinner off these floors,' said Ridcully sharply, and probably would, he added to himself.

'Only the collectors get so annoyed if there is a speck of dust on them and I give mine to the butler's little boy,' Henry went on blithely. He turned the pasteboard over and frowned. 'Notable Wizards of our

---

* This diagram was devised to chart the tendency of wizards, who start out small and pale, to progress through the craft getting bigger and cholerically redder until at last they swell up and explode in a cloud of pomposity.

Time, No. 9 of 50: Dr Able Baker, BC (Hons), Fdl, Kp, PdF (escrow), Director of Blit Studies, Brazeneck. I'm sure he's already got this one.' He dropped it into a waistcoat pocket. 'Never mind, good for swapsies.'

Ridcully could assess things quite fast, especially when fuelled by banked fires of rage.

'The Wizla tobacco, snuff and rolling paper company,' he said, 'of Pseudopolis. Hmm, clever idea. Who's in this from UU?'

'Ah. Well, I have to admit that the Assembly and people of Pseudopolis are rather . . . patriotic in their outlook—'

'I think the word is "parochial", don't you?'

'Harsh words, considering that Ankh-Morpork's the smuggest, most self-satisfied city in the world.' This was self-evidently true, so Ridcully decided he hadn't heard it.

'You on one of these cards, then?' he grunted.

'They insisted, I'm afraid,' said Henry. 'I was born there, you see. Local boy and all that.'

'And no one from UU,' said Ridcully flatly.

'Technically no, but Professor Turnipseed is in there as the inventor of Pex.' As Henry said it, guilt and defiance fought for space in the sentence.

'Pex?' said Ridcully slowly. 'You mean like Hex?'

'Oh, no, not at all like Hex. Certainly not. The principle is quite different.' Henry cleared his throat. 'It's run by chickens. They trigger the morphic resonator, or whatever it's called. Your Hex, as I recall, utilizes ants, which are far less efficient.'

'How so?'

'We get eggs we can eat.'

'That doesn't sound all that different, you know.'

'Oh, come now. They are hundreds of times bigger! And Pex is in a purpose-built room, not strung haphazardly all over the place. Professor Turnipseed knows what he is doing, and even you, Mustrum, must acknowledge that the river of progress is fed by a thousand springs!'

'And they didn't all rise in bloody Brazeneck!' said Ridcully.

They glared at one another. Professor Turnipseed poked his head around the corner and pulled it back very quickly.

'If we were the men our fathers were, we'd be throwing fireballs by now,' said Henry.

'The point is taken,' said Ridcully. 'Although, I must point out, our fathers were not wizards.'

'That's right, of course,' said the former Dean. 'Your father was a butcher, as I recall.'

'That's right. And your father owned a lot of cabbage fields,' said Ridcully.

There was a moment's silence and then the former Dean said, 'Remember the day we both turned up at UU?'

'We fought like tigers as I recall,' said Ridcully.

'Good times, when you come to remember them,' said the Dean.

'Of course, we've all passed a lot of water over the bridge since then,' said Ridcully. There was another pause and he added, 'Fancy a drink?'

'I don't mind if I do,' said the former Dean.

'So you are trying to play football?' said Henry as they progressed majestically towards the Archchancellor's office. 'I did see something about it in the paper, but I thought it was a joke.'

'Why, pray?' said Ridcully as they began to walk across the Great Hall. 'We have a fine sporting tradition, as well you know!'

'Ah yes, tradition is the scourge of endeavour. Be sensible, Mustrum. The leopard may change his shorts, but I think he'd have a job getting into the ones he wore forty years ago. Oh, I see that you still have Mister Stibbons here?'

'Er . . .' began Ponder, looking from one to the other.

Ponder Stibbons had once got one hundred per cent in a prescience exam by getting there the previous day. He could see a little storm cloud when it was beginning to grow.

'How's the football going, lad?'

'Oh, it seems to be going very well, Archchancellor. Good to see you again, Dean.'

'Archchancellor,' purred the former Dean. 'I wonder how good you would be against *my* university.'

'Well, we have a pretty nifty team built here,' said Ridcully, 'and, while it is our intention to play our first game against a local side, I would take great pleasure in showing Brazeneck a thing or two on the field.' By now they were almost in the middle of the Great Hall and their presence, not unexpectedly, had stopped play.

'Archchancellor, I really feel that it might be a good idea to—' Ponder began, but his voice was drowned out by the roar of approval that rang out from all sides around the Great Hall.

'And the prize would be?' said Henry, smiling at the crowd.

'What?' spluttered the Archchancellor. 'What prize?'

'We picked up a few rowing trophies when we were lads, didn't we?'

'I believe the Patrician has got something planned for the league, yes.'

'I think that refreshments will be laid out in the Blue refectory shortly,' said Ponder with a kind of desperate, sweaty cheerfulness. 'There will, of course, be cake, but also, I believe, an interesting assortment of curries.'

On many occasions this might have worked, but the two senior wizards had locked glares and would not so much as blink, even for a slice of Ploughman's Pie.

'But we men of craft are not interested in such paltry baubles as cups and medals, are we?' said Henry. 'For us it's huge great big baubles or nothing, is that not right, Mustrum?'

'You are after the Hat,' said Ridcully flatly. The air between them was humming.

'Yes, of course.'

There followed the menacing silence of a clash of wills, but Ponder Stibbons decided that as he was, technically, twelve important people at the university, he formed, all by himself, a committee, and since he was therefore, de facto, very wise, he should intervene.

'And *your* stake, Dea— Sir, would be . . .?'

Ridcully turned his head slightly and growled, 'He doesn't have to have one. I have rather walked into this . . .'

There was a stirring from the more senior wizards, and Ponder heard a whispered phrase. 'Dead man's pointy shoes?'

'No, I forbid it!' said Ponder.

'You forbid it?' said Henry. 'You are but a chick, young Stibbons.'

'The accumulated votes of all the posts I hold on the University Council mean that I do, technically, control it,' said Ponder, trying to stick out a skinny chest that was never built for sticking, but still buoyed up and awash with righteous rage and a certain amount of terror about what might happen when it ran out of steam.

The contenders relaxed a little more in the presence of this turning worm.

'Didn't anyone notice that you were getting all this power?' said Ridcully.

'Yes, sir, me. Only I thought it was responsibility and hard work. None of you ever bother with details, you see. Technically, I have to report to other people, but usually the other people are *me*. You have no idea, sirs. I'm even the Camerlengo, which means that if you drop dead, Archchancellor, from any cause other than legitimate succession under the Dead Man's Pointy Shoes tradition, I run this place until a successor is elected which, given the nature of wizardry, will mean a job for life, in which case the Librarian, as an identifiable and competent member of the senior staff, will try to discharge his duties, and if he fails, the official procedure is for wizards everywhere to fight among themselves for the Hat, causing fire, destruction, doves, rabbits and billiard balls to appear from every orifice and much loss of life.' After a short pause he continued. 'Again. Which is why some of us get a little worried when we see powerful wizards squabbling like this. To conclude, gentlemen, I have spoken at some length in order to give you time to consider your intentions. *Somebody* has to.'

Ridcully cleared his throat. 'Thank you for your input, Stibbons. We shall discuss this matter further. Definitely something that needed to be said. These aren't the old days, after all.'

'Your point is taken,' said Henry, 'except that, technically, these are going to be somebody else's old days.'

Ponder's chest was still going up and down.

'A very good point,' said Ridcully.

'I believe I heard mention of a curry?' said Henry, with equal care. It was like listening to two ancient dragons talking to each other with the help of an even older book of etiquette written by nuns.

'It's a long time until lunch.* I tell you what, why don't you accept the hospitality of my university? I believe we have left your room *exactly* as it was, although I understand some quite amazing things have crawled out under the door. And perhaps you might like to stay on for tomorrow's banquet?'

'Oh? Are you having a banquet?' said Henry.

'Indeed so, and I would be delighted if you would accept, old boy. We'll be entertaining some of the solid citizenry. Salt-of-the-earth fellows, you understand. Wonderful people if you don't watch them eat, but quite good conversationalists if you give them enough beer.'

'Funnily enough, I find that works with wizards too. Well, I must accept, of course. I haven't been to a banquet in ages.'

'You haven't?' said Ridcully. 'I thought *you* would have a banquet every night.'

'We have a limited budget, you know,' said the Archchancellor of Brazeneck. 'It's a governmental grant thing, you see.'

The wizards fell silent. It was as if a man had just told you his mother had died.

Ridcully patted him on the hand. 'Oh, I'm so sorry.' He paused at the doors of the Hall and turned back to Ponder. 'We will be having some high-level discussions, Stibbons. Keep them on their toes! The lads will help! Find out what football wants to be!'

The older members of the faculty exhaled as the two heads left. Most of them were old enough to recall at least two pitched battles among factions of wizards, the worst of which had only been brought to a conclusion by Rincewind, wielding a half-brick in a sock . . .

---

* This may not be true. Wizards tend to think it's a long time to the next meal, right up until they are consuming it.

Ponder looked across at Rincewind now, and he was hopping awkwardly on one leg, trying to put a sock back on. He thought it better not to comment. It was probably the same sock.

The Chair of Indefinite Studies slapped Ponder on the back. 'Well done, lad. Could have been a nasty incident there.'

'Thank you, sir.'

'I'm sorry we seem to have loaded you down a bit. I'm sure it wasn't deliberate.'

'I'm sure it wasn't, too, sir. Very little around here is.' Ponder sighed. 'I'm afraid that unthinking delegation and prevarication and procrastination are standard practice here.' He looked expectantly at the remaining members of the Council. He wanted to be disappointed, but knew he wouldn't be.

'A very bad state of affairs indeed,' said the Lecturer in Recent Runes.

The Chair looked grave. 'Hm . . .'

So go on, thought Ponder, say it. I know you're going to, you just won't be able to stop yourself, you really won't—

'I think, Stibbons, that you should sort it out when you have a moment,' said the Chair.

'Bingo!'

'I beg your pardon, Stibbons?'

'Oh, nothing, sir, not really. I was just pondering, as it were, on the unchangeable nature of the universe.'

'I'm glad somebody is. Keep it up.' The Lecturer in Recent Runes looked around and added, 'It all seems to have quietened down. That curry sounds amusing.'

There was a general movement towards the doors on the part of those wizards who were well endowed with years, gravitation or both, but the scratch match went on among those less magnetically attracted to knives and forks.

Ponder sat down, his clipboard balanced on his lap. 'I don't have the faintest idea what I'm doing here,' he declared to the world around him.

'May I be of some worth, sir?'

'Mister Nutt? Oh, well, it's very kind of you, but I don't think that your skill with a candle can be of much—'

'In games of this nature there are three classes of things to be considered: one, the rules of the game in all their detail; two the correct skills, actions and philosophies required for success, and three, an understanding of the real nature of the game. May I continue?'

'Huh,' said Ponder, in that slight daze that overcame everyone hearing a Nutt lecture for the first time.

'Got a fine jaw on him, ain't he?' said Trev. 'He can say the long words where the likes of you an' me would 'ave to stop for a rest 'alfway through! Me, anyway,' he trailed off.

'Er, do continue, Mister Nutt.'

'Thank you, sir. As I understand it, the purpose of this game is to score at least one more goal than your opponents. But our two teams just ran around, with everyone trying to kick the ball at once. Oh, goals were scored, but only opportunistically. As in chess, you must secure the king, your goal. Yes, you are going to say that you have the custodian of the goal, but he is only one man, figuratively speaking. Every ball he saves shames the team members who let the opponents get so close. Yet at the same time, they must maximize their chances of getting the ball into the opposing goal. This is a problem I will have to address. I have mentioned chess, but this game, and particularly the ease with which the ball takes flight, means that the activity can go from one end of the play to the other in seconds, just as one dwarf piece can upset the whole board in a game of Thud.'

He smiled up at their expressions and added, 'You know, this game is surely one of the simplest. Any little boy knows how to play it . . . and yet playing it optimally requires superhuman talents.' He thought for a moment and added, 'Or possibly subhuman. Certainly the willing sublimation of the ego, which takes us into the realms of the metaphysical. So simple and yet so complex. You know, this is wonderful. I am quite thrilled!'

The ring of silence around him was not ominous, but the air choked with bafflement. Finally, the wizard Rincewind said, 'Er, Mister Nutt,

I thought you told us we just had to get the ball between the pointy hats?'

'Professor Rincewind, you run very well, but you don't do anything with it. Professor Macarona, you attempt to score as soon as you get the ball irrespective of anything else that is happening. Dr Hix, you cheat and foul constantly—'

'Excuse me, skull ring,' Hix intervened. 'I am required to attempt to break the rules, under college statutes.'

'Within acceptable limits,' Ponder added quickly.

'Bledlow Nobbs (no relation), you have a furiously powerful kick,' Nutt continued, 'but you don't seem to care where the ball goes so long as it gets there. All of you have strengths and weaknesses and it might be possible to make use of both of them. That is, if you want to win. But for now, a good exercise would be to get a lot more of these balls and learn how to control them. Running while kicking the ball ahead of you simply means that you will lose it to an opponent. You must learn to keep it at your feet. You were all looking down to check that you had the ball. Gentlemen, if you need to check that you still have the ball, you either do not have it or you will lose it in the next fraction of a second. Now, if you will excuse me, Mister Trev and I will get into trouble if we don't get the chandelier back up soon.'

The spell broke.

'What?' said Ponder. 'I mean, what? Stay there, Mister Nutt!'

Nutt immediately hunched and stared at his feet in their clumsy shoes. 'I am sorry if I have transgressed in any way. I was only seeking worth.'

'Worth?' said Ponder, looking at Trev for some kind of map of this new territory.

'That's how he talks, that's all,' said Trev. 'He 'asn't done anythin' wrong, so why shout at him like that? They were some bloody good ideas! You shouldn't pick on 'im just 'cos he's small and talks posh.'

Nutt seemed noticeably taller a little while ago, Ponder thought. Is he really just hunched up? 'I wasn't exactly shouting at him,' he said. 'I just wondered what he's doing dribbling candles! I mean, I know that's what he's doing, but why?'

'Ah, you have to have dribbled candles, sir,' said Bledlow Nobbs (no relation), 'and to my mind, the dribbling has been particularly fine just lately. Often, when I'm walking the corridors of a night, I think to myself—'

'Good heavens, man, he's erudite! He radiates learning! He's a polymath!' said Ponder.

'Are you saying he's too smart to be a candle dribbler?' said the bledlow, a militant look in his eye. 'You wouldn't want a stupid dribbler, would you? You'd get, like, manky dribbles all over the place.'

'I simply meant that—'

'. . . and blobs,' said the bledlow firmly.

'But you must admit that it is strange that—'

Probably everyone wants him dead.

Ponder stopped as the chasm of memory opened. 'That makes no sense. It can't be true!'

'Sir?'

He realized that all the footballers were staring at him. Ridcully had refused to say any more, and in Ponder's crowded mind he'd settled for believing that Nutt was on the run in some way. It was not unknown. Occasionally a novice wizard working in a small town might find it a good idea to hurry back for a swift refresher course in the safety of the university's hospitable stones until his little mistake had been rectified/forgotten/erased/caught and bottled. There had always been others given sanctuary for mysterious reasons. The politics of wizardry were either very simple, and resolved by someone ceasing to breathe, or as complex as one ball of yarn in a room with three bright-eyed little kittens.

But Nutt . . . What crime could he have done? And then you had to factor in that it was Ridcully who had allowed him to come here and indeed had put Ponder in this position. The sensible thing, therefore, was to – just get on with it.

'I think Mister Nutt has some very good ideas,' he said carefully, 'and I think he should continue. Do carry on, Mister Nutt.'

Watching Nutt look up was like watching the sun rise, but a hesitant sun afraid that any moment the gods might slap it back down into the night, and hungry for reassurance that this would not be so.

'I am worthy?'

'Well, er . . .' Ponder began, and saw Trev nodding frantically.

'Well, er, yes, it would seem so, Mister Nutt. I'm amazed at your insight in so short a time.'

'I have a talent for pattern recognition in developing situations.'

'Really? Oh. Good. Carry on, then.'

'Excuse me, I have a question, if you would be so good?'

Looks like a bag of second-hand clothes, talks like a retired theologian, Ponder thought. 'Ask away, Mister Nutt.'

'Can I carry on with the dribbling?'

'What? Do you want to?'

'Yes, thank you. I enjoy it and it does not take me long.'

Ponder glanced at Trev, who shrugged, made a face and nodded.

'But I have a favour to ask,' Nutt went on.

'I rather expected you would,' said Ponder, 'but I'm sorry to say that the budget this term means—'

'Oh no, I don't want any money,' said Nutt. 'I don't really spend it anyway. I just want Mister Trev in the team. He is very modest, but you should know that he is a genius with his feet. I cannot see how you could lose with him in the team.'

'Oh no,' said Trev, waving his hands and backing away. 'No! Not me! I'm not a footballer! I just kick tin cans around!'

'Thought that was at the heart and soul of foot-the-ball, isn't it?' said Ponder, who'd never been allowed to play in the street.

'I thought it was when early blokes kicked a dead enemy's head around,' Bledlow Nobbs (no relation) volunteered.

A throat was cleared. 'Unlikely in my opinion,' said Hix. 'Unless it's in a bag or some sort of metal brace, and then you have the problem of weight, because a human head comes in at around ten pounds, which is a pain in the foot, I should think. Scooping it out would work for a while, of course, but mind you wire the jaw, because no one wants to be bitten in the foot. I do have some heads on ice if anyone wants to experiment. It's amazing, but there are still those who leave their bodies to necromancy. There's some strange people out there.'

At this point, the head of the Department of Post-Mortem Communications realized that he was not taking his audience with him.

'There's no need to look at me like that,' he grumbled. 'Skull ring, remember? I have to know this wretched stuff.'

Ponder coughed politely. 'Mister, er, Likely, isn't it? Your colleague speaks very highly of you. Won't you join us?'

'Sorry, guv, but I promised my old mum that I'd never play football. It's a good way of gettin' your head caved in!'

'Trev Likely?' roared Bledlow Nobbs (no relation). 'Are you Dave Likely's lad? He—'

'Scored four goals, yeah, yeah, yeah,' said Trev. 'And then died in the street with the rain washing his blood down the gutter and someone's smelly overcoat over him. The Prince of Football?'

'Do we need a little talk, Mister Trev?' Nutt said urgently.

'No. No. I'm okay. Okay?'

'This isn't that kind of football, Trev,' said Nutt soothingly.

'Yeah, I know. But I promised my old mum.'

'Then at least show them your moves, Mister Trev,' Nutt pleaded. He turned to the players. 'You must see this!'

Trev sighed, but Nutt knew just how to wheedle. 'All right, if it shuts you up,' he said, and pulled a tin can out of his pocket, to much laughter.

'See?' he complained to Nutt. 'They just think it's a joke.'

Nutt folded his arms. 'Show them.'

Trev dropped the can on to his foot and with hardly any effort flicked it on to his shoulder, where it rolled around his neck to his other shoulder and, after a tiny pause, righted itself. He shrugged it on to his other foot, spun it into the air, and let it tumble and spin on the toe of his boot with a faint rattling noise.

Trev winked at Ponder Stibbons. 'Don't move, guv.'

The can sprang off the boot and up into the air, then, as it fell, he hit it with a roundhouse kick, driving it at Ponder. The people behind Ponder dived out of the way as it growled past his face and went into orbit, appearing for a moment to give him a silver necklace until it broke away and dropped into Trev's hand like a beached salmon.

In the silence, Ponder pulled his thaumometer out of his pocket and glanced at it.

'Natural background,' he said flatly. 'No magic involved. How did you do that, Mister Likely?'

'You just 'ave to get the hang of it, guv. Getting the spins is the thing, but if I 'ave to think too much it don't work.'

'Can you do it with a ball?'

'Dunno, never tried. But prob'ly no. Can't get the long spin and the short spin, see? But you ort to be able to get somethin' out of a ball.'

'But how would that help us?' said Hix.

'Mastery of the ball is everything,' said Nutt. 'The planned rule will, I think, allow the keeper of the goal to handle the ball. This is vital. There is, however, no explicit ban on nodding the ball, kneeing the ball or blocking the ball with the chest and letting it drop neatly on to the foot. Remember, gentlemen, this ball flies. It will spend a lot of time in the air. You must learn not to think just about the ground.'

'I feel sure that using the head would be considered illegal,' said Ponder.

'Sir, you presume a rule where there is none. Remember what I said about the real nature of the game.'

Ponder saw Nutt's little half-smile, and gave in. 'Mister Nutt, I am delegating the selection and training of our football team to you. You will report to me, of course.'

'Yes, sir. Thank you, sir. I will need the power to sequester team members from their normal duties when required.'

'Well, I suppose I must agree to that. Very well, I shall leave the team in your hands,' said Ponder, thinking: how many bags of old clothes use the word 'sequester' as if they're used to it? Still, Ridcully likes the little goblin, if that's what he is, and I've never seen the point of team games.

'May I also, sir, request a very small budget?'

'Why?'

'With all due respect to the exigencies of university finances,' said Nutt, 'I believe it is very necessary.'

'Why?'

'I wish to take the team to the ballet.'

'That's ridiculous!' Ponder snapped.

'No, sir, it's essential.'

The next day there was a piece in the *Times* about the mysterious disappearance of the fabulous 'Jewels', which made Glenda smile. They just haven't read their fairy stories, she thought as she left the house. If you want to find a beauty, you look for her in the ashes. Because Glenda was Glenda and would always irredeemably be Glenda to the core, she added: although the ovens in the Night Kitchen are scrupulously maintained at all times and all ashes are immediately disposed of.

To her surprise, Juliet stepped out of her doorway at almost the same time and looked as if she was almost awake. 'Do you think they'll let me in on the banquet?' she said as they waited for the bus.

Theoretically yes, Glenda thought, but probably no, because she was a Night Kitchen girl. Even though she was Juliet, she would be tarred by Mrs Whitlow as a Night Kitchen girl. 'Juliet, you shall go to the banquet,' she said aloud, 'and so shall I.'

'But I think Mrs Whitlow won't like that,' said Juliet.

Something was still bubbling inside Glenda. It had started in Shatta and lasted all day yesterday and there was still some left today. 'I don't care,' she said.

Juliet giggled and looked around in case Mrs Whitlow was hiding near the bus stop.

And I really don't care, Glenda thought. I don't care. It was like drawing a sword.

*

Ponder's office always puzzled Mustrum Ridcully. The man used filing cabinets for heavens' sake. Ridcully worked on the basis that anything you couldn't remember wasn't important and had developed the floor-heap method of document storage to a fine art.

Ponder looked up. 'Ah, good morning, Archchancellor.'

'Just had a look in at the Hall,' said Ridcully.

'Yes, Archchancellor?'

'Our lads were all doing ballet.'

'Yes, Archchancellor.'

'And there were some girls from the Opera House with those short dresses.'

'Yes, Archchancellor. They're helping the team.'

Ridcully leaned over and put huge knuckles either side of the paper Ponder was working on. '*Why?*'

'Mister Nutt's idea, Archchancellor. Apparently they must learn balance, poise and elegance.'

'Have you ever seen Bledlow Nobbs try to stand on one leg? Let me tell you, it's an immediate cure for melancholy.'

'I can imagine,' said Ponder, not looking up.

'I thought the idea was to learn how to kick the ball into the goal.'

'Ah, yes, but Mister Nutt has a philosophy.'

'Does he?'

'Yes, sir.'

'They're runnin' about all over the place, I know that,' said Ridcully.

'Yes, Mister Nutt and Mister Likely are preparing a little something extra for the banquet,' said Ponder, getting up and opening the top drawer of a filing cabinet. The sight of filing cabinets opening tended to remind Ridcully that he should be elsewhere, but on this occasion the ruse failed to work.

'Oh, and I believe we have some fresh balls.'

'Mister Snorrisson knows an opportunity when he sees one.'

'So it's all going well, then?' said Ridcully, in a kind of mystified voice.

'Apparently so, sir.'

'Well, I suppose I'd better leave it alone,' said Ridcully. He hesitated, feeling at a bit of a loose end, and found another thread to pull. 'And how are those rules coming along, Mister Stibbons?'

'Oh, quite well, thank you, Archchancellor. I'm keeping in some of the ones from the street game, of course, to keep everybody happy. Some of them are quite strange.'

'Mister Nutt is quite a decent chap, it appears.'

'Oh yes, Archchancellor.'

'Very good idea of his to redesign the goal, I thought. Makes it more fun.'

'Aren't you going to train, sir?' said Ponder, pulling another document towards him.

'I am the captain! I do not need to train.' Ridcully turned to leave and stopped with his hand on the doorknob. 'Had a long chat with the former Dean last night. Decent soul at heart, of course,' he said.

'Yes, I understand the atmosphere in the Uncommon Room was very convivial, Archchancellor,' said Ponder. And expensive, he added to himself.

'You know young Adrian Turnipseed is a professor?'

'Oh, yes, Archchancellor.'

'You wanna be one?'

'Not really, Archchancellor. I think there should be one or two posts in this institution that I don't hold.'

'Yes, but they've just called their machine Pex! Hardly a great leap of ingenuity, is it?'

'Oh, there are some significant differences. I believe he's using chickens to generate the blit diametric,' said Ponder.

'Apparently so,' said Ridcully. 'Something like that, anyway.'

'Hmmm,' said Ponder. And it was quite a solid hmmm, possibly one you could moor a small boat to.

'Something wrong?' said Ridcully.

'Oh, er, not really, Archchancellor. Did the former Dean mention anything about the need to totally rebuild the morphic resonator to allow for the necessary changes in the blit/slood interface?'

'Shouldn't think so,' said Ridcully.

'Oh,' said Ponder, his face blank. 'Well, Adrian is bound to get round to that. He *is* very clever.'

'Yes, but it was all based on *your* work. *You* built Hex. And now they're putting out that he's some big clever clogs. He's even on a cigarette card.'

'That's nice, sir. It's good when researchers get recognition.'

Ridcully felt like a mosquito that was trying to sting a steel breast-plate. 'Hah, wizardry has certainly changed since my day,' he said.

'Yes, sir,' said Ponder noncommittally.

'And by the way, Mister Stibbons,' said Ridcully as he opened the door, 'my day isn't over yet.'

There was a yell in the distance. And then a crash. Ridcully smiled. The day had suddenly brightened up.

When he and Ponder reached the Great Hall, most of the team were gathered around one of their members lying on the floor, with Nutt kneeling over him.

'What's happened here?' Ridcully demanded.

'Badly bruised, sir. I shall put a compress on it.'

'Ah.' His gaze fell upon a large, brass-bound chest. It looked at first sight like any other chest, until you saw the tiny little toes poking out.

'Rincewind's luggage,' he growled. 'And where that is, Rincewind can't be far in front. Rincewind!'

'Actually, it wasn't my fault,' said Rincewind.

'He's right, sir,' said Nutt. 'I have to apologize for the fact that this was a group misapprehension. I understand it is a remarkably magical chest on hundreds of little legs and I am afraid that the gentlemen here believed that it would play football like stink, as they put it. In which surmise, I have to say, they were proved wrong.'

'I tried to tell them,' said the former Dean from the edge of the crowd. 'Morning, Mustrum. Good team you have here.'

'All its feet do is get in each other's way,' said Bengo Macarona. 'And if it does get on top of the ball, it spins out of control and, alas, it crashed into Mister Sopworthy here.'

'Oh, well, we learn by our mistakes,' said Ridcully. 'And now, do you happen to have something *nice* to show me?'

'I think I have the very thing, Archchancellor,' said a cheerful but reedy voice behind him.

Ridcully turned and looked into the face of a man with the shape and urgency of a piccolo. He seemed to be vibrating on the spot.

'Professor Ritornello, Master of the Music,' Ponder whispered into Ridcully's ear.

'Ah, Professor,' said Ridcully smoothly, 'and I see you have the choir with you.'

'Yes indeed, Archchancellor, and I must tell you, I am thrilled and filled with inner light by what I have witnessed this morning! Without ado, I have penned a chant, such as you asked for!'

'Did I?' said Ridcully, out of the corner of his mouth.

'You will remember that chanting was mentioned and so I thought it best to alert the professor,' whispered Ponder.

'Another pp, eh? Oh, well.'

'Happily, it is based on the traditional plainchant or stolation form and is a valedicta, or hail to the winner. May I?' said Professor Ritornello. 'It is a cappella, of course.'

'Go ahead, by all means,' said Ridcully.

The Master of the Music pulled a short baton out of his sleeve. 'I've put the name of Bengo Macarona in there for a marker at the moment, because he has apparently scored two fine "goals", as I believe they are called,' he said, dealing carefully with the word as one might deal with a large spider in the bathtub. Then he caught the eyes of his little flock, nodded, and:

Hail the unique qualities of Magister Bengo Macarona! Of Macarona the unique qualities Hail! Hail the! Hail the! The singular talent possessed by no other! Hail! Hail the! Hail the bountiful gods! Who to the, two the— SINGULA SINGULAR SINGULA!

After a minute and a half of this Ridcully coughed loudly, and the Master waved the choir into a stuttering silence.

'Is there something untoward, Archchancellor?'

'Er, not as such, Master, but, er, do you not feel that it is a bit too, well, long?' Ridcully was aware that the former Dean was not trying very hard to suppress a snigger.

'Not at all. In fact, sir, I intend that when it is finished it will be scored for forty voices and, though I dare to say so, will be my masterwork!'

'But it is something for *football fans* to sing, you see?' said Ridcully.

'Well then,' said the Master, holding his baton in a rather threatening manner, 'is it not the duty of the educated classes to raise the standards of the lower orders?'

'He's got a point there, Mustrum,' said the Chair of Indefinite Studies, and Ridcully felt his grandfather kick him in the heredity, and was glad that maid wasn't here – what was her name now? Oh, yes, Glenda, smart woman – but although she was not there he saw something of her expression in Trev Likely's face.

'During the week, possibly,' he snapped, 'but not on Saturdays, I think. But very well done, anyway, and I look forward to hearing more of your efforts.'

The Master of the Music flounced out with the choir flouncing out in perfect unison behind him.

Ridcully rubbed his hands together. 'Well, gentlemen, perhaps you could show me your moves.'

While the players spread out in the Hall, Nutt said, 'I must say that Professor Macarona is excelling at the game. He clearly has excellent ball skills.'

'I'm not surprised,' said Ridcully brightly.

'The Librarian is, of course, an excellent keeper of the goal. Especially since he can stand in the middle and reach either side of it. I believe that it will be very hard for any of our opponents to get past him. And, of course, you will be partaking also, Archchancellor.'

'Oh, you don't become Archchancellor if you don't get the hang of things quickly. I will just watch for now.'

He watched. After the second occasion when Macarona, like a silver streak, ran the length of the Hall to flick the ball into the opponents' goal, Ridcully turned to Ponder and said, 'We're going to win, aren't we?'

'If indeed he is still playing for you,' put in the former Dean.

'Oh, come now, Henry. Can we at least agree to just play one game at a time here?'

'Well, I think today's session should end pretty soon, sir,' said Ponder. 'It's the banquet tonight after all and it will take some time to get the place ready.'

'Excuse me, guv, that's right,' said Trev behind him, 'and we've got to get the chandelier down an' put new candles in.'

'Yes, but we have been practising a little demonstration for tonight. Maybe the Archchancellor would like to see it,' said Nutt.

Ridcully looked at his watch. 'Well, yes, Mister Nutt, but time is getting on and so I look forward to seeing it later. Splendid effort all round, though,' he boomed.

The night market was setting up in Sator Square as Glenda and Juliet arrived for work. Ankh-Morpork lived on the street, where it got its food, entertainment and, in a city with a ferocious housing shortage, a place to hang around until there was space on a floor. Stalls had been set up anywhere, and flares filled the early-evening air with stink and, almost as a by-product, a certain amount of light.

Glenda could never resist looking, especially now. She was very good at all sorts of cookery, she really was, and it was important to keep that knowledge at the calm centre of her spinning brain. And there was Verity Pushpram, queen of the sea.

Glenda had a lot of time for Miss Pushpram, who was a self-made woman, although she could have used some help when it came to her eyes, which were set so far apart that she rather resembled a turbot.

But Verity, like the ocean that was making her fortune these days, had hidden depths, because she'd made enough to buy a boat, and then another boat and a whole aisle in the fish market. But she still woman-handled her barrow to the square most evenings, where she sold whelks, shrimps, leather crabs, blossom prawns, monkey clams and her famous hot fish sticks.

Glenda often bought from her; there was the kind of respect you give to an equal who is, crucially, no threat to your own position.

'Going to the big bun fight, girls?' said Verity cheerfully, waving a halibut at them.

'Yes,' said Juliet proudly.

'What, both of you?' said Verity, with a glance towards Glenda, who said, firmly, 'The Night Kitchen is expanding.'

'Oh well, so long as you're having fun,' said Verity, looking, in theory, from one to the other. 'Here, have one of these, they're lovely. My treat.'

She reached down and picked a crab out of a bucket. As it came up it turned out that three more were hanging on to it.

'A crab necklace?' giggled Juliet.

'Oh, that's crabs for you,' said Verity, disentangling the ones who had hitched a ride. 'Thick as planks, the lot of them. That's why you can keep them in a bucket without a lid. Any that tries to get out gets pulled back. Yes, as thick as planks.' Verity held the crab over an ominously bubbling cauldron. 'Shall I cook it for you now?'

'No!' said Glenda, much louder than she had intended.

'Are you okay, dear?' Verity enquired. 'You look a bit ill.'

'I'm fine. Fine. Just a touch of a sore throat, that's all.' Crab bucket, she thought. I thought Pepe was talking nonsense. 'Erm, can you just truss it up for us? It's going to be a long night.'

'Right you are,' said Miss Pushpram, expertly wrapping the un-resisting crab in twine. 'You know what to do, that's certain. Lovely crabs, these, real good eating. But thick as planks.'

Crab bucket, thought Glenda as they hurried towards the Night Kitchen. That's how it works. People from the Sisters *disapproving* when a girl takes the trolley bus. That's crab bucket. Practically everything my mum ever told me, that's crab bucket. Practically everything I've ever told Juliet, that's crab bucket, too. Maybe it's just another word for the Shove. It's so nice and warm on the inside that you forget that there's an outside. The worst of it is, the crab that mostly keeps you down is you . . . The realization had her mind on fire.

A lot hinges on the fact that, in most circumstances, people are not allowed to hit you with a mallet. They put up all kinds of visible and invisible signs that say 'Do not do this' in the hope that it'll work, but if it doesn't, then they shrug, because there is, really, no real mallet at all. Look at Juliet talking to all those nobby ladies. She didn't know that she shouldn't talk to them like that. And it worked! Nobody hit her on the head with a hammer.

And custom and practice as embodied by Mrs Whitlow was that the Night Kitchen staff should not go above stairs, to where the light was comparatively clean and had not already been through a lot of other eyeballs. Well, Glenda had done that, and nothing bad had happened, had it? So now Glenda strode towards the Great Hall, her serviceable shoes hitting the floor enough to hurt. The Day girls said nothing as she marched in behind them. There was nothing for them to say. The real unwritten rule was that girls on the dumpy side didn't serve at table when guests were present, and Glenda had decided tonight that she couldn't read unwritten rules. Besides, there was a row already going on. The servants who were laying out the cutlery were trying to keep an eye on it, which subsequently meant that more than one guest had to eat with two spoons.

Glenda was amazed to see the Candle Knave waving his hands at Trev and Nutt, and she headed for them. She did not like Smeems very much; a man could be dogmatic, and that was all right, or he could be stupid, and no harm done, but stupid and dogmatic at the same time was too much, especially fluxed with body odour.

'What's this all about?'

It worked. The right tone from a woman with her arms folded always bounces an answer out of an unprepared man before he has time to think, and even before he has time to think up a lie.

'They raised the chandelier! They raised it without lighting the candles! We won't have enough time now to get it down and up again before the guests come in!'

'But, Mister Smeems—' Trev began.

'And all I get is talking back and lies,' Smeems complained bitterly.

'But I can light them from here, Mister Smeems.' Nutt spoke quietly, even his voice huddling.

'Don't give me that! Even wizards can't do that without getting wax all over the place, you little—'

'That's enough, Mister Smeems,' said a voice that to Glenda's surprise turned out to be hers. '*Can* you light them, Mister Nutt?'

'Yes, miss. At the right time.'

'There you are, then,' said Glenda. 'I suggest you leave it to Mister Nutt.' Smeems looked at her, and she could see there was, as it were, an invisible mallet in his thinking, a feeling that he might get into some trouble here.

'I should run along now,' she said.

'I can't stand around. I'm a man with responsibilities.' Smeems looked wrong-footed and bewildered, but from his point of view absence was a good idea. Glenda almost saw his brain reach the conclusion. Not being there diluted the blame for whatever it was that was going to go wrong. 'Can't stand around,' he repeated. 'Ha! You'd all be in the dark if it wasn't for me!' With that, he grabbed his greasy bag and scuttled off.

Glenda turned to Nutt. He can't possibly make himself smaller, she told herself. His clothes would fit him even worse than they do already. I must be imagining it.

'Can you really light the candles from here?' she said aloud. Nutt carried on staring at the floor.

Glenda turned to Trev. 'Can he really—' but Trev was not there, because Trev was leaning against the wall some distance away talking to Juliet.

She could read it all at a glance, his possessive stance, her modestly downcast eyes: not hanky panky, as such, but certainly overture and beginners to hanky panky. Oh, the power of words . . .

As you watch, so are you watched. Glenda looked down into the penetrating eyes of Nutt. Was that a frown? What had he seen in her expression? More than she wanted, that was certain.

The tempo in the Hall was increasing. The football captains would be assembling in one of the anterooms, and she could imagine them there, in clean shirts, or at least in shirts less grubby than usual, dragged here from the various versions of Botney Street all over the city, staring up at the wonderful vaulting and wondering if they were going to walk out of there dead. Huh, she tagged on to that thought, more likely it would be dead drunk. And, just as her brain began to pivot around that new thought, a severe voice behind her said, 'Hwe do not usually expect to see you in the Great Hall, Glenda?'

It had to be Mrs Whitlow. Only the housekeeper would pronounce 'we' with an H and finish a plain statement as if it were a question. Besides, without turning round, Glenda heard the clink of her silver chatelaine, reputed to hold the one key that could open any lock in the university, and the creaking of her fearsome corsetry.*

Glenda turned. There is no mallet! 'I thought you might need a few extra hands tonight, Mrs Whitlow,' she said sweetly.

'Nevertheless, custom and practice—'

'Ah, dear Mrs Whitlow, I think we're ready to let them through now. His lordship's coach will shortly be leaving the palace,' said the Archchancellor, behind them.

Mrs Whitlow could loom. But mostly only horizontally. Mustrum Ridcully could out-loom her by more than two feet. She turned hurriedly and gave the little half-curtsy which, he'd never dared tell her, he always found mildly annoying.

'Oh, and Miss Glenda, isn't it?' said the Archchancellor happily. 'Good to see you up here. Very useful young lady, Mrs Whitlow. Got initiative, fine grasp of things.'

'How kind of you to say so. She is one of my best girls,' said the housekeeper, spitting teeth and taking care not to meet Glenda's suddenly cherubic gaze.

* It is said that if you want to stand up to someone you should picture them naked. In the case of Mrs Whitlow this would be, as Ponder Stibbons might put it, contra-indicated.

'Big chandelier not lit, I see,' said Ridcully.

Glenda stepped forward. 'Mister Nutt is planning a surprise for us, sir.'

'Mister Nutt is full of surprises. We've had an amazing day here today, Miss Glenda,' said Ridcully. 'Our Mister Nutt has been teaching the lads to play football *his* way. Do you know what he did yesterday? You'll never guess. Tell them, Mister Nutt.'

'I took them along to the Royal Opera House to watch the dancers in training,' said Nutt nervously. 'You see, it is very important that they learn the skills of movement and poise.'

'And then when they came back,' said Ridcully, with the same, slightly threatening joviality, 'he had them playin' here in the Hall blindfolded.'

Nutt coughed nervously. 'It is vital for them to keep track of every other player,' he said. 'It is essential that they are a team.'

'And then he took them to see Lord Rust's hunting dogs.'

Nutt coughed again, even more embarrassed. 'When they hunt, every dog knows the position of every other dog. I wanted them to understand the duality of team and player. The strength of the player is the team and the strength of the team is the player.'

'Did you hear that?' said Ridcully. 'Great stuff! Oh, he's had them running up and down here all day long. Balancing balls on their heads, doing big diagrams on a blackboard. You'd think it was some kind of battle being planned.'

'It is a battle,' said Nutt. 'I mean, not with the opposing team, as such, but it is a battle between every man and himself.'

'That sounds very Uberwaldian,' said Ridcully. 'Still, they all seem full of vim and vigour and ready for the evening. I think Mister Nutt is planning one of those sunny luminair things.'

'Just a little something to capture people's attention,' said Nutt.

'Anything going to go off bang?' said Ridcully.

'No, sir.'

'Promise? Personally I like the occasional bit of Sturm and

222

Drang, but Lord Vetinari is a tad particular about that sort of thing.'

'No thunder and lightning, sir. Possibly a brief haze, high up.'

It seemed to Glenda that the Archchancellor was paying some thoughtful attention to Nutt.

'How many languages do you speak, you . . . Nutt?'

'Three dead and twelve living, sir,' said Nutt.

'Really. Really,' said Ridcully, as though filing this away and trying not to think *How many of them were alive before you murdered them?* 'Well done. Thank you, Mister Nutt, and you too, ladies. We will bring them in shortly.'

Glenda took this opportunity to get out of Mrs Whitlow's way. She was not pleased to see that Trev and Juliet had already taken a slightly earlier opportunity to get out of hers.

'Do not worry about Juliet,' said Nutt, who had followed her.

'Who said I was worried?' Glenda snapped.

'You did. Your expression, your stance, the set of your body, your . . . reactions, your tone of voice. Everything.'

'You have no business to be looking at my everything – I mean the set of my body!'

'It is simply the way you stand, Miss Glenda.'

'And you can read my mind?'

'It may appear that way. I am so sorry.'

'And Juliet. What was she thinking?'

'I am not sure, but she likes Mister Trev, she thinks he is funny.'

'So have you read Trev's everything? Bet that was a dirty book!'

'Er, no, miss. He is worried and confused. I would say he is trying to see what kind of man he is going to be.'

'Really? He's always been a scallywag.'

'He is thinking of his future.'

Across the Hall, the big doors opened just as the last scurrying servants reached their stations.

This made no impression on Glenda, lost in thought as she wrestled with the prospect that a leopard might change his shorts. He has been a bit quiet lately, I must admit. And he did write her that lovely poem . . . That should mean a lot, a poem. Who'd have thought it? It's not like him at all—

With atomic speed Nutt was suddenly missing, and the doors stood wide, and here came the captains with their retinues, and all of them were nervous and some of them were wearing unaccustomed suits, and some of them were walking a little unsteadily even now, because the wizards' idea of an aperitif had bite, and in the kitchen plates would be being filled and the chefs would be cursing and the ovens clanging as they . . . as they . . . What was the menu, anyway?

Life as an unseen part of Unseen University was a matter of alliances, feuds, obligations and friendships, all stirred and twisted and woven together.

Glenda was good at it. The Night Kitchen had always been generous to other toilers and right now the Great Hall owed her favours, even if all she had done was keep her mouth shut. Now she bore down on Shiny Robert, one of the head waiters, who gave her the cautious nod due to someone who knew things about you that you wouldn't want your mother to know.

'Got a menu?' she asked. One was produced from under a napkin. She read it in horror.

'That's not the stuff they like!'

'Oh dear, Glenda,' Robert smirked. 'Are you saying it's too good for them?'

'You're giving them Avec. Nearly every dish has got Avec in it, but stuff with Avec in the name is an acquired taste. I mean, do these look to you like people who habitually eat in a foreign language? Oh dear, and you are giving them beer! Beer with Avec!'

'A choice of wines is available. They are choosing beer,' said Robert coldly.

Glenda stared at the captains. They seemed to be enjoying themselves now. Here was free food and drink and if the food tasted strange there was plenty of it, and the beer tasted welcomely familiar and there was lots of that, too.

She didn't like this. Heavens knew that football had got pretty disgusting these days, but . . . well, she couldn't quite work out what she was uneasy about, but—

''scuse me, miss?'

She looked down. A young footballer had decided to confide in the only uniformed woman he could see who was not carrying at least two plates at once.

'Can I help?'

He lowered his voice. 'This chutney tastes of fish, miss.'

She looked at the other grinning faces around the table. 'It's called caviar, sir. It'll put lead in your pencil.'

The table, as one well-oiled drinker, guffawed, but the youth only looked puzzled. 'I haven't got a pencil, miss.' More amusement.

'There's not a lot of them around,' said Glenda, and left them laughing.

'So kind of you to invite me, Mustrum,' said Lord Vetinari, waving away the hors d'œuvres. He turned to the wizard on his right. 'And the Archchancellor formerly known as Dean is back with you, I see. That is capital.'

'You may remember that Henry went to Pseudopolis – Brazeneck, you know. He is, er . . .' Ridcully slowed.

'The new Archchancellor,' said Vetinari. He picked up a spoon and perused it carefully, as if it were a rare and curious object. 'Dear me. I thought that there could be only one Archchancellor. Is this not so? One above all others and one Hat, of course? But these are wizardly matters, of which I know little. So do excuse me if I have misunderstood.' In the gently turning bowl of the spoon his nose went from long to short. 'However, it occurs to me, as an onlooker, that this could lead to a little friction, perhaps.' The spoon stopped in mid twirl.

'A soupçon, perhaps,' said Ridcully, not looking in the direction of Henry.

'That much, indeed? But I surmise from the absence of people being turned into frogs that you gentlemen have forgone the traditional option of magical mayhem. Well done. When it comes to the pinch, old friends, united by the bonds of mutual disrespect, cannot bring themselves to actually kill one another. We have hope. Ah, soup.'

There was a brief interregnum as the ladle went from bowl to bowl, and then the Patrician said, 'Could I assist you? I am without any bias in this matter.'

'Excuse me, my lord, but I think it might be said that you would favour Ankh-Morpork,' said the Archchancellor formerly known as Dean.

'Really? It might also be said that it would be in my interest to weaken the perceived power of this university. You take my meaning? The delicate balance between town and gown, the unseen and the mundane? The twin foci of power. It might be said that I could take the opportunity to embarrass my learned friend.' He smiled a little smile. 'Do you still own the official Archchancellor's Hat, Mustrum? I notice that you don't wear it these days and tend to prefer the snazzy number with the rather attractive drawers and the small drinks cabinet in the point.'

'I never liked wearing the official one. It grumbled all the time.'

'It really can talk?' said Vetinari.

'I think the word "nag" would be far more accurate, since its only topic of conversation has been how much better things used to be. My only comfort here is that every Archchancellor over the last thousand years has complained about it in exactly the same way.'

'So it can think and speak?' said Vetinari innocently.

'Well, I suppose you could put it like that.'

'Then you can't own it, Mustrum: a hat that thinks and speaks cannot be enslaved. No slaves in Ankh-Morpork, Mustrum.' He waved a finger waggishly.

'Yes, but it is the look of the thing. What would it look like if I gave up the uniqueness of Archchancellorship without a fight?'

'I really could not say,' said Lord Vetinari, 'but since just about every genuine battle between wizards has hitherto resulted in wholesale destruction, I feel that you would at least look a little embarrassed. And, of course, I will remind you that you were quite happy that Archchancellor Bill Rincewind at Bugarup University cheerfully calls himself Archchancellor.'

'Yes, but he's a long way away,' said Ridcully. 'And Fourecks doesn't really count as anywhere, whereas in Pseudopolis we are talking about a Johnny-come-lately of an organization and its—'

'So are we then merely arguing over the question of distance?' said Vetinari.

'No, but—' said Ridcully and stopped.

'Is this worth the argument, I ask you?' said Vetinari. 'What we have here, gentlemen, is but a spat between the heads of a venerable and respected institution and an ambitious, relatively inexperienced, and importunate new school of learning.'

'Yes, that's what we've got all right,' said Ridcully.

Vetinari raised a finger. 'I hadn't finished, Archchancellor. Let me see now. I said that what we have here is a spat between an antique and somewhat fossilized, elderly and rather hidebound institution and a college of vibrant newcomers full of fresh and exciting ideas.'

'Here, hang on, you didn't say that the first time,' said Ridcully.

Vetinari leaned back. 'Indeed I did, Archchancellor. Do you not remember our talk about the meaning of words a little while ago? Context is everything. I suggest, therefore, that you allow the head of Brazeneck University the opportunity to wear the official Arch-chancellor's Hat for a short time.'

You had to pay close attention to what Lord Vetinari said. Sometimes the words, while clearly docile, had a tendency to come back and bite.

'Play the football for the Hat,' said Vetinari.

He looked at their faces. 'Gentlemen. Gentlemen. Do take a moment to consider this. The importance of the Hat is enhanced. The means by which the wizards strive are not primarily magical. The actual striving and indeed the rivalry will, I think, be good for both universities and people will be interested, whereas in the past when wizards have argued they have had to hide in the cellars. Please do not answer me too quickly, otherwise I will think you have not thought about this enough.'

'As a matter of fact, I can think very fast indeed,' said Ridcully. 'It will simply be no contest. It will be totally unfair.'

'It certainly will,' said Henry.

'Ah, you both feel that it will be totally unfair,' said Vetinari.

'Indeed. We have a much younger faculty and the brisk and healthy playing fields of Pseudopolis.'

'Capital,' said Lord Vetinari. 'It seems to me that we have a challenge. University against university. City, as it were, against city. Warfare, as it were, without the tedious necessity of picking up all those heads and limbs afterwards. All things must strive, gentlemen.'

'I suppose I have to agree,' said Ridcully. 'It's not as if I'm going to lose the Hat in any case. I must note, though, Havelock, that you do not allow many challenges to your position.'

'Oh, but I am challenged very frequently,' said Lord Vetinari. 'It's just that they don't win. Incidentally, gentlemen, I did notice in today's paper that the new voters of Pseudopolis yesterday voted not to have to pay taxes. When you see the president again, please don't hesitate to tell him that I will be more than happy to advise him when he feels it is necessary. Cheer up, gentlemen. Neither of you has got exactly what you want, but both of you have got exactly what you deserve. If the leopard can change his shorts, a wizard can change his hat. And the leopard must change his shorts, gentlemen, or we are all doomed.'

'Are you referring to the Loko business?' said Henry. 'You needn't look surprised.'

'I don't intend to. I am surprised,' said Vetinari, 'but please credit me with not looking surprised unless, of course, there is some advantage in doing so.'

'We are going to have to do something. The expedition found a nest of the damn things!'

'Yes. Children, which they killed,' said Vetinari.

'Pups that they exterminated!'

'Indeed? And what do you suggest?'

'We are talking about a very evil force here!'

'Archchancellor, I see evil when I look in my shaving mirror. It is, philosophically, present everywhere in the universe in order, apparently, to highlight the existence of good. I think there is more to this theory, but I tend to burst out laughing at this point. I take it that you are behind the idea of an expeditionary force to Far Uberwald?'

'Of course!' said the former Dean.

'It has been tried once before. It was tried twice before that. Why is there a certain cast of the military mind which leads sensible people to do again, with gusto, what didn't work before?'

'Force is all they understand. You must know that.'

'Force is all that's been tried, Archchancellor Henry. Besides, if they are animals, as some people claim, then they understand nothing, but if, as I am convinced, they are sapient creatures, then some understanding is surely required by us.'

The Patrician took a sip of his beer. 'I have told this to few people, gentlemen, and I suspect never will again, but one day when I was a young boy on holiday in Uberwald I was walking along the bank of a stream when I saw a mother otter with her cubs. A very endearing sight, I'm sure you will agree, and even as I watched, the mother otter dived into the water and came up with a plump salmon, which she subdued and dragged on to a half-submerged log. As she ate it, while of course it was still alive, the body split and I remember to this day the sweet pinkness of its roes as they spilled out, much to the delight of the baby otters who scrambled over themselves to feed on the delicacy. One of nature's wonders, gentlemen: mother and children dining upon mother and children. And that's when I first learned about evil. It is built in to the very nature of the universe. Every world spins in pain. If there is any kind of supreme being, I told myself, it is up to all of us to become his moral superior.'

The two wizards exchanged a glance. Vetinari was staring into the depths of his beer mug and they were glad that they did not know what he saw in there.

'Is it me or is it rather dark in here?' said Henry.

'Good heavens, yes! I forgot about the chandelier!' exclaimed Ridcully. 'Where is Mister Nutt?'

'Here,' said Nutt, rather closer than Ridcully would have preferred. 'Why?'

'I said I would be ready when you needed me, sir.'

'What? Oh, yes, of course you did.' He's short and polite and amazingly helpful, he told himself. Nothing to worry about at all . . . 'Well, show us how to light the candles, Mister Nutt.'

'Could I possibly have a fanfare, sir?'

'I doubt it, young man, but I will bring the Hall to attention.'

Ridcully picked up a spoon and tapped the side of a wine glass, in the time-honoured 'Look, everybody, I'm trying to make a loud noise very quietly!' procedure, which has successfully eluded after-dinner speakers ever since the invention of glasses, spoons and dinners.

'Gentlemen, pray silence, an expectant one, followed by appreciative applause for the lighting of the chandelier!'

There was the silence.

As a round of applause was followed by some more silence, people turned around in their chairs for a better view of nothing to see.

'Would you please puff on your pipe and hand it to me, sir?' said Nutt.

Shrugging, Ridcully did so. Nutt took it, raised it in the air and—

What happened? It was a topic of conversation for days. Did the red fire come up from the pipe or down from the ceiling or simply out of the walls? All that was certain was that the darkness was suddenly fractured by glowing zigzags that vanished in a blink, leaving a total blackness which cleared like the sky at dawn as all at once every candle, in perfect unison, glowed into life.

As the applause began to mount, Ridcully looked along the table at Ponder, who waved his thaumometer, shook his head and shrugged.

Then the Archchancellor turned to Nutt, took him out of earshot of the table and for the benefit of watchers shook him by the hand.

'Well done, Mister Nutt. Just one thing: that wasn't magic, because we would know, so how was it done?'

'Well, initially, dwarfish alchemy, sir. You know, the kind that works? It is how they light the big chandeliers in the caverns under Bonk. I worked that out by tests and analysis. All the candle wicks are con-nected by a network of black cotton thread, which terminates in one single thread, which barely shows up in this Hall. You see, the thread is soaked in a formula which burns with extreme but brief ferocity when dry. My slightly altered solution burns considerably faster even than that, consuming the thread until it is nothing but gas. It is quite safe. Only the tips of the candle wicks are treated, you see, and they light as normal. You might be interested, sir, in the fact that the flame travels so fast as to be instantaneous by any human measure. Certainly faster than twenty miles a second, I calculate.'

Ridcully was good at looking blank. You couldn't deal with Vetinari on a regular basis without being able to freeze your expression at will. But, right now, he didn't have to try.

Nutt looked concerned. 'Have I failed to achieve worth, sir?'

'What? Ah. Well.' Ridcully's face thawed. 'A wonderful effort, Nutt. Well done! Er, how did you get hold of the ingredients?'

'Oh, there is an old alchemy room in the cellars.'

'Hmm. Well, thank you again,' said Ridcully. 'But as Master of this university I must ask you not to talk to anyone about this invention until we have spoken again on the matter. Now, I must get back to the events in hand.'

'Don't you worry, sir, I will see that it does not fall into the wrong hands,' said Nutt, bustling off.

Except, of course, that *you* are the wrong hands, Ridcully thought, as he returned to the table.

'An impressive display,' said Vetinari, as Ridcully took his seat again. 'Am I right in thinking, Mustrum, that the Mister Nutt you referred to is indeed, as it were, *the* Mister Nutt?'

'That's right, yes, quite a decent chap.'

'And you're letting him do alchemy?'

'I think it was his own idea, sir.'

'And he's been standing here all this time?'

'Very keen. Is there a problem, Havelock?'

'No, no, not at all,' said Vetinari.

It was indeed an impressive display, Glenda acknowledged, but while she watched it she could feel Mrs Whitlow's gaze on her. In theory Glenda's activities would merit another kind of firework display later on, but it wasn't going to happen, was it? She had nailed the invisible hammer. But there were other, if less personal, matters on her mind.

Stupid, silly, and thoughtless though some of her neighbours were, it was up to her, as ever, to protect their interests. They had been dropped into a world they didn't understand, so she had to understand it for them. She thought this because as she prowled between the tables she could make out a certain type of *clink, clink* noise, and, sure enough, the amount of silverware on the tables appeared to be diminishing. After watching carefully for a moment or two, she walked up behind Mr Stollop and without ceremony pulled three silver spoons and a silver fork out of his jacket pocket.

He spun around and then had the decency to look a bit embarrassed when he saw that it was her.

Glenda didn't have to open her mouth.

'They've got so many,' he protested. 'Who needs all those knives and forks?'

She reached into the man's other pocket and pulled out three silver knives and a silver salt cellar.

'Well, there's such a lot,' said Stollop. 'I didn't think they'd miss one or two.'

Glenda stared at him. The clinking of cutlery disappearing from the tables had been a small but noticeable part of the ambient noise for some time. She leaned down until her face was an inch away from his.

'Mr Stollop. I wonder if that's what Lord Vetinari is expecting you all to do.' His face went white. She nodded. 'Just a word to the wise,' she said.

And words spread fast. As Glenda walked on she was gratified to hear behind her, spreading along the tables, more clinking as a tide of cutlery flowed swiftly out of pockets and back on to the tables. The tinkling flew up and down the tables like little fairy bells.

Glenda smiled to herself and hurried off to dare everything. Or at least everything that she dared.

Lord Vetinari stood up. For some inexplicable reason he needed no fanfare. No 'Would you put your hands together for', no 'Lend me your ears', no 'Be upstanding for'. He simply stood up and the noise went down. 'Gentlemen, thank you for coming, and may I thank you, Archchancellor Ridcully, for being such a generous host this evening. May I also take this opportunity to put your minds at rest.

'You see, there appears to be a rumour going around that I am against the playing of football. Nothing could be further from the truth. I am completely in favour of the traditional game of football and, indeed, would be more than happy to see the game leave the fusty obscurity of the back streets. Moreover, while I know you have your own schedule of games, I personally propose a league, as it were, of senior teams, who will valiantly vie with one another for a golden cup—'

There were cheers, of a beery nature.

'—or should I say gold-ish cup—'

More cheers and more laughter.

' based on the recently discovered ancient urn known as The Tackle, which, I am sure, you have all seen?'

General sniggering.

'And if you haven't, then your wives certainly have.'

Silence, followed by a tsunami of laughter which, like most tidal waves, had a lot of froth on the top.

Glenda, lurking among the serving girls, was taken aback and affronted at the same time, which was a bit of a squeeze, and wondered . . . So, he's planning something. They're lapping it up along with the beer, too.

'Never seen that before,' said a wine waiter beside her.

'Seen what before?'

'Seen his lordship drinking. He doesn't even drink wine.'

Glenda looked at the skinny black figure and said, enunciating carefully, 'When you say he does not drink wine, do you mean he does not *drink* wine, or he does not drink . . . *wine*?'

'He doesn't have a bloody drink. That's all I'm saying. That's Lord Vetinari, that is. He's got ears everywhere.'

'I can only see two, but he's quite handsome, in a way.'

'Oh, yeah, the ladies like him,' said the waiter and sniffed. 'Everyone knows he's got something going on with that vampire up in Uberwald. You know? The one who invented the Temperance League? Vampires who don't suck blood? Hello, what's this . . . ?'

'Let no one suppose that I am alone in a desire to see a better future for this great game,' Vetinari was saying. 'Tonight, gentlemen, you will see football, hear football and if you don't duck, gentlemen, you might even eat football. Here to display a marriage of football from the past and I dare hope from the future, I present to you the first team of Unseen University . . . Unseen Academicals!'

The candles went out, all at once, even the ones high up in the chandelier; Glenda could see pale ghosts of smoke rising in the gloom. Beside her, Nutt started counting under his breath. One, two . . . At the count of three, the candles at the far end of the Hall burst into life again, revealing Trevor Likely, wearing his most infectious grin.

'Evenin' all,' he said, 'an' to you too, your lordship. My, but ain't you lookin' quite the swell tonight.' As breaths were indrawn all around the Hall Trev pulled out his tin can, dropped it on to his foot and flicked it up on to his shoulder, where it travelled around the back of his neck and down his other arm.

'At the start people used to kick rocks. That was sort of stupid. Then they tried skulls, but you had to get 'em off people and that led to fightin'.'

Beside Glenda, Nutt was still counting . . .

'An' now we've got what we call a ball,' Trev continued, as his tin can rolled and climbed around him, 'but it ain't all that, 'cos it's a lump of firewood. You can't kick it 'less you've got big heavy boots on. It's slow. It's heavy. It don't live, gentlemen, and football should live . . .'

The doors at the other end of the Hall opened and Bengo Macarona trotted in, bouncing the new football. Its *gloing, gloing* echoed around the Hall. Some of the football captains had got to their feet, craning for a better view.

'And with the old football, you couldn't do this,' said Trev, and dived for the floor as Macarona spun in one balletic movement and sent the ball screaming up the aisle like an angry hornet.

Some scenes are only ever a memory rather than an experience, because they happen too fast for immediate comprehension, and Glenda watched the subsequent events on the internal screen of horrified recollection. There were the two Archmages and the Tyrant of the city, watching with frozen interest as the spinning globe hummed towards them, dragging terrible consequences in its wake, and then there was the Librarian rising out of nowhere, stopping it dead in mid air with a hand like a shovel.

'That's us, gentlemen. And we'll take on the first team that joins us on the Hippo on Saturday at one o'clock. We'll be training all around the city. You can join in if you like. And don't worry if you don't have the balls! We'll give you some!' The candle flames went out, which was just as well because it is hard to riot in the dark. When the flames rose again in their eerie way, shouting, arguments, laughter and even discussion were taking place on every table. Quietly, too, the servants went to and fro with their flagons. There always seemed to be another one, Glenda noticed.

'What have they been drinking?' she whispered to the nearest waiter.

'Winkle's Old Peculiar, Mages' Special. It's top stuff.'

'What about his lordship?'

He grinned. 'Ha. Funny thing, some of 'em have asked me that, too. Just the same as the guests. Poured out of the same flagon, just like for everyone else, so it's—' He stopped.

Lord Vetinari was on his feet again. 'Gentlemen, who among you will accept the challenge? It need not be Dimwell, it need not be Dolly Sisters, it need not be the Nappers, it just has to be a team, gentlemen; the Unseen Academicals will take on the best of you, in the best traditions of sportsmanship. I have set the date of the game for Saturday. As far as the Academicals are concerned, you can watch them train and Mister Stibbons will give you all the advice you may need. This will be a fair match, gentlemen, you have my word on it.' He paused. 'Did I mention that when it is presented, the very nearly gold urn will be full of beer? The concept is quite popular, I gather, and I predict that for a reasonable period the golden cup will quite miraculously stay full of beer, no matter how many drink thereof. I shall personally see to it.'

This got a big cheer, too. Glenda felt embarrassed for the men, but angry at them too. They were being led by the nose. Or, more accurately, by the beer.

Vetinari didn't need whips and thumbscrews; he just needed Winkle's Old Peculiar, Mages' Special, and he was leading them like little lambs – and matching them pint for pint. How could he manage that? *Hey, look at me*, he's saying, *I'm just like you*, and he's not like them at all. They can't have someone killed – she paused the thought to allow consideration of some of the street fights when the pubs shut, and amended it to – and get away with it.

'My friend the Archchancellor has just informed me that, of course, the Unseen Academicals will not on any account resort to magic! Nobody wants to see a team of frogs, I am sure!'

There was general laughter at this lame joke, but the plain fact was that right now they would have laughed at a paper bag.

'This will be a proper football match, gentlemen, no trickery, only skills,' said the Patrician, his voice sharp again. 'And on that note I am decreeing a new code, based on the hallowed and traditional rules of football so recently rediscovered, but including many familiar ones of more recent usage. The office of referee is there to ensure obedience to the rules. There must be rules, my friends. There must be. There is no game without rules. No rules, no game.'

And there it was. No one else seemed to notice, through the fumes, the razor blade glittering for a moment in the candyfloss. Rules? thought Glenda. What are these new rules? I never knew there were rules. But Lord Vetinari's assistant, whoever he was, was quietly putting a few sheets of paper in front of each man.

She remembered old Stollop's bafflement when confronted with a mere envelope. Some of them could read, surely? But how many of them could read *now*?

His lordship had not finished. 'Finally, gentlemen, I would like you to peruse and sign the copies of the rules Mister Drumknott has given you. And now I understand the Archchancellor and his colleagues are looking forward to seeing you in the Uncommon Room for cigars and, I believe, an exceptionally rare brandy!'

Well, that would about wrap it up, wouldn't it? The footballers were used to just beer. To be fair, they were used to lots of just beer. Nevertheless, if she was any judge, and she was pretty good, they would now be very nearly falling-down drunk. Although some seasoned captains could stand up for some time while being, technically, falling-down drunk. And there is nothing more embarrassing than seeing a falling-down drunk except for when it is a falling-down drunk who is still standing up. And that was amazing: the captains were the type of men who drank in quarts, and could belch the national anthem and bend steel bars with their teeth, or even somebody else's teeth. Okay, they had never had much in the way of schooling, but why did they have to be so dumb?

'Tell me,' murmured Ridcully to Vetinari as they watched the guests file out unsteadily, 'are you behind the discovery of the urn?'

'We have known one another for quite some time, Mustrum, have we not,' said Vetinari, 'and as you know, I would not lie to you.' He paused for a moment and added, 'Well, of course I *would* lie to you in acceptable circumstances, but on this occasion I can truthfully say that the discovery of the urn came as a surprise to me as well, albeit a pleasant one. Indeed, I assumed that you gentlemen had had something to do with it.'

'We didn't even know it was there,' said Ridcully. 'Personally, I suspect that religion is involved.'

Vetinari smiled. 'Well, of course, classically, gods play with the fates of men, so I suppose there is no reason why it shouldn't be football. We play and are played and the best we can hope for is to do it with style.'

It might have been possible to cut the air in the Uncommon Room with a knife, had anyone been able to find a knife. Or hold a knife the right way if found. From the point of view of the wizards, it was business as usual, but while a number of captains were being wheeled away in a wheelbarrow, thoughtfully stationed there earlier in the evening, there were enough visitors still standing to make for a damp, hot hubbub. In an unregarded corner, the Patrician and the two Archchancellors had found a space where they could relax unheeded in the big chairs and settle a few matters.

'You know, Henry,' said Vetinari to the former Dean, 'I think it would be a very good idea if you were to referee the match.'

'Oh, come on! I think that would be most unfair,' said Ridcully.

'To whom, pray?'

'Well, er,' said Ridcully. 'There could be a question of rivalry between wizards.'

'But on the other hand,' said Vetinari, his voice all smoothness, 'it might also be said that, for political reasons, another wizard would have a vested interest in not allowing a fellow Archmage to be seen to be bested by people who, despite their often amazing talents, skills, features and histories, are nevertheless lumped together in the term ordinary people.'

Ridcully raised a very big brandy glass in the general direction of the edge of the universe. 'I have every faith in my friend Henry,' he said. 'Even though he's a little bit on the tubby side.'

'Oh, unfair!' snapped Henry. 'A large man may be quite light on his feet. Is there any chance of me having the poisoned dagger?'

'In these modern times,' said Vetinari, 'I'm sorry to say that a whistle of some sort will have to suffice.'

At which point someone tried to slap Vetinari on the back.

It happened with remarkable speed and ended possibly even faster than it began, with Vetinari still seated in his chair with his beer mug in one hand and the man's wrist gripped tightly at head height. He let go and said, 'Can I help you, sir?'

'You're that Lord Veterinary, ain't ya? I seed you on them postage stamps.'

Ridcully glanced up. Some of Lord Vetinari's clerks were briskly heading towards them, along with some of the slurred speaker's friends, who could be defined at this point as people who were slightly more sober than he was and right now were sobering up very, very fast, because when you have just slapped a tyrant on the back you need all the friends you can get.

Vetinari nodded at his gentlemen, who evaporated back into the crowd, and then he snapped his fingers at one of the waiters. 'A chair here, please, for my new friend.'

'Are you sure?' said Ridcully, as a chair was pushed under the man who, by happy coincidence, was falling backwards in any case.

'I mean,' said the man, 'everary one saysh you're a bit of a wnacker, but I saysh you're awright over thish football fing. 'Sno future in jus' shlogging away. I should know, I got kicked inna head quite a few times.'

'Really?' said Lord Vetinari. 'And what is your name?'

'Swithin, shir,' said the man.

'Any other name, by any chance?' said Vetinari.

'Dustworthy,' he said. He raised a finger in a kind of salute. 'Captain, the Cockbill Boars.'

'Ah, you aren't having a good season,' said Vetinari. 'You need fresh blood in the squad, especially since Jimmy Wilkins got put into the Tanty after eating someone's nose. Naphill walked all over you because you lost your backbone when both of the Pinchpenny brothers were taken to the Lady Sybil, and you've been stuck down in the mud for three seasons. Okay, everyone says that Harry Capstick is making a very good showing since you bought him from Treacle Mine Tuesday for two crates of Winkle's Old Peculiar and a sack of pork scratchings, which is not bad for a man with a wooden leg, but there's never anyone in support.'

A circle of silence spread outwards from Vetinari and the swaying Swithin. Ridcully's mouth had dropped open and Henry's brandy glass remained half empty, an unusual occurrence for a glass that's been in the hands of a wizard for more than fifteen seconds.

'Also, I'm hearing that your pies are leaving a lot to be desired, such as dead, cooked, organic content,' continued Vetinari. 'Can't get the Shove behind you when the pies are seen to walk about.'

'My ladsh,' said Swithin, 'are the besht there ish. It'sh not their fault they're up againsht better people. They never getsh a chance to play shomeone they can beat. They alwaysh gives it one hundred and twenty pershent and you can't give more than that. Anyhow, how come you know all this shtuff? It's not like we're big in the league.'

'Oh, I take an interest,' said Vetinari. 'I believe that football is a lot like life.'

'There ish that, shir, there ish that. You does your besht and then shomeone kicksh you inna fork.'

'Then I strongly advise you to take an interest in our new football,' said Vetinari, 'which will be about speed, skill and thinking.'

'Oh, yeah, right, I can do all them,' said Swithin, at which point he fell off his chair.

'Does this poor man have any friends here?' said Vetinari, turning to the crowd.

There was some diffidence among them concerning whether or not it was a good idea to be friends with Swithin at this point.

Vetinari raised his voice: 'I would just like a couple of people to take him back to his home. I would like them to put him to bed and see that no trouble comes to him. Perhaps they ought to stay with him until morning too, because he just might try to commit suicide when he wakes up.'

'New Dawn For Football' said the *Times* when Glenda picked it up the next morning. As was its wont when it was reporting something it thought was particularly important, the paper's headline was followed by two others in descending sizes of font: 'Footballers Sign Up For The New Game' was on the next line down and then on the next 'New Balls A Success'.

To Glenda's surprise and dismay, Juliet still had a place on the front page, with the picture of her used smaller than yesterday, under the headline 'Mystery Lady Vanishes', and a paragraph which simply said that no one had seen the mystery model, Jewels, since her debut (Glenda had to look this one up) two days ago. Honestly, she thought, not finding somebody is news? And she was surprised that there was room for even this, since most of the front page was dedicated to the football, but the *Times* liked to start several stories on the front page and then, just when they were getting interesting, whisk them off to page 35, or somewhere, to end their days behind the crossword and the permanent advert for surgical trusses.

The leader column inside was headed 'Score One For Vetinari'. Glenda never normally read the leader column because there was only a certain number of times she was prepared to see the word 'however' used in a 120-word article.

She read the front-page story at first glumly and then with rising anger. Vetinari had done it. He had got them drunk and the fools had signed away their football for a pale variety cooked up by the palace and the university. Of course, minds are never quite that simple. She had to admit to herself that she hated the stupidity of the present game. She hated the idiot fighting and mindless shoving, but it was hers to hate. It was something that people themselves had put together and rickety and stupid though it was, it was theirs. And now the nobs were again picking up something that wasn't theirs and saying how wonderful it was. The old football was going to be banned. That was another little razor blade in Lord Vetinari's alcoholic candyfloss.

She was also deeply suspicious about the urn, the picture of which, for some reason, was still on her kitchen table. Since what was claimed to be the original rules was written in an ancient language, how could anyone other than a nob know what they meant? She ran her eye down the description of the new rules. Some of the rules of old street football had survived in there like monsters from another era. She recognized one that she had always liked: the ball shall be called the ball. The ball is the ball that is played as the ball by any three consecutive players, at which point it is the ball. She'd loved it when she first read it for the sheer stupidity of its phraseology. Apparently, it had been added on a day, centuries ago, when an unfortunately severed head had rolled into play and had rather absent-mindedly replaced the ball currently in play on account of some body, formerly belonging to the head, now lying on the original ball. That kind of thing stuck in the memory, especially because after the match the owner of the head was credited with scoring the winning goal.

That rule and a few others stood out as remnants of a vanished glory in the list of Lord Vetinari's new regulations. A few nods at the old game had been left in as a kind of sop to public opinion. He should not be allowed to get away with it. Just because he was a tyrant and capable of having just about anybody killed on a whim, people acted as if they were scared of him. Someone ought to tell him off. The world had turned upside down several times. She hadn't quite got her bearings, but making sure that Lord Vetinari did not get away with it was suddenly very important. It was up to the people to decide when they were being stupid and old-fashioned; it wasn't up to nobs to tell them what to do.

With great determination she put on her coat over her apron and, after a moment's thought, took two freshly made Jammy Devils from her cupboard. Where a battering ram cannot work, really good short-crust pastry can often break through.

In the Oblong Office, the Patrician's personal secretary looked at the stopwatch.

'Fifty seconds slower than your personal best, I'm afraid, my lord.'

'Proof indeed that strong drink is a mocker, Drumknott,' said Vetinari severely.

'I suspect that no further proof is needed,' said Drumknott, with his little secretarial smile.

'Although I would, in fairness, point out that Charlotte of the *Times* is emerging as the most fearsome crossword compiler of all time, and they are a pretty fearsome lot. But her? Initialisms, odds and evens, hidden words, container reverses, and now diagonals! How does she do it?'

'Well, you did it, sir.'

'I undid it. That is much easier.' Vetinari raised a finger. 'It is that woman who runs the pet shop in Pellicool Steps, depend upon it. She hasn't been mentioned as a winner recently. She must be compiling the things.'

'The female mind is certainly a devious one, my lord.'

Vetinari looked at his secretary in surprise. 'Well, of course it is. It has to deal with the male one. I think—'

There was a gentle tap at one of the doors. The Patrician turned back to the *Times* while Drumknott slipped out of the room. After some whispered exchanges, the secretary returned.

'It would appear that a young woman has got in via the back gate by bribing the guards, sir. They accepted the bribes, as per your standing orders, and she has been shown into the anteroom, which she will soon find is locked. She wishes to see you because, she says, she has a complaint. She is a maid.'

Lord Vetinari looked over the top of the paper. 'Tell her I can't help her with that. Perhaps, oh, I don't know, a different perfume would help?'

'I mean she is a member of the serving classes, sir. Her name is Glenda Sugarbean.'

'Tell her—' Vetinari hesitated, and then smiled. 'Ah, yes, Sugarbean. Did she bribe the guards with food? Something baked, perhaps?'

'Well done, sir! A large Jammy Devil apiece. May I ask how—?'

'She is a cook, Drumknott, not a maid. Show her in, by all means.'

The secretary looked a little resentful. 'Are you sure this is wise, sir? I have already told the guards to throw the foodstuffs away.'

'Food cooked by a Sugarbean? You may have committed a crime against high art, Drumknott. I shall see her now.'

'I must point out that you have a full schedule this morning, my lord.'

'Quite so. It is your job to point this out, and I respect that. But I did not return until half past four this morning and I distinctly remember stubbing my toe on the stairs. I am as drunk as a skunk, Drumknott, which of course means skunks are just as drunk as I. I must say the term is unfamiliar to me, and I had not thought hitherto of skunks in this context, but Mustrum Ridcully was kind enough to enlighten me. Allow me, then, a moment of indulgence.'

'Well, you are the Patrician, sir,' said Drumknott. 'You can do as you please.'

'That is kind of you to say so, but I did not, in fact, need reminding,' said Vetinari, with what was almost certainly a smile.

When the severe thin man opened the door, it was too late to flee. When he said, 'His lordship will see you now, Miss Sugarbean,' it was too late to faint. What had she been thinking of? Had she been thinking at all?

Glenda followed the man into the next room, which was oak panelled and sombre and the most uncluttered office she had ever seen. The room of the average wizard was so stuffed with miscellaneous things that the walls were invisible. Here, even the desk was clear, apart from a pot of quill pens, an inkwell, an open copy of the *Ankh-Morpork Times* and – her eye stayed fixed on this one, unable to draw itself away – a mug with the slogan 'To the world's Greatest Boss'. It was so out of place it might have been an intrusion from another universe.

A chair was quietly placed behind her. This was just as well, because when the man at the desk looked up she sat down abruptly.

Vetinari pinched the bridge of his nose and sighed. 'Miss . . . Sugarbean, there are whole rooms in this palace full of people who want to see me, and they are powerful and important people, or at least they think they are. Yet Mister Drumknott has kindly inserted in my schedule, ahead of the Postmaster General and the Mayor of Sto Lat, a meeting with a young cook with her coat on over her apron and an intent, it says here, of "having it out with me". And this is because I take notice of incongruity, and you, Miss Sugarbean, are incongruous. What is it you want?'

'Who says I want anything?'

'Everyone wants something when they are in front of me, Miss Sugarbean, even if it is only to be somewhere else.'

'All right! You made all the captains drunk last night and got them to sign that letter in the paper!'

The stare did not flicker. That was much worse than, well, anything.

'Young lady, drink levels all mankind. It is the ultimate democrat, if you like that sort of thing. A drunk beggar is as drunk as a lord, and so is a lord. And have you ever noticed that all drunks can understand one another, no matter how drunk they are and how different their native tongues? I take it for a certainty that you are a relation to Augusta Sugarbean?' The question, tagged on to the praises of inebriation, hit her between the eyes, scattering her thoughts.

'What? Oh. Well, yes. That's right. She was my grandmother.'

'And she was a cook at the Guild of Assassins when she was younger?'

'That's right. She always made a joke about how she wouldn't let them use any—' She stopped quickly, but Vetinari finished the sentence for her.

'—of her cakes to poison people. And we always obeyed, too, because as you surely know, miss, no one likes to upset a good cook. Is she still with us?'

'She passed on two years ago, sir.'

'But since you are a Sugarbean, I assume you have acquired a few more grandmothers as a replacement? Your grandmother was always a stalwart in the community and you must take all those little dainties for someone?'

'You can't know that, you're only guessing. But all right, they're for all the old ladies that don't get out much. Anyway, it's a perk.'

'Oh, but of course. Every job has its little perks. Why, I don't expect Drumknott here has bought a paperclip in his life, eh, Drumknott?'

The secretary, tidying papers in the background, gave a wan little smile.

'Look, I only take leftovers—' Glenda began, but this was waved away.

'You are here about the football,' said Vetinari. 'You were at the dinner last night, but the university likes its serving girls to be tall and I have an eye for such things. Therefore, I assume you made it your business to be there without bothering your superiors. Why?'

'You're taking their football away from them!'

The Patrician steepled his fingers and rested his chin on them while he looked at her.

He's trying to make me nervous, she thought. It's working, oh, it's working.

Vetinari filled in the silence. 'Your grandmother used to do people's thinking for them. That trait runs in families, always on the female side. Capable women, scurrying about in a world where everyone else seems to be seven years old and keeps on falling over in the playground, picking them up and watching them run right out there again. I imagine you run the Night Kitchen? Too many people in the big one. You want spaces you can control, beyond the immediate reach of fools.'

If he'd added 'Am I right?' like some windbag seeking applause, she would have hated him. But he was reading her from the inside of her head, in a calm, matter-of-fact way. She had to suppress a shiver, because it was all true.

'I'm taking nothing from anybody, Miss Sugarbean. I am simply changing the playground,' the man went on. 'What skill is there in the mob pushing and shoving? It is nothing more than a way of bringing on a sweat. No, we must move with the times. I know the *Times* moves with me. The captains will moan, no doubt, but they are getting old. Dying in the game is a romantic idea when you are young, but when you are older the boot is in the other ear. They know this, even if they won't admit it, and while they will protest, they will take care not to be taken seriously. In fact, far from taking, I am giving much. Acceptance, recognition, a certain standing, a gold-ish cup and the chance to keep what remains of their teeth.'

All she could manage after this was, 'All right, but you tricked them!'

'Really? They did not have to drink to excess, did they?'

'You knew they would!'

'No. I *suspected* they might. They could have been more cautious.

246

They *should* have been more cautious. I'd prefer to say that I led them along the correct path with a little guile rather than drove them along it with sticks. I possess many types of stick, Miss Sugarbean.'

'And you've been spying on me! You knew about the dainties.'

'Spying? Madam, it was once said of a great prince that his every thought was of his people. Like him, I watch over my people. I am just better at it, that's all. As for the dainties business, that was a simple deduction from the known facts of human nature.'

There was a lot that Glenda wanted to say, but in some very definite way she sensed that the interview – or at least the part of it that involved her opening her mouth – was over. Nevertheless, she said, 'Why aren't you drunk?'

'I beg your pardon?'

'You must weigh about half of what they do and all of 'em went home in wheelbarrows. You drank as much as them and you look fresh as a daisy. What is the trick? Did you get the wizards to magic the beer out of your stomach?'

She had stopped pushing her luck a long time ago. Now it was out of control, like a startled carthorse that can't stop because of the huge load bouncing and rumbling along behind it.

Vetinari frowned. 'My dear lady, anyone drunk enough to let wizards, who themselves had just been partaking copiously of the fruit of the vine, I might add, take anything out of him would already be so drunk as to be dead. To forestall your next comment, the hop is also, technically, a vine. I am, in fact, drunk. Is this not so, Drumknott?'

'You did indeed consume some twelve pints of very strong malted beverage, sir. Technically, you must be drunk.'

'Idiosyncratically put, Drumknott. Thank you.'

'You don't act drunk!'

'No, but I do act sober quite well, don't you think? And I must confess that this morning's crossword was something of a tussle. Procatalepsis and pleonasm in one day? I had to use the dictionary! The woman is a fiend! Nevertheless, thank you for coming, Miss Sugarbean. I recall your grandmother's bubble and squeak with great fondness. If

247

she had been a sculptress, it would have been an exquisite statue, with no arms and an enigmatic smile. It is such a shame that some masterpieces are so transitory.'

The proud cook in Glenda rose unstoppably. 'But she passed the recipe on to me.'

'A legacy better than jewels,' said Vetinari, nodding.

Actually a few jewels would not have gone amiss, Glenda reflected. But there was a secret of Bubble and Squeak, of course, right out there in the open where everyone could miss it. And as for the Truth of Salmagundi . . .

'I believe this audience is at an end, Miss Sugarbean,' said Vetinari. 'I have so much to do and so have you, I am sure.' He picked up his pen and turned his attention to the documents in front of him. 'Goodbye, Miss Sugarbean.'

And that was it. Somehow, she was at the door, and it had almost closed behind her when a voice said, 'And thank you for your kindnesses to Nutt.'

The door clicked shut, nearly hitting her in the face as she spun round.

'Was that a wise thing for me to have said, do you think?' said Vetinari, when she had gone.

'Possibly not, sir, but she will merely assume it is her that we are watching,' said Drumknott smoothly.

'Possibly we should. That's a Sugarbean woman for you, Drumknott, little domestic slaves until they think someone has been wronged and then they go to war like Queen Ynci of Lancre, with chariot wheels spinning and arms and legs all over the place.'

'And no father,' observed Drumknott. 'Not very good for a child in those days.'

'Only served to make her tougher. One can only hope she doesn't take it into her head to enter politics.'

'Is that not what she is doing now, sir?'

'Well noted, Drumknott. Do I *appear* drunk?'

'In my opinion no, sir, but you seem unusually . . . talkative.'

'Coherently?'

'To the minutest scruple, sir. The Postmaster is waiting, sir, and some of the guild leaders want to talk to you urgently.'

'I suspect they want to play football?'

'Yes, sir. They intend to form teams. I cannot for the life of me understand why.'

Vetinari put down his pen. 'Drumknott, if you saw a ball lying invitingly on the ground, would you kick it?'

The secretary's forehead wrinkled. 'How would the invitation be couched, sir?'

'I'm sorry?'

'Would it be, for example, a written note attached to the ball by person or persons unknown?'

'I was rather inclining to the idea that you might perhaps feel simply that the whole world was silently willing you to give said ball a hearty kick?'

'No, sir. There are too many variables. Possibly an enemy or japester might have assumed that I would take some action of the kind and made the ball out of concrete or similar material, in the hope I might do myself a serious or humorous injury. So, I would check first.'

'And then, if all was in order, you would kick the ball?'

'To what purpose or profit, sir?'

'Interesting question. I suppose for the joy of seeing it fly.'

Drumknott seemed to consider this for a while, and then shook his head. 'I am sorry, sir, but you have lost me at this point.'

'Ah, you are a pillar of rock in a world of changes, Drumknott. Well done.'

'I was wondering if I could just add something, sir,' said the secretary solemnly.

'The floor is yours, Drumknott.'

'I would not like it thought that I do not buy my own paperclips, sir. I enjoy owning my own paperclips. It means that they are mine. I thought it helpful I should tell you that in a measured and non-confrontational way.'

Vetinari looked at the ceiling for a few moments and then said: 'Thank you for your frankness. I shall consider the record straightened and the matter closed.'

'Thank you, sir.'

Sator Square was where the city went when it was upset, baffled or fearful. People who had no real idea why they were doing so congregated to listen to other people who also did not know anything, on the basis that ignorance shared is ignorance doubled. There were clusters of people there this morning and several scratch teams, for it is written, or more probably scrawled on a wall somewhere, that wherever two or more are gathered together, at least one will have something to kick. Tin cans and tightly wound balls of rag were annoying adults on all sides, but as Glenda hurried nearer, the big doors of the university opened and Ponder Stibbons stepped out, somewhat inexpertly bouncing one of the wretched new leather balls. *Gloing!* Silence clanged, as rolling cans rattled on unheeded. All eyes were on the wizard and on the ball. He threw it down and there was a double *gloing!* as it bounced off the stones. And then he kicked it. It was a bit wussy as kicks went, that kick, but no one in the square had ever kicked anything even one tenth as far, and every male chased after it, propelled by ancient instinct.

They've won, Glenda thought glumly. A ball that goes *gloing!* when others go *clunk* . . . Well, where's the contest?

She hurried on to the back entrance. In a world that was getting too complicated, where she could barge in on the black-hearted Tyrant and walk out unscathed, she needed a place to go that wasn't spinning. The Night Kitchen was as familiar as her bedroom, *her* place, under *her* control. She could face anything there.

There was a figure lounging against the wall by the rubbish bins, and for some reason she identified it right away, despite the heavy cloak and the hat pulled down over the eyes; no one she had ever met could relax as perfectly as Pepe.

'Wotcher, Glenda,' said a voice from under the hat.

'What are you doing here?' she said.

'Do you know how hard it is to find somebody in this city when you can't tell anyone what they look like and aren't really sure you can remember their name?' said Pepe. 'Where's Jools?'

'I don't know,' she said. 'I haven't seen her since last night.'

'It might be a good idea to find her before other people do,' said Pepe.

'What people?' said Glenda.

Pepe shrugged. '*Everybody*,' he said. 'They're mostly looking in the dwarf districts right now, but it can only be a matter of time. We can't move down at the shop for them and it was all I could do to sneak out.'

'What are they after her for?' said Glenda, panic rising. 'I saw in the paper that people were trying to find her, but she hasn't done anything wrong!'

'I don't think you exactly grasp what's going on,' said the (possible) dwarf. 'They want to find her to ask her a lot of questions.'

'Has this got anything to do with Lord Vetinari?' said Glenda suspiciously.

'I wouldn't have thought so,' said Pepe.

'What sort of questions, then?'

'Oh, you know – What is your favourite colour? What do you like to eat? Are you an item with anybody? What advice do you have for young people today? Do you wax? Where do you get your hair done? What is your favourite spoon?'

'I don't think she's got a favourite spoon,' said Glenda, waiting for the world to make some sense.

Pepe patted her on the shoulder. 'Look, she's on the front page of the paper, isn't she? And the *Times* keeps on at us about wanting to do a lifestyle profile of her. That might not actually be a bad thing, but it's up to you.'

'I don't think she's got a lifestyle,' said Glenda, a little bewildered. 'She's never said. And she doesn't wax. She hardly even dusts. Anyway, just tell them all that she doesn't want to talk to anybody.'

251

Pepe's expression went strange for a moment, then he said with care, like a man, or dwarf, struggling to be heard across a cultural divide, 'Do you think I was talking about furniture?'

'Well, what else? And I don't think her housework is anyone else's business.'

'Don't you understand? She's popular, and the more we tell people they can't talk to her, the more they want to, and the more you say no the more interested they become. People want to know all about her,' said Pepe.

'Like what her favourite spoon is?' said Glenda.

'I might have been a bit ironic,' said Pepe. 'But there's newspaper writers all over the city looking for her and *Bu-bubble* want to do a two-page spread on her.' He paused. 'That means they'll write about her and it'll take two pages,' he volunteered helpfully. 'The Low King of the dwarfs has said that she is an icon for our times, according to *Satblatt*.'

'What's *Satblatt*?' said Glenda.

'Oh, the dwarf newspaper,' said Pepe. 'You'll probably never see it.'

'But she was just in a fashion show!' wailed Glenda. 'She was just walking up and down! I'm sure she doesn't want to get involved in all that sort of thing.'

Pepe gave her a sharp look. 'Are you?' he said.

And then she thought, really thought about Juliet, who would read *Bu-bubble* from cover to cover, wouldn't generally go near the *Times*, but would absorb all kinds of rubbish about frivolous and silly people. People that glittered. 'I don't know where she is,' she said. 'I really haven't seen her since yesterday.'

'Ah, a mystery disappearance,' said Pepe. 'Look, we're already learning about this sort of thing down at the shop. Can we go somewhere a bit more private? I hope none of them followed me up here.'

'Well, I can smuggle you in through the back entrance, as long as there isn't a bledlow around,' said Glenda.

'Fine by me. I'm used to that sort of thing.'

She led him through the doorway and into the maze of cellars and yards that contrasted rather interestingly with the fine frontage of Unseen University.

'Got anything to drink?' said Pepe behind her.

'Water!' snapped Glenda.

'I'll drink water when fish climb out of it to take a piss, but thank you all the same,' said Pepe.

And then Glenda caught the smell of baking coming from the Night Kitchen. She was the only one who *baked* in *her* kitchen! No one else was supposed to bake in *her* kitchen. Baking was her responsibility. Hers. She ran up the steps with Pepe behind her and noted that the mystery cook had yet to master the second most important rule of cooking, which was to tidy things up afterwards. The place was a mess. There were even lumps of dough on the floor. In fact, it looked as though it had been possessed by some kind of frenzy. And in the middle of it all, curled up on Glenda's battered and slightly rancid old armchair, was Juliet.

'Just like *Sleeping Beauty*, ain't it?' said Pepe behind her.

Glenda ignored him and hurried along the rows of ovens. 'She's been baking pies. What on earth did she want to come along and bake pies for? She's never been any good at baking pies.' That's because I've never let her bake a pie, she told herself. *That's because as soon as she found anything difficult you took it away and did it yourself*, her inner voice scolded.

Glenda opened oven door after oven door. They had arrived just in time. By the smell of it, a couple of dozen assorted pies were cooked to a turn.

'How about a drink?' said Pepe, in whom thirst sprang eternal. 'I'm sure there's brandy. Every kitchen has some brandy in it somewhere.'

He watched as Glenda pulled the pies out, using her apron to protect her hands. Pepe regarded the pies with the indifference of a man who likes to drink his meals and listened to Glenda's sotto voce monologue as pie after pie was laid out on the table.

'I never told her to do this. Why did she do this?' Because I did tell her to do this, sort of, that's why. 'And these are not half bad pies,' she said more loudly. In surprise.

Juliet opened her eyes, looked around blearily, and then her face contorted in panic.

'It's okay, I've taken them all out,' said Glenda. 'Well done.'

'I didn't know what else to do and Trev was busy with the footballing and I thought they would be wantin' pies tomorrow and I thought I better do some,' said Juliet. 'Sorry.'

Glenda took a step backwards. How to begin? she wondered. How to unravel it and then ravel it all back up again in a better shape because she had been wrong? Juliet hadn't just walked up and down with clothes on, she had become some kind of a dream. A dream of clothes. Sparkling and alive and tantalizingly possible. And in Glenda's memory of the fashion show, she literally shone, as if being lit from the inside. It was a kind of magic and it shouldn't be making pies. She cleared her throat.

'I've taught you a lot of things, haven't I, Juliet?' said Glenda.

'Yes, Glenda,' said Juliet.

'And they've always been useful, haven't they?'

'Yes, Glenda. I remember it was you that said I should always keep my hand on my ha'penny and I'm very glad that you did.'

There was a strange noise from Pepe, and Glenda, feeling her face go red, didn't dare look at him.

'Then I've got a bit more advice for you, Juliet.'

'Yes, Glenda.'

'First, never, ever apologize for anything that doesn't need apologizing for,' said Glenda. 'And especially never apologize for just being yourself.'

'Yes, Glenda.'

'Got that?'

'Yes, Glenda.'

'No matter what happens, always remember that you now know how to make a good pie.'

'Yes, Glenda.'

'Pepe is here because *Bu-bubble* wants to write something about you,' said Glenda. 'Your picture was in the paper again this morning and—' Glenda stopped. 'She is going to be all right, isn't she?' she said.

Pepe paused in the act of surreptitiously removing a bottle from a cupboard. 'You can trust me and Madame on that,' he said. 'Only people who are very trustworthy would dare to look as untrustworthy as me and Madame.'

'And all she will have to do is show off clothes— Don't drink that, that's cider vinegar!'

'I'm only drinking the cider bit,' said Pepe. 'Yes, all she'll have to do is show off clothes, but to judge from the mob back at the shop there's going to be people who want her to show off shoes, hats, hairstyles . . .'

'No hanky panky,' said Glenda.

'I don't think you'll find, anywhere in the world, a greater expert in both hanky and panky than Madame. In fact, I would be surprised if you, Glenda, knew one hundredth of the hanky and panky that she does, especially as she invented quite a lot of it herself. And since we'll notice it when we see it, we'll keep an eye on her.'

'And she's got to eat proper meals and get a good night's sleep,' said Glenda.

Pepe nodded, although she expected that both those concepts were quite alien to him.

'And paid,' she added.

'We'll cut her in on the profits if she works exclusively for us,' said Pepe. 'Madame wants to talk to you about that.'

'Yes, someone might want to pay her more than you do,' said Glenda.

'My, my, my. How fast we learn. I'm sure Madame will have great fun talking to you.'

Juliet looked from one to the other, sleep still wreathing her face. 'You want me to go back to the shop?'

'I don't want you to do anything,' said Glenda. 'It's up to you, okay? It's just up to you, but it seems to me that if you stay here then basically what you'll be doing is pies.'

'Well, not just pies,' said Juliet.

'Well, no, fair enough, there are also flans, bubble and squeak and assorted late-night dainties,' said Glenda. 'But you know what I mean. On the other hand, you could go and show off all these fancy clothes and go to lots of fancy places a long, long way from here and see a lot of new people and you'd know that if it all goes pear-shaped you could always make it pie-shaped.'

'Hah, nice one,' said Pepe, who'd found another bottle.

'I really would like to go,' said Juliet.

'Then go *now*. I mean right *now*, or at least as soon as he's finished drinking the ketchup.'

'But I'll have to go back for my stuff!'

Glenda reached down inside her vest and pulled out a burgundy-coloured booklet with the seal of Ankh-Morpork on it.

'What's that?' said Juliet.

'Your bank book. Your money's safe in the bank and you can take it out any time you want.'

Juliet turned the bank book over and over in her hands. 'I don't fink anyone in my family's ever been in a bank except for Uncle Geoffrey and they caught up with 'im even before he got home.'

'Keep quiet about it. Don't go home. Buy yourself lots of new stuff. Get yourself sorted out and then go back and see your dad and everybody when you have. The point is, even if you don't go right away, in your mind you should always be going. But the important thing is to go right now. Move out. Get on. Climb up. All the things I should have done.'

'What about Trev?' said Juliet.

Glenda had to think about that. 'How are things with you and Trev, then? I saw you two talking last night.'

'Talking is allowed,' said Juliet defensively. 'Anyhow, he was only telling me how he was going to get himself a better job.'

'Doing what?' said Glenda. 'I've never seen him doing a straight day's work in all the years I've known him.'

'He says he's going to find something,' said Juliet. 'He said Nutt told 'im to. He said Nutt said that when Trev finds out who Trev is, like, he will, like, know what he can do. So I told 'im he was Trevor Likely, and he said that was, you know, helpful.'

I'm stuck, aren't I? Glenda told herself. I'm talking about changing and getting out, so I have to allow that maybe he's going to, too. Aloud, she said, 'It's up to you. It's all up to you, but just mind that he keeps his hands to himself.'

'He always keeps his hands to himself,' said Juliet. 'It's a bit worryin'. I've never had to think about kneeing him in the tonker, not once.'

There was a strangled laugh from Pepe, who had just discovered the wow-wow sauce. The bottle was almost empty and, in theory, he should have no stomach left.

'Never, ever?' said Glenda, mystified at this unnatural history.

'No, he's always very polite and just a bit sad.'

That must mean he's planning something, Glenda's inner self provided. She said, 'Well, it's up to you. I can't help here, but remember, you've always got your knee.'

'And what about . . . ?' Juliet began.

'Look,' said Glenda firmly, 'either you go off now and see the world and earn lots of money and get your picture in the papers and all of the other things I know you would really like to do, or you have to sort it out for yourself.'

'We're going to be here for some time,' said Pepe. 'You know, this sauce would be nice with a little bit of vodka in it. It really would give it a little bit of zest. A little bit of sparkle. Come to think of it, a lot of vodka would be even better.'

'But I love 'im!' Juliet wailed.

'That's all right, then, stay here,' said Glenda. 'Have you even kissed?'

'No! He never quite gets round to it.'

'Perhaps he's one of those gentlemen who don't like the ladies,' said Pepe primly.

'And we could really do without your input,' snapped Glenda, turning on him.

'I mean, for some of the others, like Rotten Johnny, I nearly wear my knee out, but Trev's just . . . sweet, all the time.'

'Look, I know you told me to keep out of this, and I know I've been a terrible sinner in my time and hope to remain so, but I have been around the houses more times than a postman and the reason for this imp ass is obvious,' Pepe volunteered. 'He's got the nous to see that she's so beautiful that she should be painted standing on some shell somewhere without her vest on and little fat pink babies inexplicably zooming around all over the place and he's some kid with nothing more than a bit of street smarts. I mean, it's pointless, isn't it? He's not going to stand a chance and he knows it, even if he doesn't know he knows it.'

'I'd give him a kiss if he wanted one and would definitely not knee him in the tonker,' said Juliet.

'You have to sort it out,' said Glenda. 'I can't sort it out for you. If I tried, it would get sorted out all wrong.'

'But—' Juliet began.

'No, that's it,' said Glenda. 'Off you go, buy yourself lots of nice stuff – it's your money. And if you don't look after her, Mister Pepe, a knee would only be the start.'

Pepe nodded and very gently tugged Juliet away and down the stone steps.

Now what would I do at this point if I were in a romantic novel? Glenda said to herself as the footsteps died away. Her reading had left her pretty much an expert on what to do if you were in a romantic novel, although one of the things that really annoyed her about romantic novels, as she had confided to Mr Wobble, was that no one did any cooking in them. After all, cooking was important. Would it hurt to have a pie-making sequence? Would a novel called *Pride and Buns* be totally out of the question? Even a few tips on how to make fairy cakes would help, and be pretty much in period as well. She'd be a little happier if, even, the lovers could be thrown into the mixing bowl of life. At least it would be some acknowledgement that people actually ate food.

Around about now she knew, and knew all through her body, that she should be dissolving into a flood of tears. She started cleaning up the floor. Then she cleaned up the ovens. She always left them sparkling, but that was no reason not to clean them again. She used an old toothbrush to ease minute amounts of dirt from odd corners, scoured every pot with fine sand, emptied the grates, riddled the cinders, swept the floor, tied two brooms together to dislodge the spider's webs of years from the high wall, and scrubbed again until the soapy water poured down the stone stairs and washed away the footprints.

Oh, yes – and one other thing. There were some anchovies on the freezing slab. She warmed up a couple and went to the large three-legged cauldron in the corner of the kitchen where last night she had chalked the words 'Do Not Touch'. She took off the lid and peered into its depths. The crab that Verity Pushpram had given her last night, which seemed a very long time ago now, waved its eyeballs at her.

'I wonder what would have happened if I had left the lid off?' she said. 'I wonder how fast crabs learn?'

She dropped in the soggy anchovies, which seemed to meet with crabby approval. With that done, she stood in the middle of the kitchen and looked for something else to clean. The black iron would never shine, but every surface had been scrubbed and dried. As for the plates, you could eat your dinner off them. If you wanted a job done properly, you had to do it yourself. Juliet's version of cleanliness was next to godliness, which was to say it was erratic, past all understanding and was seldom seen.

Something brushed against her face. She absent-mindedly swiped at it and found her fingers holding a black feather. Those wretched things in the pipes. Someone ought to do something about them. She took her longest broom and banged on a pipe. 'Go on! Get out of there!' she yelled. There was a scuffling in the darkness and a faint 'Awk! Awk!'

''scuse me, miss,' said a voice, and she looked down the steps into the misshapen face of . . . What was his name? Oh, yes. 'Good morning, Mister Concrete,' she said to the troll. She couldn't help but notice the brown stains coming from his nose.

'Can't find Mister Trev,' Concrete stated.

'Haven't seen him all morning,' said Glenda.

'Can't find Mister Trev,' the troll repeated, louder.

'Why do you need him?' said Glenda. As far as she knew, the vats just

259

about ran themselves. You told Concrete to dribble candles and he dribbled candles until he'd run out of candles.

'Mister Nutt sick,' said Concrete. 'Can't find Mister Trev.'

'Take me to Mister Nutt right now!' said Glenda.

It's a bit harsh to call anybody a denizen, but the people who lived and worked in the candle vats fitted the word to a T. The vats were, in fact, their den. If you ever saw them anywhere in the underground maze, they were always scuttling very fast, but most of the time they just worked and slept and stayed alive. Nutt was lying on an old mattress with his arms wrapped tightly around himself. Glenda took one look and turned to the troll. 'Go and find Mister Trev,' she said.

'Can't find Mister Trev,' said the troll.

'Keep on looking!' She knelt down beside Nutt. His eyes had rolled back inside his head. 'Mister Nutt, can you hear me?'

He seemed to wake. 'You must go away,' he said. 'It will be very dangerous. The door will open.'

'What door is that?' she said, trying to remain cheerful. She looked at the denizens, who were watching her with a kind of meek horror. 'Can't one of you find something to put over him?' The mere question sent them scurrying in panic.

'I have seen the door, so it will open again,' said Nutt.

'I can't see any door, Mister Nutt,' said Glenda, looking around.

Nutt's eyes opened wide. 'It's in my head.'

There was no privacy to the vats; it was just a wider room off the long, endless corridor. People went past all the time.

'I think you may have been overdoing it, Mister Nutt,' said Glenda. 'You rush around working all hours, worrying yourself sick. You need a rest.' To her surprise, one of the denizens turned up holding a blanket, quite large parts of which were still flexible. She put it over him just as Trev arrived. He had no choice about arriving as Concrete was dragging him by the collar. He looked down at Nutt and then up at Glenda. 'What's happened to him?'

'I don't know.' She raised a finger to her head and swivelled it a little, the universal symbol for 'gone nuts'.

'You must go away. Things will be very dangerous,' Nutt moaned.

'Please tell us what is going on,' said Glenda. 'Please tell me.'

'I can't,' said Nutt. 'I cannot say the words.'

'There are words you want to say?' said Trev.

'Words that don't want to be said. Strong words.'

'Can't we help?' Glenda persevered.

'Are you sick?' said Trev.

'No, Mister Trev. I passed an adequate bowel motion this morning.' That was a flash of the old Nutt – precise, but slightly odd.

'Sick in the head?' said Glenda. That came out of desperation.

'Yes. In the head,' said Nutt. 'Shadows. Doors. Can't tell you.'

'Is there anyone who can cure that kind of sickness?'

Nutt didn't answer for a while and then said, 'Yes. You must find me a philosopher trained in Uberwald. They will help the thoughts come straight.'

'Isn't that what you did for Trev?' said Glenda. 'You told him what he was thinking about his dad and everything, and that made him a lot happier, didn't it, Trev?'

'Yes, it did,' said Trev. 'And there's no need to elbow me in the ribs like that. It really did help. Couldn't you be hypnotized?' he said to Nutt. 'I saw a man in the music hall once and he just waved his shiny watch at them and it's amazing the kind of things they did. Barked like dogs, even.'

'Yes. Hypnosis is an important part of the philosophy,' said Nutt. 'It helps to relax the patient so that the thoughts get a chance to be heard.'

'Well, there you are, then,' said Glenda. 'Why not try doing it on yourself? I'm sure I could find something shiny for you to wave.'

Trev pulled his beloved tin can out of his pocket. 'Tra-la. And I think I've got a piece of string here somewhere.'

'That is all very well, but I would not be able to ask myself the right kinds of questions because I will have been hypnotized. How the questions are posed is very important,' said Nutt.

'I know what,' said Trev. 'I'll tell you to ask yourself to ask the right questions. You'd know what questions to ask if it was someone else, wouldn't you?'

'Yes, Mister Trev.'

'You didn't need to hypnotize Trev,' Glenda pointed out.

'No, but his thoughts were close to the surface. I fear that mine will not be so easy to access.'

'Can you really be hypnotized to ask yourself the right questions?'

'In *The Doors of Deception*, Fussbinder did report on a way of hypnotizing himself,' said Nutt. 'It is conceivably possible . . .' His voice trailed off.

'Then let's get on with it,' said Trev. 'Better out than in, as my old granny used to say.'

'I think perhaps that it is not such a good idea.'

'Didn't do me any harm,' said Trev robustly.

'The things that I do not know . . . The things that I do not know . . .' muttered Nutt.

'What about them?' said Glenda.

'The things that I do not know . . .' said Nutt, 'I think are behind the door, because I think I put them there because I think I do not want to know them.'

'So you must know what it is you don't want to know?' said Glenda.

'Yes.'

'Well, how bad could it be?' said Trev.

'Perhaps it is very bad,' said Nutt.

'What would you say if it was me?' said Glenda. 'I want the truth, now.'

'Well,' said Nutt, stuttering slightly, 'I think I would say that you should look behind the door to face the things that you do not want to know so we may confront them together. That would certainly be the advice of Von Kladpoll in *Doppelte Berührungssempfindung*. Indeed, doing so would almost be a fundamental part of the analysis of the hidden mind.'

'Well then,' said Glenda, standing back.

'But what sort of bad things could possibly be in your head, Miss Glenda?' said Nutt, managing gallantry even in the fetid circumstances of the vats.

'Oh, there's a few,' said Glenda. 'You don't go through life without picking up a few.'

'I've had dreams in the night,' said Nutt.

'Oh, well, everyone has bad dreams,' said Glenda.

'These were more than dreams,' said Nutt. He unfolded his arms and held up a hand.

Trev whistled.

Glenda said, 'Oh,' and then, 'Should they be like that?'

'I have no idea,' said Nutt.

'Do they hurt?'

'No.'

'Well, maybe that sort of thing 'appens when goblins get a bit older,' said Trev.

'Yes, perhaps they need claws,' said Glenda.

'Yesterday was wonderful,' said Nutt. 'I was part of the team. The team were around me. I was happy. And now . . .'

Trev held up a piece of grubby string and the battered but shiny tin can. 'Perhaps you *should* find out?'

'I might be getting all this wrong,' said Glenda, 'but if you don't want to know what the things are that you don't want to know, then that means that there are going to be even more things that you don't want to know and I imagine that sooner or later, if that goes on, your head will cave in around the hole.'

'There is something in what both of you say,' said Nutt reluctantly.

'Then give me a hand to put him on the couch,' said Trev. 'Should he be covered in sweat like that?'

'I don't think so,' said Glenda.

'I would be happier if you chained me down,' said Nutt.

'What? Why do you think we should do that?' said Glenda.

'I think you should beware. Some things leak around the door. They may be bad.'

263

Glenda looked at the claws. They were a shiny black and, in their way, quite neat, but it was hard to imagine them being used for, say, painting a picture or cooking an omelette. They were claws, and claws were for clawing, weren't they? But this was Mr Nutt. Even with claws it was still Mr Nutt.

'Shall we get started?' said Trev.

'I insist on the chains,' said Nutt. 'There are all sorts of metal things in the old storeroom four doors down. I saw chains there. Please hurry.'

Automatically Glenda looked down at the claws and saw they had grown longer. 'Yes, Trev, please hurry.'

Trev followed her gaze and said brightly, 'I'll be back before you know I've gone.'

In fact, it was less than a couple of minutes, and she could hear the clanking as he dragged them all the way down the passageway.

Glenda was fighting tears at the simple strangeness of the whole business. Nutt lay there, looking at the ceiling, as they lifted him on to the couch and carefully wrapped the chains around him.

'There's padlocks, but there's no keys. I can close them, but I can't open them.'

'Close them,' said Nutt.

Glenda had very seldom cried, and she was trying not to now. 'I don't think we should be doing this,' she said. 'Not here in the vats. People are watching.'

'Please swing your pendulum, Mister Trev,' said Nutt.

Trev shrugged and did so.

'Now you have to start telling me that I am feeling sleepy, Mister Trev,' said Nutt.

Trev cleared his throat and swung the shiny can back and forth. 'You are definitely feelin' sleepy. Extremely sleepy.'

'That is good. I am feeling enormously sleepy,' said Nutt wearily. 'And now you must ask me to analyse myself.'

'What does that mean?' said Glenda sharply, always on the lookout for dangerous words.

'I'm sorry,' said Nutt. 'I mean, help me examine in detail the

264

workings of my own mind by means of question and answer.'

'But I don't know the questions to ask,' said Trev.

'I do,' said Nutt patiently, 'but you must instruct me to do it.'

Trev shrugged. 'Mister Nutt, you must find out what is wrong with Mister Nutt,' he said.

'Ah yes,' said Nutt, his tone of voice changing slightly. 'Are ve comfortable, Mister Nutt? Yes, thank you. The chains hardly chafe at all. Verrry good. Now, tell me about your mother, Mister Nutt. I am familiar with the concept, but I never had a mother as I recall. Thank you for asking anyway,' said Nutt.

And so the monological dialogue began. The other two sat on the stone steps as the quiet voice unravelled itself until: 'Ah yes, ze library. Is zere something in ze library, Mister Nutt?'

'There are many books in the library.'

'What else is in ze library, Mister Nutt?'

'There are many chairs and ladders in the library.'

'And what is in ze library zat you do not want to tell me about, Mister Nutt?'

They waited. At last, the voice said, 'There's a cupboard in the library.'

'Is zere anything special about zis cupboard, Mister Nutt?'

Another pause, another faint little voice: 'I must not open the cupboard.'

'Why is half of him talking like someone from Uberwald?' said Glenda to Trev, forgetting the notoriously acute sense of hearing.

'Questions asked in a mild Uberwaldian accent in examinations of zis nature appear to put ze patient more at ease,' said Nutt. 'And now I would be pleased if you would not make wiz ze interruptions.'

'Sorry,' said Glenda.

'Don't mention it. So, why must you not open ze cupboard, Mister Nutt?'

'Because I promised Ladyship that I would not open the cupboard.'

'And did you open ze cupboard, Mister Nutt?'

'I promised Ladyship that I would not open the cupboard.'

'And did you open ze cupboard, Mister Nutt?'

A much longer pause this time. 'I promised Ladyship that I would not open the cupboard.'

'Did you learn many things in ze castle, Mister Nutt?'

'Many things.'

'Did you learn how to make ze lockpicks, Mister Nutt?'

'Yes.'

'Where is ze door now, Mister Nutt?'

'It is in front of me.'

'You opened ze door, Mister Nutt. You think you did not, but you did. And now it is very important zat you open ze door again.'

'But what is inside the door is wrong!'

The two eavesdroppers craned to hear.

'Nothing is wronk. Nothing is wronk at all. In ze past, you opened ze door in the foolishness of chilthood. Now, to understand ze door, you must open it with ze wisdom of ze adult. Open ze door, Mister Nutt, and I will walk with you to it.'

'But I no longer have the lockpick.'

'Nature will provide, Mister Nutt.'

Glenda shivered. It had to be her imagination, but they didn't seem to be in the candle vats any more.

A corridor stretched in front of Nutt. He felt everything drop away from him. Chains, clothes, flesh, thoughts. All there was was the corridor and, drifting gently towards him, the cupboard. It was glass-fronted. Light glinted off the bevelled edges. He raised a hand and extended the claw. It cut through wood and glass as if they were air. There was one shelf in the cupboard and one book on the shelf. There was a title on it in silver and chains around it in steel. These were much easier to break through than last time as well. He sat down on a chair that had not been there until he sat down and he began to read the book. The book was called *ORC*.

When the scream came, it didn't come from Nutt, but from overhead in the tangle of pipes. A skinny woman in a long black robe, perhaps a witch, Glenda thought, shocked by the suddenness, dropped down on to the flagstones and looked around like a cat.

No, more like a bird, Glenda thought. Jerky.

And then it opened its mouth and screamed: 'Awk! Awk! Danger! Danger! Beware! Beware!' It made a lunge towards the couch, but Trev stepped in the way. 'Foolish! The orc will eat your eyes!'

And now this was a duet, because another of the creatures had slid down out of the gloom on what might have been a billowing cloak, or might have been wings. They never stopped moving, each in a different direction, trying to get closer to the couch.

'Do not be afraaaid,' squawked one of them, 'we are on your siiide. We are here to protect you.'

Glenda, trembling in shock, managed to stand up. She folded her arms. She always felt better like that. 'Who do you think you are – dropping out of the ceiling and shouting at people? And you're shedding feathers. That's disgusting. This is a— this is quite near a food-preparation area.'

'Yeah, push off,' said Trev.

'That's telling them,' said Glenda out of the corner of her mouth. 'I bet that took a lot of thinking.'

'You do not understand,' said a creature. The faces really were strange, as if someone had made a bird out of a woman. 'You are in great danger! Awk!'

'From you?' said Glenda.

'From the orc,' said the creature. And the word was a scream. 'Awk!'

In the shadows in front of the open cupboard the soul of Nutt turned a page. He felt someone at his elbow and looked up into the face of Ladyship.

'Why did you tell me not to open the book, Ladyship?'

'Because I wanted you to read it,' said her voice. 'You had to find the truth for yourself. That is how we all find the truth.'

'And if the truth is terrible?'

'I think you know the answer to that one, Nutt,' said the voice of Ladyship.

'The answer is that, terrible or not, it is still the truth,' said Nutt.

'And then?' said her voice, like a teacher encouraging a promising pupil.

'And then the truth can be changed,' said Nutt.

'Mister Nutt is a goblin,' said Trev.

'Yeah, right,' said the creature. And the phrase seemed incredibly exotic for someone whose face was looking more birdlike all the time.

'If I scream, a lot of people will come running,' said Glenda.

'And what will they do?' said the creature.

And what would they do? Glenda thought. They would stand around saying 'What's all this then?' and asking all the same questions we are. She shuffled again as one of the things tried to get to the couch.

'The orc will kill,' said a third voice, and another of the things dropped down almost in front of Glenda's face. Its breath was like carrion.

'Mister Nutt is kind and gentle and has never hurt anyone,' said Glenda.

'Who didn't deserve it,' said Trev hurriedly.

'But now the orc knows it is an orc,' said a creature. And now they were milling backwards and forwards in a ghastly pavane.

'I don't think you're allowed to touch us,' said Trev. 'I really don't think you can touch us.'

He sat down suddenly beside the recumbent Nutt and dragged Glenda down next to him. 'I think you 'ave to obey rules,' said Trev. The moving figures stopped instantly. That was somehow creepier than their movement. They stood there as frozen as statues.

'They've got talons,' said Glenda, quietly. 'I can see their talons.'

'Pounces,' said Trev.

'What're you talking about?'

'Those big claws are called pounces. The ones at the back are called talons – the ones they carry the prey off with. Everyone gets that wrong.'

'Except you,' said Glenda. 'You're like the big expert on horrible bird-like creatures all of a sudden.'

'I can't help it. Sometimes you just pick stuff up,' said Trev.

'We must protect you,' said one of the females.

'We don't need protecting from Mister Nutt! He's our friend,' said Glenda.

'And how many of your friends have claws?'

'What have we got to worry about here, in Unseen University, which has got great big thick walls and is pretty much generally crawling with wizards?'

One of the women stretched her neck until her face was a few inches from Trev's. 'There is an orc in here with you.'

There was a clink of chain. Nutt had moved slightly.

'You work for somebody, don't you?' said Trev. 'You've got tiny little heads. You can't 'ave enough brains to think this up for yourself. Do the wizards know you're here?'

Glenda screamed. She had never screamed before, not in a proper way, straight up from the bottom of her terror. Cutting her finger while using the knife carelessly didn't count and almost certainly would never have been so loud. The scream echoed along the passages, bounced into the cellars and made the undercrofts ring.*

Glenda screamed a second time and, as her lungs had got into practice, she managed to make this one even louder. There were hurrying footsteps from both directions.

That was reassuring.

She was not certain how reassuring was the little clink and sliding of metal that suggested a chain had broken.

The creatures went into an instant panic, trying to take wing at once. They were as clumsy as herons and got in one another's way.

'And don't come back!' she yelled as they disappeared back into the dark. Then she turned to Trev, her heart thumping, and said, 'What *is* an orc?'

---

* Contrary to popular belief and hope, people don't usually come running when they hear a scream. That's not how humans work. Humans look at other humans and say, 'Did you hear a scream?' because the first scream might just have been you screaming inside your head, or a horse backfiring.

'I dunno. I think it's some kind of old bogey man,' said Trev.

'And what were those things?'

'I know it sounds silly,' said Trev, 'but we saw one of them the other night, and he seems to think they're, like . . . friends.'

Butchers, bakers, butlers and bledlows came hurrying out of the dark corridors and one of them was Bledlow Nobbs (no relation), who was inexplicably wearing just his official hat, a string vest and a pair of shorts, far too short and far too tight for a man the size of Bledlow Nobbs (no relation).

He looked at Glenda and then glared at Trev. People like Trev were, as far as Bledlow Nobbs (no relation) was concerned, an automatic enemy. 'Did you scream? What's been going on?' he said.

'I'm sorry, I made an improper suggestion,' Trev said. He looked at Glenda, his expression saying, 'Help me out here.'

'I'm afraid I let my girlish modesty get the better of me,' she said, cursing him with her eyes.

'It must have been a pretty strange suggestion,' said a baker, who seemed to think that an extremely long loaf would have been a suitable aid to combat, but he was grinning – and grinning was good.

If this ends up with no more than sniggering and grinning then we'll all be happy, Glenda thought. Hard to live down afterwards, but still good.

'But what's that bloke chained to that bed for?' said the bledlow.

'Yeah, what kind of improper suggestions go on around here?' said the baker. He really was having fun.

I am going to kill someone before the end of all this and it might just have to be myself, thought Glenda.

'Isn't that Mister Nutt?' said the bledlow. 'We're supposed to be in training in five minutes.'

There was another clink behind Glenda and Nutt's voice said, 'Don't worry, Alphonse, I often do this trick. Dynamic tension you know, helps build up the muscles.'

'Alphonse?' said the baker, looking incredulously at the bledlow. 'I thought your name was Alfred, Alf for short. Alphonse is a Quirmian name if ever I've heard one. You're not from there, are you?' That was an accusation as much as a question.

'What's wrong with Alf being short for Alphonse?' said the bledlow. He had very large hands that might have troubled even Mustrum Ridcully in a game of pat-a-cake. Also, his ears were going red, never a good sign in a man of his size.

'Oh, I never said it wasn't a nice name,' said the baker, belatedly using his loaf. 'But I would never have figured you for an Alphonse. It just goes to show that you never can tell.'

'I am an orc,' said Nutt quietly.

'Actually, Alphonse is quite a nice name,' the baker went on. 'The phonse spoils it a bit, but the Alf I quite like.' He paused and turned to Nutt. 'What do you mean, "orc"?'

'An orc,' said Nutt again.

And away in the distant central heating pipes there was a scream of 'Awk! Awk!'

'Don't be daft, there's no such thing as orcs any more. They all got killed off hundreds of years ago. Bloody hard to kill, too, I read somewhere,' said a butler.

'In the latter part of your statement you are substantially correct,' said Nutt, still chained to the couch. 'However, nevertheless, I am an orc.'

Glenda looked down. 'You told me you're a goblin, Mister Nutt. You told me you're a goblin.'

'I was misinformed,' said Nutt. 'I *know* I am an orc. I think I have always known that I am an orc. I have opened the door and read the book and I know the truth of my soul and I am an orc, and for some reason I am an orc with a terrible urge to smoke a cigar.'

'But they were like these big horrible monsters that wouldn't stop fighting and were quite happy to tear off their own arm to use as a weapon,' said Bledlow Nobbs (no relation). 'There was an article about them in *Bows & Ammo*.'

Every eye turned to Nutt's arms. 'Certainly that is the judgement of history,' said Nutt. He looked up at Glenda. 'I am so sorry,' he said. 'I disobeyed, everybody does it, you see. Schnouzentintle says as much in his book *The Obedience of Disobedience*. So I wondered what was in the cupboard. And I already had some expertise with lockpicks. I opened the cupboard, I read the book and . . .' His chains clinked as he shifted position. 'I disobeyed. I think everybody does it. We are very good at hiding from ourselves what we do not want to know. Believe me; I was very good at keeping that from myself. But it leaks out, you see, in dreams and things when you have dropped your guard. I *am* an orc. There is no doubt about that.'

'Okay, right, if you are an orc, right, then why are you not tearing my head off?' said Bledlow Nobbs (no relation).

'Would you like me to?' said Nutt.

'Well, as it happens, no!'

'Who cares?' said Trev. 'It's all ancient history anyway. These days you see vampires hangin' around all over the place. An' we've got trolls and golems and zombies and all kinds of people just graftin' away. Who cares what 'appened 'undreds of years ago?'

'Hang on a minute. Hang on a minute,' said the butler. 'He's not tearing your head off 'cos he's chained down.'

'So, why did you get us to chain you down?' said Glenda.

'So I wouldn't tear off anybody's head. I suspected the truth, although I didn't know what it was that I suspected. At least, I think it works like that.'

'So that means you can't escape and tear us all limb from limb,' said Bledlow Nobbs (no relation). 'No offence meant, but does this mean you won't be training us?'

'I am sorry,' said Nutt, 'but as you can see, I'm rather inconvenienced.'

'Have you all gone loony?' Astonishingly, this came from Juliet, standing in the corridor. 'He's Nutt. He potters around making candles and stuff. I see 'im around all the time and 'e's never 'olding someone else's leg *or* head. And 'e likes his football, too!'

Glenda thought she could actually hear Trev's heartbeat. She hurried over to the girl. 'I told you to go,' she hissed.

'I've come back to tell Trev about everythin'. After all, he did write such a lovely poem.'

'She's got a point,' said a man in a butcher's apron. 'I've seen him running around everywhere and I've never seen him carrying any limbs.'

'That's true,' said the baker. 'And anyway, didn't he do all those lovely candles at the banquet last night? That doesn't sound very orc-like to me.'

'And,' said Bledlow Nobbs (no relation), 'he was training us yesterday and he never once said, "Get in there, lads, and tear their 'eads off".'

'Oh, yes,' said the butler, who was making no friends as far as Glenda was concerned. 'Humans don't tear off heads, not like orcs.'

An 'Awk! Awk!' echoed in the distance.

'He's been teaching us kinds of stuff you'd never think about,' said the bledlow, 'like playing the game with a blindfold on. Amazing stuff. More like filosopy than football, but damn good stuff.'

'Tactical thinking and combat analysis is part of the orc make-up,' said Nutt.

'See! No one who uses make-up is going to tear your head off, right?'

'Didn't you meet my ex-wife?' said the baker.

'Well, I'd draw the line if you wore make-up,' said the butcher to general amusement. 'Being an orc is one thing, but we don't want a funny one.'

Glenda looked down at Nutt. He was crying.

'My friends, I thank you for your trust in me,' he said.

'Well, you know, you're like part of the team,' said Bledlow Nobbs (no relation), whose smile almost managed to conceal his nervousness.

'Thank you, Mister Nobbs, that means a lot to me,' said Nutt, standing up.

That was quite a complex movement.

It stayed in Glenda's mind for ever afterwards as a kind of slow-motion scene of bursting chains and cracking wood when Nutt stood up as though he had been restrained by cobwebs. Pieces of chain spun off and hit the wall. Padlocks broke. As for the couch, barely one piece remained attached to another. It dropped to the floor as so much firewood.

'RUN FOR IT, LADS!'

You would have needed some kind of special micrometer to work out which man said it first, but the stampede along the corridor was swift and over very quickly.

'You know,' said Trev, after a few moments' silence, 'at one point I thought this was all goin' very well.'

'Those women,' said Glenda, 'what were they?'

Nutt stood forlornly in the wreckage; a length of chain slithered off him like a serpent and landed on the flagstones. 'Them?' he said. 'They are the Little Sisters of Perpetual Velocity. They come from Ephebe. I think the name for their species is Furies. I think Ladyship sent them in case I tried to hurt anybody.' The words came out without emphasis or emotion.

'But you haven't hurt anyone,' said Glenda.

'But they ran away,' said Nutt, 'because of what I am.'

'Well, you know, they're ordinary people,' said Glenda. 'They're—'

'Twits,' said Trev.

Nutt turned and walked down the opposite corridor, kicking off the remnants of wood and chain. 'But the world is *full* of ordinary people.'

'You can't just let 'im go like that,' said Juliet. 'You just can't. Look at 'im! 'e looks like 'e's been kicked.'

'I'm 'is boss, that's my job,' said Trev.

Glenda caught Trev by the arm. 'No, I'll sort this out. Now, you listen to me, Trev Likely, under all that gab, you're a decent sort, so I'll tell you this: see Juliet over there? You know her, she works in the kitchens. You wrote her a lovely poem, *didn't you*? Ever heard of Emberella? Everyone's heard of Emberella. Well, you might not be my first choice for Prince Charming, but there's probably plenty worse.'

'What the hell are you talkin' about?' said Trev.

'Juliet's going to be leaving soon, isn't that right, Jools?'

Juliet's face was a picture. 'Well, er—'

'And that's because she's been that girl in the papers.'

'What, the shiny dwarf one? With a beard?'

'That's her!' said Glenda. 'She's going to go off with the circus, well, you know what I mean. With the fashion show, at least.'

'But she hasn't got a beard,' said Trev.

Blushing, Juliet delved into her apron and to Glenda's surprise produced the beard. 'They let me keep it,' she said, with a nervous giggle.

'*Right*,' said Glenda. 'You say you love him. Trev, I don't know whether you love her or not, time to make up your mind. You're both grown up, well, strictly speaking, and so you better sort yourselves out, 'cos I don't see any fairy godmothers around. As for Mister Nutt, he hasn't got *anyone*.'

'She's gonna leave the city?' said Trev, realization dawning slowly through a male mind.

'Oh, yes. For quite a long time, I suspect,' said Glenda.

She watched his face carefully. You haven't got much learning and you haven't opened a book in your life, Trevor Likely, but you are smart and you must know there is a wrong way and a right way to reply to what I have just told you.

She watched the high-speed changes around his eyes as he thought, and then he said, 'Well, that's nice. It's the kind of thing she's always dreamed of. I'm very happy for her.'

You cunning bastard, you actually got it right, Glenda thought. You're not appearing to be thinking about yourself at all, 'cos you know I'd have no time for you if you were. And who knows, you might just be genuine. In fact, heavens help me, I think you are, but I'd pull all my own teeth out rather than tell you.

'She likes you, you like her and I've made a lot of silly mistakes. The two of you, sort out what you want to do. And now, if I were you I'd run, before anyone else beats you to it. And can I offer you a word of advice, Trev? Don't be smart, be clever.'

Trev took Glenda by the shoulders and kissed her on both cheeks. 'Was that smart *or* clever?'

'Get away with you, Trev Likely!' she said, pushing him away, in the hope that he wouldn't notice her blush. 'And now I'm going to see where Mister Nutt has gone.'

'I know where he's gone,' said Trev.

'I thought I just told you two to go off and live happily ever after,' said Glenda.

'You won't find 'im without me,' said Trev. 'I'm sorry, Glenda, but we like him too.'

'Do you think we should tell somebody?' said Juliet.

'And what will they do?' Glenda snapped. 'It'll just be like that lot back there. All hanging around in the hope that somebody will come up with an idea. Anyway,' she added, 'I'm sure the wizards upstairs know all about him. Oh yes, I bet they do.'

She had to admit, ten minutes later, that Trev had been right. She probably wouldn't have noticed the door on the other side of another cluttered, abandoned cellar. Light shone from under the door.

'I followed 'im once,' said Trev. 'Everyone should have a place to call their own.'

'Yes,' said Glenda, and she pushed open the door. She might as well have opened an oven. There were candles of every size and every colour and many of them were burning.

And in the middle of it was Nutt, sitting behind a ramshackle table, which was covered with candles. In front of him they burned in every colour. He was staring at them with a blank expression, and did not look up as they approached. 'You know, I fear that I will never really get the hang of blue,' he said, as if to the air. 'Orange, of course, is ridiculously easy and red goes without saying and green is not difficult at all, but the best blue I could achieve, I have to admit, is very largely green . . .' His voice trailed off.

'Are you all right?' said Glenda.

'Do you mean, am I all right apart from being an orc?' said Nutt, with a very small smile.

'Well, yes, but that's not really your fault.'

'It can't really be true, can it?' said Trev.

Glenda turned on him.

'What good is it saying that?' she said.

'Well, they were supposed to have died out hundreds of years ago.'

'Annihilated,' said Nutt. 'But some survived. I fear that when this oversight is revealed, there will be those who will endeavour to rectify the situation.'

Trev looked blankly at Glenda. 'He means he thinks they're going to try to kill him,' she said.

Nutt stared at his candles. 'I must accumulate worth. I must be helpful. I must be friendly. I must make friends.'

'If anyone comes to hurt you,' said Glenda, 'I will kill them. I'm sure you won't try to pull a leg off, but I might. Trev, this needs a woman's touch.'

'Yes, I can see that.'

'That wasn't clever, Trev Likely. No, Mister Nutt, you stay there,' said Glenda, dragging Trev and Juliet back out into the corridor. 'Off you go, I want to talk to him alone.'

Nutt hung his head as she stepped back in. 'I'm sorry I'm spoiling it for everyone,' he said.

'What's happened to your claws, Mister Nutt?'

He stretched out his arm and with a faint noise the claws extended.

'Oh, well, that's convenient,' said Glenda. 'At least that means you can change your shirt.'

She thumped the table so the candles jumped. 'And now, get up!' she screamed. 'You are supposed to be training the team, Mister Nutt, don't you remember? You're supposed to be going out there and showing them how to play the football!'

'I must accumulate worth,' said Nutt, staring at the candles.

'Then train the team, Mister Nutt! How can you be so certain that the orcs were that bad in any case?'

'We did terrible things.'

'They,' said Glenda. 'They, not we, not you. And one thing I am certain of is that in a war no one is going to say that the other side is made up of very nice people. Now, how about you just run along to training? How hard can it be?'

'You saw what happened,' said Nutt. 'It could be very bad indeed.' He picked up a nearly blue candle. 'I must think.'

'Okay,' said Glenda.

She shut the door carefully behind her, walked a little way along the corridor and looked up at the dripping pipes. 'I know someone is listening. I could hear the creaking pipes. Come out right now.'

There was no reply. She shrugged and then hurried along the labyrinth until she reached the steps to the Library, ran up them and headed for the Librarian's desk.

As she approached it, his big grinning face appeared above it.

'I want—' she began.

The Librarian rose slowly, put a finger to his lips and placed a book on the table in front of her. The three-letter title, silver on black, was *ORC*.

He looked her up and down, as if trying to reach a conclusion, then opened the book, and turned the pages with exquisite care, given the thickness of those fingers, until he found the page he had been looking for. He held it up in front of her. There had been no time for breakfast today, but it's still possible to throw up when there's nothing left to throw. And if you needed to vomit, the woodcut held up beneath the Librarian's hands would be a sure-fire medicine.

He put the book down on the desktop, reached down again and produced a barely used handkerchief and, after some rummaging around, a glass of water.

'I don't have to believe that,' said Glenda. 'It's a drawing. It's not real.'

The Librarian's thumb went up and he nodded. He put the book under one arm and grabbed her with another and led her with surprising speed out of the door into the great maze of halls and corridors of the university.

Their breathless journey finished in front of a door on which was painted 'Department of Post-Mortem Communications'. The paint, however, had peeled somewhat and under the bright new title could just be made out the letters **NECR** and what could possibly be one half of a skull.

The door opened – any door pushed by the Librarian would assuredly open. Glenda heard the clink of the catch falling on to the floor inside.

In the middle of the floor that was revealed stood a hideous figure. Its horrifying countenance had less than the effect it might have done, because from it dangled a quite readable label that said 'Boffo Novelty and Joke Emporium. Improved Necromancer's Mask. Sale Price AM$3'. This was removed to reveal the more salubrious countenance of Dr Hix.

'There really is no need to —' he said, and then spotted the Librarian. 'Oh, can I help you?'

The Librarian held up the book and Dr Hix groaned. 'That again,' he said. 'All right, what do you want?'

'We've got an orc down in the cellars,' said Glenda.

'Yes, I know,' said Dr Hix.

The Librarian had a big face, but it nevertheless was not large enough to accommodate all of the surprise he wished to show. The head of the Department of Post-Mortem Communications shrugged and sighed. 'Look,' he said, as if weary of having to explain so often, and sighed again. 'I am supposed to be the bad person as defined by university statute, right? I am supposed to listen at doors. Supposed to dabble in the black arts. I've got the skull ring. I've got the staff with the silver skull on it—'

'And a joke-shop mask?' said Glenda.

'Quite serviceable as a matter of fact,' said Hix, haughtily. 'Rather more frightening than the original thing and washable, which is always a consideration in this department. Anyway, the Archchancellor was down here weeks ago, after the same stuff you are, I very much imagine.'

'Were the orcs terrible creatures?' said Glenda.

'I think I can probably show you,' said Hix.

'This gentleman has already shown me the picture in the book,' said Glenda.

'Was it the one with the eyeballs?'

Glenda found the memory only too vivid. 'Yes!'

'Oh, there's worse than that,' said Hix happily. 'And I suppose you want the proof?' He half turned his head. 'Charlie?' A skeleton walked out through black curtains at the far end of the room. It was holding a mug. There was something curiously depressing about the slogan on said mug, which ran: 'Necromancers Do It All Night'.

'Don't be scared,' said Dr Hix.

'I'm not,' Glenda said, terrified to her insteps. 'I've seen the insides of a slaughterhouse. It's part of the job and, anyway, he's polished.'

'Thank you very much,' the skeleton articulated.

'But "Necromancers Do It All Night"? That's a bit pathetic, isn't it? I mean, don't you think it's trying a bit too hard?'

'It was hard enough to get that one made,' said Dr Hix. 'We're not the most popular department in the university. Charlie, the young lady wants to know about orcs.'

'Again?' said the skeleton, handing the mug to the doctor. It had a rather hoarse voice, but on the whole far less dreadful than it might have been. Apart from anything else, his bones were, well, apart from anything else, and floated in the air as if they were the only visible parts of an invisible body. The jaw moved as Charlie went on: 'Well, I think we've still got the memory in the sump 'cos, you remember, we called it up for Ridcully. I haven't got round to wiping it yet.'

'Memory of what?' said Glenda.

'It's a kind of magic,' said Hix loftily. He continued. 'It would take too long to explain.'

Glenda didn't like this. 'Let's have it in a nutshell, then.'

'Okay. We're now quite certain that what we call the passage of time is in fact the universe being destroyed and instantly rebuilt in the smallest instant of eventuality that it is possible to have. While the process is instant at every point, nevertheless to renew the whole Universe takes approximately five days, we believe. Interestingly enough—'

'Can I have it in a smaller nut?'

'So you don't want to hear about Houseman's theory of the Universal Memory?'

'Possibly the size of a walnut,' said Glenda.

'Very well, then, can you imagine this: current thinking is that the old universe is not destroyed in the instant the new universe is created, a process which, incidentally, has been happening an untold billion number of times since I have been talking—'

'Yes, I can believe that. Can we try for a pistachio?' said Glenda.

'Copies of the universe are kept. We don't know how, we don't know where, and it beats the hell out of me trying to imagine how it all works. But we're finding that it is sometimes possible to, er, read this memory in certain circumstances. How am I doing in terms of nut dimensions?'

'You've got some kind of magic mirror?' said Glenda flatly.

'That's it, if you want the size of a pine nut,' said Hix.

'Pine nuts are actually seeds,' said Glenda smugly. 'So, what you're saying is that everything that happens stays happened somewhere and you can look at it if you have the knowing?'

'That is a magnificent distillation of the situation,' said Hix. 'Which is incredibly helpful while at the same time inaccurate in every possible way. But, as you put it, we use a' – and here he gave a little shudder – 'magic mirror, as you put it. We recently looked at the battle of Orc Deep for the Archchancellor. That was the last known battle in which the race known as orcs were deployed.'

'Deployed?' said Glenda.

'Used,' said Hix.

'*Used?* And you can find something like that in the total history of everything there has ever been?'

'Ahem. It helps to have an anchor,' said Hix. 'Something that was present. And all I am going to tell you, young lady, is that there was a piece of a skull found on that battlefield, and since it was a skull that firmly puts it into the responsibility of my department.' He turned to the Librarian. 'It's okay to show her, isn't it?' he said. The Librarian shook his head. 'Good. That means I can do it, then, under university statute. A certain amount of surreptitious disobedience is demanded of me. We have it set up on an omniscope. Since my colleague is so certain that I should not be doing this, he will not mind if I do. It's only a very brief fragment of time, but it did impress the Archchancellor, if impress is the right word.'

'I just want to get something clear,' said Glenda. 'You can actually disobey the orders of someone like the Archchancellor?'

'Oh, yes,' said Hix. 'I am under instruction to do so. It is *expected* of me.'

'But how can that possibly work?' said Glenda. 'What happens when he gives you an instruction that he doesn't want you to disobey?'

'It works by common sense and good will on all sides,' said Hix. 'If, for example, the Archchancellor gives me a command that absolutely must not be disobeyed, he will add something like, "Hix, you little worm (by university statute), if you disobey this one, I'll smack your head." Though in reality, a word to the wise, madam, is sufficient. It's all done on the basis of trust, really. I am trusted to be untrustworthy. I don't know what the Archchancellor would do without me.'

'Yeah, right,' said Charlie, grinning.

A few minutes later, Glenda was in another dark room, standing in front of a round, dark mirror, at least as high as she was. 'Is this going to be like the Moving Pictures?' she said sarcastically.

'An amusing comparison,' said Hix. 'Except for, one, there is no popcorn and, two, you would not want to eat it if there was. What might be called the camera in this case was the last thing one of the human fighters saw.'

'Is this the person whose skull you've got?'

'Well done! I see you have been following things,' said Hix.

There was a moment of silence. 'This is going to be scary, isn't it?'

'Yes,' said Hix. 'Nightmares? Very probably. Even I think it's extremely disconcerting. Are you ready, Charlie?'

'Ready,' said Charlie, from somewhere in the darkness. 'Are you sure, miss?'

Glenda wasn't sure, but anything would be better than facing Hix's know-it-all smile. 'Yes,' she said, keeping her voice firm.

'The fragment we are able to show lasts less than three seconds, but I doubt whether you will want to see it again. Are we ready? Thank you, Charlie.'

Glenda's chair went backwards very quickly and Hix, who had been hovering, caught her. 'The only known representation of an orc in battle,' said Hix, standing her upright. 'Well done, by the way. Even the Archchancellor swore out loud.'

Glenda blinked, trying to slice slightly less than three seconds out of her memory. 'And that's true, is it?' But it had to be true. There was something about the way the image was sticking to the back of her brain that declared the truth of it.

'I want to see it again.'

'You what?!' said Hix.

'There's more to it,' said Glenda. 'It's only a part of a picture.'

'It took us hours to work that out,' said Hix severely. 'How did you spot it the very first go?'

'Because I knew it had to be there,' said Glenda.

'She's got you there, boss,' said Charlie.

'All right. Show it again and this time magnify the right-hand corner. It's very blurry,' he said to Glenda.

'Can you stop it?' said Glenda.

'Oh, yes. Charlie has worked that one out.'

'Then you know the bit I mean.'

'Oh, yes.'

'Then show me it again.'

Charlie disappeared behind his curtain. There were a few flashes of light and then . . .

'There!' She pointed at the frozen image. 'That's men on horseback, isn't it? And they've got whips. I know it's blurry, but you can tell that they've got whips.'

'Well, yes, of course,' said Hix. 'It's quite hard to get anything to run into a hail of arrows unless you give it some encouragement.'

'They were weapons. Living creatures as weapons. And they don't look so different from humans.'

283

'A lot of really interesting stuff happened under the Evil Emperor,' said Hix, conversationally.

'Evil stuff,' said Glenda.

'Yes,' said Hix, 'that was rather the point. Evil Emperor. Evil Empire. It did what it said on the iron maiden.'

'And what happened to them?'

'Well, officially they're all dead,' said Hix. 'But there have been rumours.'

'And men drove them into battle,' said Glenda.

'If you want to put it like that, I suppose so,' said Hix, 'but I'm not certain that changes anything.'

'I think it changes everything,' said Glenda. 'It does if all that people talk about are the monsters and not the whips. Things that look very much like people, well, a kind of people. What can you make from people if you really try?'

'It's an interesting theory,' said Hix. 'But I don't think you can prove it.'

'When Kings fight other Kings and win, they chop off the other King's head, don't they?' said Glenda.

'Sometimes,' said Hix.

'I mean, you can't blame a weapon for how it's used. What's it they say? People can't help how they were made. I think the orcs were made.'

Glenda glanced at the Librarian, who looked at the ceiling.

'You work as a cook, don't you? Would you like to work for my department?'

'Everyone knows women can't be wizards,' said Glenda.

'Ah, yes, but Necro— Post-Mortem Communications is different,' said Hix proudly. And added, 'We could do with some sensible people here, heavens know. And the feminine touch would be very welcome. And don't think I would require you to just come and do the dusting. We treasure our dust in this place and your cookery skills will be invaluable. After all, basic butchery is all part of the job. And I do believe that Boffo's shop has a rather good female Necromancer's costume in their sale, isn't that right, Charlie?'

'Ten dollars including lace-up bodice. A bargain in anybody's money,' said Charlie from behind his curtain. 'Very slinky.'

There had been no reply because Glenda's mouth had stuck in the act of opening, but she finally managed a polite, but firm, 'No.'

The head of the Department of Post-Mortem Communications gave a little sigh. 'I thought as much, but we are part of the scheme of things. Light and dark. Night and day. Sweet and sour. Good and evil (within acceptable college statutes). It just helps if you can have sensible and reliable people on both sides, but I'm glad that we've been able to be of assistance. We don't see many people down here. Well, not people as such.'

This time Glenda walked along the corridor. 'Orc,' she thought. 'A thing that just kills.' Every time she blinked, the image came back to her. The teeth and claws of a creature in full leap seen, as far as one could tell, by whoever it was it was leaping at. Fighters you couldn't stop. And Nutt had been killed, according to Trev, and then sort of became unkilled again before going back to Unseen University and eating all the pies.

There was an awfully big gap in all this, but men with whips filled it. You can't have something that just fights, she thought. It has to do other things as well. And Nutt isn't any stranger than most of the people you see around these days. It's not a lot to go on, though, but then again, the Evil Emperor was a sorcerer, everyone knew that. Everyone knows you can't help how you're made. Well, it's worth a try. It's a little bit of uncertainty.

As soon as she arrived back outside Nutt's special place, she sensed that it would be empty. She pushed the door open and there was a definite absence of candles and, more importantly, a very noticeable absence of Nutt. But I told him to go and help them train. That's where he's gone, to go and train, definitely, she said to herself. So no need to worry, then.

On edge, feeling that something was nevertheless wrong, she forced herself back to the Night Kitchen.

*

She was nearly there when she met Mr Ottomy, his scrawny Adam's apple as red and glistening as chicken giblets.

'So, we've got a man-eating orc down here, have we?' he said. 'People aren't going to stand for that. I heard somewhere that they could go on fighting while their heads are chopped off.'

'That's interesting,' said Glenda. 'How did they know which way to go?'

'Ah-ah! They could smell their way,' said the bledlow.

'How could they do that with their heads chopped off? Are you telling me they had a nose up their arse?' She was shocked at herself for saying that, it was bad language, but Ottomy was bad language made solid.

'I don't hold with it,' he said, ignoring the question. 'You know something else I heard? They were kind of made. When the Evil Emperor wanted fighters he got some of the Igors to turn goblins into orcs. They're not really proper people at all. I'm going to complain to the Archchancellor.'

'He already knows,' said Glenda. Well, he must do, she thought. And Vetinari, too, she added to herself. 'You're not going to make trouble for Mister Nutt, are you?' she said. 'Because if you are, Mister Ottomy' – she leaned forward – 'you will never be seen again.'

'You shouldn't threaten me like that,' he said.

'You're right, I shouldn't,' said Glenda. 'I should have said that you will never be seen again, you egregious slimy little twerp. Go and tell the Archchancellor if you like and see how much good that does you.'

'They ate people alive!' said Ottomy.

'So did trolls,' said Glenda. 'Admittedly they spat them out again, but not in much of a state to enjoy life. We used to fight dwarfs once and when they cut you off at the knees they weren't joking. We know, Mister Ottomy, that the leopard can change his shorts,' she sniffed, 'and it might be a good idea if you did, too. And if I hear of any trouble from you, you will hear from me. Up there it's the Archchancellor. Down here in the dark, it's cutlery.'

'I'll tell him what you said,' said the luckless bledlow, backing away.

'I would be very grateful if you did,' said Glenda. 'Now push off.'

Why do we tell one another that the leopard cannot change his shorts? she mused as she watched him scurry away. Has anyone ever seen a leopard wearing shorts? And how would they be able to put them on if they had them? But we go on saying it as if it was some kind of holy truth, when it just means that we've run out of an argument.

There was something she had to do, now what was it? Oh, yes. She went over once again to the cauldron on which she had chalked 'Do Not Touch' and lifted up the lid. The beady eyes stared up at her from the watery depths and she went away and got a few scraps of fish, which she dropped towards the waiting claws. 'Well, I know what to do with you, at least,' she said.

A fully working kitchen holds a great many things, not least of which is a huge collection of ways of committing horrible murder, plus multiple ways of getting rid of the evidence. This wasn't the first time the thought had crossed her mind. She was quite glad about it. For now, she selected a really thick pair of gloves from a drawer, put her old coat on again, reached into the cauldron and picked up the crab. It snapped at her. She knew it would. Never, ever expect gratitude from those you help.

'Tide's turning,' she told the crustacean, 'so we're going to take a little walk.' She dropped it into her shopping bag and headed across the university lawns.

A couple of graduate wizards were working in the university boat-yard nearby. One looked at her and said, 'Are you supposed to be walking on the university lawns, madam?'

'No, it is absolutely forbidden to kitchen staff,' said Glenda.

The students looked at one another. 'Oh, right,' said one of them.

And that was it.

As easy as that.

It was only a metaphorical hammer. It only hit you if you allowed it to be there.

She pulled the crab out of her bag and it waved its claws irritably. 'See that over there?' she said, waving her own spare hand. 'That's Hen and Chickens Field.' It's doubtful whether the crab's beady eyes could focus on the grassy waste across the river, but at least she pointed it in the right direction. 'People think it's because there was chickens kept there,' she went on conversationally while the two wizards looked at one another. 'As a matter of fact, that's not so. It used to be where people were hanged, and so when they walked out from the old gaol that used to be over there, the priest in front of the procession with his billowing robes seemed to lead the line of doomed men and gaolers like a hen leading its chicks. That sort of thing is what we call a droll sense of humour in these parts and I haven't got the faintest idea why I'm talking to you. I've done my best. You now know more than any other crab.'

She walked down to the very edge of what passed for water as the river flowed through the city, and dropped the crab into it. 'Stay clear of crab pots and don't come back.' She turned round and realized the wizards had been watching her. 'Well?' she snapped. 'Is there any law about talking to crabs around here?' She then gave them a little smile as she walked past.

Back in the long corridors she wandered, feeling a little light-headed, towards the vats. Some of its denizens eyed her nervously as she passed through, but there was no sign of Nutt, not that she was looking for him at all. As she walked on towards the Night Kitchen, Trev and Juliet appeared. Glenda couldn't help but notice that Juliet had a somewhat bright-eyed and ruffled look. That is, she couldn't help but notice because she made a point of noticing every time. Semi-parental responsibility was a terrible thing.

'What are you *still* doing here?' she said.

They looked at her and there was more in their expressions than mere embarrassment.

'I come back to say goodbye to the girls and I 'ad to wait for Trev because of the training.'

Glenda sat down. 'Make me a cup of tea, will you?' And because old habits died hard she added, 'Boil water in the kettle, two spoons of tea in the pot. Pour water from kettle into pot when it boils. Do not put tea in kettle.' She turned to Trev. 'Where's Mister Nutt?' she said, non-chalance booming in her voice.

Trev looked down at his feet. 'I don't know, Glenda,' he said. 'I've been—'

'Busy,' Glenda completed.

'But no hanky panky,' said Juliet quickly.

Glenda realized that right now she would not have minded if there had been hanky panky or even spanky. There were things that were important and things that weren't, and times when you knew the difference.

'So, how did Mister Nutt get on, then?'

Trev and Juliet looked at one another. 'We don't know. He wasn't there,' said Trev.

'We kind of thought 'e might be with you,' said Juliet, handing her a cup of what you get when you ask for a cup of tea from someone who tends to confuse the recipe even at the best of times:

'He wasn't in the Great Hall?' said Glenda.

'No, 'e wasn't there— Wait one moment.' Trev ran down the steps and after a few seconds they heard his footsteps coming back. 'His tool-box 'as gone,' said Trev. 'I mean, it wasn't much. He made it outta bits he found in the cellars, but as far as I know it's all 'e owned.'

I knew it, thought Glenda. Of course I knew it. 'Where could he be? He's got nowhere else to go but here,' she said.

'Well, there is that place up in Uberwald he talks about quite a lot,' said Trev.

'That's getting on for about a thousand miles away,' said Glenda.

'Well, I suppose he thinks he might as well be there as here,' said Juliet innocently. 'I mean, Orc, I'd want to run away from a name like that if I was me.'

'Look, I'm sure he's just wandered off somewhere in the building,' Glenda said, believing absolutely that he hadn't. But if I believe he's going to be around the next corner or has just nipped off to . . . powder his nose, or has just wandered away for half an hour – which, of course, is his right; perhaps he needs to go and buy a pair of socks? – if I keep believing he'll turn up any minute, he might, even though I know he won't.

She put down the cup. 'Half an hour,' she said. 'Juliet, you go and check around the Great Hall. Trev, you go down the tunnels that way. I'll go down the tunnels this way. If you find anyone you can trust, ask 'em.'

A little more than half an hour later, Glenda was the last to turn up back in the Night Kitchen. She very nearly half expected that he would be there and knew that he wouldn't. 'Would he know about getting on a coach?' she said.

'I doubt 'e's ever seen one,' said Trev. 'You know what I would do if I was 'im? I'd just run. It was like when Dad died, I spent all night walkin' around the city. I wasn't bothered where I went. Just went. Wanted to run away from bein' me.'

'How fast can an orc run?' said Glenda.

'Much faster than a man, I bet,' said Trev. 'An' for a long time, too.'

'Listen.' This was Juliet. 'Can't you 'ear it?'

'Hear what?' said Glenda.

'Nothing,' said Juliet.

'Well?'

'What happened to Awk! Awk!?'

'I think we'll find them where we find him,' said Trev.

'Well, he can't run all the way back to Uberwald,' said Glenda. '*You* couldn't.'

At last Glenda said it: 'I think we should go after him.'

'I'll come,' said Trev.

'Then I'm goin' to come, too,' insisted Juliet. 'Besides, I've still got the money and you're goin' to need it.'

'Your money's in the bank,' said Glenda, 'and the bank is shut. But I think I've got a few dollars in my purse.'

'Then, excuse me,' said Trev, 'I won't be a moment. I think there's somethin' we ought to take . . .'

*

The driver of the horse bus to Sto Lat looked down and said, 'Two dollars fifty pence each.'

'But you only go to Sto Lat,' said Glenda.

'Yes,' said the man calmly. 'That's why it says Sto Lat on the front.'

'We might 'ave to go a lot further,' said Trev.

'Just about every coach in this part of the world goes through Sto Lat,' he said.

'How long will it take to get there?'

'Well, this is the late-night bus, okay? It's for people who've got to be in Sto Lat early and haven't got much money, and there's the rub, see? The less the money, the slower the travel. We get there in the end. Somewhere around about dawn, in fact.'

'All night? I think I could walk it faster.'

The man had the quiet, friendly air about him of someone who had found the best way to get through life was never to give much of a stuff about anything. 'Be my guest,' he said. 'I'll wave to you as we go past.'

Glenda looked down the length of the coach. It was half full of the kind of people who took the overnight bus because it wasn't very expensive; the kind of people, in fact, who had brought their own dinner in a paper bag, and probably not a new paper bag at that.

The three of them huddled. 'It's the only one we can afford,' said Trev. 'I don't think we can even afford travel for one on the mail coaches.'

'Can't we try and bargain with him?' said Glenda.

'Good idea,' said Trev. He walked back to the coach.

'Hello again,' said the driver.

'When are you gonna leave?' said Trev.

'In about five minutes.'

'So everyone who's gonna be riding is on the coach.'

Glenda glanced past the driver. The passenger behind him was very meticulously peeling a hardboiled egg.

'Could be,' said the driver.

'Then why not leave right now,' said Trev, 'and go faster? It's very important.'

'*Late-night*,' said the driver. 'That's what I said.'

'Supposing I was to threaten you with this lead pipe, would you go any faster?' said Trev.

'Trevor Likely!' said Glenda. 'You can't go around threatening people with lead pipes!'

The driver looked down at Trev and said, 'Can you run that past me again?'

'I told you that I had this length of lead pipe,' said Trev, banging it gently against the bus's door. 'Sorry, but we really need to get to Sto Lat.'

'Oh, right, yes,' said the driver, 'I see your lead pipe,' and he reached down to the other side of his seat, 'and I will raise you this battle-axe and would remind you that if I were to cut you in arf, the law would be on my side, no offence meant. You must think I am some kind of fool, but you're all hopping about like nits on a griddle, so what's this all about then?'

'We've got to catch up with our friend. He could be in danger,' said Trev.

'And it's very romantic,' said Juliet.

The driver looked at her.

'If you 'elp us catch up wiv him, I'll give you a big kiss,' she said.

'There!' said the driver to Trev. 'Why didn't *you* think of that?'

'All right, I'll give you a kiss as well,' said Trev.

'No thanks, sir,' said the driver, clearly enjoying himself. 'In your case I think I'll go for the lead pipe, although please don't try anything 'cos it's a devil's own job to get the bloodstains off the seats. Nothing seems to shift them.'

'Okay, I'll try to hit you with the lead pipe,' said Trev. 'We're desperate.'

'And we'll give you some money,' said Juliet.

'Sorry?' said the driver. 'Do I get the kiss, the money *and* the lead pipe? I mean, I'd rather forgo the lead pipe for another kiss.'

'Two kisses, a whole three dollars and no lead pipe,' said Juliet.

'Or just the lead pipe and I'll take my chances,' said Trev.

Glenda, who had been watching them with a fascinated horror, said,

'And I'll give you a kiss as well if you like.' She couldn't help noticing that this didn't move the stakes either way.

'But what about my passengers?' said the driver.

All four of them looked into the back of the bus and realized that they were the subject of at least a dozen fascinated stares. 'Go for the kiss!' said a woman, holding a large laundry basket in front of her.

'And the money!' said one of the men.

'I don't give a stuff if she kisses him or hits him on the head with the lead pipe, so long as they drop us off first,' said an old man towards the back of the bus.

'Do any of us get kissed as well?' said one half of a couple of giggling boys.

'If you like,' said Glenda viciously. They slumped back into their seats.

Juliet grabbed the driver's face and there was, for what seemed slightly too long, by the internal clocks of both Glenda and Trev, the sound of a tennis ball being sucked through the strings of a tennis racket. Juliet stepped back. The driver was smiling, in a slightly stunned and cross-eyed way. 'Well, that was pretty much of a lead pipe!'

'Perhaps I'd better drive,' said Trev.

The driver smiled at him. 'I'll drive, thank you very much, and don't kid yourself, mister, I know a dicey one when I see one and you don't come close. My old mum would be more likely to hit me with a lead pipe than you. Throw it away, why don't you, or someone will give you a centre parting you won't forget in a hurry.'

He winked at Juliet. 'What with one thing or another it's a good idea to give the horses a bit of a run every now and again. All aboard for Sto Lat.'

The horse buses did not usually travel very fast and the driver's definition of a run was only marginally faster than what most people would call a walk, but he managed to get them up to something that at least meant they did not have the time to get bored by a passing tree.

The bus was for people, as the driver had pointed out, who couldn't afford speed but could afford time. In its construction, therefore, no expense had been attempted. It was really no more than a cart with double seats all the way along it from the driver's slightly elevated bench. Tarpaulins on either side kept out the worst of the weather but fortunately still let in enough of the wind to mitigate the smell of the upholstery, which had experienced humanity in all its manifold moods and urgencies.

Glenda got the impression that some of the travellers were regulars. An elderly woman was sitting quietly knitting. The boys were still engaged in the furtive giggling appropriate to their age, and a dwarf was staring out of the window without looking at anything in particular. No one really bothered about talking to anybody, except a man right at the back, who was having a continuous conversation with himself.

'This isn't fast enough!' Glenda shouted after ten minutes of bouncing over the potholes. 'I could run faster than this.'

'I don't think he's gonna get that far,' said Trev.

The sun was going down and the shadows were already drawing across the cabbage fields, but there was a figure on the road ahead, struggling. Trev jumped off.

'Awk! Awk!'

'It's those wretched things,' said Glenda, running up behind him. 'Give me that lead pipe.'

Nutt was half crouched in the dust on the road. The Sisters of Perpetual Velocity were half flying and half flapping around him while he tried to protect his face with his hands. The passengers of the bus were quite unnoticed until the lead pipe arrived, followed very shortly by Glenda. It didn't have the effect she'd hoped. The Sisters were indeed like birds. She couldn't so much hit them as bat them through the air.

'Awk! Awk!'

'You stop trying to hurt him!' she screamed. 'He hasn't done anything wrong!'

Nutt raised an arm and grabbed her wrist. There wasn't much pressure, but somehow she couldn't move it at all. It was as if it had suddenly been embalmed in stone. 'They're not here to hurt me,' he said. 'They're here to protect you.'

'Who from?'

'Me. At least that's how it's supposed to go.'

'But I don't need any protection from you. That doesn't make any sense.'

'They think you might,' said Nutt. 'But that is not the worst of it.'

The creatures were circling and the other passengers, sharing the endemic Ankh-Morpork taste for impromptu street theatre, had piled out and had become an appreciative audience, which clearly discomforted the Sisters.

'What is the worst of it, then?' said Glenda, waving the pipe at the nearest Sister, which jumped back out of the way.

'They may be right.'

'All right, so you're an orc,' said Trev. 'So they used to eat people. Have you eaten anyone lately?'

'No, Mister Trev.'

'Well, there you are, then.'

'You can't arrest someone for something he hasn't done,' said one of the bus passengers, nodding sagely. 'A fundamental law, that.'

'What's an orc?' said the lady next to him.

'Oh, back in the olden days up in Uberwald or somewhere they used to tear people to bits and eat them.'

'That's foreigners for you,' said the woman.

'But they're all dead now,' said the man.

'That's nice,' said the woman. 'Would anyone like some tea? I've got a flask.'

'All dead, except me. But I am afraid that I am an orc,' said Nutt. He looked up at Glenda. 'I'm sorry,' he said. 'You have been very kind, but I can see that being an orc will follow me around. There will be trouble. I would hate you to be involved.'

'Awk! Awk!'

The woman unscrewed the top of her flask. 'But you're not about to eat anyone, are you, dear? If you feel really hungry I've got some macaroons.' She looked at the nearest Sister and said, 'What about you, love? I know none of us can help how we're made, but how come you've been made to look like a chicken?'

'Awk! Awk!'

'Danger! Danger!'

'Dunno about that,' said another passenger. 'I don't reckon he's going to do anything.'

'Please, please,' said Nutt. There was a box lying on the road beside him. He tore it open frantically and started to pull things out of it.

They were candles. Knocking them over in his haste, picking them up in shaking fingers only to knock them over again, he finally had them upright on the flints of the road. He pulled matches out of another pocket, knelt down and once again got his shaking fingers tangled in themselves as he struggled to strike a match. Tears streamed down his face as the light of the candles rose.

Rose . . . and changed.

Blues, yellows, greens. They would go out for a few smoky seconds and then light again a different colour, to the oohs and aahs of the crowd.

'See! See!' said Nutt. 'You like them? You like them?'

'I think you could make yourself a lot of money out of that,' said one of the passengers.

'They're lovely,' said the old lady. 'Honestly, the things you young people can do today.'

Nutt turned to the nearest Sister and spat, 'I am not worthless, I have worth.'

'My brother-in-law runs a novelty shop down in the smoke,' said the erstwhile expert in orcs. 'I'll write his address down for you if you like? But I reckon that thing would go down very well on the kiddies' birthday circuit.'

Glenda had watched all of this open-mouthed, as the kind of democracy practised by reasonable and amiable but not very clever people, the people whose education had never involved a book but had involved lots of other people, surrounded Nutt in its invisible, beneficent arms.

It was heartwarming, but Glenda's heart was a little bit calloused on this score. It was the crab bucket at its best. Sentimental and forgiving; but get it wrong – one wrong word, one wrong liaison, one wrong thought – and those nurturing arms could so easily end in fists. Nutt was right: at best, being an orc was to live under a threat.

'You lot have got no right treating the poor little devil like that,' said the old lady, waving a finger at the nearest Sister. 'If you want to live here, you have to do things our way, all right? And that means no pecking at people. That's not how we do things in Ankh-Morpork.'

Even Glenda smiled at that one. Pecking was a picnic compared with what Ankh-Morpork could offer.

'Vetinari's letting all sorts in these days,' said another passenger. 'I won't hear a word said against the dwarfs—'

'Good,' said a voice at his back. He moved aside and Glenda saw the dwarf standing behind him.

'Sorry, mate, I didn't see you there, what with you being so little,' said the man who had nothing against dwarfs. 'As I was saying, you lot just settle down and get on with it and are no trouble to anybody, but we're getting some weird ones now.'

'That woman they put in the Watch last month, for one,' said the old lady. 'The weird one from out Ephebe way. Gust of wind caught her sunglasses and three people turned into stone.'

'She was a Medusa,' said Glenda, who had read about that in the *Times*. 'The wizards managed to turn them back again, though.'

'Well, what I'm saying is,' started the man who had nothing against dwarfs, 'we don't mind anyone, so long as they mind their own business and don't do any funny stuff.'

This was the rhythm of the world to Glenda; she'd heard it so many times. But the feeling of the crowd was now very much against the Sisters. Sooner or later somebody was going to pick up a stone. 'I'd get out of here now,' she said, 'get out and go back to the lady you work for. I should do that right now, if I were you.'

'Awk! Awk!' one of them screeched.

But there were brains in those strange-shaped heads. And the three

Sisters were clearly bright enough to want to keep them there and ran for it, hopping and leaping like herons until what seemed like cloaks turned out to be wings, which pounded on the air as they sought for height. There was a final scream of 'Awk! Awk!'

The driver of the horse bus coughed. 'Well, if that's all sorted out then I suggest you all get back on board, please, ladies and gentlemen. And whoever. And don't forget your candles, mister.'

Glenda helped Nutt on to a wooden seat. He was holding his toolbox tightly across his knees, as if it would offer some sort of protection. 'Where were you trying to go?' she said as the horses began to move.

'Home,' said Nutt.

'Back to Her?'

'She gave me worth,' said Nutt. 'I was nothing and she gave me worth.'

'How can you say you were nothing?' said Glenda. On the pair of seats in front of them, Trev and Juliet were whispering together.

'I *was* nothing,' said Nutt. 'I *knew* nothing, I *understood* nothing, I had no understanding, I had no skill—'

'But that doesn't mean someone is worthless,' said Glenda firmly.

'It does,' said Nutt. 'But it does not mean they are bad. I was worthless. She showed me how to gain worth and now I have worth.'

Glenda had a feeling they were working from two different dictionaries. 'What does "worth" mean, Mister Nutt?'

'It means that you leave the world better than when you found it,' said Nutt.

'Good point,' said the lady with the macaroons. 'There's far too many people around the place who wouldn't dream of doing a hand's turn.'

'All right, but what about people who're blind, for example?' This from the hardboiled-egg man, sitting on the other side of the bus.

'I know a blind bloke in Sto Lat who runs a bar,' said an elderly gentleman. 'Knows where everything is and when you put your money on the counter he knows if it's the right change just by listening. He does all right. It's amazing, he can pick out a dud sixpence halfway across a noisy bar.'

'I don't think there are absolutes,' said Nutt. 'I think what Ladyship meant was that you do the best you can with what you have.'

'Sounds like a sensible lady,' said the man who had nothing against dwarfs.

'She's a vampire,' said Glenda maliciously.

'Nothing against vampires, just so long as they keep themselves to themselves,' said the macaroon lady, who was now engaged in licking something revoltingly pink. 'We've got one working down at the kosher butcher's on our street, and she's as nice as you like.'

'I don't think it's about what you end up with,' said the dwarf. 'It's about what you end up with compared with what you started with.'

Glenda leaned back with a smile as attempts at philosophy bounced their way from seat to seat. She wasn't at all certain about the whole thing, but Nutt was sitting there looking far less bedraggled and the rest of them were treating him as one of themselves.

There were dim lights ahead in the darkness. Glenda slipped from her seat and went up ahead to the driver. 'Are we nearly there yet?'

'Another five minutes,' said the driver.

'Sorry about all that silly business with the lead pipe,' she said.

'Didn't happen,' said the man cheerfully. 'Believe me, we get all sorts on the night bus. At least no one's thrown up. Quite an interestin' lad you've got back there with you.'

'You've no idea,' said Glenda.

'Of course, all he's saying is you've got to do your best,' said the driver. 'And the more best you're capable of, the more you should do. That's it, really.'

Glenda nodded. That did seem to be it, really. 'Do you go straight back?' she said.

'No. Me and the horses are stopping here and will go back in the morning.' He gave her the wry look of a man who's heard a great many things, and surprisingly seen a great many things, when to those behind him he was just a head facing forward keeping an eye on the road. 'That was a wonderful kiss she give me. I'll tell you what, the bus will be in the yard, there's plenty of straw around and if anyone was to have a bit of a kip, I wouldn't know about it, would I? We'll leave at six with fresh horses.' He grinned at her expression. 'I told you, we get all sorts on the late-night bus: kids running away from home, wives running away from husbands, husbands running away from other wives' husbands. It's called an omnibus, see, and omni means everything and damn near everything happens on this bus, that's why I have the axe, see? But the way I see it, life can't be all axe.' He raised his voice: 'Sto Lat coming up, folks! Return trip six o'clock prompt.' He winked at Glenda. 'And if you're not there, I'll go withoutcha,' he said. 'You've got to catch the bus at bus-catching time.'

'Well, this hasn't been so bad, has it?' said Glenda, as the lights of the city grew bigger.

'My dad's going to fret,' said Juliet.

'He'll think you're with me.'

Trev said nothing. By the rules of the street, being exposed in front of your want-to-be girlfriend as the kind of man who can so easily be seen not to be the kind of man that would have the guts to belt someone over the head with a length of lead pipe was extremely shaming, although no one seemed to have noticed this.

'Looks like a bit of trouble ahead,' the driver called back. 'The Lancre Flyer ain't gone.'

All they could see were flares and lantern lights, illuminating the big coaching inn outside the city gate, where several coaches were standing. As they drew nearer, he called to one of the skinny, bandy-legged and weaselly-looking men who seemed to self-generate around any establishment that involved the movement of horses. 'Flyer not gone?' he enquired.

The weasely man removed a cigarette end from his mouth. ''orse frowed a shoe.'

'Well? They've got a smith 'ere, ain't they? Speed the mails and all that.'

'He's not speedin' nuffink on account of him just laminating his hand to the anvil,' said the man.

'There'll be the devil to pay if the Flyer don't go,' said the driver.

'That's post, that is. You should be able to set your watch by the Flyer.'

Nutt stood up. 'I could certainly re-shoe a horse for you, sir,' he said, picking up his wooden toolbox. 'Perhaps you had better go and tell someone.'

The man sidled off and the bus came to rest in the big yard, where a rather better dressed man came hurrying up. 'One of you a smith?' he enquired, looking directly at Glenda.

'Me,' said Nutt.

The man stared. 'You don't look much like a smith, sir.'

'Contrary to popular belief, most smiths are on the wiry side rather than bulky. It's all a matter of sinews rather than muscle.'

'And you know your way around an anvil, do you?'

'You would be amazed, sir.'

'There's shoes in the smithy,' said the man. 'You'll have to work one to size.'

'I know how to do that,' said Nutt. 'Mister Trev, I would be glad if you would come and help me with the bellows.'

The inn was huge and crowded, because as with coaching inns everywhere its day lasted for twenty-four hours and not a moment less. There were no meal times, as such. Hot food for those who could afford it was available all the time and cold cuts of meat were on a large trestle in the main room. People arrived, were emptied and refilled in the speediest time possible and sent on their way again because the space was needed for the next arrivals. There never seemed to be a moment without the jangle of harnesses. Glenda found a quiet corner. 'I tell you what,' she said to Juliet, 'go and fetch some sandwiches for the lads.'

'Fancy Mister Nutt being a blacksmith,' said Juliet.

'He's a man of many parts,' said Glenda.

Juliet's brow wrinkled. ''ow many parts?'

'It's just a figure of speech, Juliet. Off you go now.' She needed time to think. Those strange flying women. Mister Nutt. It was all a lot to take. You start the day and it's just another day and here you are, having mercifully not ended up as a highwayman, sitting in another city with nothing more than the clothes you're standing up in, not knowing what is going to happen next.

Which, in a way, was exciting. She had to analyse that feeling for several moments because excitement was not a regular feature of her life. Pies, on the whole, do not excite. She got up and wandered unheeded through the crowds, with the vague idea of seeing what the kitchens were like, but found her path blocked by someone whose sweating face, flustered air and rotund body suggested he was the innkeeper. 'If you could just wait a moment, ma'am,' he said to her and then addressed a woman who was emerging from what looked like a private dining room. 'So nice to see you again, your ladyship,' he said, bobbing up and down a little. 'It's always an honour to have you grace our humble establishment.'

Ladyship.

Glenda looked up at the woman who was everything she had pictured when Nutt had first talked about her. Tall, thin, dark, forbidding, to be feared. Her expression was stern and she said, in what to Glenda were posh tones, 'Far too noisy in here.'

'But the beef was superb,' said another voice and Glenda realized that Ladyship had almost eclipsed a smaller woman, quite pleasant, not particularly tall and with a slightly fussy air about her.

'Are you Lady Margolotta?' said Glenda.

The tall lady gave her a look of brief disdain and swept on towards the main doors, but her companion stopped and said, 'Do you have business with her ladyship?'

'Is she coming to Ankh-Morpork?' Glenda asked. 'Everybody knows she's Lord Vetinari's squeeze.' She felt instantly embarrassed as she said the word; it conjured up images that simply could not fit into the available space in her brain.

'Really?' said the woman. 'They are certainly very close friends.'

'Well, I want to talk to her about Mister Nutt,' said Glenda.

The woman gave her a worried look and pulled her over to an empty bench. 'There has been a problem?' she said, sitting down and patting the wood beside her.

'She told him he was worthless,' said Glenda. 'And sometimes I think all he worries about is being worthy.'

'Are you worthy?' said the woman.

'What sort of question is that to ask a stranger?'

'An interesting and possibly revealing one. Do you think the world is a better place with you in it, and would you do me the courtesy of actually thinking about your answer rather than pulling one off the "affronted" rack? I'm afraid there's far too much of that these days. People believe that acting and thinking are the same thing.'

Faced with that, Glenda settled for, 'Yes.'

'You've made it better, have you?'

'Yes. I've helped lots of people and I invented the Ploughman's Pie.'

'Did the people you helped want to be helped?'

'What? Yes, they came and asked.'

'Good. And the Ploughman's Pie?'

Glenda told her.

'Ah, you must be the cook at Unseen University,' said the woman. 'Which means that you have access to rather more than the average cook and, therefore, I would deduce that to keep the pickled onions crisp in the pie you put them in a cold room at very nearly freezing point for some time immediately before baking, possibly wrapping them in cheese for the sake of temporary insulation, and, if you have assembled your pie correctly and paid attention to temperatures, I think that would do the trick.' She paused. 'Hello?'

'Are you a cook?' said Glenda.

'Good grief, no!'

'So you worked it out, just like that? Mister Nutt told me her lady-ship employs *very* clever people.'

'Well, I'm embarrassed to say it, but that is true.'

'But she shouldn't have told Mister Nutt that he's worthless. She shouldn't say that to people.'

'But he was worthless, yes? He couldn't even talk properly when he was found. Surely what she has done has helped him?'

'But he frets all the time and it's got out now that he's an orc. What's that all about?'

'And is he, in your mind, doing anything particularly orcish?'

Reluctantly, Glenda said, 'Sometimes his fingernails turn into claws.'

The woman looked suddenly concerned. 'And what does he do then?'

'Well, nothing,' said Glenda. 'They just sort of . . . go back in again. But he makes wonderful candles,' she added quickly. 'He's always making things. It's as if . . . worth is something that drains away all the time so you have to keep topping it up.'

'Possibly, now you put it that way, she has been a little too brisk with him.'

'Does she love him?' asked Glenda.

'I beg your pardon?'

'I mean, has anyone ever loved him?'

'Oh, I think she does, in her way,' said the woman. 'Although she's a vampire, you know. They tend to see the world rather differently.'

'Well, if I met her I'd give her a piece of my mind,' said Glenda. 'Muddling him about. Setting those wretched flying ladies on him. I wouldn't let her do that sort of thing.'

'She's immensely strong, I'm led to believe,' said the woman.

'That doesn't give her the right,' said Glenda. 'And shall I tell you something? Mister Nutt is right here. Oh yes, out in the yard, shoeing one of the horses for the Lancre Flyer. He really is amazing.'

'It sounds like it,' said the woman with a faint little smile. 'You certainly seem to be a vehement supporter.'

Glenda hesitated. 'Is that something to do with foxes?' she said.

'It means with great passion,' said the woman. 'Do you have a great passion for Mister Nutt, Miss Sugarbean? And remember, please, I do like people to do me the honour of thinking before they speak.'

'Well, I like him a lot,' said Glenda hotly.

'That is charming,' said the woman. 'It does occur to me that Mister Nutt might have achieved more worth than I had previously thought.'

'So you tell her ladyship what I said,' said Glenda, feeling her neck on fire with blushes. 'Mister Nutt has got friends.'

'Indeed I will,' said the woman, standing up. 'And now if you'll excuse me, I'm sure our coach is about to depart. I must fly.'

'Remember to tell her what I said!' Glenda shouted after her.

She saw the woman turn to smile at her and then she was lost as a party arriving from a new coach hurried in from the cold night air.

Glenda, who had stood up at the same time as the woman, sat down heavily. Who on earth did that woman think she was? Her ladyship's librarian, probably. Nutt had mentioned her several times. Altogether too many ideas above her station for Glenda's liking. She hadn't even had the decency to give Glenda her name.

The faint, distant hunting horns of sheer terror began to sound in the back of her mind. Had the woman asked Glenda her name? No! But she'd certainly known it and how would she know about the 'cook' at Unseen University? And she'd been so quick, she'd worked out the Ploughman's Pie with a snap of her fingers. That little part of her that had first been liberated by the sherry chimed in with, *The trouble with you is that you make assumptions. You see something and you think you know what you've seen. She certainly didn't sound like a librarian, did she?*

Very slowly, Glenda raised her right hand into a fist and lowered it into her mouth, and bit down very hard in an attempt to somehow retrieve the last fifteen minutes from the records of the universe and replace them with something far less embarrassing, like her knickers falling down.

Even here, late into the night, the forge was the heart of attention. Coaches were arriving and leaving constantly. The inn did not run according to the sun, it ran according to the timetable, and aimless people waiting for their connections gravitated to the forge as a free show and a place of comfort in the chilly night air.

Nutt was shoeing a horse. Trev had seen horses being shod before, but never like this. The animal stood as if transfixed, trembling very slightly. When Nutt wanted it to move, he clicked his tongue. When he wanted its leg raised, another click caused this to happen. Trev felt that he wasn't watching a man shoeing a horse, but a master demonstrating his skills to a world of amateurs. When the shoe was on, the horse walked backwards in front of the crowd, for all the world like a fashion model, turning as Nutt moved a hand or made a clicking noise. It didn't seem to be a particularly happy horse, but, great heavens, it was certainly an obedient one. 'Yes, that all seems fine,' Nutt said.

'How much is that going to cost us?' said the coachman. 'Wonderful job, if I may say so.'

'How much? How much? How much?' said Nutt, turning it over in his mind. 'Have I earned worth, sir?'

'I should say so, mate. I've never seen a horse shod as smooth as that.'

'Then worth will do,' said Nutt. 'And a ride for myself and my three friends back to Ankh-Morpork.'

'An' five dollars,' said Trev, coming away from his lounging spot near the wall with the speed of money.

The coachman sniffed. 'A bit steep,' he said.

'What?' said Trev. 'For a late-night job? To better than Burleigh and Stronginthearm specification? Not a bad deal, I think.'

A murmur from the other watchers backed Trev up. 'I never seen anyone do anything like that,' said Juliet. 'He'd 'ave 'ad that 'orse dancing if you'd asked 'im.'

The coachman winked at Trev. 'All right, lad. What can I say? Old Havacook there is a good lad, but a bit bad tempered, as it goes. Once kicked a coachman through the wall. I never thought I'd see him stand there and lift 'is leg up like a trained lap-dog. Your chum has earned his money and his ride.'

'Please take him away,' said Nutt. 'But hold him with care because when he gets a little way away from me he might get a tiny bit frisky.'

The crowd dispersed. Nutt methodically damped down the forge and started to pack his tools into the box. 'If we're going to go back, we'd better go now. Has anyone seen Miss Glenda?'

'Here,' said Glenda, advancing out of the shadows. 'Trev, you and Jools go and get us some seats on the coach. I need to talk to Mister Nutt.'

'Her ladyship was here,' said Glenda when they'd gone.

'I would not be surprised,' said Nutt calmly, snapping the catches shut on his box. 'Just about everybody passes through here and she travels a great deal.'

'Why were you running away?'

'Because I know what will happen,' said Nutt. 'I am an orc. It's as simple as that.'

'But the people on the bus were on your side,' said Glenda.

Nutt flexed his hands and the claws slid out, just for a moment. 'And tomorrow?' he said. 'And if something goes wrong? Everybody knows orcs will tear your arms off. Everybody knows orcs will tear your head off. Everybody knows these things. That is not good.'

'Well, then, why are you coming back?' Glenda demanded.

'Because you are kind and came after me. How could I refuse? But it does not change the things that everybody knows.'

'But every time you make a candle and every time you shoe a horse, you change the things that everybody knows,' said Glenda. 'You know that orcs were—' She hesitated. 'Sort of made?'

'Oh, yes, it was in the book.'

She nearly exploded. 'Well, then, why didn't you tell me?!'

'Is it important? We are what we are now.'

'But you don't have to be!' Glenda yelled. 'Everybody knows trolls eat people and spit them out. Everybody knows dwarfs cut your legs off. But at the same time everybody knows that what everybody knows is wrong. And orcs didn't decide to be like they are. People will understand that.'

'It will be a dreadful burden.'

'*I'll help!*' Glenda was shocked at the speed of her response and then mumbled, 'I'll help.'

The coals in the forge crackled as they settled down. Fires in a busy forge seldom die out completely. After a while, Glenda said, 'You wrote that poem for Trev, didn't you?'

'Yes, Miss Glenda. I hope she liked it.'

Glenda thought she'd better raise this carefully. 'I think I ought to tell you that she didn't understand a lot of the words *exactly*. I sort of had to translate it for her.' It hadn't been too difficult, she reckoned. Most love poems were pretty much the same under the curly writing.

'Did *you* like it?' said Nutt.

'It was a wonderful poem,' said Glenda.

'I wrote it for you,' said Nutt. He was looking at her with an expression that stirred together fear and defiance in equal measure.

The cooling embers brightened up at this. After all, a forge has a soul. As if they had been waiting there, the responses lined themselves up in front of Glenda's tongue. Whatever you do next is going to be very important, she told herself. Really, extremely, very important. Don't start wondering about what Mary the bloody housemaid would do in one of those cheap novels you read, because Mary was made up by someone with a name suspiciously like an anagram for people like you. She is not real and you are.

'We had better get on the coach,' said Nutt, picking up his box.

Glenda gave up on the thinking and burst into tears. It has to be said that they were not the gentle tears they would have been from Mary the housemaid, but the really big long-drawn-out blobby ones you get from someone who very rarely cries. They were gummy, with a hint of snot in there as well. But they were *real*. Mary the housemaid would just not have been able to match them.

So, of course, it will be just like Trev Likely to turn up out of the shadows and say, 'They're calling the coach now— Are you two all right?'

Nutt looked at Glenda. Tears aren't readily retractable, but she managed to balance a smile on them. 'I believe this to be the case,' said Nutt.

Travelling on a fast coach, on even a mild autumn night, those passengers on the roof experience the temperature that can freeze doorknobs. There are leather covers and rugs of various age, thickness and smell. Survival is only possible by wrapping yourself in the biggest cocoon you can achieve, preferably with somebody else next to you;

two people can heat up faster than one. In theory, all of this could lead to hanky panky, but the seats of the coach and the rockiness of the road mean that such things are not uppermost in the traveller's mind, which dreams longingly of cushions. Furthermore, there was a fine rain now.

Juliet craned her head to look at the seats behind, but there were just the mounds of damp rugs that were the coach company's answer to the cold night air. 'You don't think they're sweet on each other, do you?' she said.

Trev, who was himself cocooned in rugs, only managed a grunt, but then went on, 'I think 'e admires her. He always seems a bit tongue-tied when 'e's near her, that's all I know.'

This *had* to be a romance, Glenda thought. It wasn't like the ones peddled every week by Iradne Comb-Buttworthy. It felt more real – more real and very, very strange.

'Did you know that all of the orcs were hunted down after the war? All of them, children too,' Nutt said.

And people don't say things like that in a romantic situation, thought Glenda. But it still *is*, she added.

'But they were forced,' she replied. 'They had children. Okay?' Should I tell him about the magic mirror? she wondered. Would it make things better? Or worse?

'They were very bad times,' said Nutt.

'Well, look at it like this,' said Glenda. 'Most of the people who talk about orcs now don't know what they're on about, but the only orc they are ever going to *see* is you. You making beautiful candles. You training the football team. That will mean a lot. You'll show them that orcs don't go around pulling people's heads off. That'll be something to be proud of.'

'Well, in fairness, I have to say that when I think of the amount of radial force that must have been necessary to effectively unscrew a human head against its owner's wishes, I am a little impressed. But that's now, sitting here with you. Then, I wanted to go up to the hills. I think that's how we must have survived. If you didn't keep away from humans you died.'

'Yes, that's a very good point,' said Glenda, 'but I think you should keep it to yourself for now.' She noticed a surprised owl, lit up briefly by the coach's lamps.

Then she said, keeping her eyes straight ahead, 'The thing about the poem . . .'

'How did you know, Miss Glenda?' said Nutt.

'You talk about kindness a lot.' She cleared her throat. 'And under the circumstances, I think Glenda is sufficient.'

'You were kind to me,' said Nutt. 'You are kind to everybody.'

Glenda swiftly put aside a vision of Mr Ottomy and said, 'No, I'm not, I'm shouting at everyone all the time!'

'Yes, but it's for their own good.'

'What do we do now?' Glenda said.

'I have no idea. But can I tell you something very interesting about ships?'

It wasn't exactly what Glenda had expected, but somehow it was one hundred per cent Nutt. 'Please tell me the interesting thing about ships,' she said.

'The interesting thing about ships is that the captains of ships have to be very careful when two ships are close together at sea, particularly in calm conditions. They tend to collide.'

'Because of the wind blowing, and that?' said Glenda, thinking: In theory this is a romantic-novel situation and I am about to learn about ships. Iradne Comb-Buttworthy never puts a ship in her books. They probably don't have enough reticules.

'No,' said Nutt. 'In fact, to put it simply, each ship shields the other ship from lateral waves on one side, so by small increments outside forces bring them together without their realizing it.'

'Oh! It's a metaphor?' said Glenda, relieved. 'You think we're being pushed together.'

'It's something like that,' said Nutt. They rocked as the coach hit a particularly nasty pothole.

'So, if we don't do anything we'll just get closer and closer?'

'Yes,' said Nutt.

The coach jumped and rattled again, but Glenda felt as if she was travelling over very thin ice. She'd hate to say the wrong thing.

'You know Trev said that I'd died?' Nutt continued. 'Well, that was true. Probably. Ladyship said that we were made from goblins for the Evil Emperor. The Igors did it. And they put in something very strange. It's a part of you that isn't quite a part of you. They called it the Little Brother. It's tucked in deep inside and absolutely protected and it's like having your own hospital with you all the time. I know that I was hit very hard, but the Little Brother kept me alive and simply cured things again. There are ways to kill an orc, but there are not many of them and anyone trying them out on a living orc is not going to have very much time to get it right. Does that worry you at all?'

'No, not really,' said Glenda. 'I don't really understand it. I think it's more important just to be who you are.'

'No, I don't think I should be who I am, because I am an orc. But I have some plans in that direction.'

Glenda cleared her throat again. 'This thing with the ships . . . Does it happen quite quickly?'

'It starts quite slowly, but it's quite quick towards the end,' said Nutt.

'The thing is,' said Glenda, 'I mean, I can't just walk away from my job, and there's old ladies I go and visit, and you'll be busy with the football . . .'

'Yes. I think we should be doing the things we should be doing, and it's the last training day tomorrow, which is actually today now,' said Nutt.

'And I've got to make a lot of pies.'

'It's going to be a very busy time for both of us,' said Nutt solemnly.

'Yes. Um, er, do you mind me saying . . . in your lovely poem . . . the line "The crypt's a handsome place to be, but none I think leave after tea" didn't quite—'

'Didn't quite work? I know,' said Nutt. 'I feel rather bad about that.'

'Oh, please don't! It's a wonderful poem!' Glenda burst out, and felt the ripples in the calm sea.

*

The rising sun managed to peek around the vast column of smoke that forever rose from Ankh-Morpork, City of Cities, illustrating almost up to the edge of space that smoke means progress or, at least, people setting fire to things. 'I think we're going to be so busy that we're not going to have much time for . . . ourselves,' said Glenda.

'I quite agree,' said Nutt. 'Leaving things alone would definitely be our wisest move.'

Glenda felt light as air as the coach trundled down Broad Way, and it wasn't just from lack of sleep. *That stuff about boats, I really hope he doesn't think it's all about ships.*

There was a crowd outside the university when they arrived, just as yesterday, but it seemed to have a different complexion now. People were staring at her and Nutt, and there was something wrong with the way they were looking.

She reached over to the mound that was Trev, pretended not to hear a girlish giggle and said, 'Trev. Could you, er, have a look at this. I think there's going to be trouble.'

Trev, very tousled, stuck his head out and said, 'Hmm, me too. Let's all nip in around the back.'

'We could stay on and get off at the Post Office,' said Glenda.

'No,' said Trev. 'We 'aven't done anythin' wrong.'

As they dismounted from the coach a small boy said to Nutt, 'Are you the orc, mister?'

'Yes,' said Nutt, as he helped Glenda down. 'I am an orc.'

'Cool! Have you ever twisted someone's head off?'

'I don't believe so. I am sure I would have remembered,' said Nutt.

This got if not applause then a certain amount of approval from some of the bystanders. *It's his voice,* thought Glenda. *He sounds posher than a wizard. You can't imagine a voice like that with its hands around somebody's head.*

At this point the back gate opened and Ponder Stibbons came hurrying through. 'We saw you from the Hall,' he said, grabbing Nutt. 'Come in quick. Where have you all been?'

'We 'ad to go to Sto Lat,' said Trev.

'On business,' said Juliet.

'Personal,' said Glenda, daring Ponder to object. 'Is there something wrong?'

'There was something in the paper this morning. We have not been having a very nice time,' said Ponder, towing them into the relative safety of the undercrofts.

''ave they been sayin' somethin' nasty about Mister Nutt?' said Trev.

'Not exactly,' said Ponder. 'The editor of the *Times* came round, in person, and was knocking on the door to see the Archchancellor at midnight. He wanted to know all about you.' This was said directly to Nutt.

'I bet it was bloody Ottomy that told them,' growled Glenda. 'What have they done?'

'Well, of course, you know there was all that trouble over the Medusa in the Watch a little while ago,' Ponder began.

'Yes, but you wizards sorted that out,' said Trev.

'But no one likes being turned into stone, even if it's just for half an hour.' Ponder sighed. 'The *Times* has done one of their thoughtful pieces. I suppose it isn't too bad. It quoted the Archchancellor, who says that Mister Nutt is a hardworking member of the university staff and there have been no incidents of anyone's leg being torn off.'

'They put it like that?' said Glenda, wide-eyed.

'Oh, you know the sort of thing if you read the papers a lot,' said Ponder. 'I seriously think they think that it's their job to calm people down by first of all explaining why they should be overexcited and very worried.'

'Oh, yes, I know they do that,' said Glenda. 'How would people get worried if they weren't told how to be?'

'Well, it wasn't all that bad,' said Ponder, 'but a few of the other papers have picked it up as well and some of the facts have become . . . elastic. The *Inquirer* said Nutt is training the football team.'

'That's true,' said Glenda.

'Well, actually it's me. I am merely delegating the task to him. I hope that's understood? Anyway, they did a cartoon about it.'

Glenda put a hand over her eyes. She hated cartoons in newspapers. 'Was it a football team of orcs?' she said.

Ponder's look was almost admiring. 'Yes,' he said. 'And they did an article about raising important questions about Vetinari's open-door policy, while saying at the same time that rumours that Mister Nutt had to be chained down were quite likely false.'

'What about the *Tanty Bugle*?' said Glenda. 'They never write anything unless it's got blood and horrible murder in it.' She paused and then added, 'Or pictures of girls without their vests on.'

'Oh, yes,' said Ponder. 'They did a rather grainy picture of a young lady with enormous melons.'

'D'you mean—' Trev began.

'No, they were just enormous melons. The green ones. Slightly warty. She won a contest for growing them, apparently, but in the caption it said that she's worried that she won't be able to sleep easily in her bed now that orcs are coming into the city.'

'Is Lord Vetinari doing anything about this?'

'I haven't heard,' said Ponder. 'Oh, and *Bu-bubble* want to interview Mister Nutt. What they call a lifestyle piece.' He said the words as if trying to hold them at arm's length.

'Have people turned up for training?' said Nutt calmly.

'Oh, yes. The ground is heaving.'

'So we'll go and train them,' said Nutt. 'Don't worry, I won't twist anybody's head off.'

'No, don't make jokes,' said Glenda. 'I think this could be terribly bad.'

'We know something's going on with the teams,' said Ponder. 'And there were lots of fights during the night.'

'About what?'

'About who's going to play us.' Ponder stopped and looked Nutt up and down. 'Commander Vimes is back in town and would like to lock you up,' he said. 'Only in protective custody, of course.'

'You mean put him somewhere where they can all find him?' said Glenda.

'I would say that the chances of a mob breaking into Pseudopolis Yard are remote,' said Ponder.

'Yes, but you're locking him up. That's what it would be. He'd be locked up and coppers chat like everyone else. The orc would be locked up in prison and if people don't know why, they'll make it up, that's how people are. Can't you wizards do something?'

'Yes,' said Ponder. 'We can do practically anything, but we can't change people's minds. We can't magic them sensible. Believe me, if it were possible to do that, we would have done it a long time ago. We can stop people fighting by magic and then what do we do? We have to go on using magic to stop them fighting. We have to go on using magic to stop them being stupid. And where does all that end? So we make certain that it doesn't begin. That's why the university is here. That's what we do. We have to sit around not doing things because of the hundreds of times in the past it's been proved that once you get beyond the abracadabra, hey presto, changing-the-pigeons-into-ping-pong-balls style of magic you start getting more problems than you've solved. It was bad enough finding ping-pong balls nesting in the attics.'

'Ping-pong balls nestin'?' said Trev.

'I don't want to talk about it,' said Ponder glumly.

'I remember when one of you gentlemen got hungry in the night and cast a spell for a baked potato,' said Glenda.

Ponder shuddered. 'That was the Bursar,' he said. 'He really does get confused about the decimal point.'

'I remember all those wheelbarrows,' said Glenda, slightly amused at Ponder's discomfort. 'Days and days it took to get them all out. I heard we were feeding every beggar in the city and every pig farm out as far as Sto Lat for weeks.'

Ponder nearly gave a harrumph. 'Well, yes, there's an example of why we have to be careful.'

'But there's still going to be a match tomorrow and I would like to conclude my training programme,' said Nutt.

'Ah, there's another problem. You know Lord Vetinari is allowing the Hippo to be used for the game? Well, some of the teams are doing their training there now. You know, a bit of a kick-about, and so on. It's all about who will be playing Unseen Academicals.'

'But that's the other side of the city,' said Glenda.

'Commander Vimes has said the Watch will provide an escort,' said Ponder. 'Just for protection, you know?'

'Whose?' said Glenda. 'You can see what's going on here. People will see Mister Nutt as the problem.'

'Oh, it's all fun and games until someone loses a head,' said a voice behind Glenda. She recognized that voice and it always sounded as if it was trying to put its hand up her jumper.

'Pepe? What the hell are you doing here?'

'And how did you get in?' Ponder demanded. 'The Watch are all around this place.'

Pepe barely gave him a glance. 'And who are you, smart boy?'

'I run this university!'

'Then I should go away and run it, because you're not going to be any good around here.'

'Is this – person – known to you, miss?' Ponder demanded.

'Er, yes. He, er, designs clothes.'

'I am a fashionista,' said Pepe. 'I can do things with clothing that you wouldn't think were possible.'

'I'd believe that, at least,' said Trev.

'And I know a thing or two about riots and mobs.'

An idea struck Glenda and she whispered to the irate Ponder, 'Very big in dwarf circles, sir. Knows a lot of influential people.'

'So do I,' said Ponder. 'Actually, I am one,' he wailed. 'But *I* had to do the training *myself* yesterday and I couldn't remember all of the things Mister Nutt comes up with so I had them running on the spot, which I don't think is very helpful.'

'There's somethin' goin' bad,' said Trev. 'I know about this city. I'll go and check a few things out. It's not as if you really need me.'

'I do,' said Juliet.

Trev hesitated, but Nutt had shown him how to do this. He extended a hand and blew her a kiss as he went through the door.

'Did you see that?' said Juliet. 'He blew me.'

Glenda looked at Pepe, whose eyes were turned up so far in his head that she could see the whites – although they were red.

A short while later, when most of the UU squad headed for the Hippo with Glenda and Juliet trailing after them like camp followers, half a dozen watchmen appeared from the various places that they had selected for a quiet smoke and fell in after them, trying to make it look as if they all just happened to be strolling in the same direction.

Trev was right, Glenda thought. *It is going bad.*

Trev had not gone very far when his street sense told him he was being followed. He jinked in and out of a few alleys and waited at the next corner to confront the follower . . . The follower who wasn't there. The alley behind him was empty all the way to the last street. He realized this at the same time as someone pressed what definitely felt like a knife to his neck.

'Cor, this takes me back and so it does,' said a voice. 'I reckon I can still remember every back alley in this place.'

'I know you, it's Pepe, isn't it? You're a dwarf?' said Trev, trying not to turn round.

'Sort of a dwarf,' said Pepe.

'But I don't have no argument with you, do I?' said Trev.

Something small and shiny appeared on the edge of Trev's vision. 'Sample piece of moonsilver,' said Pepe's voice. 'I could do more damage with a broken champagne bottle – and I have, believe you me. I wouldn't threaten a bloke like you with a knife, not with that little girl doting on you like she is. She seems very happy with you and I'd like to keep her happy.'

'Somethin's goin' down on the street,' said Trev.

'What, the whole street? Sounds like fun.'

'Somethin's gone wrong, 'asn't it?' said Trev.

Only now did Pepe enter his field of view. 'Not really my problem at all,' he said. 'But there're some kinds of people I just don't like. I've seen too many of 'em, bullies and bastards. If you want to learn athletics very quickly, be born around here with a talent for design and maybe a few other little preferences. Lord Vetinari has got it all wrong. He thought he could take on the football and it's not working. It's not like the Thieves' Guild, see. He had it easy with the Thieves' Guild. That's because the Thieves' Guild is organized. Football ain't organized. Just because he's won over the captains don't mean that everyone's going to meekly get into line after them. There was fights all over the place last night. Your chums with their shiny new football and their shiny new jerseys are going to get creamed tomorrow. No, worse than creamed – cheesed.'

'I thought you were just someone who made clothes?' said Trev.

'Just. Someone. Who. Made. Clothes. Just someone?! I am not any-one. I am Pepe and I don't make clothes. I create gorgeous works of art that just happen to require a body to show them off as they should be seen. Tailors and dressmakers make clothes. I forge history! Have you heard about micromail?'

'Got yer. Yep,' said Trev.

'Good,' said Pepe. 'Now, what have you heard about micromail?'

'Well, it doesn't chafe.'

'It's got one or two other little secrets, too . . .' said Pepe. 'Anyway, I can't say I've got any time for the wizards, myself. Snooty lot. But it's not going to be a game out there tomorrow, it's going to be a war. Do you know a bloke called Andy? Andy Shank?'

Trev's heart sank. 'What's he gotta do with it?'

'I just heard the name, but I reckon I know the type. Lord Vetinari has done what he wanted. He's broken the football, but that's leaving a lot of sharp bits, if you get my meaning.'

'The Watch'll be there tomorrow,' said Trev.

'What's this? What's this? A street face like you being glad that the Watch is going to be anywhere?'

'There'll be a lot of people watching.'

'Yeah, won't that be fun?' said Pepe. 'And, you know, there's people in this city that would watch a beheading and hold their kiddies up for a better view. So I'll tell you what I'll do. I'm not going to give you an edge, the last thing you'll want to see tomorrow is an edge. I'll give you something that's much better than an edge. After all, you're Dave Likely's lad.'

'I'm not playing,' said Trev. 'I promised my ol' mum.'

'You promised your old mum?' said Pepe. There wasn't even any attempt to hide the disdain. 'And you think that makes any difference, do you? You've got a star in your hand, lad. You'll play, all right, so I'll tell you what I'll do. You come along and see me round the back entrance of Shatta, sorry about that, it sounds better in Dwarfish, and kick on the door round about midnight. You can bring a chum with you if you like, but you better bloody well come.'

'Why do I 'ave to kick the door?' said Trev.

'Because you'll have a bottle of best brandy in each hand. Don't thank me. I'm not doing it for you. I'm protecting my investment and, on the way, that means protecting yours as well. Off you go, boy. You're late for training. And me? I'm a soddin' genius!'

Trev noticed more watchmen around as he headed onwards. They could be absolute bastards if they felt like it, but Sam Vimes had no use for coppers that couldn't read the streets. The Watch was jumpy.

Carter used to live in his mum's cellar until she rented it out to a family of dwarfs, and now he lived in the attic, which baked in the summer and froze in the winter. Carter survived because the walls were insulated with copies of *Bows & Ammo*, *Back Street Pins*, *Stanley Howler's Stamp Monthly*, *Giggles*, *Girls and Garters*, *Golem Spotter Weekly*, and *Fretwork Today*. These were only the top layer. In self-defence against the elements, he glued old copies over the larger cracks and holes in the roof. As far as Trev knew, Carter had never persevered beyond a week with any of the hobbies indicated by his rather embarrassing library except, possibly, the one notoriously associated with the centrefolds of *Giggles, Girls and Garters*.

319

Mrs Carter opened the door to him and indicated the stairs with all the hearty welcome and hospitality that mothers extend to their sons' no-good street friends. 'He's been ill,' she announced, as if it were a matter of interest rather than concern.

This turned out to be an understatement. One of Carter's eyes was a technicolor mess and there was a livid scar on his face. It took some time for Trev to find this out because Carter kept telling him to go away, but since the ramshackle door was held shut with a piece of string, the application of Trev's shoulder had seen to that, at least.

Trev stared at the boy, who shrank back into his unspeakably dreadful bed as if he was expecting to be hit. He didn't like Carter. No one liked Carter. It was impossible. Even Mrs Carter, who in theory at least should entertain some lukewarm affability to her son, didn't like Carter. He was fundamentally unlikeable. It was a sad thing to have to say, but Carter, farting or otherwise, was a wonderful example of charisntma. He could be fine for a day or two and then some utterly stupid comment or off-key joke or entirely inappropriate action would break the spell. But Trev put up with him, seeing in him, perhaps, what Trev might have been had he not been, in fact, Trev. Maybe there was a bit of Carter the Farter in every bloke at some time in his life he had thought, but with Carter it wasn't just a bit, it was everything.

'What 'appened?' Trev said.

'Nuffin'.'

'This is Trev. I know about nothin' 'appenin'. You need to get to the hospital with that.'

'It's worse than it looks,' Carter moaned.

Trev cracked. 'Are you bloody stupid? That cut's a quarter of an inch from your eye!'

'It was my fault,' Carter protested. 'I upset Andy.'

'Yeah, I can see where that'd have been your fault,' Trev said.

'Where were you last night?' said Carter.

'You wouldn't believe me.'

'Well, it was a bloody war, that's what it was.'

'I found it necessary to spend a little time down the Lat. There was fightin', wasn't there?'

'The clubs 'ave signed up to this new football and some people ain't 'appy.'

Trev said, 'Andy?' and looked at the livid, oozing scar again. Yep, that looked like Andy being unhappy.

It was hard to feel sorry for someone as basically unlikeable as Carter, but just because he had been born with Kick Me Up The Arse tattooed on to his soul was no reason for doing it. Not to Carter. That was like pulling wings off flies.

'Not just Andy,' said Carter. 'There's Tosher Atkinson and Jimmy the Spoon and Spanner.'

'Spanner?' said Trev.

'And Mrs Atkinson.'

'*Mrs Atkinson?*'

'And Willy Piltdown, Harry Capstick and the Brisket Boys.'

'Them? But we *hate* them. Andy hates them. They hate Andy. One foot on their turf and you get sent home in a sack!'

'Well, you know what they say,' said Carter. 'My enemy's enemy is my enemy.'

'I think you got that wrong,' said Trev. 'But I know what you mean.'

Trev stared at nothing, utterly aghast. The subjects of that litany of names were Faces. Hugely influential in the world of the teams and, more importantly, among the supporters. They owned the Shove. Pepe had been right. Vetinari thought the captains were in charge and the captains were not in charge. The Shove was in charge and the Faces ran the Shove.*

'There's going to be a team put together for tomorrow and they'll try to get as many of them in as possible,' Carter volunteered.

'Yeah, I heard.'

---

* One other reason that you could call them Faces was that crude drawings of them appeared on Watch posters, with hopeful messages asking people to let the Watch know if said person had been seen around and about.

321

'They're going to show Vetinari what they think of his new football.'

'I didn't hear the name of the Stollops there,' Trev said.

'I hear their dad's got them doing choir practice every night,' said Carter.

'The captains did sign up,' said Trev, 'so it'll look bad for them. But 'ow much do you think Andy and his little chums care 'bout that?' He leaned forward. 'Vetinari's got the Watch, though, 'asn't he? And you know about the Watch. Okay, so there's some decent bastards among 'em when you get 'em by theirselves, but if it all goes wahoonie-shaped they've got big, big sticks and big, big trolls and they've not got to bother too much about who they hit because they're the Watch, which means it's all legal. And, if you get 'em really pissed off, they'll add a charge of damaging their truncheons with your face. And talking of faces, exactly 'ow come you're a quarter-inch away from being a candidate for a white stick?'

'I told Andy I didn't think it was a good idea,' said Carter.

Trev couldn't hide his surprise. Even that much bravery was alien to Carter. 'Well, as it 'appens, it might be a blessin' in disguise. You just stay here in bed and you won't end up stuck between the Old Sam and Andy.'

He stopped because of a rustling noise.

Since Carter glued pages of his used magazines to the walls with flour-and-water paste, the attic was home to some quite well fed mice, and for some reason, one of them had just gnawed its way to freedom via the chest of last year's Miss April, thus giving her a third nipple, which was, in fact, staring at Trev and wobbling. It was a sight to put anyone off their tea.

'What're you goin' to do?' said Carter.

'Anything I can,' said Trev.

'You know Andy's out to get you? You and that weird bloke.'

'I'm not afraid of Andy,' said Trev. As a statement, this was entirely true. He was not frightened of Andy. He was mortally terrified to his boots and back again, with a visceral fear that dripped off his ribs like melting snow.

'Everyone's afraid of Andy, Trev. If they're smart,' said Carter.

'Hey, Fartmeister, I'm Trevor Likely!'

'I think you're goin' to need a lot more than that.'

I am going to need a lot more than that, thought Trev, travelling at speed across the city. If even Pepe knew there was something on the boil, then surely the Old Sam would know too? Oops.

He sprinted quickly to the horse bus's rear platform and landed in the road before the conductor was anywhere near. If they didn't catch you on the bus then they couldn't catch you at all, and while they were issued with those big shiny choppers to deter non-paying passengers, everyone knew that a) they were too scared to use them and b) the amount of trouble they would get into if they actually whacked a respectable member of society did not bear thinking of.

He darted through the alley into Cockbill Street, spotted another bus plodding its way in the right direction, jumped on to the running board and held on. He was lucky this time. The conductor gave him a look and then very carefully did not see him.

By the time he reached the big junction known as Five Ways, he had travelled almost the width of the city at an average speed faster than walking pace and had hardly had to run very far at all. A near perfect result for Trev Likely, who wouldn't walk if he could ride.

And there, right in front of him, was the Hippo. It used to be a race-track until all that was moved up to the far end of Ankh. Now, it was just a big space that every large town needs for markets, fairs, the occasional insurrection and, of course, the increasingly popular cart-tail sales, which were very fashionable with people who wanted to buy their property back.

It was full today, without even a stolen shovel to be seen. All over the field, people were kicking footballs about. Trevor relaxed a little. There were pointy hats in the distance and no one seemed to be doing any murder.

'Wotcher, howya doing?'

He adjusted his eyeline down a little bit. 'How's it goin', Throat?'

'I'm hearing you're kind of associated with Unseen Academicals,' said Cut-Me-Own-Throat Dibbler, the city's most enterprising but inexplicably least successful businessman.

'Don't tell me you've come to sell pies?'

'Nah, nah, nah,' said Dibbler. 'Too many amateurs here today. My pies aren't just knocked up out of rubbish for a load of drunken old football fans.'

'So *your* pies are for—?' Trev left the question hanging in the air with a noose on the end of it.

'Anyway, pies are so yesterday,' said Dibbler dismissively. 'I am on the ground floor of football memorabilityness.'

'What's that, then?'

'Like genuine autographed team jerseys and that sort of thing. I mean, look here.' Dibbler produced from the large tray around his neck a smaller version of what one of the new *gloing! gloing!* footballs would be if it were about a half of the size and had been badly carved out of wood. 'See those white patches? That's so they can be signed by the team.'

'You're goin' to get them signed, are you?'

'Well, no, I think people would like to get that done themselves. The personal touch, you know what I mean?'

'So they're actually just painted balls of wood and nothin' else?' said Trev.

'But authentic!' said Dibbler. 'Just like the shirts. Want one? Five dollars to you, and that's cutting me own throat.' He produced a skimpy red cotton item and waved it enticingly.

'What's that?'

'Your team colours, right?'

'Two big yellow Us on the front?' said Trev. 'That's wrong! Ours has got two little Us interlocked on the left breast like a badge. Very stylish.'

'Pretty much the same,' said Dibbler airily. 'No one'll notice. And I had to keep the price down for the kiddies.'

He leaned closer. 'Anything you can tell me about the game tomorrow, Trev? Looks like the teams are putting together a tough squad. Vetinari's not going to get it all his own way for once?'

324

'We'll play a good game, you'll see,' said Trev.

'Right! Can't lose with a Likely playing, right?'

'I just help around the place. I'm not playin'. I promised my ol' mum after Dad died.'

Dibbler looked around at the crowded stadium of the Hippo. He appeared to have something else on his mind other than the need for the next dollar. 'What happens if your lot lose?' he said.

'It's only a game,' said Trev.

'Ah, but Vetinari's got his reputation based on it.'

'It's a game. One side wins, one side loses. Just a game.'

'A lot of people aren't thinking like that,' said Dibbler. 'Things always come out well for Vetinari,' he went on, staring at the sky. 'And that's the magic, see? Everyone thinks he always gets it right. What do you think will happen if he gets things wrong?'

'It's *just* a game, Throat, only a game . . . Be seein' you.' Trev wandered onwards. People were putting up tiers of wooden stands on one side of the arena, and because this was Ankh-Morpork, when two or more people gathered together thousands turned up just to wonder why.

And there was Mr Ponder Stibbons, sitting at a long table with some of the football captains. Oh, yes, the Rules Committee. There had been talk about that. Even with the rules written down, and half of them as old as the game itself, there were a few things that had to be made clear. He arrived in time to hear Ponder say, 'Look, you can't have a situation in the new game where people hang around right next to the other team's goal.'

'Worked all right before,' said one of the captains.

'Yes, but the ball flies. One really good kick would send it down half the length of the Hippo. If someone gets that right the goalkeeper wouldn't have a chance.'

'So, what you're saying,' said Mr Stollop, who had become a kind of spokesman for the captains, 'is that there's got to be two blokes from team A in front of a bloke from team B before he scores?'

'Yes, that's about right,' said Ponder stiffly, 'but one of them is the goalkeeper.'

'So, what happens if one of them fellers nips past him downfield before he kicks the ball?'

'Then he will be what is traditionally known as off his side,' said Ponder.

'Off his head, more like,' said one of the captains. And since this had the same shape as humour, it got a laugh. 'If that's true, you could end up with loads of blokes rushing past one another, all trying to get the other poor buggers into an unlawful position without any of the poor devils moving, right?'

'Nevertheless, we are standing by this rule. We have tried it out. It allows for free movement on the field. In the old game it wasn't unusual for players to bring their lunch and a copy of *Girls, Giggles and Garters* and just wait for the ball to come along.'

'Hello, Trev, how are you getting on?' It was Andy, and he was standing behind Trev.

There must be a thousand people here today, Trev thought in a curiously slow and blissful sort of way. And a lot of watchmen. I can see a couple of them from here. Andy isn't going to try anything right here, is he?

Well, yes, he might, because that's what made him Andy. The little bee that buzzed in his brain might bang against the wrong bit and he would carve your face off. Oh, yes, and there was Tosher Atkinson and his mum, strolling about as if out for a walk.

'Haven't seen you about much lately, Trev,' said Andy. 'Been busy, I suspect?'

'I thought you were lyin' low?' said Trev hopelessly.

'Well, you know what they say. Sooner or later all sins are forgiven.'

In your case, quite a bit later, Trev thought.

'Besides,' said Andy, 'I'm turning over a new leaf, ain't I?'

'Oh, yeah?'

'Got out of the Shove,' said Andy. 'Gotta put aside my scallywag ways. Time to fit in.'

'Glad to hear it,' said Trev, waiting for the knife.

'So I'm a key player for Ankh-Morpork United.' It wasn't a knife, but it had a rather similar effect. 'Apparently his lordship gave them the idea,' Andy said, still speaking in the same greasy, friendly tone. 'Of course, no one wants to be the team playing you wizards. So there is, like, a new one just for the occasion.'

'I thought you never played?' said Trev weakly.

'Ah, but that was in the bad old days before football was open to more individual effort and enterprise. See this shirt?' he said.

Trev looked down. He hadn't thought much about what the man was wearing, just that he was there.

'White with blue trim,' said Andy cheerfully. 'Very snazzy.' He turned around. The numeral 1 was on the back in blue with the name Andy Shank above it. 'My idea. Very sensible. Means we'll know who we are from the back.'

'And I told your wizards that your gentlemen ought to do the same,' said Mrs Atkinson, surely one of the most feared Faces who had ever wielded a sharpened umbrella with malice aforethought. Grown men would back away from Mrs Atkinson, otherwise grown men bled.

Just what we need, thought Trev. Our names on the back as well. Saves them having the trouble to go round the front before they stab.

'Still, I can't stand here chattin' all day with you. Got to talk to the team. Got to think about tactics.'

There will be a referee, thought Trev. The Watch will be there. Lord Vetinari will be there. Unfortunately, Andy Shank will be there, too, and Nutt wants me as his assistant and so I've got to be there. If it all goes wrong, the floor of the arena isn't going to be the place to be and I'll be in it.

'And if you're wondering where that dim little girl of yours is, she's back there with the fat girl. Honestly, what must you think of me?'

'Nothing, right up until you said that,' said Trev. 'And now I do.'

'Give my best to the orc,' said Andy. 'Shame to hear he's the last one.'

They strolled on, but Trev was quick enough to get out of the way before Mrs Atkinson sliced at his leg with her stick.

Find Juliet. Find Nutt. Find Glenda. Find help. Find a ticket to Fourecks.

Trev had never fought. Never *really* fought. Oh, there had been times when he was younger when he was drawn into a bit of a ruck and it was politic to be among the other kids, holding a makeshift weapon in his hands. He'd been so good at appearing to be everywhere, shouting a lot and then running into the thick of the fray, but never actually catching up with the real action. He could go to the Watch and tell them . . . that Andy had been threatening? Andy was *always* threatening. When trouble struck in the Shove as it sometimes did, when two tribes were brought into conjunction, there was always the forest of legs to dive between and once, when Trev had been really desperate, a number of shoulders to run across . . . What was he thinking? He wouldn't be there. He wasn't going to play. He'd promised his old mum. Everyone knew he'd promised his old mum. He'd like to play, but his old mum wouldn't like it. It was as if his old mum had written him a note: Dear Andy, please do not knife Trevor today because he has promised not to play.

He blinked away the sensation that a knife was already hurtling towards him and heard the voice of Nutt saying, 'Oh, I have heard about *Bu-bubble*.' There was Glenda and Juliet and Nutt and Juliet and a slightly worried young lady with a notebook and Juliet. There was also Juliet, but it was hard to even notice her because Juliet was there.

'She says she wants to write an article,' said Glenda, who had clearly waylaid the journalist. 'Her name is Miss—'

'Roz,' said the girl. 'Everyone's talking about you, Mister Nutt. Would you answer a few questions, please? We have a very now audience.'*

'Yes?' he ventured.

'How does it feel to be an orc, Mister Nutt?'

'I am not sure. How does it feel to be human?' said Nutt.

'Have your experiences as an orc affected the way you will play football?'

'I will only be playing as a substitute. My role is merely that of a

---

* An archbishop in a house of negotiable affection might have looked a little more puzzled than Nutt right now, but the amount of said puzzlement depends on how many archbishops you know.

328

trainer. And, I have to say, in answer to your question, I'm not sure I have had many experiences as an orc up until now.'

'But are you advising the players to rip opponents' heads off?' the girl giggled.

Glenda opened her mouth, but Nutt said solemnly, 'No, that would be against the rules.'

'I hear they think you're a very good trainer. Why do you think this is?'

Despite the patent stupidity of the question, Nutt seemed to think deeply. 'One must consider the horizons of possibility,' he said slowly. '*E Pluribus Unum*, the many become one, but it could just as easily be said that the one becomes many, *Ex uno multi*, and indeed, as Von Sliss said in *The Effluence of Reality*, the one, when carefully considered, may in fact be a many in different clothing.'

Glenda looked at the girl's face. Her expression hadn't moved and neither had her pencil. Nutt smiled to himself and continued. 'Now let us consider this in the light, as it may be, of the speeding ball. Where it has come from we believe we know, but where it will land is an ever-changing conundrum, even if only considered in four-dimensional space. And there we have the existential puzzle that confronts the striker, for he is both striker and struck. As the ball flies, all possibilities are inexorably linked, as Herr Frugal said in *Das Nichts des Wissens*, "Ich kann mich nicht genau erinnern, aber es war so etwas wie eine Vanillehaltige süsse Nachspeisenbeigabe," although I believe he was on some medication at the time. Who is mover and who is moved? Given that the solution can only be arrived at through conceptual manifestation using, I believe, some perception of transfinite space, it can clearly be seen that among the possibilities is that the ball will land everywhere at the same time or turn out never to have been kicked at all. It is my job to reduce this metaphysical overhead, as it were, and to give my lads some acceptable paradigm, such as, it might be, whack it right down the middle, my son, and at least if the goalie stops it you will have given him a hot handful he won't forget in a hurry.

'You see, the thing about football is that it is not about football. It is a most fascinating multi-dimensional philosophy, an extrusion, as it were, of what Doctor Maspinder promulgated in *Das Meer von Unvermeidlichkeit*. Now, you would say to me, I am sure,' he went on, 'What of the 4–4–2 or even the 4–1–2–1–2, yes? And my answer to that would be, there is only the one. Traditionally we say there are eleven players in the team, but that is because of our rather feeble perceptions. In truth, there is only the one and therefore, I would say,' he gave a little laugh, 'daring to adapt a line from *The Doors of Deception*: it does not matter whether you win or lose so long as you score the most goals.'

The girl looked down at her notepad. 'Could you give that to me a little bit more simply?'

'Oh, I'm sorry,' said Nutt. 'I thought I had.'

'And I think that's about enough,' said Glenda, taking the girl by the arm.

'But I haven't asked him about his favourite spoon,' she wailed.

Nutt cleared his throat. 'Well, I would have appreciated some notice of that question because it is quite a large field, but I think the Great Bronze Spoon of Cladh, which weighed more than a ton, would definitely have to be a runner, though we must not forget the set of spoons, each one smaller than a grain of rice, crafted by some unknown genius for the concubines of the Emperor Whezi. But undoubtedly, from what I can gather, these were surpassed by the notorious clock-work spoon, devised by Bloody Stupid Johnson, which could apparently stir coffee so fast that the cup would actually rise up from the saucer and hit the ceiling. Oh, to be a fly on that wall, but not too close, obviously. Possibly less well known is the singing spoon of the learned sage Ly Tin Wheedle, which could entertain the dinner table by singing comic songs. Among other great spoons—'

'That *is* enough,' said Glenda, tugging the girl away for her own good.

'He's an orc?' the girl said.

'So everyone says,' said Glenda.

'Were they all like that? I thought it was all about twisting heads off?'

'Well, I suspect people get bored with the same old thing.'

'But how does he know all about spoons?'

'Believe me, if anyone has ever written *Great Spoons of the World*, Mister Nutt has read it.'

Trev heard the girl's plaintive voice as Glenda almost forcibly led her away, or at least away from Nutt. 'I really wanted to talk to Jewels,' Trev heard the girl say, as she walked past Juliet without a glance. 'But she's hiding out, everyone says.'

He hurried across and pulled the other two in a huddle towards him. 'There's gonna be murder tomorrow,' he said. 'The wizards can't use magic and Ankh-Morpork United is gonna be made up out of the toughest, nastiest bunch of buggers that're outside of the Tanty.'

'We shall have to change our tactics to suit, then,' said Nutt.

'Are you nu— insane? I'm talkin' about people like Andy, Nutt. An' he might not be the worst one.'

'But everything is a matter of tactics. A respect for strengths and weaknesses and the proper utilization of the knowledge,' said Nutt.

'Listen!' said Trev. 'There won't be time for that sort of thing.'

'If I may quote—' Nutt began.

'I said listen! Do you know any quotes by people who have been knifed in the back an' then kicked in the nu—' He stopped and then continued. 'Kicked when they're lyin' on the ground, yes? Because that's what you need to be thinkin' about at the moment.'

'The Watch will be there,' said Nutt.

'But generally their way of dealing with a complicated event is to get everyone lyin' on the ground,' said Trev. 'That makes it simpler.'

'I feel certain that we could beat any team at football,' said Nutt soothingly.

Trev looked around him in a desperate search for anyone who might have a grip. 'It doesn't work like that! It's not about the football!'

'I don't think I want to see anyone hurt,' said Juliet.

'Then you'll have to close your eyes,' said Trev. 'Nutt, you think that everythin' is going to be nice and sportsmanlike 'cos that's how the new football has been designed, but it's the same old people out there. You know what I think?'

'My dad says it won't look very good for Vetinari if the Academicals lose,' said Juliet.

'An' will he be glad about that?' said Trev.

'Well, I suppose, yes, but even Dad says prob'ly better to have bloody Vetinari than most of the buggers we've had.'

That was because the city *worked*, thought Trev. It had been a mess before Vetinari had taken over and no one knew exactly how he'd done it. He'd got the Watch working properly. He'd got the war between the dwarfs and the trolls sorted out. He let people do whatever they liked, provided they did whatever *he* liked. And above all, the city was crammed with people and money. Everyone wanted to live in Ankh-Morpork. Could he really be shaken down because the new football went bad? Well, the answer was, of course, yes – because that's how people were.

Trev mentioned this to Glenda as she came back from ushering the bemused Roz out of the range of more of Nutt's philosophy. She looked at Trev and said, 'Do you think Vetinari knows about this?'

'Dunno,' said Trev. 'Well, I know he's s'posed to have lots of spies, but I dunno whether they'd know about this.'

'Do you think someone ought to tell him?' said Glenda.

Trev laughed. 'What are you suggestin'? That we go over to the palace, walk right up to him and say, "Excuse us, mister, there are a few things that have escaped your attention?" '

'Yes,' said Glenda.

'Thank you, Drumknott, that will be all for now,' said Vetinari.

'Yes, sir,' said Drumknott. He nodded at Lady Margolotta and oiled his way noiselessly out of the room.

'Havelock, I appreciate that Drumknott is very competent, but he always seems to me to be a rather strange little man.'

'Well, it would be a funny old world if we were all alike, madam, although I admit not very funny if we were all like Drumknott. But he is loyal and excessively trustworthy,' said Vetinari.

'Hmm,' said her ladyship. 'Does he have much of a personal life?'

'I believe that he collects different types of stationery,' said Vetinari. 'I have sometimes speculated that he might change his life for the better should he meet a young lady willing to dress up as a manila envelope.'

They were on the balcony outside the Oblong Office, which offered a perfect view of the centre of the city while leaving the viewer almost invisible.

'The accord is going ahead?' said Vetinari.

'Certainly,' said her ladyship. 'Peace at last between dwarfs and trolls.'

Vetinari smiled. 'The word "peace" is generally defined as a period of rest and rearmament before the next war. Were many assassinations necessary?'

'Havelock, sometimes you are too direct!'

'I do beg your pardon, it's just that the progress of history requires butchers as well as shepherds.'

'There were no assassinations,' said her ladyship. She turned her eyes upwards. 'There was, however, a terrible mining accident and a rather unusual rock slide. But, of course, there is still the Loko business to sort out. The dwarfs still want total extermination.'

'How many orcs are there?'

'Nobody knows. Perhaps Nutt will be able to find them.'

'We must not have genocide,' said Vetinari. 'History has a way of repaying.'

'He is turning out to be quite a surprise.'

'So I understand. From the reports I have been receiving, all that the orcs were not, he is.'

'But he will remain an orc underneath it all,' said her ladyship.

'I wonder what remains under all of us?' said Vetinari.

'You've taken a very big risk, you know,' said Lady Margolotta.

'Madam, this city is all risk, I assure you.'

'And power is a game of smoke and mirrors,' said her ladyship, reaching for the wine.

'Oddly enough, Commander Vimes reminds me of that nearly every day. No civil police force could hold out against an irate and resolute population. The trick is not to let them realize that. Yes?'

There was a knock at the door. It was Drumknott again. 'I am sorry to interrupt, sir, madam, but in the circumstances I thought it would be a good idea.' He sniffed. 'It's the lady with the pies.'

'Ah, Miss Sugarbean, legendary inventor of the famous Ploughman's Pie,' said Vetinari. He glanced at her ladyship. 'And Mister Nutt's friend.'

'I have met her, Havelock. She harangued me.'

'Yes, she does it very well. You feel as if you've had a nice cold bath. Do show her in, Drumknott.'

'And there is a young man with her. I recognize him as Trevor Likely, son of the famous footballer Dave Likely, and I am informed by her that she has indeed brought you a Ploughman's Pie.'

'You would take untested food from a member of the public?' said her ladyship, horrified.

'Certainly from this one,' said Vetinari. 'There is no possible way that she would ever put poison in anything. Not out of respect for me, you understand, but out of respect for the food. Don't leave. I think you will find this . . . interesting.'

The pie was still warm in Glenda's hands as she stepped into the Oblong Office. She herself almost froze at the sight of Lady Margolotta, but a certain robustness kicked in.

'Do I have to curtsy?' she said.

'Not unless you really feel the need.'

'We've come to warn you,' said Trev.

'Indeed.' Vetinari raised an eyebrow.

'Ankh-Morpork United will walk all over Unseen Academicals with great big boots on.'

'Oh, dear. Do you think that will be the case?'

'They're not yer average players!' Trev blurted out. 'They're from the Shove. They go armed.'

'Ah, yes. Football as warfare,' said Vetinari. 'Well, thank you for telling me.'

Silence fell. Vetinari broke it by saying, 'Was there anything else you would like to say?' He looked at the pie that Glenda was holding out in front of her like some kind of chastity device.

'Can't you do something?' she said.

'It's a game, Miss Sugarbean. Having suggested the match in the first place, what do you think I would look like if I intervened? There will, after all, be rules. There will, after all, be a referee.'

'They won't care,' said Trev.

'Then I suppose the Watch will have to do its duty. And now, if you will excuse me, I have affairs of state to attend to, but please leave the pie.'

'One moment,' said her ladyship. 'Why have you come to warn his lordship, young lady?'

'Isn't that the sort of thing I ought to do?' said Glenda.

'And you walked in, just like that?'

'Well, the pie helped.'

'We have met before, you know,' said her ladyship.

She stared at Glenda and Glenda stared back, and she finally managed, 'Yes, I know, and I'm not frightened and I'm not sorry.'

The battle of the stares went on for a year too long and then Lady Margolotta turned her head away sharply and said, 'Well, you have got one of them right, but I am sure I shall enjoy the pie and also the match.'

'Yes, yes,' said Vetinari. 'Thank you both for calling, but if you will excuse us we do have matters of state to discuss.'

'Well!' said Lady Margolotta as the door shut behind them. 'What type of people are you incubating in this city of yours, Havelock?'

'I imagine some of the very best,' said Vetinari.

'Two common people can barge in on you without so much as an appointment?'

'But with a pie,' said Vetinari quickly.

'You were expecting them?'

'Let us just say that I was not unduly surprised,' said Vetinari. 'I certainly know about the make-up of Ankh-Morpork United. So does the Watch.'

'And you are going to let them into an arena with a bunch of old wizards who have promised not to do magic?'

'A bunch of old wizards and Mister Nutt,' said Vetinari cheerfully. 'Apparently he's very good at tactical planning.'

'I can't allow that.'

'This is my city, Margolotta. There are no slaves in Ankh-Morpork.'

'He is my ward. I expect you will ignore that, though.'

'I have every intention of doing so. After all, it's only a game.'

'But a game is not about games. And what sort of game do you think you will get tomorrow?'

'A war,' said Vetinari. 'And the thing about war is that it's about war.'

Lady Margolotta shot out her long sleeve and a fine steel dagger was suddenly in her hand.

'I suggest you cut it in half,' said Vetinari, indicating the pie, 'and I will choose which half to pick up.'

'But what if one half has more pickled onions than the other?'

'Then I think that will be open to negotiation. Would you like some more . . . wine?'

'Did you see that she tried to stare me down?' said Margolotta.

'Yes,' said Vetinari. 'I saw that she succeeded.'

When Glenda and Trev got back to the Hippo, Nutt looked at them expectantly. 'He hardly listened,' said Trev.

'Quite so,' said Nutt. 'I am confident of our success on the morrow. I am quite certain that we will be tactically supreme.'

'I'm just glad I won't be playin', that's all,' said Trev.

'Yes, Mister Trev, that really is a great shame.'

From the nearby table where last-minute adjustments were being made by the Football League came the voice of somebody saying, 'Nah, nah. Look, you've still got it wrong. If a bloke from side B is closer to the goal-keeper – no, I tell a lie – if he's closer to the goal than the goalkeeper, then he surely puts one away there and then. Stands to reason.'

There was a sigh that could only have come from Ponder Stibbons. 'No, I don't think you understand . . .'

Another voice chipped in. 'If the goalkeeper is that far out of his goal then he's a pillock!'

'Look, let's start again,' said another voice. 'Supposing I'm this bloke here.' Trev looked across and saw one of the men flick a screwed-up piece of paper across the table. 'Like, I've kicked the ball that far and this is me, this piece of paper. Then what?' He flicked the paper once again, which hit Ponder's pencil.

'No! I've already explained that. And stop flicking bits of paper around, I find it very confusing.'

'But it must work if he dribbles on it,' said a voice.

'Hold on a minute, though,' said yet another voice. 'What happens, right, if you get the ball in your own half of the field and run all the way, not passing it to anyone else, and get it into the net?'

'That would be perfectly legal,' said Ponder.

'Yeah, but there's no way that's goin' to happen, is there?' said the man who had just flicked a soggy piece of paper and had enjoyed it so much that he'd flicked another one.

'But if he tries and succeeds it would be magnificent football, would it not?' said Ponder.

'Where's our team?' said Trev, looking around.

'I've suggested they have an early night,' said Ponder.

'An early night for wizards is two o'clock in the morning,' said Glenda.

'I have also given instructions that the team are to have a special meal this evening,' said Nutt. 'On that note, Miss Glenda, I shall have to ask you to lock the Night Kitchen.'

Stony silence hung over the dining room that evening.

'I don't eat salads,' said Bledlow Nobbs (no relation). 'They gives me the wind.'

'How can a man live without pasta?' said Bengo. 'This is barbaric!'

'I hope you notice that my plate is as barren as yours, gentlemen,' said Ridcully. 'Mister Nutt is training us and I'm allowing Mister Nutt the driver's seat. Nor is there to be any smoking this evening.'

There was a chorus of dismay and he raised his hand for silence.

'Also, his instruction here . . .' He looked closer at Nutt's rather untidy writing and gave a little smile. 'There is to be no sexual congress.' This did not meet with the reaction he had expected.

'That means talking about it, doesn't it?' said the Chair of Indefinite Studies.

'No, that's oral sex,' said Rincewind.

'No, that's listening to it.'

Bengo Macarona sat with a dazed look on his face.

'Now, I don't want any sneaking off for midnight snacks,' said Ridcully. 'There are rules. Mrs Whitlow and Miss Sugarbean have been told that I fully back Mister Nutt's authority here. Surely you gentlemen could show some backbone?'

'In an attempt to show solidarity with the rest of the team,' said the Lecturer in Recent Runes, 'I am led to believe that there is some cheese in the mousetrap in my room.'

Ridcully was left all alone with only the echo of falling chairs for company.

The Archchancellor repaired to his own room and tossed his hat on to its stand. There have to be rules, he said to himself, and there has to be a rule for them and a rule for me. He went to his eight-poster bed and opened the hatch containing the tobacco jar. It now contained a little note instead, saying,

> 'Dear Archchancellor,
> In accordance with your ratification of Mister Nutt's
> instructions that the faculty are not to be allowed food or
> the implements of smoking this evening, I've taken the
> liberty of clearing away your cigarettes and pipe tobacco.
> May I also mention that I have emptied the cool cupboard
> of the usual cold cuts and pickles to avoid temptation.'

'Bugger,' said Ridcully under his breath.

He walked to his wardrobe and rummaged in the pocket of his smoking jacket, coming up with a note that said,

'In accordance with Mister Nutt's rules, as ratified by yourself, Archchancellor [and it was remarkable how reproachful Mrs Whitlow could make her handwriting], *I have taken the liberty of removing your emergency peppermints.'*

'Change and decay!' Ridcully declared to the night air. 'I am surrounded by traitors! They thwart me at every turn.' He wandered disconsolately past his bookcase and pulled out Boddrys' *Occult Companion*, a book he knew by heart. And because he knew the book by heart, page 14 opened on to a neat little cavity, which contained a packet of extra-strong liquorice mints, an ounce of Jolly Sailor tobacco and a packet of Wizzla's . . . And, as it turned out, a small note:

'Dear Archchancellor,
I just didn't have the heart. Mrs Whitlow.'

It seemed darker than usual. Generally, the Archchancellor's rulings were obeyed, and it seemed to the members of Unseen Academicals that every door was closed, indeed slammed, as they searched for food. Every pantry was locked and spell-proofed. The team trudged helplessly from one hall to another.

'I do have some reheatable pasta in my room,' said Bengo Macarona. 'My grandmother gave it to me before I came down here. It will keep for ten years and my grandmother says that it will taste as good after ten years as it does now. I regret that she may have been telling the truth.'

'If you get it, we could cook it up in my room,' said the Lecturer in Recent Runes.

'If you like. It contains alligator testicles, for nourishment. They are very popular at home.'

'I didn't know alligators had testicles,' said the Lecturer in Recent Runes.

'They haven't got 'em any more,' said Bledlow Nobbs (no relation).

'I've got a biscuit, we could share that out,' said Ponder Stibbons. He was immediately pierced by their questioning gazes. 'No,' he said, 'I am not going to countermand the Archchancellor's orders any further than that. I would never hear the last of it, gentlemen. Without a hierarchy we are nothing.'

'The Librarian will have some bananas,' said Rincewind.

'Are you sure?' said Macarona.

'I think the Librarian has a motto in these cases: "If you try to take my bananas from me, I will reclaim them from your cold dead hands." '

Trev, who had been lurking in the shadows, waited until the rumble of stomachs died away in the distance and then hurried back and knocked on the bolted door of the Night Kitchen. 'They've all met up and they're headed for the Library.'

'Good, I think he'll share his bananas with them,' said Nutt.

'I don't really see the point,' said Glenda.

'The point is they are friends. Partners in adversity. They are a team. That is football. You have to train a team to be a team and I will have no problem with them having a very large breakfast in the morning.'

Nutt was changing, Trev thought. 'Can I ask you a personal question, Mister Nutt?'

'Nearly all the questions people ask me are personal, though do go ahead, Mister Trev.'

'Well, er, all right. Sometimes you look big and sometimes you look small. What's that all about?'

'It is something built into us,' said Nutt. 'I believe that it is a product of the morphic field contracting and expanding. It affects your perceptions.'

'When you're upset, you do look very small,' said Glenda.

'What size do I look now?'

'Pretty big,' said Trev.

'Good,' said Nutt, helping himself to a slice of pie. 'Tomorrow I intend to look even bigger.'

'There's somethin' else we have to do,' said Trev. 'Pepe wants to help me. He thinks I'm gonna play football.'

'Well, you are going to play football,' said Nutt.

'No! You know this! I promised my ol' mum and you can't break a promise to your ol' mum, Gods rest her soul. Do you 'ave keys to the wine cellar, Glenda?'

'Do you think I'd tell you, Trev Likely?'

'Thought not. I want two bottles of best brandy. And, er, could you all come with me, please? I think Pepe means well, but he, er, well, you know him, it's midnight and everythin'.'

'I think I know Pepe,' said Glenda.

There was a guard on the rear door of Shatta, but before he could even think of turning away Trev and his bodyguards, Pepe appeared. 'Cor! Three chums. I must be very frightening,' he said, leering. 'Hello, chums, got the brandy?'

'Yes, what's this all about, Pepe? You've been putting the willies up Trev,' said Glenda.

'I never have! I hardly ever put the willies up anyone these days. I just told him he was going to play in the football.'

'I promised my ol' mum,' said Trev, clinging to the declaration as if it were a tiny raft in a choppy sea.

'But you've got a star in your hand and you don't have much of a choice.'

Trev looked at his palm. 'Just a lot of lines.'

'Well there's them that has the sight and there again there's them that don't. I'm one of those that have. 's metaphorical, see. But all it is is that I would like to give you a little something that may be of use to you tomorrow. What am I saying? It might damn well save your life,' said Pepe. 'It'll certainly save your marriage. I'm sure the ladies here would like to think that us at Shatta have done the best for you.'

'For what it's worth, Trev, I trust Pepe,' said Glenda.

'And this is Mister Nutt,' said Trev. 'He's a friend.'

'Yeah. I know what Mister Nutt is,' said Pepe. 'And you can come, too. I am pleased to make your . . . acquaintance.'

He turned to Glenda. 'You girls stay here, miss,' he said. 'This is no errand for a lady.' He ushered the boys into the gloom. 'What I'm going to show you gentlemen is top secret and if you cross me, Trev Likely, I will do things that will make Andy Shank look like a playground bully.'

'Andy was a playground bully,' said Trev, as they reached what was clearly a forge.

'Micromail,' said Pepe with satisfaction. 'The world hasn't seen the half of it yet.'

'It just looks like fine chain mail,' said Nutt.

'It's strange stuff,' said the dwarf. 'I can give you a vest and pair of shorts and they better both come back here, boy, otherwise said implications will be performed on your arse and I ain't kidding. This stuff isn't just for making the girls look pretty. You would be amazed what it can do with just a little change in the alloy.' He pointed to a glistening heap. 'It's as light as a feather and doesn't chafe, you know.'

'And what else does it do?'

'I'll show you in a minute. Slip on a pair of the shorts.'

'Wot, here?' said Trev.

Somehow, Pepe looked like a small demon by the light of the forge. 'Ooh, look at Mister Bashful!' said Pepe. 'Just pull a pair on over your trousers for now and I'll tell you what I'll do, I'll even turn my back while you're doing that.' He looked away, fiddling with the tools beside the anvil. 'Got 'em on?' he said, after listening to a few minutes of heavy breathing.

'Yes, they, er, well, they feel all right.'

'Okay,' said Pepe. 'Could you just wait 'ere one moment.' He disappeared into the darkness and, after a succession of strange noises, walked back into view, slowly and awkwardly.

'What's that you're wearin', Pepe?' said Trev. 'It looks like a mass of cushions to me.'

'Oh, just a bit of protection,' said Pepe. 'Now if you could just go back a little way, Mister Nutt, and Trev, if you could oblige me by putting your hands on your head, it just helps to get the measurements right.' He turned his back on them. 'Okay, Trevor, are your hands on your head?'

'Yeah, yeah.'

At which point, Pepe spun round and hit him full force in the groin with a twenty-four-pound sledgehammer . . .

Surprisingly, the only effect was to send Pepe crashing into the opposite wall. 'Perfect!' said his voice, muffled by the padding.

Morning came, but it seemed to Glenda that there was no night and no day, no work and no play, there was just football, ahead of them all, drawing them together. In the Great Hall the team had a table all to themselves. Servants and wizards side by side, filling up as only Unseen University could.

Football owned the day. Nothing was happening that wasn't about football. There were certainly no lectures. Of course, there never were, but at least today they weren't being attended because of the excitement about the upcoming match rather than not being attended because no one wanted to go to them. And after a while, Glenda became aware of the sound which was coming from the city itself.

There were crowds outside the university; there were crowds, even now, queuing to get into the Hippo. The sound of a hundred thousand people at one purpose rose like the buzz of a distant swarm.

Glenda went back to the sanctuary of the Night Kitchen and tried to pass some time by doing some baking, but the dough fell from her fingers.

'Are you upset?' said Juliet.

'I hope we're going to win,' said Glenda.

'Well, of course we're going to win,' said Juliet.

'That's all very well up until the time we lose,' said Glenda. 'Yes, who's that?'

The door was pushed open and Pepe stepped in, looking smarter than usual. 'Hello, ladies,' he said. 'Got a little message for you. How was you expecting to watch the match?'

'Just so long as we can get close,' said Glenda.

'Tell you what, then,' said Pepe. 'Madame has got the best seats in the stadium. Nothing underhand, just open and above-board bribery.

Shatta has got to be seen out and about, you see? Got to keep micro-mail in the public eye.'

'I'd love to!' Juliet shouted. And even Glenda found that her automatic, unthinking cynicism was letting her down.

'There will be sherry,' said Pepe.

'Will there be anyone famous there?' said Juliet.

Pepe walked over and prodded her gently in the chest and said, 'Yes. You, miss. Everyone wants to see Jewels.'

It seemed as if the clocks turned backwards. All Watch leave had been suspended, but it was hard to see what crime there could be in streets where nobody could move. A flood of humanity, well, mostly humanity, poured towards the stadium, bounced off it and overflowed and backfilled more and more of the city. The game was in the Hippo, the crowd stretched back to Sator Square and eventually the pressure of so many eyeballs on the hands of so many clocks moved time forwards.

Only the team, and Trev, remained in the Great Hall, everyone else having left much earlier in a fruitless attempt at securing a seat. They milled around aimlessly prodding the ball to one another until Ponder, Nutt and the Archchancellor turned up.

'Well, big day, lads!' said Ridcully. 'Looks like there's going to be a nice day for it as well. They're all over there waiting for us to give them a show. I want you to approach this in the best traditions of Unseen University sportsmanship, which is to cheat whenever you are unobserved, though I fear that the chance of anyone being unobserved today is remote. But in any case, I want you all to give it one hundred and ten per cent.'

'Excuse me, Archchancellor,' said Ponder Stibbons. 'I understand the sense of what you are saying, but there is only one hundred per cent.'

'Well, they could give it one hundred and ten per cent if they tried harder,' said Ridcully.

'Well, yes and no, sir. But, in fact, that would mean that you had just made the one hundred per cent bigger while it would still be one hundred per cent. Besides, there is only so fast a man can run, only so high a man can jump. I just wanted to make the point.'

'Good point, well made,' said Ridcully, dismissing it instantly. He looked around at the faces. 'Ah, Mister Likely, I suppose there is nothing I can do that would get you on to the team? Dave Likely's boy playing for Unseen Academicals would be a bit of a feather in our cap. And I see my colleague Professor Rincewind has humorously already put a white one in his.'

'Well, sir, you know how I'm fixed,' Trev mumbled.

'Your old mum,' said Ridcully, nodding understandingly.

'I promised her,' said Trev. 'I know she's passed away, but I'm certain that she still watches over me, sir.'

'Well, that's nice and does you credit. Is there anything else that can be said? Let me think. Oh yes, gentlemen – Mrs Whitlow, as is her wont on these occasions, has organized her maids to dress up in appropriate costume and cheer us on from the sidelines.' His face was a blank mask as he continued. 'Mrs Whitlow unaccountably takes an enthusiastic and uncharacteristically athletic part in these things. There will be high kicking, I am told, but if you are careful where you let your gaze fall, you should see nothing that will upset you too much.'

'Excuse me, sir,' said Rincewind. 'Is it true that some of the men in Ankh-Morpork United are just a bunch of thugs from the Shove?'

'That might be a bit harsh,' Ridcully began.

'Excuse me, sir,' said Trev, 'that is quite true. I would say about half of them are honest cloggers and the rest of them are bastards.'

'Well, I'm sure we will overcome,' said Ridcully jovially.

'I would also like to make a few comments before we leave, sir,' said Nutt. 'A few words of advice, perhaps? In these few days I have taught you everything I know, even if I do not know how I know it. As you know, I am an orc and whatever else we were, we were team players. You are playing, therefore, not as individuals, but as a team. I think it was Von Haudenbrau who said—'

'I don't think we've got very much time to get through the crowds,' said Ridcully, who had been expecting this. 'Thank you, Mister Nutt, but I really think we ought to get going.'

345

Those watching from above would have seen the cramped streets of the city waver as the red caterpillar that was the Unseen Academicals made its way to the ground. There were cheers and there were boos and because this was Ankh-Morpork, usually the cheers and the booing were done alternately by everyone concerned.

By the time Lance-Constable Bluejohn of the Watch and two other trolls had forcibly prised open the gates against the pressure of bodies, the noise was just one great hammer of sound. The troll officers opened a path for them with the forethought and delicacy that has made police crowd control such a byword. It led to a fenced-off and heavily guarded area, in the centre of which was the Archchancellor formerly known as Dean, the entire team of Ankh-Morpork United and His Grace the Duke of Ankh, Commander of the City Watch, Sir Samuel Vimes, with a face like a bad lunch. 'What the hell are you clowns proposing to do to my city?' he demanded and looked up at Vetinari in his box in the middle of the stand. He raised his voice. 'I've been grafting like mad this last month on getting the KV Accord sorted out and it turns out that just when the dwarfs and the trolls are shaking hands and being jolly good pals, you lot are starting another KV of your very own.'

'Oh, come now, Sam,' said Ridcully. 'It's only a jolly day out.'

'People are queueing up at the gates,' said Vimes. 'The *actual* city gates. How much of this is magical?'

'None, Sam, as far as we're aware. There will be no magic used during the game, this has been discussed and agreed and the D—' Ridcully swallowed hard. 'The Archchancellor of Brazeneck University is making himself responsible for thaumic damping of the stadium.'

'Then let me tell you this,' said the commander. 'None of my men will set a foot on the field of play, no matter what happens. Do I make myself clear?'

'As crystal, Sam.'

'Sorry, Archchancellor, for now I am Commander of the City Watch, not Sam, if it's all the same to you,' said Vimes. 'The whole damn city is an accident waiting to— no, an accident that already has happened and anything that goes bad will get worse very quickly. I'm not going to have it said that the Watch were the problem. Honestly, Mustrum, I really would have expected better from you.'

'That will be Archchancellor,' said Ridcully coldly.

'As far as I'm concerned,' said Vimes, 'this is a scuffle between rival gangs. Do you know what my job is, Archchancellor? It's to keep the peace, and for two pins, I'd arrest the whole boiling of ya, but his lordship won't have it.'

Ridcully coughed. 'May I extend my congratulations, sir, on the very good work you have been doing in Koom Valley.'

'Thank you,' said Vimes. 'And so I suspect you can imagine how cheerful I am to see you involved in another kind of war.' The commander turned to Archchancellor Henry. 'Nice to see you again, sir,* it's good to see that you've moved up in the world. I'm formally telling you that I am laying down the law, here, and as the referee, you have to pick it up. Inside these lines it's football – step over the line and it's me.' He turned back to Ridcully. 'Mind how you go, Archchancellor.'

He departed, watchmen falling into place behind him.

'Well, now, I suspect the good commander has a lot on his mind these days,' said Archchancellor Henry, brightly. He pulled out his watch. 'I would like to speak to the team captains.'

'Well, I know I'm one of them,' said Ridcully.

A man stepped forward from the ranks of United.

'Joseph Hoggett, of the Pork Packers, as it happens. Captain, for my sins.'

Hoggett held out his hand to Ridcully and, to his credit, hardly winced when it was taken in a firm handshake.

'Well, gentlemen,' said the former Dean. 'I am sure you know the rules, we've been through them often enough. I want a good clean game. One long, er, peep from my whistle means that I am interrupting play for an infringement or injury or for some other reason at that

---

* Policemen have a way of pronouncing the word 'sir', as if they would really like to spell it 'cur'.

point known only to myself. One even longer peep, which I suppose will be more of a parrp, will mean the end of one half and time for refreshment, after which the game will recommence. During the interval, I believe that there will be a marching display by the Ankh-Morpork accordion band, but I suppose these things are sent to try us. May I remind you gentlemen that you change ends at the half-time. Also, please impress on your team that the goal they are aiming for should not be behind them. If I see any serious infringement, that player will be removed from the pitch. A considerably longer parrp, which as far as I am concerned will continue until I am out of breath, will mark the end of the game. May I also remind you, as Commander Vimes has reminded us, that within these four, rather sticky lines of chalk, I am a wielder of power second only to the gods themselves, and then only perhaps. If at any time it becomes clear that the rules themselves are impractical, I will change them. When I blow the whistle, I shall raise my staff and unleash a spell which will prevent any further magic being used within these hallowed lines until the close of play. Is that understood?'

'Yes, sir,' said Mr Hoggett.

'Mustrum?' said the former Dean, in a meaningful voice.

'Yes, yes, all right,' grumbled Ridcully. 'You are making the most of your little moment, aren't you? Let's get on with it, shall we?'

'Gentlemen, would you please form up your teams for the singing of the National Anthem. Mister Stibbons, I believe you have found me a megaphone, thank you very much.' He raised the horn to his lips and shouted through it, 'Ladies and gentlemen, be upstanding for the National Anthem.'

The singing of the National Anthem was always a ragged affair, the good people of Ankh-Morpork feeling that it was unpatriotic to sing songs about how patriotic you were, taking the view that someone singing a song about how patriotic they were was either up to something or a Head of State.*

* i.e., up to something.

An additional problem today lay in the acoustics of the arena, which were rather too good, coupled with the fact that the speed of sound at one end of the stadium was slightly off beat compared with the other end, a drawback exacerbated when both sides tried to recover the gap.

These acoustical anomalies did not count for much if you were standing next to Mustrum Ridcully, as the Archchancellor was one of those gentlemen who will sing it beautifully, correctly enunciated and very, very loudly.

' "When dragons belch and hippos flee, my thoughts, Ankh-Morpork, are of thee," ' he began.

Trev noticed, to his surprise, that Nutt was standing stiffly to attention. His own mouth operating on automatic, he looked along the massed rank of Ankh-Morpork United. About fifty-fifty, he thought. Half of them decent old cloggers and half of them Andy and his chums. His gaze lighted on Andy just as he thought that and Andy flashed him a little smile and pointed a finger briefly. But I'm not playing, Trev thought, because of my old mum. He glanced down at the palm of his hand, no star there, he was sure of that. Anyway, he thought, staring at the opponents, when it all goes bad the referee is a wizard, after all.

' "Let others boast of martial dash, for we have boldly fought with cash," ' roared the crowd at various pitches and speeds.

I mean, Trev thought, he wouldn't switch off his own magic, would he?

' "We own all your helmets, we own all your shoes." '

I mean, he really wouldn't do that, would he? The only person who could stop it if it all went wrong wouldn't have made a mistake like that?

' "We own all your generals – touch us and you'll lose." '

Yes, he has done! He has done just that!

' "Morporkia! Morporkia! Morporkia owns the day," ' Trev shouted to quell his own rising panic. He has done that, we all saw him! He's kept his own staff inside the field where you can't do magic. He looked at Andy and Andy nodded. Yes, he had worked it out as well.

' "We can rule you wholesale. Touch us and you'll pay." '

It is considered in the Sto Plains that only scoundrels know the second verse of their national anthem, since anyone spending time memorizing that would be up to no good purpose. The Ankh-Morpork national anthem, therefore, had a second verse that was deliberately written as *ner ner ners* and the occasional coherent word desperately trying to stay afloat, on the basis that this is how it would sound in any case. Trev listened to it with even more agony than usual.

But everyone joined in cheerful unison for the last line, which everybody knew, ' "We can rule you wholesale, credit where it's due." '

Glenda, one arm as far across her bosom as it would go, risked a look at what would still probably be called the Royal Box, just as Vetinari raised the gold-ish coloured urn and a cheer went up. Ankh-Morpork was not particularly keen on cheering the Patrician but it would cheer money any day of the week. Yet it seemed to Glenda that there was some strange harmonic to the cheer, coming up from under the ground itself, as if the place was one huge mouth . . . Then the feeling went away. And the day came back.

'Gentlemen? Team players to their places,' said the Archchancellor of Brazeneck, haughtily.

'Er, can I have a word with you, sir?' said Trev, sidling up as quickly as possible.

'Ah, yes. Dave Likely's boy,' said the former Dean. 'We are about to play football, Mister Likely, I'm sure you've noticed.'

'Yes, sir, well, er, but . . .'

'Do you know of any good reason why I should hold up the game?' the referee demanded.

Trev gave up.

Henry produced a coin from his waistcoat pocket. 'Mustrum?' he said.

'Heads,' said the Archchancellor, and he turned out to be wrong.

'Very well, Mister Hoggett . . . and who has the ball?'

Gloing! Gloing!

Nutt picked the ball out of the air and handed it over. 'Me, sir.'

'Ah, you are the coach for the Academicals.'

'Yes, but a player as well should it become necessary.'

'Gentlemen, you will see that I am placing the ball in the centre of the pitch.' It's true that the Archchancellor formerly known as Dean did rather relish the occasion. He took a few steps back, paused for dramatic effect, produced a whistle from his pocket and flourished it. He gave a blow that only a man of that size could give; his face began to twitch and go red. He raised his megaphone to his lips and shouted, 'ANY BOY WHO HAS NOT BROUGHT HIS KIT WILL PLAY IN HIS PANTS!' followed by Ponder Stibbons shouting, 'I want to know who gave that to him!'

The crowd roared and you could hear the laugh going away in the distance, rolling down the streets as every listener in the crowded city passed it on, bringing back such memories that at least two people started to forge letters from their mother.

In his goal, the Librarian swung himself to the top of his posts to get a better look. In his goal, Charlie Barton, goalkeeper for United, methodically lit his pipe. And the man with the biggest problem within the ground that day, apart possibly from Trev, was the editor of the *Times*, Mr William de Worde, who had not trusted any underling with the reporting of this unique, most prestigious occasion, but wasn't at all sure how it should be done.

At the whistle, he'd managed:

The United chief, should I say chief? There must be a better word for him, but I can sort that out in the office, does not actually appear to know what to do next. Archchancellor Ridcully (BF, No, no, I'll fill that in later) has kicked the ball hard towards, well, actually it has hit Jimmy Wilkins, formerly of the Miners, who seems uncertain as to what to do with it. No, no, he's picked it up! He's picked up the ball! The referee, who is the former Dean of Unseen University, has called him over for what I imagine is to be a refresher course in the rules of this new game of football.

A megaphone, thought de Worde, that's what I need, an extremely big megaphone so I can tell everyone what's going on.

The ball has been handed to, let me see, number sixty-nine, oh yes, the multi-talented Professor Bengo Macarona, who according to the regulations, the new rules, is allowed what is known as a free kick from where the infringement took place and it's, and here comes, Bengo Maca— sorry, Professor Bengo Macarona for Unseen Academicals and— oh my word! It has gone right down the pitch at shoulder height, making a noise like a partridge (check with Nature Notes correspondence on whether I have the correct simile). The ball has hit Mr Charlie 'Big Boy' Barton in the stomach with such force as to carry him into the back of the net! What a display! And this would appear to be a goal! At least one goal, I should think! And the crowd are on their feet, though technically most of them were there already, anyhow [he wrote conscientiously, with a journalist's well-known desire to get things right]. And yes, they are celebrating the hero of the moment and the refrain coming from the lips of the Academicals' supporters in their unique patois seems to be: 'One Makaronah, there's only one Makaronah, one Makaro-naah.'* No, no. Something seems to be happening; Macarona has left the pitch and is talking animatedly to the crowd. He appears to be haranguing them. Those he has been talking to look subdued.

At this point, one of the editor's assistants hurried over with a brief digest of what had transpired on the other side of the pitch. De Worde wrote quickly, hoping that his home-made shorthand would not fail him:

With that hot-blooded resolve that is so lovably typical of the native Genuan, Professor Macarona is apparently insisting that

* In his seat, the university's Master of the Music fumbled for his notebook and wrote down rapidly: Macarona Unum Est. Certes Macarona Est. And couldn't wait to get back to the choir.

any celebratory chanting should include his full name and full list of honours and is helpfully writing them down. There also appears to be a bit of a hiatus around United's goal as some of Charlie Barton's team mates help him find his pipe and also, it transpires [the editor of the *Times* liked the word transpire], the other half of the pork pie it transpired he had been eating at the time the goal was scored. It appears that, not unlike many of us, he had underestimated the speed of the new ball.

And now the ball appears to be back in the centre of the pitch where there is another argument going on.

'But they've just scored a goal!' said Mr Hoggett.

'Yes, quite so,' said the former Dean, wheezing gently. 'That means that they get to kick off next.'

'That means we don't, but we've just lost a goal!'

'Yes, but that's what the rules say.'

'But that's not fair, we want a kick, they kicked it last.'

'But it's not about the kicks, Mister Hoggett, it's what you do with them.'

And Archchancellor Ridcully runs towards the ball. He turns swiftly and has kicked the ball towards his own goal!

The editor wrote furiously:

Almost all of United's team are running up to take advantage of this strange faux pas, not entirely cognisant [the editor liked that word, too, it was so much better than aware] but the famous Librarian of Unseen University has just—

He stopped, blinked and grabbed one of his assistants who had turned up with a full list of Bengo Macarona's honours and pushed him down in the chair.

'Write down everything that I say!' he shouted. 'And I hope your shorthand is better than mine, and if it isn't you'll be sacked in the morning. This is insane!'

They did it on purpose, I'll swear they did it on purpose. He kicked the ball directly at his own goalkeeper, knowing, I swear, that he could take advantage of the Librarian's renowned upper body strength to throw the ball almost the entire length of the pitch. And there is Bengo Macarona, more or less unnoticed by his opponents, heading towards the missile while United have streamed away from their citadel, like the ill-fated Maranids during the first Prodostian war [the editor liked to think of himself as a classicist].

'I've never seen anything like it!' he shouted at his almost deafened assistant. 'They've got United all in the wrong place.'

And there goes Macarona. The ball appears to be attached to his feet. And there ahead of him appears to be the only member of the luckless United squad that knows what's going on. Mr Charles 'Big Boy' Barton, who nevertheless is staggering out of the goalmouth, like the Giant Octopal, upon seeing the hordes of the Mormidons.

The editor fell silent, forgetting everything as the ground between the two men shortened by the moment. 'Oh, no!' he said.
There was a huge cheer from the crowd. 'What happened?' said the assistant, pencil poised.
'Didn't you see it? Didn't you see it?' said the editor. His hair was dishevelled and he looked like a man nearing madness. 'Macarona ran round him! I don't know how the ball stayed at his feet.'
'Do you mean he dodged past him, sir?' said the assistant.
The noise of the crowd would have been incandescent had it been visible. 'Another goal,' said the editor slumping. 'Two goals in as many minutes! No, he didn't dodge him, he ran around him! Twice! And I'll swear, ended up going faster.'

'Ah, yes,' said the assistant, still writing. 'I went to a lecture about that sort of thing, once. It was about how things don't hit the world turtle, sir. It was like a slingshot effect, he may have picked up additional speed as he rounded the goalkeeper's enormous girth, sir.'

'And listen to the crowd roar!' said the editor. 'And write it down.'

'Yes, sir, that would be: One Professor Macarona D.Thau (Bug), D.Maus (Chubb), Magistaludorum (QIS), Octavium (Hons), PHGK (Blit), DMSK, Mack, D.Thau (Bra), Visiting Professor in Chickens (Jahn the Conqueror University (Floor 2, Shrimp Packers Building, Genua)), Primo Octo (Deux), Visiting Professor of Blit/Slood Exchanges (Al Khali), KCbfJ, Reciprocating Professor of Blit Theory (Unki), D.Thau (Unki), Didimus Supremius (Unki), Emeritus Professor in Blit Substrate Determinations (Chubb), Chair of Blit and Music Studies (Quirm College for Young Ladies), there's only one Professor Macarona D.Thau (Bug), D.Maus (Chubb), Magistaludorum (QIS), Octavium (Hons), PHGK (Blit), DMSK, Mack, D.Thau (Bra), Visiting Professor in Chickens (Jahn the Conqueror University (Floor 2, Shrimp Packers Building, Genua)), Primo Octo (Deux), Visiting Professor of Blit/Slood Exchanges (Al Khali), KCbfJ, Reciprocating Professor of Blit Theory (Unki), D.Thau (Unki), Didimus Supremius (Unki), Emeritus Professor in Blit Substrate Determinations (Chubb), Chair of Blit and Music Studies (Quirm College for Young Ladies), there's only oooonnnnnnne Professor Bengo Macarooonaah D.Thau (Bug), D.Maus (Chubb), Magistaludorum (QIS), Octavium (Hons), PHGK (Blit), DMSK, Mack, D.Thau (Bra), Visiting Professor in Chickens (Jahn the Conqueror University (Floor 2, Shrimp Packers Building, Genua)), Primo Octo (Deux), Visiting Professor of Blit/Slood Exchanges (Al Khali), KCbfJ, Reciprocating Professor of Blit Theory (Unki), D.Thau (Unki), Didimus Supremius (Unki), Emeritus Professor in Blit Substrate Determinations (Chubb), Chair of Blit and Music Studies (Quirm College for Young Ladies), oooonnnnnnnly one Professor Bengo Macaroooonaaaah D.Thau (Bug), D.Maus (Chubb), Magistaludorum (QIS), Octavium (Hons), PHGK (Blit), DMSK, Mack,

D.Thau (Bra), Visiting Professor in Chickens (Jahn the Conqueror University (Floor 2, Shrimp Packers Building, Genua)), Primo Octo (Deux), Visiting Professor of Blit/Slood Exchanges (Al Khali), KCbfJ, Reciprocating Professor of Blit Theory (Unki), D.Thau (Unki), Didimus Supremius (Unki), Emeritus Professor in Blit Substrate Determinations (Chubb), Chair of Blit and Music Studies (Quirm College for Young Ladies). But wouldn't he be off-the-side, sir?'

'That would indeed appear to be the complaint of the luckless warriors of United,' said the editor. 'They are clustering around the referee and what would I give to be a fly on that wall?'

'There is no wall, sir.'

'It would seem—' and the editor stopped dead. 'Who is that?'

'What is that, sir?'

'Look over there at the stands! The upper-class stands, I might add, to which we were not invited.'

The sun usefully took this opportunity to appear from behind the clouds and the bowl of the Hippo seemed to fill with light.

'That's the micromail girl, sir,' said the assistant.

Even some of the protesting United team were looking up at the stands now. She hurt the eyes, but they were dragged towards it again.

'I've got her picture on my bedroom wall,' said the assistant. 'Everyone has been looking for her.' He coughed. 'They say it doesn't chafe, you know.'

Now, all the footballers on the field, bar the unfortunate Charlie Barton, who was having a dizzy spell, were clustered around the referee, who said, 'I repeat; it was a perfectly acceptable goal. A trifle unkind and showy, perhaps, but nevertheless entirely within the rules. You've watched the Unseen lads training. The game moves about. It doesn't send you a clacks to tell you what's happening next.'

A voice a little lower down said, 'It is an elementary mistake to believe that even the most doughty keeper of the net can single-handedly defend against the full might of the opposing team.' This was Nutt.

'Mister Nutt, you are not supposed to tell them that sort of thing,' said Ridcully.

Mr Hoggett looked downcast. A man betrayed by team, history and expectations. 'I can see we've got a lot to learn,' he said.

Trev pulled Nutt off to one side. 'And this is where it all goes bad,' he said.

'Oh, come now, Mister Trev. We're doing very well. Bengo is, anyway.'

'I'm not watching him. I'm watching Andy and Andy is watchin' Bengo. They're bidin' their time. They're lettin' the poor old buggers get into a hell of a fix and then they'll just take over.'

And then Trev was given a short lesson in why wizards are wizards.

'I have a modest proposal and I wonder if you will hear me out, referee. While we at Unseen University are absolute novices, we have had rather more time to get to grips with the new football than our current opponents have. Therefore, I propose to give them one of our goals,' said Ridcully.

'You can't do that, sir!' said Ponder.

'Why, is it against the rules?' Ridcully's tone deepened and became noticeably more pompous. 'I ask you, are good sportsmanship, fellowship and generosity against the rules, pray?' By the end of the sentence, his voice was audible nearly to the very back of the stadium.

'Well, of course there is nothing against it, sir. There isn't a rule stopping you washing your laundry during the middle of the game – and that is because no one would do it.'

'Right. Mister Hoggett? One of our goals is now yours. We are, as it were, level.'

Hoggett, transfixed, looked around at his fellow players, 'Well, er, if you insist, sir.'

'Wouldn't dream of taking no for an answer,' said Ridcully expansively.

'What in the world made him do that?' said the editor of the *Times*, as an exhausted runner brought him the news.

'It was a very generous gesture.'

'Why did you do it?' said Ponder to Ridcully.

'I am totally transparent, Stibbons. Generous to a fault, that's me. It's not my fault that they do not know they are inferior and this will play on their minds for the rest of the game.'

'That's rather . . . cunning, sir.'

'Yes, it is, isn't it? I'm rather proud of it. And once again, we get to kick first. No wonder this is such a popular game.'

'That was a remarkable piece of psychology there,' said Nutt to Trev as they walked back to the sidelines. 'Somewhat cruel, possibly, but clever.'

Trev said nothing. There was the shrill call of the whistle for the game to resume, followed instantly by the referee screaming, 'A LITTLE BIT OF HAIL WON'T HURT YOU, BOY, IT'S HEALTHY AND WILL DO YOU GOOD.'

'That's magic,' said Trev. 'Should that be happening?'

'No,' said Ponder Stibbons behind him. 'It's just possession.'

'Yes, the game is all about possession, Mister Trev,' said Nutt.

Trev looked up again at the stand. There was the shining shape of Juliet, only a few feet away from Vetinari himself and flanked by Glenda and Pepe. She could be a goddess. It's never going to happen, is it? he said to himself. Not her and a boy from the candle vats.

Not really going to happen. Not now.

And then Bengo screamed and it seemed as though every voice in the stadium joined in one communal 'OOOOOH!'

And the whistle blew again.

'What happened, sir?' said the editorial assistant.

'Can't exactly be sure. They got the ball to Macarona again and then he collided with a couple of United players and they all ended up in a heap.'

Nutt, the first to reach the stricken Macarona, looked up at Trev gravely. 'Both patellas dislocated,' he said. 'We'll need a couple of men to take him down to the Lady Sybil.'

The former Dean looked around at the clustered footballers. 'So, what happened here, Mister Shank?' he said as perspiration dripped off his chin.

Andy momentarily lifted a finger to his forelock.

'Well, sir, I was rushing forward according to the rules to tackle Mister Macarona and I had no idea at all that Jimmy the Spoon, here, had got exactly the same idea and was coming from a different direction and suddenly we were all there together going arse over tip, if you would excuse my Klatchian.'

Trev glowered.

The look on Andy's face was transparent. He was lying. He knew he was lying. He knew everyone else knew he was lying and he didn't care. In fact, he rather enjoyed the situation. Andy's boots looked heavy enough to moor a boat.

'They got 'im like the meat in a sandwich, sir,' Trev complained to the referee.

'Can you substantiate that, young man?'

'Well, you can see what's happened to the poor bugger.'

'Yes, but do you have any evidence of collusion?'

Trev went blank and Nutt supplied in a whisper, 'Can you prove it was a set-up?'

'Can anyone?' said the referee, looking around the players. No one could. Trev wondered how many might, were it not for the fact that Andy was standing there, innocent as a shark. 'I am the referee, gentlemen, and I can only referee what I see and I saw nothing.'

'Yes, because they made sure of that,' said Trev. 'Anyway, listen to the crowd. *They* all saw it!'

'Look! They've got boots on them that could strip bark,' Ridcully protested.

'Yes, indeed, Mustrum, I mean, sorry, captain, but as yet there are no rules about which boots should be worn and at the very least these are the boots that have been traditionally worn for the game of foot-the-ball.'

'But they are man traps!'

'I can certainly see what you are getting at, but what would you like me to do?' said Henry. 'I have a suspicion that if I cancel this match at this point you and I would not get out of here alive, because even if we ourselves did escape the wrath of the crowd, we would by no means escape the wrath of Vetinari. The game *will* continue. Unseen Academicals can play a substitute and I will, let me see—' He pulled out a notebook. 'Ah, yes, I will award a free kick at the very point where this unfortunate incident took place. And may I add that I will look askance at any future "incidents". Mister Hoggett, I trust that you will make this clear to your team.'

'Blow that for a game of soldiers!' Trev yelled. 'They just took out our best player an' you're gonna let 'em walk away grinning?'

But the referee was, after all, the former Dean. A man used to head-to-head confrontations with Mustrum Ridcully. He gave Trev a chilly look and turned very deliberately to the Archchancellor and said, 'And I trust you, too, captain, will impress upon your team that my decisions are final. There will be a five-minute interlude for you to do this and can some of you fellows take poor Professor Macarona off the field and see if you can find some quack to look at him.'

A voice behind him bellowed, 'You have one right here, sir.' They turned. A figure slightly larger than life, wearing a top hat and carrying a small bag, nodded at them.

'Doctor Lawn,' said Ridcully. 'I wouldn't have expected to see you here.'

'Really?' said the doctor. 'Wouldn't have missed it for the world. Now some of you men drag him over to that corner and I'll take a look at him. I'll send my bill to you, shall I, Mustrum?'

'Wouldn't you like to take him somewhere nice and quiet?' said the referee.

'No fear! I want to keep my eye on the play.'

'They're gettin' away with it,' said Trev, as he walked back to the line. 'Everyone knows they're gettin' away with it.'

'We still have the rest of the team, Mister Trev,' said Nutt, lacing up his boots. He had, of course, made them himself. They looked like foot gloves. 'And me of course, I am the first substitute. I promise that I will do my best, Mister Trev.'

*

360

Thus far, it had been a rather boring afternoon for the Librarian after his one little moment in the sun. It really was rather dull between the goal posts and he was getting hungry and so was pleasantly surprised by the appearance of a large banana in front of the goal. It was later agreed that, in a footballing context, mysteriously appearing fruit should have been greeted with a certain amount of caution. But he was hungry, it was a banana and the metaphysics were sound. He ate it.

Glenda, up in the stand, wondered if she was the only one to have seen the startlingly yellow fruit in its trajectory and then saw, looking up at her from the crowd, with a big grin on her face, Mrs Atkinson, mother of Tosher, himself something of an unguided weapon. Anyone who had ever been in the Shove knew her as a perpetrator of all kinds of inventive assaults. She had always got away with it because no one in the Shove would hit an old lady, especially one standing next to Tosher.

'Excuse me,' said Glenda, standing up. 'I've got to get down there right now.'

'Not a chance, love,' said Pepe. 'It's shoulder-to-shoulder. A Shove and a half.'

'Look after Juliet,' said Glenda. She leaned forward and tapped on the shoulder of the nearest man. 'I've got to get to the bottom of this as soon as possible. Mind if I jump?'

He looked past her at the glittering figure of Juliet and said, 'Not at all, if you get your girlfriend to give me a big kiss.'

'No, but I'll give you one.'

'Er, don't trouble yourself, miss, but come on then, give me your hand.'

It was a reasonably fast descent, as she was passed from hand to hand, accompanied by ribaldry, much genial horseplay and a definite feeling of satisfaction on Glenda's part that she was wearing her biggest and most impenetrable pants.*

---

* This was slightly modified when she realized that none of the spectators had tried any hanky panky whatsoever.

Elbowing and kicking people out of the way, she reached the goal just as the banana was consumed in one gulp and stood panting helplessly in front of the Librarian. He gave her a wide smile, looked thoughtful for a moment and went over backwards.

High up in the stand, Lady Margolotta turned to Vetinari. 'Is that part of the game?'

'I fear not,' he said.

Ladyship yawned. 'Well, it relieves the boredom, at least. They've spent far more time arguing than playing.'

Vetinari smiled. 'Yes, madam. It does look as if football is very much like diplomacy: short periods of fighting followed by long periods of negotiation.'

Glenda prodded the Librarian. 'Hello? Are you all right?' All she could hear was a gurgling. She cupped her hands, 'Man— er, someone down, here!'

To another chorus of boos, and, because this was Ankh-Morpork, cheers, the travelling committee, which was what the game had now become, hastened over to the Unseen Academicals' goal.

'Someone threw a banana and I saw who did it and I think it's poisoned,' said Glenda, all in one breath.

'He's breathing very heavily,' said Ridcully. The comment was unnecessary as the snores were making the goal rattle.

He crouched down and put his ear to the Librarian's chest. 'I don't think he's been poisoned,' he said.

'Why's that, Archchancellor?' said Ponder.

'Because if anyone has poisoned our Librarian,' said Ridcully, 'then, although I am not, by nature, a vindictive man, I will see to it that this university hunts down the poisoner by every thaumic, mystic and occult means available and makes the rest of their life not only as horrible as they can imagine it, but as horrible as I can imagine it. And you can depend on it, gentlemen, that I have already started work on it.'

Ponder looked around until he saw Rincewind. 'Professor Rincewind. You were, I mean you are, his friend, can't you stick your fingers down his throat or something?'

'Well, no,' said Rincewind. 'I am very attached to my fingers and I like to think of them as attached to me.'

The noise of the crowd was getting louder. They were here to see football, not a debate.

'But Doctor Lawn is still here,' Rincewind volunteered. 'He makes a living out of sticking his hand in things. He's got the knack.'

'Ah, yes,' said the referee. 'Perhaps we can impose upon him to take another patient.' He turned to Ridcully. 'You must play your other substitute.'

'That would be Trevor Likely,' said the Archchancellor.

'No!' blurted out Trev. 'I promised my ol' mum.'

'I thought you were part of the team?' said Ridcully.

'Well, yes, sir, sort of . . . helpin' out and all that . . . I promised my ol' mum, sir, after Dad died. I know I was down on the list, but who would have thought it would have turned out like this?'

Ridcully stared at the sky. 'Well, it seems to me, gentlemen, that we cannot ask a man to break a promise made to an old mum. That would be a crime more heinous than murder. We will have to play with ten men. It appears that we will have to go without.'

Up in his ramshackle box, the editor of the *Times* picked up his notebook and said, 'I'm going down there. It's ridiculous to sit up here like this.'

'You're going on the pitch, sir?'

'Yes. At least that way I can see what's happening.'

'I don't think the referee will allow that, sir!'

'You're not going to play, Trev?' said Glenda.

'I told you! How many times do I need to tell people? I promised my ol' mum!'

'But you are part of the team, Trev.'

'I promised my ol' mum!'

'Yes, but I am sure she'd understand.'

'That's easy for you to say. We'll never know, will we?'

'Not necessarily,' said a voice cheerfully.

'Oh, hello, Doctor Hix,' said Glenda.

'I couldn't help overhearing your conversation, and if Mister Likely could tell me where his mother is buried, and the referee was to give us a little leeway in regard to time, well it could be possible that I—'

'Don't you put a shovel anywhere near my ol' mum!' Trev screamed, tears rolling down his face.

'I'm sure we all understand, Trev,' said Glenda. 'It's always difficult with old mums,' and she added, not really thinking what she was saying, 'and I think Juliet will understand.'

She took him by the hand and towed him off the pitch. Trev had been right. It was all going wrong. The buoyant certainties of the beginning of the game were fading.

'You gave away a goal, sir,' said Ponder as he and Ridcully lined up for the next encounter.

'I have great faith in Mister Nutt in goal,' said Ridcully. 'And I'll show them what happens to people who try to poison a wizard.'

The whistle blew.

'GET DOWN AND GIVE ME TWENTY! I'm sorry, gentlemen, I don't quite know why I said that . . .'

What happens to people who try to poison a wizard, at least in the short run, is that they have an advantage in a game of football. The absence of Professor Macarona was a deadly blow. He had been the pillar around which the university strategy had been built. Emboldened, United went for the kill.

Even so, the editor of the *Times* thought, as he lay down at the very edge of the pitch alongside his iconographer, the wizards were just about managing to hold their own. He scribbled as fast as he could, trying hard to ignore the gentle shower of pie wrappings, banana skins, empty greasy pea bags and the occasional beer bottle being tossed on to the pitch. And who is that with the ball now? He glanced at the little crib-sheet of numbers he had managed to jot down. Ah, right. United had broken into the UU side of the field and there was Andy Shank, an unpleasant man by all accounts and ... surely that wasn't a normal footballing procedure. Other players had lined up around him. So he was running in the middle of a group of bodyguards. Even the other team members themselves did not seem to know what was going on, but Mr Shack nevertheless managed a creditable strike at the goal, which was expertly snatched out of the air by ... Mister Nutt. He glanced at his crib-sheet, ah yes, the orc, and added in his notebook: 'who is clearly adept at grasping big round objects'. But then he felt ashamed and crossed it out. Despite where we are lying, he said to himself, we are *not* the gutter press.

The orc.

Nutt danced back and forth outside his goal, trying to find someone who looked in a position to be able to do something with a ball.

'Can't hang around all day, Orc,' said Andy, staying in front of him. 'Got to let it go soon, Orc. Not much help for you now, is there, Orc? They say you've got claws. Show us your claws, Orc. That will bust your ball.'

'I believe that you are a man with unresolved issues, sir.'

'What?'

Nutt dropkicked the ball over Andy's head and somewhere in the mob that fought for it there was a crunch, which was followed by a yell, which was followed by the whistle and the whistle was followed by the chant. It began somewhere in the region of Mrs Atkinson, but spread oh so quickly: 'Orc! Orc! Orc! Orc! Orc! Orc! Orc!'

Ridcully got to his feet, standing unsteadily. 'The buggers have got me, Henry,' he yelled, in a voice that could hardly be heard over the chant. 'Kneecap! Bloody kneecap!'

'Who did it?' the referee demanded.

'How should I know? It's a bloody mess, just like the old game! And can't you get them to stop that bloody chant? That's not the sort of thing we want to hear.'

Archchancellor Henry raised his megaphone. 'Mister Hoggett?'

The captain of United pushed his way through the rabble, looking very sheepish.

'Can't you control your fans?'

Hoggett shrugged. 'Sorry about that, sir, but what can you do?'

Henry looked around the Hippo. What could anyone do? It was the mob. The Shove. No one was in charge. It hadn't an arse to kick, a wrist to be slapped or even an address. It was just there and it was shouting because everybody else was.

'Well, then can you at least control your team?' he said. To his surprise Mr Hoggett looked down.

'Not entirely, sir. Sorry about that, sir, it's how things are.'

'One more incident of this kind and I will cancel the match. I suggest you leave the field of play, Mustrum. Who is the substitute captain?'

'Me!' said Ridcully, 'but under the circumstances I appoint Mister Nobbs as my deputy.'

'Not Nobby Nobbs?' exclaimed the former Dean.

'No relation,' said Bledlow Nobbs very quickly.

'Well, that was a good choice at least,' said Trev, sighing. 'Nobbsy is a clogger at heart.'

'But it's not supposed to be about clogging,' said Glenda. 'And you know what?' she added, raising her voice against the steel roar of the crowd. 'Whatever the old Dean thinks he can't stop the game, now. This place would just blow up!'

'You think so?' said Trev.

'Listen,' said Glenda. 'Yes, I think you're right. You ought to get out of here.'

'Me? Not a chance.'

'But you could make yourself useful and get Juliet out. Get her as far as Vimesy and his lot. I bet they're waiting right outside the gates. Do it right now while you can still get down the steps. Won't get a chance once they start to play again.'

As he left, Glenda walked unheeded down the touchline, to the little area where Dr Lawn was standing guard over his patients.

'You know that little bag you brought with you, sir?'

'Yes?'

'I think you're going to need a bigger bag. How's Professor Macarona?'

The professor was lying on his back, staring at the sky and wearing an expression of bland happiness. 'Sorted him out easily enough,' said the doctor. 'He won't be playing again any time soon. I've given him a little something to make him happy. Correction, I have given him a big something to make him happy.'

'And the Librarian?'

'Well, I got a couple of lads to help me turn him upside down and he's been throwing up a lot. He's still pretty groggy, but I don't think it's too bad. He's as sick as a parrot.'*

'This wasn't how it was supposed to go, you know,' said Glenda out of a feeling that she should defend the bloody mess.

'It generally isn't,' said the doctor.

They turned as the noise of the nearby crowd changed. Juliet was coming down the steps glittering. The silence followed her like a lovesick dog. So did Pepe and the reassuring bulk of Madame Sharn, who might be a useful barricade in case the Hippo became a cauldron. Trev, tagging along behind them, seemed like an afterthought in comparison.

'All right, dear, what's this all about?' said Pepe.

'I ain't going,' said Juliet, 'not while Trev's in here. I ain't leaving without Trev. Pepe says he's going to win the match.'

'What have you been saying?' said Glenda.

'He'll win,' said Pepe, winking. 'He's got a star in his hand. You want to see him do it, missy?'

'What are you playin' at?' said Trev, angrily.

'Oh, I'm a bit of a conjurer, me. Or maybe a fairy godmother.' Pepe gestured around the arena. 'See that lot? Their ancestors screamed

---

* According to *Fletcher's Avian Nausea Index*, parrot sickness stands at number five in the 'wishing yourself dead' index. The highest level of sickness is that suffered by the great Combovered Eagle which can vomit over three countries at once.

to see men killing one another and beasts tearing decent folks apart. Men with spears fighting men with nets and all that kind of ugly shite.'

'And they have cart-tail sales here every other Sunday,' added Glenda.

'It's always been the same,' said Pepe. 'It's one big creature. Never dies. Crying and screaming and loving and hating all down the generations and you can't tame it and you can't stop it. Just for you, young lady, and for the soul of Mister Trev, I'm going to throw it a bone. Won't take a mo.'

His slim and slightly spidery form disappeared back up the steps just as the whistle blew. Glenda made out Bledlow Nobbs taking the kick, but Ridcully had made the mistake of thinking that a man who was as big as he was was as clever as he was. And there it was, it was the old game all over again. United were stampeding down the pitch, the old cloggers making way for Andy's army as they bore down against Nutt. The kick took him in the chest and lifted him into the back of the goal. The whistle blew and was followed by, 'DON'T TOUCH THAT, BOYO! YOU DON'T KNOW WHERE IT'S BEEN!' which was followed by, 'I really am very sorry about that, I don't know why it happens,' which was followed by . . . absolute silence.

Which was broken by one voice, 'Likely. Likely. Likely.' It started up in the stand, somewhere near where Pepe had gone.

The beast had forgotten the name 'Orc', but certainly remembered the name 'Likely', a name that had fed it so often, a name it had given birth to and eaten, a name that was football, the very heart of the beast. And here, on this broken field, it was a name to conjure with. 'LIKELY! LIKELY! LIKELY!' Hardly a grown man hadn't seen him. He was the legend. Even after all these years, it was a name that cut through other loyalties. You told your grandchildren about him. You told them how he lay there bleeding and maybe how you dipped your handkerchief in his blood and kept it for a souvenir.

'Likely,' intoned the baritone of Madame Sharn.

'Likely,' whispered Glenda and then 'LIKELY!' She could see the little figure running along the top of the stands, the chant tailing after it.

Tears streamed down Trev's face. Mercilessly, Glenda looked him in the eye. 'Likely! Likely!'

'But my ol' mum!' Trev wept.

Then Juliet leaned over and kissed him and for a moment, the tears were silver. 'Likely?'

Trev stood clutching and unclutching his hands as the chant went on, then he gave a sort of shrug. Then he took his battered tin can out of his jacket pocket and handed it to Glenda, before turning to face the pitch again. 'I'm sorry, Mum,' he said, taking off his jacket, 'but this is football. And I don't even have a jersey.'

'We thought of that,' said Glenda. 'When they were being made.' She pulled one out of the depths of her bag.

'Number four. That was my dad's number.'

'Yes,' said Glenda. 'We know. Listen to 'em cheering, Trev.'

Trev looked like someone trying to find an escape clause. 'I've never even trained with the new football. You know me, it's always been the tin can.'

'It's a football. It's just a football,' said Nutt. 'You'll get the hang of it in a second.'

The former Dean strode up. 'Well, this is all very gratifying with a touch of welcome pathos, ladies and gentlemen, but it is time we continued this football match and I would be very grateful if all non-players could stand back behind the touchlines,' he said, shouting to make himself heard above the noise of the crowd.

Trev left Nutt at the goal. 'Don't you worry, Mister Trev,' said the orc, grinning. 'With me saving and you striking we can't lose. They won't get me the same way a second time.' He lowered his voice and grabbed Trev's shoulder. 'When it starts to get hot down this end, run like stink towards the other and I'll make sure you get the ball.' Trev nodded and walked across the turf to the cheers of the crowd.

The editor of the *Times* later reported as follows:

> At this point, United seemed to feel that they had a working strategy and poured every resource into the university

side in a mêlée that was clearly beyond the referee to control.

The plucky orc custodian had also learned a lesson and two or three times recovered the day with magnificent saves, on one occasion kicking the ball, in our opinion, directly at the head of one of the milling opponents, stunning him and then catching it upon the rebound, dropping it on to the boot and sending it far into the opposing half where Trevor Likely, son of the famous football hero, ran pell-mell towards the goal where Mr Charlie Barton had happily been provided with a chair, a table, a late lunch and two stalwart defenders, whose clear purpose it was to see that none shall pass.

All breathing in the park surely ceased as the young paladin fired off a tremendous shot, which was, alas, out by a few inches and only served to rattle the woodwork and rebounded towards the defenders. Nevertheless, Likely tackled like a man possessed and spirits lifted once again as the two defenders got in each other's way just sufficiently for the boy to once again power the sphere back towards its intended resting place.

Your correspondent believes that even the supporters of United joined in the groan as once again this second shot failed to find a slot and this time rebounded almost to the feet of H. Capstick, who lost no time in sending it screaming towards the Academicals' end before it could do more harm.

Once again, the indefatigable Mr Nutt warded off a number of attacks while the rather pathetic remnant of the university boys' defence proved that prowess with the magic wand is of little avail if you do not know what your feet are for.

At this point, Master of the Dark Arts Dr J. Hix was summarily dismissed from the field after the crowd's

persistent chant of 'Who's the bastard in the black?' alerted
the referee to his attempts at endeavouring to strike down
F. Brisket, one of the notorious Brisket boys, with the soul-
eating dagger of the Deadly Vampyre Spider Queen. Which,
as it transpired, turned out to be neither magical nor, as it
turned out, made of metal, but one of a number of similar
items available in Boffo's Joke Emporium, Tenth Egg Street.
Ranting apparently fearful oaths about university statute,
Dr Hix had to be dragged from the field by members of his
own team, leaving our spirited magicians in an even more
depleted spell of difficulty, probably wishing they had a
magic carpet to get them out of there!

At least Dr Hix's tirade and attempts to drag the ground with him
bought them some time. Glenda ran on to the pitch to a dishevelled
and downcast Trev.

'What happened, Trev?' she said. 'You had it right there in front of
you. You had it in your hands, well, on your boot, anyway.'

'It doesn't do what I want,' said Trev.

'You're supposed to make it do what you want. It's just a football.'

'Yeah, but I'm tryin' to learn with all of this goin' on.'

'Well, at least you nearly did it. We haven't lost yet and it's still only
the first half.'

When play was resumed, according to the editor of the *Times*:

A certain amount of backbone had been retrieved by the
men in pointy hats and captain Nobbs led a concerted
attack in an attempt to further interfere with Charlie
Barton's lunch, but to the dismay of all, the son of Dave
Likely still appeared to have only a nodding acquaintance
with the art of goal scoring and it appeared very much that
his only chance of putting one away would be to have the
ball wrapped up and sent via the Post Office.

And then, to the shock of all, the occult gang appeared to prove that they were far better at billiards than football when another of Likely's powerful, but directionless, attempts rebounded again off the goal on to the head of Professor Rincewind, who was, in fact, running in the opposite direction, and was in the back of the goal before anyone, including Charlie, knew where it was.

This got a cheer, but only because the game now appeared, in our opinion, to be a comedy routine. Alas, there was no comedy about the fact that in several parts of the Hippo, fights were breaking out between gangs of rival supporters, doubtless inspired by some of the shameful performances on the pitch . . .

As the two sides trooped or hobbled back to their places, the referee called the captains together. 'Gentlemen, I'm not quite sure what we are doing here, but I am quite certain that it's not exactly football and I look forward to the inquiry later on. In the meantime, before anyone else is injured and especially before the crowd start to tear this place apart and eat one another, I will tell you that the next goal scored will be the last one, even though we are still only in the first half.' He looked meaningfully at Hoggett and said, 'I sincerely hope that some players will examine their consciences. If I may coin a phrase, gentlemen, it's sudden death either way. I will give you a few minutes to impress this upon your teams.'

'I am sorry, sir,' said Hoggett, looking around, 'some of my lads are not people I would have chosen, if you get my drift. I'll give them a good talking to.'

'In my opinion that would only work if you were hitting them with a hammer at the same time, Mister Hoggett. They are a disgrace. And do you also understand me, Mister Nobbs?'

'I think we'd like to carry on, too. Never say die.'

'And I would not like to see death here, either, but I suspect that your request for extra time is in the hope that Mister Likely will learn how to play football, but I fear that will not happen in a month of Sundays.'

'Well, yes, sir, but can't you—' Hoggett began.

'Mister Hoggett, I have spoken and I am the referee and right now I am the nearest thing to the gods.'

I am the nearest thing to the gods. It came back as an echo. Softer. Brighter. He looked around, 'What? Did you chaps say something?' *Nearest thing to the gods.* There was a sound like *gloing!* But the ball was still in his hands, wasn't it? He stared at it. And was it just him, or was there something in the air? Something . . . in the air . . . the silveryness of fine winter days.

Trev did an embarrassingly jiggly little run on the spot as he waited. When he looked up, there was Andy Shank watching him.

'Your dear old dad must be 'aving a fit,' said Andy cheerfully.

'I know you, Andy,' said Trev wearily, 'I know what you do. You corner some poor tosser and taunt 'im until 'e loses 'is rag and so 'e starts it, doesn't 'e? I'm not risin' to it, Andy.'

'Not risin' to anythin' very much, are you?'

'Not listenin', Andy,' said Trev.

'Oh, I reckon you are.'

Trev sighed again. 'I've been watchin' you. You and your chums are bloody masters at stickin' the boot in when the ref ain't lookin' and what 'e don't see 'e can't do nothin' about.'

Andy lowered his voice. 'Well, I can do something about you, Trev. You won't be walking out of this place, I swear it. You'll be carried out.'

There was the sound of the whistle, followed by the unstoppable 'ANY BOY WHO HAS NOT BROUGHT HIS KIT WILL PLAY IN HIS PANTS!'

'Sudden death,' the former Dean said and the sides collided, Andy emerging with the ball at his feet and his dishonour guard flanking him at either side.

Ponder Stibbons, in the path of their advance, calculated quite a lot of things very quickly, such as speed, wind direction and the likelihood of being physically trodden into the turf. He made an effort at any rate, but ended up flat on his back after the collision. As the editor of the *Times* put it: in this scene of despair, dismay and disarray, one lone defender, Nutt, stood in the way of United's winning goal . . .

There was a roar immediately behind Nutt. He daren't look round, but someone landed on top of the goal, making it shake, dropped down and indicated by means of one huge and horny thumb that Mr Nutt's assistance was no longer required. There was a green crust around the Librarian's mouth, but this was nothing to the fire in his eyes.

At this point, according to the editor of the *Times*:

> Seemingly nonplussed by the return of the wizards' famous man of the forest, Shank essayed another attempt at the winning score, which was stopped one-handed by the Librarian and effortlessly thrown back into United's turf. With everything to play for, it seemed to us that every man on the pitch was chasing the ball as if they were a pack of boys, scuffling in the gutter for the traditional tin can. However, Mr Nobbs, who we are assured is no relation, was able to make some space to give the unlucky Mr Likely another attempt at following in his father's footsteps, which he failed to do by the width, from our estimation, of about half of one inch and the ball was snatched up by Big Boy Barton who then collapsed, choking, having stuffed, we understand, a considerable amount of pie into his face to keep his hands free.

'It shouldn't be like this,' said Glenda, and the thought echoed back in her head: *It shouldn't be like this*. 'Trev has to win, it can't go any other way.' And her voice came back again; could you get echoes in your own head? They were going to lose, weren't they? They were going to lose because Andy knew how to break the rules.

The rules.

I am the rules.

She looked around, but apart from the doctor and his groaning or,

374

in Ridcully's case, cursing charges, there was no one near her apart from Juliet who was watching the game with her normal, faint smile.

'Good heavens. All he needs is to get only one goal,' said Glenda aloud.

I am the goal, said the quiet voice from nowhere.

'Did you hear that?' said Glenda.

'Wot?' said Juliet. She turned and Glenda could see that she was crying. 'Trev's going to lose.'

I am the ball.

This time it had come from her pocket, and she pulled out Trev's tin can.

As Doctor Lawn gave a groan and hurried back up the pitch towards the choking Charlie (as the *Times* later put it), she followed him and caught up with Mr Nobbs. 'If you ever want a cup of tea and a piece of cake again in your life, Mr Nobbs, you kick the ball towards me. You will know where I am, because I will be screaming and acting silly. Do what I say, okay?'

Do what she says, okay? he heard her voice echo. 'And what will you do, throw it back?'

'Something like that,' said Glenda.

'And what good is this going to do?'

'It's going to win you the match, that's what. Can you remember rule 202?'

She left him wondering and then hurried along to Mrs Whitlow and the cheerleaders who, right now, had nothing to cheer about. 'I think we should give the boys a really good display at this time,' she suggested. 'Don't you agree, Juliet?'

Juliet, who had been dutifully following her said, 'Yes, Glenda.'

Yes, Glenda. And there it was again. One sentence. Two voices.

Mrs Whitlow was not the sort of person who would take an instruction from the head of the Night Kitchen, but Glenda leaned forward and said, 'It's the Archchancellor's special request.'

The resurrection of Big Boy Barton was not an easy job and there were possibly fewer volunteers for putting their fingers down his throat than there had been for the Librarian. And his emptying and cleaning up took a little more time.

As the referee summoned the teams back into position, Glenda arrived out of breath and handed him a piece of paper. 'What's this?'

'It's the rules, sir, but you will see that I have put a ring around one of them.'

He glanced at it, and said dismissively, 'Looks like a lot of nonsense to me.'

'It's not, sir, not if you look at it a bit at a time, sir, it's the rules, sir.'

Archchancellor Henry shrugged and stuffed the paper into his pocket.

For a moment, Bledlow Nobbs glanced at Glenda, defiantly out of place amongst the cheerleaders. Glenda was known to be generous to her friends and she made the best tea in the university. This wasn't about football, this was about a hot mug of tea and possibly a doughnut. He leaned down to Nutt. 'Glenda says I've got to remember rule 202,' he said.

Nutt's face brightened. 'Clever idea and of course it will work. Did she tell you to kick the ball out of the pitch?'

'Yes, that's right. Are we going to cheat?' said Bledlow Nobbs.

'No. We are going to stick to the rules. And the thing about sticking to the rules is that it's sometimes better than cheating.'

Nobbs's chance came soon enough, surprisingly with an obviously misdirected pass from Hoggett. Had Hoggett been standing very close when they had been talking? And had he just said 'Go for it?' It sounded very much like it. He kicked the ball straight towards the cheerleaders, where Glenda snatched it out of the air and pushed it into the folds of Mrs Whitlow's skirt. 'You haven't seen this, ladies, you haven't seen where it is and you're not moving for anyone, okay?'

As the crowd booed and cheered, she pulled the tin can out of her bag and held it up in the air. 'Ball lost!' she yelled. 'Substitute ball!' and threw the can directly towards the bledlow, who was quick enough to flick it on to Nutt. Before any other player had moved, it landed with a little *gloing!* sound on the end of Trev Likely's boot . . .

According to the editor of the *Times*:

> We have been assured that no magic was used on the day of
> the match and it is not my place to contradict the
> honourable faculty of Unseen University. All your
> correspondent will say is that Trevor Likely kicked the 'ball',
> against all probability, towards the Academicals' goal,
> where he stood, apparently waiting for the stampede of the
> enraged United squad. What followed, your correspondent
> must declare, was not just a goal, but it was a punishment
> and it was a retribution. It was writing the name Likely, for
> the second time, in the annals of football history, as Trevor,
> famous son of a famous father, wiped the floor with United,
> wrung them out and did it all over again. Running.
> Dodging. Sometimes obligingly kicking the 'ball' directly
> towards a defender who then found it heading off in quite a
> different direction, which just happened to be where Likely
> was now. He taunted them. He played with them. He caused
> them to collide with one another as they both went for a ball
> that, inexplicably, was no longer where they were sure it had
> been. And it must have come as a relief to the more steady
> members of United when he relented and skipped the 'ball'
> over the head of their standby keeper, Micky Pulford
> (latterly of the Whopping Street Wanderers) and into the
> net, where it circled and then returned to land precisely on
> the tip of Likely's boot. The silence . . .

. . . spread like warm butter. Glenda was sure she could hear distant
birdsong or, possibly, the noise of worms under the turf, but definitely
the sound from Dr Lawn's impromptu field hospital, the sound of 'Big
Boy' Barton chucking up again.

And then, where silence had reigned, sound poured like the gush of

377

water from a broken dam. It was physical and it was complex. Here and there the spectators started chanting. All the chants of all the teams, united and harmonizing in one perfect moment.

Glenda watched in amazement as Juliet . . . It was like the fashion show all over again. She seemed to light up from the inside, bars of golden light floating away from the micromail. She started to run towards Trev, tearing off her beard, and, Glenda could see, gradually rising from the ground as though she was running up a stairway.

It was a strange and wonderful sight, and not even Charlie Barton, still throwing up, could detract from it.

' 'scuse me,' said Mister Hoggett. 'That was a goal, wasn't it?'

'Yes, Mister Hoggett, I think it was,' said the referee.

Hoggett was pushed out of the way by Andy Shank. 'No! It went to one side! Are you bloody blind, or what? And it was a tin can.'

'No, Mister Shank, it was not. Gentlemen, can you not see what's happening in front of your faces? Look, everything that happened was perfectly legal under the rules of the game, rule 202, to be precise. It's a fossil, but it *is* a rule, and I can assure you that no magic was used. But right now, gentlemen, can you not see the golden lady floating up in the air?'

'Yeah, right, that's just more weird kids' stuff, just like that goal.'

'This is football, Mister Shank, it's all weird kids' stuff.'

'So the game is over,' said Mr Hoggett.

'Yes, Mister Hoggett, it is. Apart from, and I insist on drawing your attention to it, a beautiful golden lady floating over the pitch. Am I the only one seeing this?'

Hoggett glanced towards the rising Juliet. 'Yeah, right, very pretty, but we've lost, have we?'

'Yes, Mister Hoggett, you have clearly and emphatically lost.'

'And, just to be precise,' said Hoggett, 'there are no more, like, rules, are there?'

'No, Mister Hoggett, you are no longer subject to the rules of football.'

'Thank you for that clarification, your worship, and may I also thank you on behalf of United for the way you handled the trying events of this afternoon.'

With this, he turned and punched Andy full in the face. Mister Hoggett was a mild man, but years of lifting a pig carcass in each hand meant that he had a punch that even Andy's thick skin had to reckon with. Even so, after Andy had blinked a few times he managed to say, 'You bastard.'

'You lost us the game,' said Hoggett. 'We could have won fair and square, but you had to muck it up.' And those around him felt able to murmur in support of the accusation.

'Me? It wasn't me! It was that bloody Trev Likely and his little orc chum. They was using magic. You can't say that wasn't magic.'

'Just skill, I assure you,' said the former Dean. 'Amazing skill, certainly, but he is well known for his prowess with the tin can, which itself is a veritable icon of football.'

'Where is that bloody Likely, anyway?'

Glenda, eyes fixed on the centre of the pitch, said in the voice of someone half hypnotized, 'He's rising up in the air as well.'

'Look, you can't tell me that's not magic,' Andy insisted.

'No,' said Glenda. 'You know what, I think it's religion. Can't you hear?'

'I can't hear anything, dear, with all the noise from the crowd,' said the former Dean.

'*Yes*,' said Glenda. '*Listen* to the crowd.'

He did. It was a roar, a great sky-filling roar, old and animal and coming up from the gods knew where, but inside it, travelling like a hidden message, he made out the words. They swam into focus, if indeed the ear could focus and if he was actually hearing them with his ears. They might have been coming through his bones . . .

> If the striker thinks he scores
> Or if the keeper cries in shame
> They understand not the crowd's applause
> I make, and hear and earn again

For I am the crowd and I am the ball
I am the triumph and the blame
I am the turf, the pies, the All
Always and ever, I am the Game.
It matters not who won or lost
Nothing is the score you made
Fame is a petal that curls in the frost
But I will remember how you played.

And it stays there, Glenda thought, *like sound in a banner. Everybody one part of it.*

Juliet and Trev began to float down, hand in hand, turning gently until they landed lightly on the turf, still kissing. A sort of reality began to leak back into the arena, and there are some people who, even when hearing the voice of the nightingale, will say 'What's that bloody noise?'

'Cheatin' bastard,' said Andy and launched himself directly at Trev, covering the ground at speed as the boy stood there with a very bemused but happy expression on his face. He did not notice the hell-bent Andy until a huge boot kicked him squarely in the groin, so hard that the eyes of all male watchers watered in sympathetic pain.

For the second time in twenty-four hours, Trev felt the micromail *sing* as the thousands of links moved and just as quickly settled down again. It was as if a little breeze had blown up his pants. Apart from that, he hadn't felt a thing.

Andy, on the other hand, had. He was lying on the ground, bent double, making a sort of whistling noise through his teeth.

Someone slapped Trev on the back. It was Pepe.

'You *did* put my pants on, didn't you? Well, obviously not my pants. You'd have to be suicidal to want to put my pants on. Anyway, I've come up with a name for the stuff: I'm going to call it Retribushium. Can't ever say it will be an end to war, 'cos I can't imagine anything putting an end to war, but it sends the force back the way it came. Didn't chafe either, did it?'

'No,' said Trev, amazed.

'Well, it did for him! My word, though, he's a game one. That reminds me, I'll need a picture of you in them.'

Andy was rising slowly, elevating himself to the vertical almost by willpower alone. Pepe grinned, and somehow it seemed obvious to Trev that anyone who was going to get up and try any threats with Pepe grinning at him was more than suicidal.

'Got a knife, have you, you little squirt?' said Andy.

'No, Andy,' said Nutt behind him. 'No more. The game is over. Fortune has favoured Unseen Academicals and I believe the traditional ending is to exchange shirts in an atmosphere of good fellowship.'

'But not pants,' said Pepe under his breath.

'What do you know about that sort of thing?' growled Andy. 'You're a bloody orc. I know all about you people. You can tear arms and legs off. You're black magic. I'm not scared of you.' He came at Nutt with commendable speed for a man in such pain.

Nutt dodged. 'I believe there is a peaceful solution to the obvious enmity between us.'

'You what?!'

Pepe and some of the footballers were closing in. Andy had not been making friends. Nutt waved them away.

'I'm sure I could help you, Andy. Yes, you are right, I am an orc, but doesn't an orc have eyes? Doesn't an orc have ears? Doesn't an orc have arms and legs?'

'Yeah, at the moment,' said Andy, and leaped.

What happened next happened so fast that Trev didn't see the middle of it. It started with Andy jumping and finished with him sitting on the ground with Nutt's hands clamped around his head, claws out. 'Let me see now,' Nutt mused as the man struggled in vain. 'Twisting the skull with enough force to snap the spine and spinal column should not present much difficulty since it is a non-rotating joint. And, of course, the ear holes and eye sockets allow for extra grip in the manner of a bowling ball,' he added happily.

There was a horrified hush as he continued. 'Using the unit of measurement of force invented by Sir Rosewood Bunn, I should think that a mere 250 Bunns should do the trick. But, of course, and possibly surprisingly, it is the tearing of the skin, tendons and muscles that would present me with some difficulty. You are a young man and the tensile strength would be quite high. I imagine the skin alone would require a force of about a thousand Bunns.'

Andy yelped as his head was gently twisted.

'Oh, I say! Look here now!' said Ridcully. 'A joke is a joke and all that, but . . .'

'From then on it gets rather messy,' said Nutt. 'Muscle would tear off the bones comparatively easily.'

Andy gave another strangled yelp.

'But taking it all in all, I would think a force of between three to five Kilobunns should do the trick.' He paused. 'Just my little joke, Andy. I know you like a laugh. I would also, I believe, be quite capable of putting one hand down your throat and pulling out your stomach.'

'Go ahead,' croaked Andy.

And around the arena of the Hippo, the beast smelled blood. After all, it wasn't just horse racing that had taken place in the Hippo over the centuries. The comparatively small amount of blood that had been shed today was nothing compared with the oceans of the centuries gone by, but the beast knew blood when it smelled it. The cheering and the chanting now picked up, and the words grew louder and louder as people rose to their feet: *Orc! Orc! Orc!*

Nutt stood impassively and then turned to the former Dean. 'Could I please ask everyone else to leave? This may become messy.'

'Oh, come on!' said Trev. 'No way.'

'Ah, well,' said Nutt, 'maybe just the ladies?'

'Not likely,' said Glenda.

'In that case, would you please be so kind as to lend me your megaphone, referee, and I would be grateful if you would instruct some of the stronger players on the field to restrain Mister Shank who is, I believe, sadly not in his right mind.'

Wordlessly it was handed over. Nutt took it as the storm of *Orc! Orc!* grew louder, walked a little way from the rest of the group and stood there impassively with his arms folded until the taunting stopped out of sheer lack of momentum. With every eye watching him, he raised the megaphone to his lips and said, 'Gentlemen. Yes, indeed, I am an orc and will always be one. And may I say that it's been a privilege to play here today and to see you all. But I do gather now that being an orc in this city may be seen as something of a problem to some of you.' He paused. 'So I would ask you to excuse me if I request that this matter be sorted out between us now.'

There was laughter and some jeers from various parts of the ground, but also, it seemed to Glenda, the beast was calling upon itself for silence. In that pin-drop silence the thud of the megaphone hitting the ground could be heard in every corner. Then Nutt rolled up his sleeves and lowered his voice so that people had to strain to listen.

He said, 'Come on if you think you're hard enough.'

First there was shock and then the silence of disbelief and the whisper of every head turning to every other head and saying, 'Did he really say that?' and then someone high in the stands started to clap, at first slowly and then at an accelerating tempo, as it reached the crowd's tipping point, when not clapping would be unthinkable. Ceasing to clap was also unthinkable and within a minute the applause was a storm.

Nutt turned back to the rest of the team with tears streaming down his face. 'Do I have worth?' he said to Glenda.

She ran towards him and hugged him. 'You always did.'

'Then when the match is over there are things we have to do.'

'But it's been over for ages,' said Glenda.

'No, it's not over until the referee blows his whistle. Everyone knows that.'

'By Io he's right,' said Ridcully. 'Go on, Dean. Give it the works!'

The Archchancellor of Brazeneck University felt gracious enough to let that one pass. He put the gigantic whistle to his lips, filled his lungs with air and sent the pea rattling. Despite everything, the shade of

Evans the Striped had the last word: 'NO BOY IS TO FIDDLE ABOUT IN THE SHOWERS!'

As the crowd streamed down from the stands, trampling the now sacred turf, Ridcully tapped a gloomy Mr Hoggett on the shoulder and said, 'It would be my privilege to change shirts with you, sir.' He dropped his hat on the ground, pulled off his shirt and revealed a chest so hairy that it looked like two sleeping lions. The United shirt he received in return was somewhat of a tight fit, but that was unimportant because, as Andy had predicted, the Unseen Academicals were indeed picked up by the yelling crowd (except for Mrs Whitlow who fought back) and carried in glory through the city. It was a triumph. Whether you won or lost, it was still a triumph.*

---

* It is traditional on these occasions for the conquering heroes to spray bottles of champagne on the crowd. This did not happen. If a wizard succeeds in getting the cork out of a champagne bottle, he certainly does not intend to pour it away.

You think it's all over?

The wizards of Unseen University knew how to party. Pepe and Madame Sharn* were impressed. However, business was business and they had to think about Juliet. 'I can't see her anywhere,' said Madame.

'I think I saw two of her a while ago,' said Pepe. 'These fellows do themselves well – I have never seen such a large cheeseboard. It almost makes celibacy seem worthwhile.'

'Oh, do you think so?'

'No. By the way, have you noticed that very tall wizard giving you the eye, my dear?'

'That's Professor Bengo Macarona. Do you think he—' Madame began.

'Without a shadow of a doubt, my dear. I know he's hurt his legs, but I doubt if that would be a problem.'

Once again, Madame craned to search the crowd for the glittering figure. 'I do hope our young model is not getting involved in any hanky panky.'

'How could she? She's totally surrounded by admirers.'

'It's still possible.'

In fact, Juliet and Trev were sitting in the darkness of the Night Kitchen. 'I'll find somethin' to do,' said Trev. 'I'll go wherever you go.'

'You ought to stay here and play football,' said Juliet. 'You know what some people said when we were drinking? They said Dave Likely was your father.'

'Well, yes, that's true.'

'Yes,' said Juliet, 'but they used to say you were his son.'

'Well, maybe a bit of football,' Trev conceded, 'but I don't think I'll get away with the tin can again.'

They kissed.

There and then, that was all that appeared necessary.

However . . .

*

* Who was the same shape as most of the wizards and felt doubly at home.

Glenda and Nutt had also wanted to find a place a little out of the way and, if possible, dark. Fortuitously she had pulled out of her pocket a pair of tickets, placed there by Dr Hix in his attempt to spread darkness and despondency throughout the world by the means of amateur dramatics, to the Dolly Sisters Players' production of *Starcrossed* by Hwel the Playwright. They sat hand in hand, watching it solemnly, feeling the ripples move them, then discussed it as they walked back through the city, carefully skirting the chanting bands of happy, drunken supporters.

'What did you think?' said Nutt, after a while. 'About the play, I mean.'

'I don't see that it was that romantic,' said Glenda. 'To be honest, I thought it was a bit silly.'

'It is widely regarded as one of the great romantic plays of the last fifty years,' said Nutt.

'Really? But what type of example are they setting? First of all, didn't anyone in Genua, even in those days, know how to take a pulse? Is a little first-aid knowledge too much to expect? Even a hand mirror would have helped and there are quite a number of respectable places where you can take a pulse.'

'I think that's because neither of them were thinking about themselves, perhaps,' said Nutt.

'Neither of them was thinking at all,' said Glenda, 'and they certainly weren't thinking about each other as people. A little common sense and they would be alive. It's made-up, like books. I don't think anyone sensible would act like that.'

He squeezed her hand. 'Sometimes you speak like Ladyship,' he said, 'and that reminds me.'

'Reminds you of what?'

'It's time for me to meet my maker.'

Andy Shank walked unsteadily among the night-time alleys, secure in the knowledge that they contained nothing worse than him, a belief which, as it happened, was in error.

'Mister Shank?'

'Who's asking?' he said, turning around and reaching instinctively into his coat for his new cutlass.

But another knife, silver and thin, sliced twice and a foot expertly stamped the length of his shin and forced him to the ground. 'Me! I'm the happy ending. You can call me the good fairy. Don't worry, you'll be able to see by the time you wipe the blood out of your eyes and, as they say, now you won't have to pay for a drink in any bar in this town, though I suspect you never have.'

His attacker leaned nonchalantly against the wall.

'And the reason I am doing this, Mister Shank, is that I am a bastard. I am an old bugger. I am a sod. They let you get away with it because they were nice people and, you know, the world needs someone like me to set the balance square. Since before you were born I have known people like you. Tormentors, bullies and thieves. Ah yes, thieves. Thieves of other people's self-respect. Thieves of their peace of mind. Now Mister Nutt, he's an orc and I've heard that he can talk people better. Well, so be it, say I. If it works, he's a genius, but that don't square things, not in my book, so I thought you ought to meet Pepe, just to say hello. If I ever see you again, they'll never find all the pieces, but just to show that I have a decent streak, here's something to put on your wounds.'

Something landed softly near Andy's groping hand.

Andy, dripping blood and snot on to the pavement, reached around quickly as the trim little footsteps disappeared, thinking only of getting the blood out of his eyes and revenge and retribution out of his heart. And in the circumstances, therefore, he should not have wiped the half-lemon across his face.

*

You think it's all over?

It is a regrettable fact that when two people are dining at a very large and impressive dining table they sit at the opposite ends of the long axis. This is incredibly stupid and makes conversation difficult and the passing of food impossible, but even Lord Vetinari and Lady Margolotta had apparently signed up to the idea.

On the other hand, they both ate very little and so there wasn't very much to pass.

'Your secretary seems to be getting on very well with my librarian,' said Lady Margolotta.

'Yes,' observed Vetinari. 'Apparently they are comparing ring binders. He has invented a new one.'

'Well, for the proper working of the world,' said Lady Margolotta, 'it is essential that ring binders are important to at least one person.' She put down her glass and looked towards the door.

'You seem nervous,' said Vetinari. 'Are you wondering how he will come?'

'He has had a very long day and a remarkably successful one. And you say he's gone to an amateur dramatics performance?'

'Yes, with that very forthright young lady who makes the pies,' said Vetinari.

'I see,' said Lady Margolotta. 'He must know I am here and he's gone off with a cook?'

There was just a trace of a smile on Vetinari's lips. 'Not any cook. A genius amongst cooks.'

'Well, I must admit to being surprised,' said her ladyship.

'And upset?' said Vetinari. 'A little jealous, perhaps?'

'Havelock, you go too far!'

'Would you expect otherwise? Besides, you must surely realize that his triumph is yours too?'

'Did I tell you that I've seen some of them?' said Margolotta after a while.

'The orcs?'

'Yes. They really are wretched. Of course, people say that about the goblins and while it is true that they religiously save their own snot, and, frankly, just about everything else, at least there is a logic to it.'

'Well, a religious logic, at least,' murmured Vetinari. 'They tend to be quite stretchable.'

'The Igors made them from men, did you know?'

Vetinari, still holding his glass, walked to the other end of the table and picked up the pepperpot. 'No. However, now you tell me, it's patently obvious. Goblins would not have been nearly ferocious enough.'

'And they had nothing,' said Margolotta. 'No culture, no legends, no history – he could give them those.'

'Everything they are not, he is,' said Vetinari, adding, 'but that's an enormous weight you're putting on his shoulders.'

'How much is on mine? How much of a weight is on yours?'

'It's rather like being a carthorse,' said Vetinari. 'After a while one ceases to notice, it's just the way of life.'

'They deserve their chance and it must be taken now, while the world is at peace.'

'Peace?' said Vetinari. 'Ah, yes, defined as a period of time to allow for preparation for the next war.'

'Where did you learn such cynicism, Havelock?'

Vetinari spun around and began his absent-minded walk along the length of the table again. 'Well, mostly from you, madam, though I have to say that the credit is not all yours, since I have had an extended period of further education as tyrant of this city.'

'I think you allow them too much freedom.'

'Oh, yes, I do. That's why I am still tyrant of this city. The way to retain power, I have always thought, is to ensure the absolute unthinkability of oneself not being there. I shall help you in any way I can, of course. There should be no slaves, even slaves to instinct.'

'One person can make a difference,' said Margolotta. 'Look at Mister Shine who is now Diamond King of Trolls. Look at yourself. If men can fall—'

Vetinari gave a sharp laugh. 'Oh, they can, indeed.'

'—then orcs can rise,' said Margolotta. 'If that is not true then the universe is not true.'

There was a velvet-like knock at the double doors and Drumknott entered. 'Mister Nutt is here, sir.' He added with a certain disdain, 'And he's with that . . . woman, who cooks in the university.'

Vetinari glanced at Margolotta. 'Yes,' he said. 'I think we should see him in the main hall.'

Drumknott coughed. 'I think I should tell you, sir, that Mister Nutt acquired entrance to the building through gates that were securely locked.'

'Did he tear them off their hinges?' asked Vetinari with apparent enthusiastic interest.

'No, sir, he lifted the gates bodily off their hinges and stacked them neatly against the wall.'

'Ah, then there is still hope for the world.'

'And the guards?'

Drumknott glanced for a moment at Lady Margolotta. 'I have taken the precaution of stationing some of them inconspicuously in the Great Hall gallery with crossbows.'

'Stand them down,' said Vetinari.

'Stand them down?' said Margolotta.

'*Stand them down*,' said Vetinari again, directly to Drumknott. He extended his arm to her ladyship. 'I think the term is, as they put it, *alea iacta est*. The die, your ladyship, is cast, and we should both see how it falls.'

'Will you get into trouble for that?' said Glenda, staying close to Nutt as they walked up the steps.

The main hall of the palace was an intimidating place when empty, because it had been designed for exactly that purpose.

'Why didn't you just knock like everyone else?'

'My dear Glenda, I am not like anyone else and neither are you.'

'Then what are you going to do?'

'I don't know. What will Ladyship do? I have no idea, although I am becoming aware of how she thinks and there are a few possibilities I have in mind.'

They watched two figures coming down the broad staircase that extended up into the rest of the building. It had been built to accommodate hundreds; the two people coming down looked uncharacteristically small.

'Ah, Mister Nutt,' said Vetinari as they had almost reached the bottom step, 'and Miss Sugarbean. I must add my congratulations to the pair of you on the wonderful, albeit surprising, success of Unseen Academicals.'

'I think you are going to have to make a lot of changes to the rules, sir,' said Nutt.

'Such as?' said Vetinari.

'I think you need assistants for the referee. His eyes can't be everywhere,' said Nutt, 'and there do need to be some more rules. Although Mister Hoggett did the honourable thing, I think.'

'And Professor Rincewind might make a very capable attacker, if only you could persuade him to take the ball with him,' said Vetinari.

'I would never tell the Archchancellor this, my lord, but I think he may be better in a more defensive role.'

'Who would you suggest as an alternative?' said Vetinari.

'Well, Charlie, the animated skeleton who works in the Department of Post-Mortem Communications, did very well in trials. And, after all,' he paused for a moment, 'yes, after all, none of us can help how we're made.'

They turned at a tap, tap, tapping behind them. It was Lady Margolotta's foot.

Nutt gave a little bow. 'Ladyship. I trust I find you in adequate health.'

'And you likewise, Nutt,' said Lady Margolotta.

Nutt turned to Glenda. 'What was that term you used once?'

'In the pink,' said Glenda.

'Yes, that's right, I am deeply in the pink,' said Nutt. 'And it's Mister Nutt, if you please, your ladyship.'

'Would the two of you care to join us upstairs for a late supper?' asked Vetinari, watching them both very carefully.

'No, I don't think we will impose, but thank you very much. I have a lot to do. Lady Margolotta?'

'Yes?'

'Would you come here, please?'

Glenda watched the expressions: Vetinari's faint smile, her look of affront, Nutt's confidence. The rustle of her long, black dress was an audible intoxication as she walked the last few steps towards the orc and stopped. 'Do I have worth?' asked Nutt.

'Yes, Nutt, you do.'

'Thank you,' said Nutt, 'but I am learning that worth is something that must be continuously accumulated. You asked me to be becoming. Have I become?'

'Yes, Nutt, you have become.'

'And what is it you want me to do now?'

'Find the orcs that still live in Far Uberwald and bring them back out of the dark.'

'Then there are more orcs, like me?' said Nutt.

'A few dozen, perhaps,' said Margolotta, 'but in truth I could hardly say they are like you. They are a sorry bunch.'

'Is it they who should be sorry?' said Nutt.

Glenda watched the faces. Amazingly, Lady Margolotta looked taken aback.

'Many bad things were done under the Evil Empire,' she said. 'The best we can do now is undo them. Will you assist in this endeavour?'

'In every way that I can,' said Nutt.

'I would like you to teach them civilized behaviour,' said Ladyship coldly.

He appeared to consider this. 'Yes, of course, I think that would be quite possible,' he said. 'And who would you send to teach the humans?'

There was a brief outburst of laughter from Vetinari, who

immediately cupped his hand over his mouth. 'Oh, I do beg your pardon,' he said.

'But since it falls to me,' continued Nutt, 'then, yes, I shall go into Far Uberwald.'

'Pastor Oats will be very pleased to see you, I'm sure,' said Margolotta.

'He's still alive?' said Nutt.

'Oh, yes, indeed, he is still quite young after all, and walks with forgiveness at his side. I think he would feel it very appropriate if you were to join him. In fact, he has told me on one of his all too infrequent visits that he would be honoured to pass the rate of forgiveness on to you.'

'Nutt doesn't need forgiveness!' Glenda burst out.

Nutt smiled and patted her hand. 'Uberwald is a wild country for a man to travel in,' he said, 'even a holy man. Forgiveness is the name of Pastor Oats's double-headed battle-axe. For Mister Oats the crusade against evil is not a metaphor. Forgiveness cut through my chains. I will gladly carry it.'

'The kings of the trolls and the dwarfs will give you all the help that they can,' said Ladyship.

Nutt nodded. 'But first I have a small favour to ask you, my lord,' he said to Vetinari.

'By all means, ask.'

'I know the city has a number of golem horses. I wonder if I could borrow one of them?'

'Be my guest,' said the Patrician.

Nutt turned to Glenda. 'Miss Sugarbean. Juliet told me that you secretly want to ride through Quirm on a warm summer's evening, feeling the wind in your hair. We could leave now. I have saved money.'

All kinds of reasons why she shouldn't foamed in Glenda's head. Everywhere were responsibilities, commitments and the never-ending clamour of wanting. There were a thousand and one reasons why she should say no.

'Yes,' she said.

'In that case, then, we will not take up any more of your valuable time, my lord, my lady, and will head off to the stables.'

'But—' Lady Margolotta began.

'I think all that needs to be said has been,' said Nutt. 'I will, *we* will, of course, visit you shortly when I have settled my affairs here and I look forward very much to doing so.' He nodded to them and, with Glenda walking on air beside him, went back the way they had come.

'Wasn't that nice?' said Vetinari. 'Did you see that they held hands all the time?'

At the doorway, Nutt turned round. 'Oh, just one more thing. Thank you for not posting archers up in the gallery. That would have been so . . . embarrassing.'

'I shall drink to your success, Margolotta,' said Vetinari as their footsteps died away. 'You know, I seriously intended to proposition Miss Sugarbean to be my cook.' He sighed again. 'Still, what is a pie to a happy ending?'

You think it's all over?

The following morning Ponder Stibbons was at work in the High Energy Magic Building when Ridcully limped in. There was a glowing silver band around his knee. 'Grapeshot's Therapeutic Squeezer,' he announced. 'A simple little spell. I'll be right as rain in no time. Mrs Whitlow wanted me to put a stocking on it, but I told her that I'm not interested in that sort of thing.'

'I'm glad to see that you're in such good spirits, Archchancellor,' said Ponder, working his way down a long calculation.

'Have you had a chance to see the papers yet this morning, Mister Stibbons?'

'No, sir. What with the football business, I'm a little behind with my work.'

'It may interest you to know that late last night a seventy-foot-high chicken broke out of what they are pleased to call the Higher Energy Magic Building at Brazeneck and is apparently rampaging through Pseudopolis while being pursued by most of the faculty, who, I assume, would be quite capable of terrorizing the city all by themselves. Henry has just had a frantic clacks and has had to rush off.'

'Oh, that is very disturbing, sir.'

'Yes, it is, isn't it?' said Ridcully. 'Apparently it's laying eggs very fast.'

'Ah, that sounds like a quasi-expansion blit phenomenon adapting itself to a living organism,' said Ponder. He turned the page, his pencil moving neatly across the column of figures.

'The former Dean has egg all over his face,' said Ridcully.

'Well, I'm sure that Professor Turnipseed will be able to bring things back under control,' said Ponder. The tone of his voice was entirely unchanged.

There was a busy little silence and Ridcully said, 'How long do you think we should give him to get it under control?'

'What size are the eggs?'

'Eight or nine feet high, apparently,' said Ridcully.

'With calcium shells?'

'Yes, quite thick, so I'm told.'

Ponder looked thoughtfully at the ceiling. 'Hmm, that's not too bad, then. If you'd said steel it would have been rather worrying. It sounds very much like a blit devolution, possibly caused by . . . lack of experience.'

'I thought you taught Mister Turnipseed everything you know,' said Ridcully, looking happier than Ponder had seen him in a very long time.

'Well, sir, perhaps there was something he didn't quite grasp. Are people at risk?'

'The wizards have told everyone to stay indoors.'

'Well, sir, I think if I got some of my equipment together we could leave about teatime.'

'I'll come, too, of course,' said Ridcully. He looked at Ponder. 'And—'

'What?' said Ponder. He looked at Ridcully's grin. 'Yes, it might be a good idea if one of the gentlemen from the *Times* came along to take pictures. They might be very good for instructional purposes.'

'An extremely good plan, Mister Stibbons, and I think we should take the senior faculty as well. They will lend some much-needed . . .' He snapped his fingers. 'What's the word?'

'Confusion,' said Ponder.

'No, not that,' said Ridcully.

'Appetite?' said Ponder. 'Weight?'

'Something like that . . . Ah, gravitas. Oh, yes, lots of gravitas. We aren't the kind of fellows who run around chasing strange birds. I'll see you after lunch. And now I have other matters to deal with.'

'Yes, Archchancellor,' said Ponder. 'Oh, and, um . . . What about the proposed football match?'

'*Regrettably*, it appears that it will have to wait until they have rebuilt the university.'

'That's a shame, Archchancellor,' said Ponder.

He carried on with the calculation until the very last figures danced into place, made sure the Archchancellor had left, gave a very small smile, which you might not have noticed had you not expected it, and then pulled another ledger towards him.

It was another good day.

It is now!